Praise for #1 *New York Times* bestselling autnor

NORA ROBERTS

"Nora Roberts is among the best." —*Washington Post*

"Roberts has a warm feel for her characters and an eye for the evocative detail." —*Chicago Tribune*

"America's favorite writer." —*New Yorker*

"When Roberts puts her expert fingers on the pulse of romance, legions of fans feel the heartbeat." —*Publishers Weekly*

"You can't bottle wish fulfillment, but Nora Roberts certainly knows how to put it on the page." —*New York Times*

"Roberts' style has a fresh, contemporary snap." —*Kirkus Reviews*

Also available from

NORA ROBERTS

LATE SUMMER LOVE
The strongest bonds form when opposites attract

THAT SUMMER MAGIC
The Donovan family has some magical secrets

WEATHER THE STORM
Sometimes love is laced with risks

THE MacGREGOR GROOMS: Three Passionate Proposals
The meddling, matchmaking MacGregor patriarch is at it again

SOMEDAY WITH YOU
A second chance to embrace life and discover love

MacGREGOR EVER AFTER
When it's meant to be, love always finds a way

For a full list of titles by Nora Roberts,
please visit www.noraroberts.com.

NO. 1 *NEW YORK TIMES* BESTSELLING AUTHOR

NORA ROBERTS

Then There Was You

THEN THERE WAS YOU © 2025 by Harlequin Books S.A.

UNFINISHED BUSINESS
© 1992 by Nora Roberts
Australian Copyright 1992
New Zealand Copyright 1992

First Published 1992
Tenth Australian Paperback Edition 2025
ISBN 978 1 038 94027 8

MEGAN'S MATE
© 1996 by Nora Roberts
Australian Copyright 1996
New Zealand Copyright 1996

First Published 1996
Fifth Australian Paperback Edition 2025
ISBN 978 1 038 94027 8

Except for use in any review, the reproduction or utilisation of this work in whole or in part in any form by any electronic, mechanical or other means, now known or hereafter invented, including xerography, photocopying and recording, or in any information storage or retrieval system, is forbidden without the permission of the publisher.

This book is sold subject to the condition that it shall not, by way of trade or otherwise, be lent, resold, hired out or otherwise circulated without the prior consent of the publisher in any form of binding or cover other than that in which it is published and without a similar condition including this condition being imposed on the subsequent purchaser.

All rights reserved including the right of reproduction in whole or in part in any form. This edition is published in arrangement with Harlequin Books S.A..

This is a work of fiction. Names, characters, places, and incidents are either the product of the author's imagination or are used fictitiously, and any resemblance to actual persons, living or dead, business establishments, events, or locales is entirely coincidental.

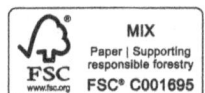

Published by
Mills & Boon
An imprint of Harlequin Enterprises (Australia) Pty Limited
(ABN 47 001 180 918), a subsidiary of HarperCollins Publishers
Australia Pty Limited (ABN 36 009 913 517)
Level 19, 201 Elizabeth Street
SYDNEY NSW 2000
AUSTRALIA

® and ™ (apart from those relating to FSC ®) are trademarks of Harlequin Enterprises (Australia) Pty Limited or its corporate affiliates. Trademarks indicated with ® are registered in Australia, New Zealand and in other countries. Contact admin_legal@Harlequin.ca for details.

Printed and bound in Australia by McPherson's Printing Group

CONTENTS

UNFINISHED BUSINESS 7

MEGAN'S MATE 205

Unfinished Business

For the Washington Romance Writers,
my extended family

Chapter 1

What am I doing here?

The question rolled around in Vanessa's mind as she drove down Main Street. The sleepy town of Hyattown had changed very little in twelve years. It was still tucked in the foothills of Maryland's Blue Ridge Mountains, surrounded by rolling farmland and thick woods. Apple orchards and dairy cows encroached as close as the town limits, and here, inside those limits, there were no stoplights, no office buildings, no hum of traffic.

Here there were sturdy old houses and unfenced yards, children playing and laundry flapping on lines. It was, Vanessa thought with both relief and surprise, exactly as she had left it. The sidewalks were still bumpy and cracked, the concrete undermined by the roots of towering oaks that were just beginning to green. Forsythia were spilling their yellow blooms, and azaleas held just the hint of the riotous color to come. Crocuses, those vanguards of spring, had been overshadowed by spears of daffodils and early tulips. People continued, as they had in her childhood, to fuss with their lawns and gardens on a Saturday afternoon.

Some glanced up, perhaps surprised and vaguely interested to see an unfamiliar car drive by. Occasionally someone waved—out of habit, not because they recognized her. Then they bent to their planting or mowing again. Through her open window Vanessa caught the scent of freshly cut grass, of hyacinths and earth newly turned. She could hear the buzzing of power mowers, the barking of a dog, the shouts and laughter of children at play.

Two old men in fielders' caps, checked shirts and work pants stood in front of the town bank gossiping. A pack of young boys puffed up the slope of the road on their bikes. Probably on their way to Lester's Store for cold drinks or candy. She'd strained up that same hill to that same destination countless times. A hundred years ago, she thought, and felt the all-too-familiar clutching in her stomach.

What am I doing here? she thought again, reaching for the roll of antacids in her purse. Unlike the town, she had changed. Sometimes she hardly recognized herself.

She wanted to believe she was doing the right thing. Coming back. Not home, she mused. She had no idea if this was home. Or even if she wanted it to be.

She'd been barely sixteen when she'd left—when her father had taken her from these quiet streets on an odyssey of cities, practice sessions and performances. New York, Chicago, Los Angeles and London, Paris, Bonn, Madrid. It had been exciting, a roller coaster of sights and sounds. And, most of all, music.

By the age of twenty, through her father's drive and her talent, she had become one of the youngest and most successful concert pianists in the country. She had won the prestigious Van Cliburn Competition at the tender age of eighteen, over competitors ten years her senior. She had played for royalty and dined with presidents. She had, in her single-minded pursuit of her career, earned a reputation as a brilliant and temperamental artist. The coolly sexy, passionately driven Vanessa Sexton.

Now, at twenty-eight, she was coming back to the home of her childhood, and to the mother she hadn't seen in twelve years.

The burning in her stomach as she pulled up to the curb was so familiar she barely noticed it. Like the town that surrounded it, the home of her youth was much the same as when she'd left it. The sturdy brick had weathered well, and the shutters were freshly painted a deep, warm blue. Along the stone wall that rose above the sidewalk were bushy peonies that would wait another month or more to bloom. Azaleas, in bud, were grouped around the foundation.

Vanessa sat, hands clutching the wheel, fighting off a desperate need to drive on. Drive away. She had already done too much on impulse. She'd bought the Mercedes convertible, driven up from her last booking in D.C., refused dozens of offers for engagements. All on impulse. Throughout her adult life, her time had been meticulously scheduled, her actions carefully executed, and only after all consequences had been considered. Though impulsive by nature, she had learned the importance of an ordered life. Coming here, awakening old hurts and old memories, wasn't part of that order.

Yet if she turned away now, ran away now, she would never have the answers to her questions, questions even she didn't understand.

Deliberately not giving herself any more time to think, she got out of the car and went to the trunk for her suitcases. She didn't have to stay if she was uncomfortable, she reminded herself. She was free to go anywhere. She was an adult, a well-traveled one who was financially secure. Her home, if she chose to make one, could be anywhere in the world. Since her father's death six months before, she'd had no ties.

Yet it was here she had come. And it was here she needed to be—at least until her questions were answered.

She crossed the sidewalk and climbed the five concrete steps. Despite the trip-hammer beating of her heart, she held herself straight. Her father had never permitted slumped shoulders. The presentation of self was as important as the presentation of music. Chin up, shoulders straight, she started up the walk.

When the door opened, she stopped, as if her feet were rooted in the ground. She stood frozen as her mother stepped onto the porch.

Images, dozens of them, raced into her mind. Of herself on the first day of school, rushing up those steps full of pride, to see her mother standing at the door. Sniffling as she limped up the walk after falling off her bike, her mother there to clean up the scrapes and kiss away the hurt. All but dancing onto the porch after her first kiss. And her mother, a woman's knowledge in her eyes, struggling not to ask any questions.

Then there had been the very last time she had stood here. But she had been walking away from the house, not toward it. And her mother hadn't been on the porch waving goodbye.

"Vanessa."

Loretta Sexton stood twisting her hands. There was no gray in her dark chestnut hair. It was shorter than Vanessa remembered, and fluffed around a face that showed very few lines. A rounder face, softer, than Vanessa recalled. She seemed smaller somehow. Not shrunken, but more compact, fitter, younger. Vanessa had a flash of her father. Thin, too thin, pale, old.

Loretta wanted to run to her daughter, but she couldn't. The woman standing on the walk wasn't the girl she had lost and longed for. She looks like me, she thought, battling back tears. Stronger, more sure, but so much like me.

Bracing herself, as she had countless times before stepping onto a stage, Vanessa continued up the walk, up the creaking wooden steps, to stand in front of her mother. They were nearly the same height. That was something that jolted them both. Their eyes, the same misty shade of green, held steady.

They stood, only a foot apart. But there was no embrace.

"I appreciate you letting me come." Vanessa hated the stiffness she heard in her own voice.

"You're always welcome here." Loretta cleared her throat, cleared it of the rush of emotional words. "I was sorry to hear about your father."

"Thank you. I'm glad to see you're looking well."

"I…" What could she say? What could she possibly say that could make up for twelve lost years? "Did you…run into much traffic on the way up?"

"No. Not after I got out of Washington. It was a pleasant ride."

"Still, you must be tired after the drive. Come in and sit down."

She had remodeled, Vanessa thought foolishly as she followed her mother inside. The rooms were lighter, airier, than she remembered. The imposing home she remembered had become cozy. Dark, formal wallpaper had been replaced by warm pastels. Carpeting had been ripped up to reveal buffed pine floors that were accented by colorful area rugs. There were antiques, lovingly restored, and there was the scent of fresh flowers. It was the home of a woman, she realized. A woman of taste and means.

"You'd probably like to go upstairs first and unpack." Loretta stopped at the stairs, clutching the newel. "Unless you're hungry."

"No, I'm not hungry."

With a nod, Loretta started up the stairs. "I thought you'd like your old room." She pressed her lips together as she reached the landing. "I've redecorated a bit."

"So I see." Vanessa's voice was carefully neutral.

"You still have a view of the backyard."

"I'm sure it's fine."

Loretta opened a door, and Vanessa followed her inside.

There were no fussily dressed dolls or grinning stuffed animals. There were no posters tacked on the walls, no carefully framed awards and certificates. Gone was the narrow bed she had once dreamed in, and the desk where she had fretted over

French verbs and geometry. It was no longer a room for a girl. It was a room for a guest.

The walls were ivory, trimmed in warm green. Pretty priscillas hung over the windows. There was a four-poster bed, draped with a watercolor quilt and plumped with pillows. A glass vase of freesias sat on an elegant Queen Anne desk. The scent of potpourri wafted from a bowl on the bureau.

Nervous, Loretta walked through the room, twitching at the quilt, brushing imaginary dust from the dresser. "I hope you're comfortable here. If there's anything you need, you just have to ask."

Vanessa felt as if she were checking into an elegant and exclusive hotel. "It's a lovely room. I'll be fine, thank you."

"Good." Loretta clasped her hands together again. How she longed to touch. To hold. "Would you like me to help you unpack?"

"No." The refusal came too quickly. Vanessa struggled with a smile. "I can manage."

"All right. The bath is just—"

"I remember."

Loretta stopped short, looked helplessly out the window. "Of course. I'll be downstairs if you want anything." Giving in to her need, she cupped Vanessa's face in her hands. "Welcome home." She left quickly, shutting the door behind her.

Alone, Vanessa sat on the bed. Her stomach muscles were like hot, knotted ropes. She pressed a hand against her midsection, studying this room that had once been hers. How could the town have seemed so unchanged, and this room, her room, be so different? Perhaps it was the same with people. They might look familiar on the outside, but inside they were strangers.

As she was.

How different was she from the girl who had once lived here? Would she recognize herself? Would she want to?

She rose to stand in front of the cheval glass in the corner. The face and form were familiar. She had examined herself carefully before each concert to be certain her appearance was perfect. That was expected. Her hair was to be groomed—swept up or back, never loose—her face made up for the stage, but never heavily, her costume subtle and elegant. That was the image of Vanessa Sexton.

Her hair was a bit windblown now, but there was no one to see or judge. It was the same deep chestnut as her mother's. Longer, though, sweeping her shoulders from a side part, it could catch fire from the sun or gleam deep and rich in moonlight. There was some fatigue around her eyes, but there was nothing unusual in that. She'd been very careful with her makeup that morning, so there was subtle color along her high cheekbones, a hint of it over her full, serious mouth. She wore a suit in icy pink with a short, snug jacket and a full skirt. The waistband was a bit loose, but then, her appetite hadn't been good.

And all this was still just image, she thought. The confident, poised and assured adult. She wished she could turn back the clock so that she could see herself as she'd been at sixteen. Full of hope, despite the strain that had clouded the household. Full of dreams and music.

With a sigh, she turned away to unpack.

When she was a child, it had seemed natural to use her room as a sanctuary. After rearranging her clothes for the third time, Vanessa reminded herself that she was no longer a child. Hadn't she come to find the bond she had lost with her mother? She couldn't find it if she sat alone in her room and brooded.

As she came downstairs, Vanessa heard the low sound of a radio coming from the back of the house. From the kitchen, she remembered. Her mother had always preferred popular music to the classics, and that had always irritated Vanessa's father. It was an old Presley ballad now—rich and lonely. Moving toward the sound, she stopped in the doorway of what had always been the music room.

The old grand piano that had been crowded in there was gone.

So was the huge, heavy cabinet that had held reams and reams of sheet music. Now there were small, fragile-looking chairs with needlepoint cushions. A beautiful old tea caddy sat in a corner. On it was a bowl filled with some thriving leafy green plant. There were watercolors in narrow frames on the walls, and there was a curvy Victorian sofa in front of the twin windows.

All had been arranged around a trim, exquisite rosewood spinet. Unable to resist, Vanessa crossed to it. Lightly, quietly, only for herself, she played the first few chords of a Chopin étude. The action was so stiff that she understood the piano was new. Had her mother bought it after she'd received the letter telling her that her daughter was coming back? Was this a gesture, an attempt to reach across the gap of twelve years?

It couldn't be so simple, Vanessa thought, rubbing at the beginnings of a headache behind her eyes. They both had to know that.

She turned her back on the piano and walked to the kitchen.

Loretta was there, putting the finishing touches on a salad she'd arranged in a pale green bowl. Her mother had always liked pretty things, Vanessa remembered. Delicate, fragile things. Those leanings showed now in the lacy place mats on the table, the pale rose sugar bowl, the collection of Depression glass on an open shelf. She had opened the window, and a fragrant spring breeze ruffled the sheer curtains over the sink.

When she turned, Vanessa saw that her eyes were red, but she smiled, and her voice was clear. "I know you said you weren't hungry, but I thought you might like a little salad and some iced tea."

Vanessa managed an answering smile. "Thank you. The house looks lovely. It seems bigger somehow. I'd always heard that things shrunk as you got older."

Loretta turned off the radio. Vanessa regretted the gesture, as it meant they were left with only themselves to fill the silence. "There were too many dark colors before," Loretta told her. "And too much heavy furniture. At times I used to feel as though the furniture was lurking over me, waiting to push me out of a room."

She caught herself, uneasy and embarrassed. "I saved some of the pieces, a few that were your grandmother's. They're stored in the attic. I thought someday you might want them."

"Maybe someday," Vanessa said, because it was easier. She sat down as her mother served the colorful salad. "What did you do with the piano?"

"I sold it." Loretta reached for the pitcher of tea. "Years ago. It seemed foolish to keep it when there was no one to play it. And I'd always hated it." She caught herself again, set the pitcher down. "I'm sorry."

"No need. I understand."

"No, I don't think you do." Loretta gave her a long, searching look. "I don't think you can."

Vanessa wasn't ready to dig too deep. She picked up her fork and said nothing.

"I hope the spinet is all right. I don't know very much about instruments."

"It's a beautiful instrument."

"The man who sold it to me told me it was top-of-the-line. I know you need to practice, so I thought... In any case, if it doesn't suit, you've only to—"

"It's fine." They ate in silence until Vanessa fell back on manners. "The town looks very much the same," she began, in a light, polite voice. "Does Mrs. Gaynor still live on the corner?"

"Oh yes." Relieved, Loretta began to chatter. "She's nearly eighty now, and still walks every day, rain or shine, to the post office to get her mail. The Breckenridges moved away, oh, about five years ago. Went south. A nice family bought their house. Three children. The youngest just started school this year. He's a pistol. And the Hawbaker boy, Rick, you remember? You used to babysit for him."

"I remember being paid a dollar an hour to be driven crazy by a little monster with buckteeth and a slingshot."

"That's the one." Loretta laughed. It was a sound, Vanessa realized, that she'd remembered all through the years. "He's in college now, on a scholarship."

"Hard to believe."

"He came to see me when he was home last Christmas. Asked about you." She fumbled again, cleared her throat. "Joanie's still here."

"Joanie Tucker?"

"It's Joanie Knight now," Loretta told her. "She married young Jack Knight three years ago. They have a beautiful baby."

"Joanie," Vanessa murmured. Joanie Tucker, who had been her best friend since her earliest memory, her confidante, wailing wall and partner in crime. "She has a child."

"A little girl. Lara. They have a farm outside of town. I know she'd want to see you."

"Yes." For the first time all day, Vanessa felt something click. "Yes, I want to see her. Her parents, are they well?"

"Emily died almost eight years ago."

"Oh." Vanessa reached out instinctively to touch her mother's hand. As Joanie had been her closest friend, so had Emily Tucker been her mother's. "I'm so sorry."

Loretta looked down at their joined hands, and her eyes filled. "I still miss her."

"She was the kindest woman I've ever known. I wish I had—" But it was too late for regrets. "Dr. Tucker, is he all right?"

"Ham is fine." Loretta blinked back tears, and tried not to be hurt when Vanessa removed her hand. "He grieved hard, but his family and his work got him through. He'll be so pleased to see you, Van."

No one had called Vanessa by her nickname in more years than she could count. Hearing it now touched her.

"Does he still have his office in his house?"

"Of course. You're not eating. Would you like something else?"

"No, this is fine." Dutifully she ate a forkful of salad.

"Don't you want to know about Brady?"

"No." Vanessa took another bite. "Not particularly."

There was something of the daughter she remembered in that look. The slight pout, the faint line between the brows. It warmed Loretta's heart, as the polite stranger had not. "Brady Tucker followed in his father's footsteps."

Vanessa almost choked. "He's a doctor?"

"That's right. Had himself a fine, important position with some hospital in New York. Chief resident, I think Ham told me."

"I always thought Brady would end up pitching for the Orioles or going to jail."

Loretta laughed again, warmly. "So did most of us. But he turned into quite a respectable young man. Of course, he was always too handsome for his own good."

"Or anyone else's," Vanessa muttered, and her mother smiled again.

"It's always hard for a woman to resist the tall, dark and handsome kind, especially if he's a rogue, as well."

"I think *hood* was the word."

"He never did anything really bad," Loretta pointed out. "Not that he didn't give Emily and Ham a few headaches. Well, a lot of headaches." She laughed. "But the boy always looked out for his sister. I liked him for that. And he was taken with you."

Vanessa sniffed. "Brady Tucker was taken with anything in skirts."

"He was young." They had all been young once, Loretta thought, looking at the lovely, composed stranger who was her daughter. "Emily told me he mooned around the house for weeks after you... after you and your father went to Europe."

"It was a long time ago." Vanessa rose, dismissing the subject.

"I'll get the dishes." Loretta began stacking them quickly. "It's your first day back. I thought maybe you'd like to try out the piano. I'd like to hear you play in this house again."

"All right." She turned toward the door.

"Van?"

"Yes?"

Would she ever call her "Mom" again? "I want you to know how proud I am of all you've accomplished."

"Are you?"

"Yes." Loretta studied her daughter, wishing she had the courage to open her arms for an embrace. "I just wish you looked happier."

"I'm happy enough."

"Would you tell me if you weren't?"

"I don't know. We don't really know each other anymore."

At least that was honest, Loretta thought. Painful, but honest. "I hope you'll stay until we do."

"I'm here because I need answers. But I'm not ready to ask the questions yet."

"Give it time, Van. Give yourself time. And believe me when I say all I ever wanted was what was best for you."

"My father always said the same thing," she said quietly. "Funny, isn't it, that now that I'm a grown woman I have no idea what that is."

She walked down the hall to the music room. There was a gnawing, aching pain just under her breastbone. Out of habit, she popped a pill out of the roll in her skirt pocket before she sat at the piano.

She started with Beethoven's "Moonlight" sonata, playing from memory and from the heart, letting the music soothe her. She could remember playing this piece, and countless others, in this same room. Hour after hour, day after day. For the love of it, yes, but often—too often—because it was expected, even demanded.

Her feelings for music had always been mixed. There was her strong, passionate love for it, the driving need to create it with the skill she'd been given. But there had always also been the equally desperate need to please her father, to reach that point of perfection he had expected. That unattainable point, she thought now.

He had never understood that music was a love for her, not a vocation. It had been a comfort, a means of expression, but never an ambition. On the few occasions she had tried to explain it, he had become so enraged or impatient that she had silenced herself. She, who was known for her passion and temper, had been a cringing child around one man. In all her life, she had never been able to defy him.

She switched to Bach, closed her eyes and let herself drift. For more than an hour she played, lost in the beauty, the gentleness and the genius, of the compositions. This was what her father had never understood. That she could play for her own pleasure and be content, and that she had hated, always hated, sitting on a stage ringed by a spotlight and playing for thousands.

As her emotions began to flow again, she switched to Mozart, something that required more passion and speed. Vivid, almost furious, the music sang through her. When the last chord echoed, she felt a satisfaction she had nearly forgotten.

The quiet applause behind her had her spinning around. Seated on one of the elegant little chairs was a man. Though the sun was in her eyes and twelve years had passed, she recognized him.

"Incredible." Brady Tucker rose and crossed to her. His long, wiry frame blocked out the sun for an instant, and the light glowed like a nimbus around him. "Absolutely incredible." As she stared at him, he held out a hand and smiled. "Welcome home, Van."

She rose to face him. "Brady," she murmured, then rammed her fist solidly into his stomach. "You creep."

He sat down hard as the air exploded out of his lungs. The sound of it was every bit as sweet to her as the music had been. Wincing, he looked up at her. "Nice to see you, too."

"What the hell are you doing here?"

"Your mother let me in." After a couple of testing breaths, he rose. She had to tilt her head back to keep her eyes on his. Those same fabulous blue eyes, in a face that had aged much too well. "I didn't want to disturb you while you were playing, so I just sat down. I didn't expect to be sucker punched."

"You should have." She was delighted to have caught him off

guard, and to have given him back a small portion of the pain he'd given her. His voice was the same, she thought, deep and seductive. She wanted to hit him again just for that. "She didn't mention that you were in town."

"I live here. Moved back almost a year ago." She had that same sexy pout. He fervently wished that at least that much could have changed. "Can I tell you that you look terrific, or should I put up my guard?"

How to remain composed under stress was something she'd learned very well. She sat, carefully smoothing her skirts. "No, you can tell me."

"Okay. You look terrific. A little thin, maybe."

The pout became more pronounced. "Is that your medical opinion, Dr. Tucker?"

"Actually, yes." He took a chance and sat beside her on the piano stool. Her scent was as subtle and alluring as moonlight. He felt a tug, not so much unexpected as frustrating. Though she sat beside him, he knew she was as distant as she had been when there had been an ocean between them.

"You're looking well," she said, and wished it wasn't so true. He still had the lean, athletic body of his youth. His face wasn't as smooth, and the ruggedness maturity had brought to it only made it more attractive. His hair was still a rich, deep black, and his lashes were just as long and thick as ever. And his hands were as strong and beautiful as they had been the first time they had touched her. A lifetime ago, she reminded herself, and settled her own hands in her lap.

"My mother told me you had a position in New York."

"I did." He was feeling as awkward as a schoolboy. No, he realized, much more awkward. Twelve years before, he'd known exactly how to handle her. Or he'd thought he did. "I came back to help my father with his practice. He'd like to retire in a year or two."

"I can't imagine it. You back here," she elaborated. "Or Doc Tucker retiring."

"Times change."

"Yes, they do." She couldn't sit beside him. Just a residual of those girlish feelings, she thought, but she rose anyway. "It's equally hard to picture you as a doctor."

"I felt the same way when I was slogging through medical school."

She frowned. He was wearing jeans and a sweatshirt and running shoes—exactly the kind of attire he'd worn in high school. "You don't look like a doctor."

"Want to see my stethoscope?"

"No." She stuck her hands in her pockets. "I heard Joanie was married."

"Yeah—to Jack Knight, of all people. Remember him?"

"I don't think so."

"He was a year ahead of me in high school. Football star. Went pro a couple of years, then bunged up his knee."

"Is that the medical term?"

"Close enough." He grinned at her. There was still a little chip in his front tooth that she had always found endearing. "She'll be crazy to see you again, Van."

"I want to see her, too."

"I've got a couple of patients coming in, but I should be done by six. Why don't we have some dinner, and I can drive you out to the farm?"

"I don't think so."

"Why not?"

"Because the last time I was supposed to have dinner with you—dinner and the senior prom—you stood me up."

He tucked his hands in his pockets. "You hold a grudge a long time."

"Yes."

"I was eighteen years old, Van, and there were reasons."

"Reasons that hardly matter now." Her stomach was beginning to burn. "The point is, I don't want to pick up where we left off."

He gave her a considering look. "That wasn't the idea."

"Good." That was just one more thing she could damn him for. "We both have our separate lives, Brady. Let's keep it that way."

He nodded, slowly. "You've changed more than I'd thought."

"Yes, I have." She started out, stopped, then looked over her shoulder. "We both have. But I imagine you still know your way out."

"Yeah," he said to himself when she left him alone. He knew his way out. What he hadn't known was that she could still turn him inside out with one of those pouty looks.

Chapter 2

The Knight farm was rolling hills and patches of brown and green field. The hay was well up, she noted, and the corn was tender green shoots. A gray barn stood behind a trio of square paddocks. Nearby, chickens fussed and pecked at the ground. Plump spotted cows lolled on a hillside, too lazy to glance over at the sound of an approaching car, but geese rushed along the bank of the creek, excited and annoyed by the disturbance.

A bumpy gravel lane led to the farmhouse. At the end of it, Vanessa stopped her car, then slowly alighted. She could hear the distant putting of a tractor and the occasional yip-yipping of a cheerful dog. Closer was the chatter of birds, a musical exchange that always reminded her of neighbors gossiping over a fence.

Perhaps it was foolish to feel nervous, but she couldn't shake it. Here in this rambling three-story house, with its leaning chimneys and swaying porches, lived her oldest and closest friend—someone with whom she had shared every thought, every feeling, every wish and every disappointment.

But those friends had been children—girls on the threshold of womanhood, where everything is at its most intense and emotional. They hadn't been given the chance to grow apart. Their friendship had been severed quickly and completely. Between that moment and this, so much—too much—had happened to both of them. To expect to renew those ties and feelings was both naive and overly optimistic.

Vanessa reminded herself of that, bracing herself for disappointment, as she started up the cracked wooden steps to the front porch.

The door swung open. The woman who stepped out released a flood of stored memories. Unlike the moment when she had started up her own walk and seen her mother, Vanessa felt none of the confusion and grief.

She looks the same, was all Vanessa could think. Joanie was still sturdily built, with the curves Vanessa had envied throughout adolescence. Her hair was still worn short and tousled around a pretty face. Black hair and blue eyes like her brother, but with softer features and a neat Cupid's-bow mouth that had driven the teenage boys wild.

Vanessa started to speak, searched for something to say. Then she heard Joanie let out a yelp. They were hugging, arms clasped hard, bodies swaying. The laughter and tears and broken sentences melted away the years.

"I can't believe—you're here."

"I've missed you. You look... I'm sorry."

"When I heard you—" Shaking her head, Joanie pulled back, then smiled. "Oh, God, it's good to see you, Van."

"I was almost afraid to come." Vanessa wiped her cheek with her knuckles.

"Why?"

"I thought you might be polite and offer me some tea and wonder what we were supposed to talk about."

Joanie took a rumpled tissue out of her pocket and blew her

nose. "And I thought you might be wearing a mink and diamonds and stop by out of a sense of duty."

Vanessa gave a watery laugh. "My mink's in storage."

Joanie grabbed her hand and pulled her through the door. "Come in. I might just put that tea on, after all."

The entryway was bright and tidy. Joanie led Vanessa into a living room of faded sofas and glossy mahogany, of chintz curtains and rag rugs. Evidence that there was a baby in the house was found in teething rings, rattles and stuffed bears. Unable to resist, Vanessa picked up a pink-and-white rattle.

"You have a little girl."

"Lara." Joanie beamed. "She's wonderful. She'll be up from her morning nap soon. I can't wait for you to see her."

"It's hard to imagine." Vanessa gave the rattle a shake before setting it down again. It made a pretty, musical sound that had her smiling. "You're a mother."

"I'm almost used to it." She took Vanessa's hand again as they sat on the sofa. "I still can't believe you're here. Vanessa Sexton, concert pianist, musical luminary and globe-trotter."

Vanessa winced. "Oh, please, not her. I left her in D.C."

"Just let me gloat a minute." She was still smiling, but her eyes, eyes that were so like her brother's, were searching Vanessa's face. "We're so proud of you. The whole town. There would be something in the paper or a magazine, something on the news—or an event like that PBS special last year. No one would talk about anything else for days. You're Hyattown's link to fame and fortune."

"A weak link," Vanessa murmured, but she smiled. "Your farm, Joanie—it's wonderful."

"Can you believe it? I always thought I'd be living in one of those New York lofts, planning business lunches and fighting for a cab during rush hour."

"This is better." Vanessa settled back against the sofa cushions. "Much better."

Joanie toed off her shoes, then tucked her stockinged feet under her. "It has been for me. Do you remember Jack?"

"I don't think so. I can't remember you ever talking about anyone named Jack."

"I didn't know him in high school. He was a senior when we were just getting started. I remember seeing him in the halls now and then. Those big shoulders, and that awful buzz haircut during the football season." She laughed and settled comfortably. "Then, about four years ago, I was giving Dad a hand in the office. I was doing time as a paralegal in Hagerstown."

"A paralegal?"

"A former life," Joanie said with a wave of her hand. "Anyway, it was during Dad's Saturday office hours, and Millie was sick— You remember Millie?"

"Oh, yes." Vanessa grinned at the memory of Abraham Tucker's no-nonsense nurse.

"Well, I jumped into the breach for the weekend appointments, and in walks Jack Knight, all six foot three, two hundred and fifty pounds of him. He had laryngitis." A self-satisfied sigh escaped her. "There was this big, handsome hulk trying to tell me, in cowboy-and-Indian sign language, that no, he didn't have an appointment, but he wanted to see the doctor. I squeezed him in between a chicken pox and an earache. Dad examined him and gave him a prescription. A couple hours later he was back, with these raggedy-looking violets and a note asking me to the movies. How could I resist?"

Vanessa laughed. "You always were a soft touch."

Joanie rolled her big blue eyes. "Tell me about it. Before I knew it, I was shopping for a wedding dress and learning about fertilizer. It's been the best four years of my life." She shook her head. "But tell me about you. I want to hear everything."

Vanessa shrugged. "Practice, playing, traveling."

"Jetting off to Rome, Madrid, Mozambique—"

"Sitting on runways and in hotel rooms," Vanessa finished for her. "It isn't nearly as glamorous as it might look."

"No, I guess partying with famous actors, giving concerts for the queen of England and sharing midnight schmoozes with millionaires gets pretty boring."

"Schmoozes?" Vanessa had to laugh. "I don't think I ever schmoozed with anyone."

"Don't burst my bubble, Van." Joanie leaned over to brush a hand down Vanessa's arm. All the Tuckers were touchers, Vanessa thought. She'd missed that. "For years I've had this image of you glittering among the glittery. Celebing among the celebrities, hoitying among the toity."

"I guess I've done my share of hoitying. But mostly I've played the piano and caught planes."

"It's kept you in shape," Joanie said, sensing Vanessa's reluctance to talk about it. "I bet you're still a damn size four."

"Small bones."

"Wait until Brady gets a load of you."

Her chin lifted a fraction. "I saw him yesterday."

"Really? And the rat didn't call me." Joanie tapped a finger against her lips. There was laughter just beneath them. "So, how did it go?"

"I hit him."

"You—" Joanie choked, coughed, recovered. "You hit him? Why?"

"For standing me up for his senior prom."

"For—" Joanie broke off when Vanessa sprang to her feet and began pacing.

"I've never been so angry. I don't care how stupid it sounds. That night was so important to me. I thought it would be the most wonderful, the most romantic night of my life. You know how long we shopped for the perfect dress."

"Yes," Joanie murmured. "I know."

"I'd been looking forward to that night for weeks and weeks."

On a roll now, she swirled around the room. "I'd just gotten my license, and I drove all the way into Frederick to get my hair done. I had this little sprig of baby's breath behind my ear." She touched the spot now, but there was no sentiment in the gesture. "Oh, I knew he was unreliable and reckless. I can't count the number of times my father told me. But I never expected him to dump me like that."

"But, Van—"

"I didn't even leave the house for two days after. I was so sick with embarrassment, so hurt. And then, with my parents fighting. It was—oh, it was so ugly. Then my father took me to Europe, and that was that."

Joanie bit her lip as she considered. There were explanations she could offer, but this was something Brady should straighten out himself. "There might be more to it than you think" was all she said.

Recovered now, Vanessa sat again. "It doesn't matter. It was a long time ago." Then she smiled. "Besides, I think I got the venom out when I punched him in the stomach."

Joanie's lips twitched in sisterly glee. "I'd like to have seen that."

"It's hard to believe he's a doctor."

"I don't think anyone was more surprised than Brady."

"It's odd he's never married…" She frowned. "Or anything."

"I won't touch 'anything,' but he's never married. There are a number of women in town who've developed chronic medical problems since he's come back."

"I'll bet," Vanessa muttered.

"Anyway, my father's in heaven. Have you had a chance to see him yet?"

"No, I wanted to see you first." She took Joanie's hands. "I'm so sorry about your mother. I didn't know until yesterday."

"It was a rough couple of years. Dad was so lost. I guess we all were." Her fingers tightened, taking comfort and giving it. "I know you lost your father. I understand how hard it must have been for you."

"He hadn't been well for a long time. I didn't know how serious it was until, well...until it was almost over." She rubbed a hand over her stomach as it spasmed. "It helped to finish out the engagements. That would have been important to him."

"I know." She was starting to speak again when the intercom on the table crackled. There was a whimper, a gurgle, followed by a stream of infant jabbering. "She's up and ready to roll." Joanie rose quickly. "I'll just be a minute."

Alone, Vanessa stood and began to wander the room. It was filled with so many little, comforting things. Books on agriculture and child-rearing, wedding pictures and baby pictures. There was an old porcelain vase she remembered seeing in the Tucker household as a child. Through the window she could see the barn, and the cows drowsing in the midday sun.

Like something out of a book, she thought. Her own faded wish book.

"Van?"

She turned to see Joanie in the doorway, a round, dark-haired baby on her hip. The baby swung her feet, setting off the bells tied to her shoelaces.

"Oh, Joanie. She's gorgeous."

"Yeah." Joanie kissed Lara's head. "She is. Would you like to hold her?"

"Are you kidding?" Van came across the room to take the baby. After a long suspicious look, Lara smiled and began to kick her feet again. "Aren't you pretty?" Van murmured. Unable to resist, she lifted the baby over her head and turned in a circle while Lara giggled. "Aren't you just wonderful?"

"She likes you, too." Joanie gave a satisfied nod. "I kept telling her she'd meet her godmother sooner or later."

"Her godmother?" Confused, Vanessa settled the baby on her hip again.

"Sure." Joanie smoothed Lara's hair. "I sent you a note right after she was born. I knew you couldn't make it back for the christening, so we had a proxy. But I wanted you and Brady to be her godparents." Joanie frowned at Vanessa's blank look. "You got the note, didn't you?"

"No." Vanessa rested her cheek against Lara's. "No, I didn't. I had no idea you were even married until my mother told me yesterday."

"But the wedding invitation—" Joanie shrugged. "I guess it could have gotten lost. You were always traveling around so much."

"Yes." She smiled again while Lara tugged at her hair. "If I'd known... I'd have found a way to be here if I'd known."

"You're here now."

"Yes." Vanessa nuzzled Lara's neck. "I'm here now. Oh, God, I envy you, Joanie."

"Me?"

"This beautiful child, this place, the look in your eyes when you talk about Jack. I feel like I've spent twelve years in a daze, while you've made a family and a home and a life."

"We've both made a life," Joanie said. "They're just different ones. You have so much talent, Van. Even as a kid I was awed by it. I wanted so badly to play like you." She laughed and enveloped them both in a hug. "As patient as you were, you could barely get me through 'Chopsticks.'"

"You were hopeless but determined. And I'm so glad you're still my friend."

"You're going to make me cry again." After a sniffle, Joanie shook her head. "Tell you what, you play with Lara for a few minutes and I'll go fix us some lemonade. Then we can be catty and gossip about how fat Julie Newton got."

"Did she?"

"And how Tommy McDonald is losing his hair." Joanie hooked

an arm through Vanessa's. "Better yet, come in the kitchen with me. I'll fill you in on Betty Jean Baumgartner's third husband."

"Third?"

"And counting."

There was so much to think about. Not just the funny stories Joanie had shared with her that day, Vanessa thought as she strolled around the backyard at dusk. She needed to think about her life and what she wanted to do with it. Where she belonged. Where she wanted to belong.

For over a decade she'd had little or no choice. Or had lacked the courage to make one, she thought. She had done what her father wanted. He and her music had been the only constants. His drive and his needs had been so much more passionate than hers. And she hadn't wanted to disappoint him.

Hadn't dared, a small voice echoed, but she blocked it off.

She owed him everything. He had dedicated his life to her career. While her mother had shirked the responsibility, he had taken her, he had molded her, he had taught her. Every hour she had worked, he had worked. Even when he had become desperately ill, he had pushed himself, managing her career as meticulously as ever. No detail had ever escaped his notice—just as no flawed note had escaped his highly critical ear. He had taken her to the top of her career, and he had been content to bask in the reflected glory.

It couldn't have been easy for him, she thought now. His own career as a concert pianist had stalled before he'd hit thirty. He had never achieved the pinnacle he'd so desperately strived for. For him, music had been everything. Finally he'd been able to see those ambitions and needs realized in his only child.

Now she was on the brink of turning her back on everything he had wanted for her, everything he had worked toward. He would never have been able to understand her desire to give up a glowing career. Just as he had never been able to understand, or tolerate, her constant terror of performing.

She could remember it even now, even here in the sheltered quiet of the yard. The gripping sensation in her stomach, the wave of nausea she always battled back, the throbbing behind her eyes as she stood in the wings.

Stage fright, her father had told her. She would outgrow it. It was the one thing she had never been able to accomplish for him.

Yet, despite it, she knew she could go back to the concert stage. She could endure. She could rise even higher if she focused herself. If only she knew it was what she wanted.

Perhaps she just needed to rest. She sat on the lawn glider and sent it gently into motion. A few weeks or a few months of quiet, and then she might yearn for the life she had left behind. But for now she wanted nothing more than to enjoy the purple twilight.

From the glider she could see the lights glowing inside the house, and the neighboring houses. She had shared a meal with her mother in the kitchen—or had tried to. Loretta had seemed hurt when Vanessa only picked at her food. How could she explain that nothing seemed to settle well these days? This empty, gnawing feeling in her stomach simply wouldn't abate.

A little more time, Vanessa thought, and it would ease. It was only because she wasn't busy, as she should be. Certainly she hadn't practiced enough that day, or the day before. Even if she decided to cut back professionally, she had no business neglecting her practice.

Tomorrow, she thought, closing her eyes. Tomorrow was soon enough to start a routine. Lulled by the motion of the glider, she gathered her jacket closer. She'd forgotten how quickly the temperature could dip once the sun had fallen behind the mountains.

She heard the whoosh of a car as it cruised by on the road in front of the house. Then the sound of a door closing. From somewhere nearby, a mother called her child in from play. Another light blinked on in a window. A baby cried. Vanessa smiled, wishing she could dig out the old tent she and Joanie had used and pitch it in the backyard. She could sleep there, just listening to the town.

She turned at the sound of a dog barking, then saw the bright fur of a huge golden retriever. It dashed across the neighboring lawn, over the bed where her mother had already planted her pansies and marigolds. Tongue lolling, it lunged at the glider. Before Vanessa could decide whether to be alarmed or amused, it plopped both front paws in her lap and grinned a dog's grin.

"Well, hello there." She ruffled his ears. "Where did you come from?"

"From two blocks down, at a dead run." Panting, Brady walked out of the shadows. "I made the mistake of taking him to the office today. When I went to put him in the car, he decided to take a hike." He paused in front of the glider. "Are you going to punch me again, or can I sit down?"

Vanessa continued to pet the dog. "I probably won't hit you again."

"That'll have to do." He dropped down on the glider and stretched out his legs. The dog immediately tried to climb in his lap. "Don't try to make up," Brady said, pushing the dog off again.

"He's a pretty dog."

"Don't flatter him. He's already got an inflated ego."

"They say people and their pets develop similarities," she commented. "What's his name?"

"Kong. He was the biggest in his litter." Hearing his name, Kong barked twice, then raced off to chase the shadows. "I spoiled him when he was a puppy, and now I'm paying the price." Spreading his arms over the back of the glider, he let his fingers toy with the ends of her hair. "Joanie tells me you drove out to the farm today."

"Yes." Vanessa knocked his hand away. "She looks wonderful. And so happy."

"She is happy." Undaunted, he picked up her hand to play with her fingers. It was an old, familiar gesture. "You got to meet our godchild."

"Yes." Vanessa tugged her hand free. "Lara's gorgeous."

"Yeah." He went back to her hair. "She looks like me."

The laugh came too quickly to stop. "You're still conceited. And will you keep your hands off me?"

"I never was able to." He sighed, but shifted away an inch. "We used to sit here a lot, remember?"

"I remember."

"I think the first time I kissed you, we were sitting here, just like this."

"No." She folded her arms across her chest.

"You're right." As he knew very well. "The first time was up at the park. You came to watch me shoot baskets."

She brushed casually at the knee of her slacks. "I just happened to be walking through."

"You came because I used to shoot without a shirt and you wanted to see my sweaty chest."

She laughed again, because it was absolutely true. She turned to look at him in the shadowy light. He was smiling, relaxed. He'd always been able to relax, she remembered. And he'd always been able to make her laugh.

"It—meaning your sweaty chest—wasn't such a big deal."

"I've filled out some," he said easily. "And I still shoot hoops." This time she didn't seem to notice when he stroked her hair. "I remember that day. It was at the end of the summer, before my senior year. In three months you'd gone from being that pesty little Sexton kid to Sexy Sexton with a yard of the most incredible chestnut hair, and these great-looking legs you used to show off in teeny little shorts. You were such a brat. And you made my mouth water."

"You were always looking at Julie Newton."

"No, I was pretending to look at Julie Newton while I looked at you. Then you just happened to stroll by the court that day. You'd been to Lester's Store, because you had a bottle of soda. Grape soda."

She lifted a brow. "That's quite a memory you've got."

"Hey, these are the turning points in our lives. You said, 'Hi, Brady. You look awful hot. Want a sip?'" He grinned again. "I almost took a bite out of my basketball. Then you flirted with me."

"I did not."

"You batted your eyes."

She struggled with a giggle. "I've never batted my eyes."

"You batted them then." He sighed at the memory. "It was great."

"As I remember it, you were showing off, doing layups and hook shots or whatever. Macho stuff. Then you grabbed me."

"I remember grabbing. You liked it."

"You smelled like a gym locker."

"I guess I did. It was still my most memorable first kiss."

And hers, Vanessa thought. She hadn't realized she was leaning back against his shoulder and smiling. "We were so young. Everything was so intense, and so uncomplicated."

"Some things don't have to be complicated." But sitting there with her head feeling just right on his shoulder, he wasn't so sure. "Friends?"

"I guess."

"I haven't had a chance to ask you how long you're staying."

"I haven't had a chance to decide."

"Your schedule must be packed."

"I've taken a few months." She moved restlessly. "I may go to Paris for a few weeks."

He picked up her hand again, turning it over. Her hands had always fascinated him. Those long, tapering fingers, the baby-smooth palms, the short, practical nails. She wore no rings. He had given her one once—spent the money he'd earned mowing grass all summer on a gold ring with an incredibly small emerald. She'd kissed him senseless when he'd given it to her, and she'd sworn never to take it off.

Childhood promises were carelessly broken by adults. It was foolish to wish he could see it on her finger again.

"You know, I managed to see you play at Carnegie Hall a couple of years ago. It was overwhelming. You were overwhelming." He surprised them both by bringing her fingers to his lips. Then hastily dropped them. "I'd hoped to see you while we were both in New York, but I guess you were busy."

The jolt from her fingertips was still vibrating in her toes. "If you had called, I'd have managed it."

"I did call." His eyes remained on hers, searching, even as he shrugged it off. "It was then I fully realized how big you'd become. I never got past the first line of defense."

"I'm sorry. Really."

"It's no big deal."

"No, I would have liked to have seen you. Sometimes the people around me are too protective."

"I think you're right." He put a hand under her chin. She was more beautiful than his memory of her, and more fragile. If he had met her in New York, in less sentimental surroundings, would he have felt so drawn to her? He wasn't sure he wanted to know.

Friends was what he'd asked of her. He struggled to want no more.

"You look very tired, Van. Your color could be better."

"It's been a hectic year."

"Are you sleeping all right?"

Half-amused, she brushed his hand aside. "Don't start playing doctor with me, Brady."

"At the moment I can't think of anything I'd enjoy more, but I'm serious. You're run-down."

"I'm not run-down, just a little tired. Which is why I'm taking a break."

But he wasn't satisfied. "Why don't you come into the office for a physical?"

"Is that your new line? It used to be 'Let's go parking down at Molly's Hole.'"

"I'll get to that. Dad can take a look at you."

"I don't need a doctor." Kong came lumbering back, and she reached down for him. "I'm never sick. In almost ten years of concerts, I've never had to cancel one for health reasons." She buried her face in the dog's fur when her stomach clenched. "I'm not going to say it hasn't been a strain coming back here, but I'm dealing with it."

She'd always been hardheaded, he thought. Maybe it would be best if he simply kept an eye—a medical eye—on her for a few days. "Dad would still like to see you—personally, if not professionally."

"I'm going to drop by." Still bent over the dog, she turned her head. In the growing dark, he caught the familiar gleam in her eye. "Joanie says you've got your hands full with women patients. I imagine the same holds true of your father, if he's as handsome as I remember."

"He's had a few...interesting offers. But they've eased off since he and your mother hooked up."

Dumbfounded, Vanessa sat up straight. "Hooked up? My mother? Your father?"

"It's the hottest romance in town." He flicked her hair behind her shoulder. "So far."

"My mother?" she repeated.

"She's an attractive woman in her prime, Van. Why shouldn't she enjoy herself?"

Pressing a hand against her stomach, she rose. "I'm going in."

"What's the problem?"

"No problem. I'm going in. I'm cold."

He took her by the shoulders. It was another gesture that brought a flood of memories. "Why don't you give her a break?" Brady asked. "God knows she's been punished enough."

"You don't know anything about it."

"More than you think." He gave her a quick, impatient shake. "Let go, Van. These old resentments are going to eat you from the inside out."

"It's easy for you." The bitterness poured out before she could control it. "It's always been easy for you, with your nice happy family. You always knew they loved you, no matter what you did or didn't do. No one ever sent you away."

"She didn't send you away, Van."

"She let me go," she said quietly. "What's the difference?"

"Why don't you ask her?"

With a shake of her head, she pulled away. "I stopped being her little girl twelve years ago. I stopped being a lot of things." She turned and walked into the house.

Chapter 3

Vanessa had slept only in snatches. There had been pain. But she was used to pain. She masked it by coating her stomach with liquid antacids, by downing the pills that had been prescribed for her occasional blinding headaches. But most of all, she masked it by using her will to ignore.

Twice she had nearly walked down the hall to her mother's room. A third time she had gotten as far as her mother's door, with her hand raised to knock, before she had retreated to her own room and her own thoughts.

She had no right to resent the fact that her mother had a relationship with another man. Yet she did. In all the years Vanessa had spent with her father, he had never turned to another woman. Or, if he had, he had been much too discreet for her to notice.

And what did it matter? she asked herself as she dressed the next morning. They had always lived their own lives, separate, despite the fact that they shared a house.

But it did matter. It mattered that her mother had been content all these years to live in this same house without contact with her only child. It mattered that she had been able to start a life, a new life, that had no place for her own daughter.

It was time, Vanessa told herself. It was time to ask why.

She caught the scent of coffee and fragrant bread as she reached the bottom landing. In the kitchen she saw her mother standing by the sink, rinsing a cup. Loretta was dressed in a pretty blue suit, pearls at her ears and around her throat. The radio was on low, and she was humming even as she turned and saw her daughter.

"Oh, you're up." Loretta smiled, hoping it didn't look forced. "I wasn't sure I'd see you this morning before I left."

"Left?"

"I have to go to work. There're some muffins, and the coffee's still hot."

"To work?" Vanessa repeated. "Where?"

"At the shop." To busy her nervous hands, she poured Vanessa a cup of coffee. "The antique shop. I bought it about six years ago. The Hopkinses' place, you might remember. I went to work for them when—some time ago. When they decided to retire, I bought them out."

Vanessa shook her head to clear it of the grogginess. "You run an antique shop?"

"Just a small one." She set the coffee on the table. The moment they were free, her hands began to tug at her pearl necklace. "I call it Loretta's Attic. Silly, I suppose, but it does nicely. I closed it for a couple of days, but... I can keep it closed another day or so if you'd like."

Vanessa studied her mother thoughtfully, trying to imagine her owning a business, worrying about inventory and bookkeeping. Antiques? Had she ever mentioned an interest in them?

"No." It seemed that talk would have to wait. "Go ahead."

"If you like, you can run down later and take a look." Loretta began to fiddle with a button on her jacket. "It's small, but I have a lot of interesting pieces."

"We'll see."

"Are you sure you'll be all right here alone?"

"I've been all right alone for a long time."

Loretta's gaze dropped. Her hands fell to her sides. "Yes, of course you have. I'm usually home by six-thirty."

"All right. I'll see you this evening, then." She walked to the sink to turn on the faucet. She wanted water, cold and clear.

"Van."

"Yes?"

"I know I have years to make up for." Loretta was standing in the doorway when Vanessa turned. "I hope you'll give me a chance."

"I want to." She spread her hands. "I don't know where either of us is supposed to start."

"Neither do I." Loretta's smile was hesitant, but less strained. "Maybe that's its own start. I love you. I'll be happy if I can make you believe that." She turned quickly and left.

"Oh, Mom," Vanessa said to the empty house. "I don't know what to do."

"Mrs. Driscoll." Brady patted the eighty-three-year-old matron on her knobby knee. "You've got the heart of a twenty-year-old gymnast."

She cackled, as he'd known she would. "It's not my heart I'm worried about, Brady. It's my bones. They ache like the devil."

"Maybe if you'd let one of your great-grandchildren weed that garden of yours."

"I've been doing my own patch for sixty years—"

"And you'll do it another sixty," he finished for her, setting the blood pressure cuff aside. "Nobody in the county grows better tomatoes, but if you don't ease up, your bones are going to ache." He picked up her hands. Her fingers were wiry, not yet touched by arthritis. But it was in her shoulders, in her knees, and there was little he could do to stop its march.

He completed the exam, listening to her tell stories about her family. She'd been his second-grade teacher, and he'd thought then she was the oldest woman alive. After nearly twenty-five years, the gap had closed considerably. Though he knew she still considered him the little troublemaker who had knocked over the goldfish bowl just to see the fish flop on the floor.

"I saw you coming out of the post office a couple of days ago, Mrs. Driscoll." He made a notation on her chart. "You weren't using your cane."

She snorted. "Canes are for old people."

He lowered the chart, lifted a brow. "It's my considered medical opinion, Mrs. Driscoll, that you *are* old."

She cackled and batted a hand at him. "You always had a smart mouth, Brady Tucker."

"Yeah, but now I've got a medical degree to go with it." He took her hand to help her off the examining table. "And I want you to use that cane—even if it's only to give John Hardesty a good rap when he flirts with you."

"The old goat," she muttered. "And I'd look like an old goat, too, hobbling around on a cane."

"Isn't vanity one of the seven deadly sins?"

"It's not worth sinning if it isn't deadly. Get out of here, boy, so I can dress."

"Yes, ma'am." He left her, shaking his head. He could hound her from here to the moon and she wouldn't use that damn cane. She was one of the few patients he couldn't bully or intimidate.

After two more hours of morning appointments, he spent his lunch hour driving to Washington County Hospital to check on two patients. An apple and a handful of peanut butter crackers got him through the afternoon. More than one of his patients mentioned the fact that Vanessa Sexton was back in town. This information was usually accompanied by smirks, winks and leers. He'd had his stomach gouged several times by teasing elbows.

Small towns, he thought as he took five minutes in his office between appointments. The people in them knew everything about everyone. And they remembered it. Forever. Vanessa and he had been together, briefly, twelve years before, but it might as well have been written in concrete, not just carved in one of the trees in Hyattown Park.

He'd forgotten about her—almost. Except when he'd seen her name or picture in the paper. Or when he'd listened to one of her albums, which he'd bought strictly for old times' sake. Or when he'd seen a woman tilt her head to the side and smile in a way similar to the way Van had smiled.

But when he had remembered, they'd been memories of childhood. Those were the sweetest and most poignant. They had been little more than children, rushing toward adulthood with a reckless and terrifying speed. But what had happened between them had remained beautifully innocent. Long, slow kisses in the shadows, passionate promises, a few forbidden caresses.

Thinking of them now, of her, shouldn't make him ache. And yet he rubbed a hand over his heart.

It had seemed too intense at the time, because they had faced such total opposition from her father. The more Julius Sexton had railed against their blossoming relationship, the closer they had become. That was the way of youth, Brady thought now. And he had played the angry young man to perfection, he remembered with a smirk. Defying her father, giving his own a lifetime of headaches. Making threats and promises as only an eighteen-year-old could.

If the road had run smoothly, they would probably have forgotten each other within weeks.

Liar, he thought with a laugh. He had never been so in love as he had been that year with Vanessa. That heady, frantic year, when he had turned eighteen and anything and everything had seemed possible.

They had never made love. He had bitterly regretted that after she had been swept out of his life. Now, with the gift of hindsight, he realized that it had been for the best. If they had been lovers, how much more difficult it would be for them to be friends as adults.

That was what he wanted, all he wanted, he assured himself. He had no intention of breaking his heart over her a second time.

Maybe for a moment, when he had first seen her at the piano, his breath had backed up in his lungs and his pulse had scrambled. That was a natural enough reaction. She was a beautiful woman, and she had once been his. And if he had felt a yearning the night before, as they had sat on the glider in the growing dusk, well, he was human. But he wasn't stupid.

Vanessa Sexton wasn't his girl anymore. And he didn't want her for his woman.

"Dr. Tucker." One of the nurses poked a head in the door. "Your next patient is here."

"Be right there."

"Oh, and your father said to stop by before you leave for the day."

"Thanks." Brady headed for examining room 2, wondering if Vanessa would be sitting out on the glider that evening.

Vanessa knocked on the door of the Tucker house and waited. She'd always liked the Main Street feeling of the home, with its painted porch and its window boxes. There were geraniums in them now, already blooming hardily. The screens were in the open windows. As a girl, she had often seen Brady and his father removing the storms and putting in the screens—a sure sign that winter was over.

There were two rockers sitting on the porch. She knew Dr. Tucker would often sit there on a summer evening. People strolling by would stop to pass the time or to relay a list of symptoms and complaints.

And every year, over the Memorial Day weekend, the Tuckers would throw a backyard barbecue. Everyone in town came by to eat hamburgers and potato salad, to sit under the shade of the big walnut tree, to play croquet.

He was a generous man, Dr. Tucker, Vanessa remembered. With

his time, with his skill. She could still remember his laugh, full and rich, and how gentle his hands were during an examination.

But what could she say to him now? This man who had been such a larger-than-life figure during her childhood? This man who had once comforted her when she'd wept over her parents' crumbling marriage? This man who was now involved with her mother?

He opened the door himself, and stood there studying her. He was tall, as she remembered. Like Brady, he had a wiry, athletic build. Though his dark hair had turned a steely gray, he looked no older to her. There were lines fanning out around his dark blue eyes. They deepened as he smiled.

Unsure of herself, she started to offer him a hand. Before she could speak, she was caught up in a crushing bear hug. He smelled of Old Spice and peppermint, she thought, and nearly wept. Even that hadn't changed.

"Little Vanessa." His powerful voice rolled over her as he squeezed. "It's good to have you home."

"It's good to be home." Held against him, she believed it. "I've missed you." It came with a rush of feeling. "I've really missed you."

"Let me have a look at you." Still standing in the doorway, he held her at arm's length. "My, my, my..." he murmured. "Emily always said you'd be a beauty."

"Oh, Dr. Tucker, I'm so sorry about Mrs. Tucker."

"We all were." He rubbed her hands briskly up and down her arms. "She always kept track of you in the papers and magazines, you know. Had her heart set on you for a daughter-in-law. More than once she said to me, 'Ham, that's the girl for Brady. She'll straighten him out.'"

"It looks like he's straightened himself out."

"Mostly." Draping an arm over her shoulder, he led her inside. "How about a nice cup of tea and a piece of pie?"

"I'd love it."

She sat at the kitchen table while he brewed and served. The house hadn't changed on the inside, either. It was still neat as a pin. It was polished and scrubbed, with Emily's collection of knickknacks on every flat surface.

The sunny kitchen looked out over the backyard, with its big trees leafing and its spring bulbs blooming. To the right was the door that led to the offices. The only change she saw was the addition of a complicated phone and intercom system.

"Mrs. Leary still makes the best pies in town." He cut thick slabs of chocolate meringue.

"And she still pays you in baked goods."

"Worth their weight in gold." With a contented sigh, he sat across from her. "I guess I don't have to tell you how proud we all are of you."

She shook her head. "I wish I could have gotten back sooner. I didn't even know Joanie was married. And the baby." She lifted her teacup, fully comfortable for the first time since her return. "Lara's beautiful."

"Smart, too." He winked. "Of course, I might be a tad prejudiced, but I can't remember a smarter child. And I've seen my share of them."

"I hope to see a lot of her while I'm here. Of all of you."

"We're hoping you'll stay a good long time."

"I don't know." She looked down at her tea. "I haven't thought about it."

"Your mother hasn't been able to talk about anything else for weeks."

Vanessa took a smidgen of the fluffy meringue. "She seems well."

"She is well. Loretta's a strong woman. She's had to be."

Vanessa looked up again. Because her stomach had begun to jump, she spoke carefully. "I know she's running an antique shop. It's hard to imagine her as a businesswoman."

"It was hard for her to imagine, but she's doing a good job of it. I know you lost your father a few months ago."

"Cancer. It was very difficult for him."

"And for you."

She moved her shoulders. "There was little I could do...little he would allow me to do. Basically he refused to admit he was ill. He hated weaknesses."

"I know." He laid a hand on hers. "I hope you've learned to be more tolerant of them."

He didn't have to explain. "I don't hate my mother," she said with a sigh. "I just don't know her."

It was a good answer. One he appreciated. "I do. She's had a hard life, Van. Any mistakes she made, she's paid for more times than any one person should have to. She loves you. She always has."

"Then why did she let me go?"

His heart went out to her, as it always had. "That's a question you'll have to ask her yourself. And one she needs to answer."

With a little sigh, Vanessa sat back. "I always did come to cry on your shoulder."

"That's what shoulders are for. Mostly I was vain enough to think I had two daughters."

"You did." She blinked the tears away and took a soothing drink of tea. "Dr. Tucker, are you in love with my mother?"

"Yes. Does that upset you?"

"It shouldn't."

"But?"

"It's just that it's difficult for me to accept. I've always had such a clear picture of you and Mrs. Tucker as a set. It was one of my constants. My parents...as unhappy as they were together, for as long as I can remember..."

"Were your parents," he said quietly. "Another permanent set."

"Yes." She relaxed a little, grateful that he understood. "I know that's not reasonable. It's not even reality. But..."

"It should be," he finished for her. "My dear child, there is far too much in life that's unfair. I had twenty-eight years with Emily, and had planned for twenty-eight more. It wasn't to be. During the time I had with her, I loved her absolutely. We were lucky enough to grow into people each of us could continue to love. When she died, I thought that a part of my life was over. Your mother was Emily's closest and dearest friend, and that was how I continued to look at Loretta, for several years. Then she became mine—my closest and dearest friend. I think Emily would have been pleased."

"You make me feel like a child."

"You're always a child when it comes to your parents." He glanced down at her plate. "Have you lost your sweet tooth?"

"No." She laughed a little. "My appetite."

"I didn't want to sound like an old fogy and tell you you're too thin. But you are, a bit. Loretta mentioned you weren't eating well. Or sleeping well."

Vanessa raised a brow. She hadn't realized her mother had noticed. "I suppose I'm keyed up. The last couple of years have been pretty hectic."

"When's the last time you had a physical?"

Now she did laugh. "You sound like Brady. I'm fine, Dr. Tucker. Concert tours makes you tough. It's just nerves."

He nodded, but promised himself that he'd keep an eye on her. "I hope you'll play for me soon."

"I'm already breaking in the new piano. In fact, I should get back. I've been skimping on my practice time lately."

As she rose, Brady came through the connecting door. It annoyed him to see her there. It wasn't bad enough that she'd been in his head all day. Now she was in his kitchen. He nodded to her, then glanced down at the pie.

"The dependable Mrs. Leary." He grinned at his father. "Were you going to leave any for me?"

"She's my patient."

"He always hoards the goodies," Brady said to Vanessa, dipping a finger in the meringue on her plate. "You wanted to see me before I left?"

"You wanted me to look over the Crampton file." Ham tapped a finger on a folder on the counter. "I made some notes."

"Thanks."

"I've got some things to tie up." He took Vanessa by the shoulders and kissed her soundly. "Come back soon."

"I will." She'd never been able to stay away.

"The barbecue's in two weeks. I expect you to be here."

"I wouldn't miss it."

"Brady," he said as he left, "behave yourself with that girl."

Brady grinned as the door closed. "He still figures I'm going to talk you into the backseat of my car."

"You did talk me into the backseat of your car."

"Yeah." The memory made him restless. "Any coffee?"

"Tea," she said. "With lemon verbena."

With a grunt, he turned and took a carton of milk from the refrigerator. "I'm glad you stopped by to see him. He's crazy about you."

"The feeling's mutual."

"You going to eat that pie?"

"No, I was just—" he sat down and dug in "—leaving."

"What's your hurry?" he asked over a forkful.

"I'm not in a hurry, I just—"

"Sit down." He poured an enormous glass of milk.

"Your appetite's as healthy as ever, I see."

"Clean living."

She should go, really. But he looked so relaxed, and relaxing, sitting at the table shoveling in pie. Friends, he'd said. Maybe they *could* be friends. She leaned back against the counter.

"Where's the dog?"

"Left him home. Dad caught him digging in the tulips yesterday, so he's banished."

"You don't live here anymore?"

"No." He looked up and nearly groaned. She was leaning on the counter in front of the window, the light in her hair. There was the faintest of smiles playing on that full, serious mouth of hers. The severe tailoring of her slacks and shirt made her seem that much softer and feminine. "I, ah..." He reached for the milk. "I bought some land outside of town. The house is going up slow, but it's got a roof."

"You're building your own house?"

"I'm not doing that much. I can't get away from here long enough to do much more than stick up a couple of two-by-fours. I've got a couple of guys hammering it together." He looked at her again, considering. "I'll drive you out some time so you can take a look."

"Maybe."

"How about now?" He rose to put his dishes in the sink.

"Oh, well... I really have to get back...."

"For what?"

"To practice."

He turned. Their shoulders brushed. "Practice later."

It was a challenge. They both knew it, both understood it. They were both determined to prove that they could be in each other's company without stirring up old yearnings.

"All right. I'll follow you out, though. That way you won't have to come back into town."

"Fine." He took her arm and led her out the back door.

He'd had a secondhand Chevy sedan when she'd left town. Now he drove a sporty four-wheel drive. Three miles out of town, when they came to the steep, narrow lane, she saw the wisdom of it.

It would be all but impassable in the winter, she thought as her Mercedes jolted up the graveled incline. Though the leaves were little more than tender shoots, the woods were thick. She could see the wild dogwoods blooming white. She narrowly avoided a rut. Gravel spit out from under her wheels as she negotiated the last sweeping turn and came to a halt behind Brady.

The dog came racing, barking, his tail fanning in the breeze.

The shell of the house was up. He wasn't contenting himself with a cabin in the woods, she noted. It was a huge, spreading two-story place. The windows that were in place were tall, with half-moon arches over them. What appeared to be the skeleton of a gable rose up from the second story. It would command a majestic view of the distant Blue Mountains.

The grounds, covered with the rubble of construction, sloped down to a murmuring creek. Rain would turn the site into a mud pit, she thought as she stepped from her car. But, oh, when it was terraced and planted, it would be spectacular.

"It's fabulous." She pushed back her hair as the early evening breeze stirred it. "What a perfect spot."

"I thought so." He caught Kong by the collar before he could leap on her.

"He's all right." She laughed as she bent down to rub him. "Hello, fella. Hello, big boy. You've got plenty of room to run around here, don't you?"

"Twelve acres." He was getting that ache again, just under his heart, watching her play with his dog. "I'm going to leave most of it alone."

"I'm glad." She turned a full circle. "I'd hate to see you manicure the woods. I'd nearly forgotten how wonderful they are. How quiet."

"Come on." He took her hand, held it. "I'll give you the tour."

"How long have you had the land?"

"Almost a year." They walked across a little wooden bridge, over the creek. "Watch your step. The ground's a mess." He looked down at her elegant Italian flats. "Here." He hoisted her up and over the rubble. She felt the bunching of his arm muscles, he the firm length of her legs.

"You don't have to—" He set her down, hastily, in front of a pair of atrium doors. "Still Mr. Smooth, aren't you?"

"You bet."

Inside there was subflooring and drywall. She saw power tools, sawhorses and piles of lumber. A huge stone fireplace was already built into the north wall. Temporary stairs led to the second level. The scent of sawdust was everywhere.

"The living room," he explained. "I wanted plenty of light. The kitchen's over there."

He indicated a generous space that curved off the main room. There was a bay window over the sink that looked out into the woods. A stove and refrigerator were nestled between unfinished counters.

"We'll have an archway to keep in tune with the windows," he went on. "Then another will lead around to the dining room."

She looked up at the sky through a trio of skylights. "It seems very ambitious."

"I only intend to do it once." Taking her hand again, he led her around the first floor. "Powder room. Your mother found me this great pedestal sink. The porcelain's in perfect shape. And this is a kind of a den, I guess. Stereo equipment, books." When he narrowed his eyes, he could see the finished product perfectly. And oddly, so could she. "Do you remember Josh McKenna?"

"Yes. He was your partner in crime."

"Now he's a partner in a construction firm. He's doing all these built-ins himself."

"Josh?" She ran a hand over a shelf. The workmanship was beautiful.

"He designed the kitchen cabinets, too. They're going to be something. Let's go up. The stairs are narrow, but they're sturdy."

Despite his assurances, she kept one hand pressed against the wall as they climbed. There were more skylights, more arches. The eyebrow windows, as he called them, would go over the bed in the master suite, which included an oversize bathroom with a tiled sunken tub. Though there were a mattress and a dresser in the bedroom, the bath was the only finished room. Vanessa stepped off subflooring onto ceramic.

He'd chosen cool pastels with an occasional vivid slash of navy. The huge tub was encircled by a tiled ledge that sat flush against another trio of windows. Vanessa imagined soaking there with a view of the screening woods.

"You've pulled out all the stops," she commented.

"When I decided to move back, I decided to do it right." They continued down the hall, between the studded walls. "There are two more bedrooms on this floor, and another bath. I'm going to use glass brick in that one. The deck will run all around, then drop down to the second level on the west side for sunset." He took her up another flight of splattered steps into the gable. "I'm thinking about putting my office up here."

It was like a fairy tale, Vanessa thought, circular in shape, with more arching windows. Everywhere you stood there was a lofty view of the woods and the mountains beyond.

"I could live right here," she said, "and feel like Rapunzel."

"Your hair's the wrong color." He lifted a handful. "I'm glad you never cut it. I used to dream about this hair." His gaze shifted to hers. "About you. For years after you left, I used to dream about you. I could never figure it out."

She turned away quickly and walked to one of the windows. "When do you think you'll have it finished?"

"We're shooting for September." He frowned at her back. He hadn't thought of her when he'd designed the house, when he'd chosen the wood, the tiles, the colors. Why was it that now that she was here it was as if the house had been waiting for her? As if he'd been waiting for her? "Van?"

"Yes," she answered, keeping her back to him. Her stomach was in knots, her fingers were twisted. When he said nothing else, she forced herself to turn, made her lips curve. "It's a fabulous place, Brady. I'm glad you showed it to me. I hope I get the chance to see it when it's done."

He wasn't going to ask her if she was going to stay. He didn't want to know. He couldn't let it matter. But he knew that there was unfinished business between them, and he had to settle it, at least in his own mind.

He crossed to her slowly. He saw the awareness come into her eyes with his first step. She would have backed away if there had been anywhere to go.

"Don't," she said when he took her arms.

"This is going to hurt me as much as it does you."

He touched his lips to hers, testing. And felt her shudder. Her taste, just that brief taste, made him burn. Again he kissed her, lingering over it only seconds longer. This time he heard her moan. His hands slid up her arms to cup her face. When his mouth took hers again, the testing was over.

It did hurt. She felt the ache through every bone and muscle. And damn him, she felt the pleasure. A pleasure she had lived without for too long. Greedy for it, she pulled him closer and let the war rage frantically inside her.

She was no longer kissing a boy, however clever and passionate that boy had been. She wasn't kissing a memory, no matter how rich and clear that memory had been. It was a man she held now. A strong, hungry man who knew her much too well.

When her lips parted for his, she knew what he would taste like. As her hands dug into his shoulders, she knew the feel of those muscles. With the scent of sawdust around them, and the light gentle through the glass, she felt herself rocked back and forth between the past and present.

She was all he remembered, and more. He had always been generous, always passionate, but there seemed to be more innocence now than there had been before. It was there, sweet, beneath the simmer of desire. Her body trembled even as it strained against his.

The dreams he thought he had forgotten flooded back. And with them the needs, the frustrations, the hopes, of his youth.

It was her. It had always been her. And yet it had never been.

Shaken, he pulled back and held her at arm's length. The color had risen over her cheekbones. Her eyes had darkened, clouded, in that way that had always made him churn. Her lips were parted, soft, unpainted. His hands were lost, as they had been countless times before, in her hair.

And the feeling was the same. He could have murdered her for it. Twelve years hadn't diluted the emotion she could pull out of him with a look.

"I was afraid of that," he murmured. He needed to keep sane, he told himself. He needed to think. "You always could stop my heart, Vanessa."

"This is stupid." Breathless, she stepped back. "We're not children anymore."

He dipped his hands in his pockets. "Exactly."

She ran an unsteady hand through her hair. "Brady, this was over a long time ago."

"Apparently not. Could be we just have to get it out of our systems."

"My system's just fine," she told him. It was a lie. "You'll have to worry about your own. I'm not interested in climbing into the backseat with you again."

"That might be interesting." He surprised himself by smiling, and meaning it. "But I had more comfortable surroundings in mind."

"Whatever the surroundings, the answer's still no."

She started toward the steps, and he took her by the arm. "You were sixteen the last time you said no." Slowly, though impatience simmered through him, he turned her to face him. "As much as I regret it, I have to say you were right. Times have changed, and we're all grown up now."

Her heart was beating too fast, she thought. His fault. He had always been able to tie her into knots. "Just because we're adults doesn't mean I'll jump in your bed."

"It does mean that I'll take the time and make the effort to change your mind."

"You are still an egotistical idiot, Brady."

"And you still call me names when you know I'm right." He

pulled her close for a hard, brief kiss. "I still want you, Van. And this time, by God, I'm going to have you."

She saw the truth of it in his eyes before she jerked away. She felt the truth of it inside herself. "Go to hell."

She turned and rushed down the stairs.

He watched from the window as she raced across the bridge to her car. Even with the distance, he heard her slam the door. It made him grin. She'd always had a devil of a temper. He was glad to see it still held true.

Chapter 4

She pounded the keys. Tchaikovsky. The first piano concerto. The first movement. Hers was a violently passionate interpretation of the romantic theme. She wanted the violence, wanted to let it pour out from inside her and into the music.

He'd had no right. No right to bring everything back. To force her to face feelings she'd wanted to forget. Feelings she'd forgotten. Worse, he'd shown her how much deeper, how much more raw and intense, those feelings could be now that she was a woman.

He meant nothing to her. Could be nothing more to her than an old acquaintance, a friend of her childhood. She would not be hurt by him again. And she would never—never—allow anyone to have the kind of power over her that Brady had once had.

The feelings would pass, because she would make them pass. If there was one thing she had learned through all these years of work and travel, it was that she and she alone was responsible for her emotions.

She stopped playing, letting her fingers rest on the keys. While she might not have been able to claim serenity, she was grateful that she had been able to exorcise most of the anger and frustration through her music.

"Vanessa?"

She turned her head to see her mother standing in the doorway. "I didn't know you were home."

"I came in while you were playing." Loretta took a step forward. She was dressed as she had been that morning, in her sleek suit and pearls, but her face showed a hesitant concern. "Are you all right?"

"Yes, I'm fine." Vanessa lifted a hand to push back her hair. Looking at her mother, she felt flushed, untidy and vulnerable. Automatically, defensively, she straightened her shoulders. "I'm sorry. I guess I lost track of the time."

"It doesn't matter." Loretta blocked off the urge to move closer and smooth her daughter's hair herself. "Mrs. Driscoll stopped by the shop before I closed. She mentioned that she saw you going into Ham Tucker's house."

"She still has an eagle eye, I see."

"And a big nose." Loretta's smile was hesitant. "You saw Ham, then."

"Yes." Vanessa turned on the stool, but didn't rise. "He looks wonderful, almost unchanged. We had some pie and tea in the kitchen."

"I'm glad you had a chance to visit with him. He's always been so fond of you."

"I know." She took a bracing breath. "Why didn't you tell me you were involved with him?"

Loretta lifted a hand to her pearls and twisted the strand nervously. "I suppose I wasn't sure how to bring it up. To explain. I thought you might be…might feel awkward about seeing him again if you knew we were…" She let her words trail off, certain the word *dating* would be out of place at her age.

Vanessa merely lifted a brow. "Maybe you thought it was none of my business."

"No." Her hand fell to her side. "Oh, Van..."

"Well, it isn't, after all." Slowly, deliberately, Vanessa patched up the cracks in her shield. "You and my father had been divorced for years before he died. You're certainly free to choose your own companions."

The censure in her daughter's voice had Loretta's spine straightening. There were many things, many, that she regretted, that had caused her shame. Her relationship with Abraham Tucker wasn't one of them.

"You're absolutely right," she said, her voice cool. "I'm not embarrassed, and I certainly don't feel guilty, about seeing Ham. We're adults, and both of us are free." The tilt of her chin as she spoke was very like her daughter's. "Perhaps I felt odd about what started between us, because of Emily. She had been my oldest and dearest friend. But Emily was gone, and both Ham and I were alone. And maybe the fact that we both had loved Emily had something to do with our growing closer. I'm very proud that he cares for me," she said, color dotting her cheeks. "In the past few years, he's given me something I've never had from another man. Understanding."

She turned and hurried up the stairs. She was standing in front of her dresser, removing her jewelry, when Vanessa came in.

"I apologize if I seemed too critical."

Loretta slapped the pearls down on the wood. "I don't want you to apologize like some polite stranger, Vanessa. You're my daughter. I'd rather you shouted at me. I'd rather you slammed doors or stormed into your room the way you used to."

"I nearly did." She walked farther into the room, running a hand over the back of a small, tufted chair. Even that was new, she thought—the little blue lady's chair that so suited the woman who was her mother. Calmer now, and more than a little ashamed, she chose her next words carefully. "I don't resent your relationship with Dr. Tucker. Really. It surprised me, certainly. And what I said before is true. It's none of my business."

"Van—"

"No, please." Vanessa held up a hand. "When I first drove into town, I thought nothing had changed. But I was wrong. It's difficult to accept that. It's difficult to accept that you moved on so easily."

"Moved on, yes," Loretta said. "But not easily."

Vanessa looked up, passion in her eyes. "Why did you let me go?"

"I had no choice," Loretta said simply. "And at the time I tried to believe it was what was best for you. What you wanted."

"What I wanted?" The anger she wanted so badly to control seeped out as bitterness. "Did anyone ever ask me what I wanted?"

"I tried. In every letter I wrote you, I begged you to tell me if you were happy, if you wanted to come home. When you sent them back unopened, I knew I had my answer."

The color ran into and then out of Vanessa's face as she stared at Loretta. "You never wrote me."

"I wrote you for years, hoping that you might find the compassion to open at least one."

"There were no letters," Vanessa said, very deliberately, her hands clenching and unclenching.

Without a word, Loretta went over to an enameled trunk at the foot of her bed. She drew out a deep box and removed the lid. "I kept them," she said.

Vanessa looked in and saw dozens of letters, addressed to her at hotels throughout Europe and the States. Her stomach convulsing, she took careful breaths and sat on the edge of the bed.

"You never saw them, did you?" Loretta murmured. Vanessa could only shake her head. "He would deny me even such a little thing as a letter." With a sigh, Loretta set the box back in the trunk.

"Why?" Vanessa's throat was raw. "Why did he stop me from seeing your letters?"

"Maybe he thought I would interfere with your career." After a moment's hesitation, Loretta touched her shoulder. "He was wrong.

I would never have stopped you from reaching for something you wanted and deserved so much. He was, in his way, protecting you and punishing me."

"For what?"

Loretta turned and walked to the window.

"Damn it, I have a right to know." Fury had her on her feet and taking a step forward. Then, with an involuntary gasp, she was clutching her stomach.

"Van?" Loretta took her shoulders, moving her gently back to the bed. "What is it?"

"It's nothing." She gritted her teeth against the grinding pain. It infuriated her that it could incapacitate her, even for a moment, in front of someone else. "Just a spasm."

"I'm going to call Ham."

"No." Vanessa grabbed her arm. Her long musician's fingers were strong and firm. "I don't need a doctor. It's just stress." She kept one hand balled at her side and struggled to get past the pain. "And I stood up too fast." Very carefully, she relaxed her hand.

"Then it won't hurt to have him look at you." Loretta draped an arm over her shoulders. "Van, you're so thin."

"I've had a lot to deal with in the last year." Vanessa kept her words measured. "A lot of tension. Which is why I've decided to take a few months off."

"Yes, but—"

"I know how I feel. And I'm fine."

Loretta removed her arm when she heard Vanessa's dismissive tone. "All right, then. You're not a child anymore."

"No, I'm not." She folded her hands in her lap as Loretta rose. "I'd like an answer. What was my father punishing you for?"

Loretta seemed to brace herself, but her voice was calm and strong when she spoke. "For betraying him with another man."

For a moment, Vanessa could only stare. Here was her mother, her face pale but set, confessing to adultery. "You had an affair?" Vanessa asked at length.

"Yes." Shame rushed through her. But she knew she could deal with it. She'd lived with shame for years. "There was someone... It hardly matters now who it was. I was involved with him for almost a year before you went to Europe."

"I see."

Loretta gave a short, brittle laugh. "Oh, I'm sure you do. So I won't bother to offer you any excuses or explanations. I broke my vows, and I've been paying for it for twelve years."

Vanessa lifted her head, torn between wanting to understand and wanting to condemn. "Did you love him?"

"I needed him. There's a world of difference."

"You didn't marry again."

"No." Loretta felt no regret at that, just a vague ache, as from an old scar that had been bumped once too often. "Marriage wasn't something either of us wanted at the time."

"Then it was just for sex." Vanessa pressed her fingers against her eyes. "You cheated on your husband just for sex."

A flurry of emotions raced over Loretta's face before she calmed it again. "That's the least common denominator. Maybe, now that you're a woman, you'll understand, even if you can't forgive."

"I don't understand anything." Vanessa stood. It was foolish to want to weep for something that was over and done. "I need to think. I'm going for a drive."

Alone, Loretta sat on the edge of the bed and let her own tears fall.

She drove for hours, aimlessly. She spent most of the time negotiating curving back roads lined with budding wildflowers and arching trees. Some of the old farms had been sold and subdivided since she'd been here last. Houses and yards crisscrossed over what had once been sprawling corn or barley fields. She felt a pang of loss on seeing them. The same kind of pang she felt when she thought of her family.

She wondered if she would have been able to understand the

lack of fidelity if it had been some other woman. Would she have been able to give a sophisticated little shrug and agree that the odd affair was just a part of life? She wasn't sure. She hadn't been raised to see a sanctified state. And it wasn't some other woman. It was her mother.

It was late when she found herself turning into Brady's lane. She didn't know why she'd come here, come to him, of all people. But she needed someone to listen. Someone who cared.

The lights were on. She could hear the dog barking from inside the house at the sound of her car. Slowly she retraced the steps she had taken that evening. When she had run from him, and from her own feelings. Before she could knock, Brady was at the door. He took a long look at her through the glass before pulling it open.

"Hi."

"I was out driving." She felt so completely stupid that she took a step back. "I'm sorry. It's late."

"Come on in, Van." He took her hand. The dog sniffed at her slacks, wagging his tail. "Want a drink?"

"No." She had no idea what she wanted. She looked around, aware that she'd interrupted him. There was a stepladder against a wall, and a portable stereo set too loud. Rock echoed to the ceiling. She noted there was a fine coat of white dust on his hands and forearms, even in his hair. She fought a ridiculous urge to brush it out for him. "You're busy."

"Just sanding drywall." He walked over to turn off the music. The sudden silence made her edgy. "It's amazingly therapeutic." He picked up a sheet of sandpaper. "Want to try it?"

She managed to smile. "Maybe later."

He stopped by the refrigerator to pull out a beer. He gestured with it. "Sure?"

"Yes. I'm driving, and I can't stay long."

He popped the top and took a long drink. The cold beer eased through the dust in his throat—and through the knot that had lodged there when he saw her walking to his door. "I guess you decided not to be mad at me anymore."

"I don't know." Hugging her arms, Vanessa walked to the far window. She wished she could see the moon, but it was hiding behind a bank of clouds. "I don't know what I feel about anything."

He knew that look, that set of her shoulders, that tone of voice. It had been the same years before, when she would escape from one of the miserable arguments between her parents. "Why don't you tell me about it?"

Of course he would say that, she thought. Hadn't she known he would? And he would listen. He always had. "I shouldn't have come here," she said with a sigh. "It's like falling back into an old rut."

"Or slipping into a comfortable pair of shoes." He winced a little at his own words. "I don't think I like that much better. Look, do you want to sit down? I can dust off a sawhorse, or turn over a can of drywall compound."

"No. No, I couldn't sit." She continued to stare out the window. All she could see was her own pale reflection ghosted on the glass. "My mother told me she'd had an affair before my father took me to Europe." When he didn't respond, she turned to study his face. "You knew."

"Not at the time." The hurt and bewilderment on her face had him crossing to her to brush at her hair. "Not long after you were gone, it came out." He shrugged. "Small towns."

"My father knew," Vanessa said carefully. "My mother said as much. That must have been why he took me away the way he did. And why she didn't come with us."

"I can't comment on what went on between your parents, Van. If there are things you need to know, you should hear them from Loretta."

"I don't know what to say to her. I don't know what to ask." She turned away again. "In all those years, my father never said a thing about it."

That didn't surprise him, but he doubted Julius's motives had been altruistic. "What else did she tell you?"

"What else is there to tell?" Vanessa countered.

Brady was silent for a moment. "Did you ask her why?"

"I didn't have to." She rubbed a chill from her arms. "She told me she didn't even love the man. It was just physical. Just sex."

He contemplated his beer. "Well, I guess we should drag her out in the street and shoot her."

"It's not a joke," Vanessa said, whirling around. "She deceived her husband. She cheated on him while they were living together, while she was pretending to be part of a family."

"That's all true. Considering the kind of woman Loretta is, it seems to me she must have had some very strong reasons." His eyes stayed on hers, calm and searching. "I'm surprised it didn't occur to you."

"How can you justify adultery?"

"I'm not. But there are very few situations that are simple black and white. I think once you get over the shock and the anger, you'll ask her about those gray areas."

"How would you feel if it was one of your parents?"

"Lousy." He set the beer aside. "Want a hug?"

She felt the tears rise to burn the backs of her eyes. "Yes," she managed, and went gratefully into his arms.

He held her, his arms gentle, his hands easy as they stroked along her back. She needed him now, he thought. And the need was for friendship. However tangled his emotions were, he could never refuse her that. He brushed his lips over her hair, enchanted by the texture, the scent, the warm, deep color. Her arms were tight around him. Her head was nestled just beneath his.

She still fitted, he thought. She was still a perfect fit.

He seemed so solid. She wondered how such a reckless boy could have become such a solid, dependable man. He was giving her, without her even having asked, exactly what she needed. Nothing more, nothing less.

Her eyes closed, she thought how easy, how terrifyingly easy, it would be to fall in love with him all over again.

"Feeling any better?"

She didn't know about better, but she was definitely feeling. The hypnotic stroke of his hands up and down her spine, the steady rhythm of his heart against hers.

She lifted her head, just enough to see his eyes. There was understanding in them, and a strength that had developed during the time she had been without him.

"I can't make up my mind whether you've changed or whether you're the same."

"Some of both." Her scent was waltzing through his system. "I'm glad you came back."

"I didn't mean to." She sighed again. "I wasn't going to get near you again. When I was here before, I was angry because you made me remember—and what I remembered was that I'd never really forgotten."

If she looked at him that way five more seconds, he knew, he'd forget she'd come looking for a friend. "Van...you should probably try to straighten this out with your mother. Why don't I drive you home?"

"I don't want to go home tonight." Her words echoed in her head. She had to press her lips tightly together before she could form the next words. "Let me stay here with you."

The somewhat pleasant ache that had coursed through him as he'd held her turned sharp and deadly. With his movements slow and deliberate, he put his hands on her shoulders and stepped back.

"That's not a good idea." When her mouth turned into a pout, he nearly groaned.

"A few hours ago, you seemed to think it was a very good idea." She shrugged his hands off her shoulders before she turned. "Apparently you're still a lot of talk and no action."

He spun her around quickly, threats hovering on his tongue.

As she watched, the livid fury in his eyes died to a smolder. "You still know what buttons to push."

She tilted her head. "And you don't."

He slipped a hand around her throat. "You're such a brat." When she tossed back her head, he was tempted to give her throat just one quick squeeze. He reminded himself that he was a doctor. "It would serve you right if I dragged you upstairs and made love to you until you were deaf, dumb and blind."

She felt a thrill of excitement mixed with alarm. What would it be like? Hadn't she wondered since the first moment she'd seen him again? Maybe it was time to be reckless.

"I'd like to see you try."

Desire seared through him as he looked at her, her head thrown back, her eyes hooded, her mouth soft and sulky. He knew what it would be like. Damn her. He'd spent hours trying not to imagine what now came all too clearly to his mind. In defense he took a step backward.

"Don't push it, Van."

"If you don't want me, why—?"

"You know I do," he shouted at her as he spun away. "Damn it, you know I always have. You make me feel like I'm eighteen and itchy again." When she took a step forward, he threw up a hand. "Just stay away from me." He snatched up his beer and took a long, greedy swallow. "You can take the bed," he said more calmly. "I've got a sleeping bag I can use down here."

"Why?"

"The timing stinks." He drained the beer and tossed the empty bottle into a five-gallon drum. It shattered. "By God, if we're going to have another shot at this, we're going to do it right. Tonight you're upset and confused and unhappy. You're angry with your mother, and you're not going to hate me for taking advantage of all of that."

She looked down at her hands and spread them. He was right.

That was the hell of it. "The timing's never been right for us, has it?"

"It will be." He put a hand on either side of her face. "You can count on it. You'd better go up." He dropped his hands again. "Being noble makes me cranky."

With a nod, she started toward the stairs. At the base, she stopped and turned. "Brady, I'm really sorry you're such a nice guy."

He rubbed at the tension at the back of his neck. "Me, too."

She smiled a little. "No, not because of tonight. You're right about tonight. I'm sorry because it reminds me how crazy I was about you. And why."

Pressing a hand to the ache in his gut, he watched her go upstairs. "Thanks a lot," he said to himself. "That's just what I needed to hear to make sure I don't sleep at all tonight."

Vanessa lay in Brady's bed, tangled in Brady's sheets. The dog had deserted him to sleep at her feet. She could hear the soft canine snoring as she stared into the deep, deep country dark.

Would she—could she—have gone through with her invitation to come to this bed with him? A part of her yearned to. A part of her that had waited all these years to feel as only he could make her feel.

Yet, when she had offered herself to him, she had done so recklessly, heedlessly, and in direct opposition to her own instinct for survival.

She had walked away from him just this evening, angry, even insulted, at his cocky insistence that they would become lovers. What kind of sense did it make for her to have come back to him in emotional turmoil and rashly ask to do just that?

It made no sense at all.

He had always confused her, she thought as she turned restlessly in his bed. He had always been able to make her ignore her own common sense. Now that she was sleeping—or trying to—

alone, her frustration was tempered by gratitude that he understood her better than she understood herself.

In all the years she had been away, in all the cities where she had traveled, not one of the men who had escorted her had tempted her to open the locks she had so firmly bolted on her emotions.

Only Brady. And what, for God's sake, was she going to do about it?

She was sure—nearly sure—that if things stayed as they were she would be able to leave painlessly when the time came. If she could think of him as a friend, a sometimes maddening friend, she could fly off to pick up her career when she was ready. But if he became her lover, her first and only lover, the memory might haunt her like a restless ghost throughout her life.

And there was more, she admitted with a sigh. She didn't want to hurt him. No matter how angry he could make her, no matter how deeply he had, and could, hurt her, she didn't want to cause him any real pain.

She knew what it was like to live with that kind of pain, the kind that spread and throbbed, the kind that came when you knew someone didn't care enough. Someone didn't want you enough.

She wouldn't do to Brady what had been done to her.

If he had been kind enough to allow her to hide in his home for a few hours, she would be kind enough to repay the favor by making sure they kept a reasonable distance between them.

No, she thought grimly, she would not be his lover. Or any man's. She had her mother's example before her. When her mother had taken a lover, it had ruined three lives. Vanessa knew her father had never been happy. Driven, yes. Obsessed with his daughter's career. And bitter, Vanessa thought now. Oh, so bitter. He had never forgiven his wife for her betrayal. Why else had he blocked the letters she had sent to her daughter? Why else had he never, never spoken her name?

As the gnawing in her stomach grew sharper, she curled up

tight. Somehow she would try to accept what her mother had done, and what she hadn't done.

Closing her eyes, she listened to the call of an owl in the woods, and the distant rumble of thunder on the mountain.

She awoke at first light to the patter of rain on the roof. It sent music playing in her head as she shifted. Though she felt heavy with fatigue, she sat up, hugging her knees as she blinked at the gloom.

The dog was gone, but the sheets at her feet were still warm from him. It was time for her to go, as well.

The big tiled tub was tempting, but she reminded herself to be practical and turned instead to the glassed-in corner shower. In ten minutes she was walking quietly downstairs.

Brady was flat on his stomach in his twisted sleeping bag, his face buried in a ridiculously small pillow. With his dog sitting patiently beside him, he made a picture that turned her heart upside down.

Kong grinned and thumped his tail as she came to the bottom of the steps. She put a warning finger to her lips. Kong obviously wasn't up on sign language, as he let out two sharp, happy barks, then turned to lick Brady's face wherever he could reach.

Swearing, Brady shoved the dog's face away from his. "Let yourself out, damn it. Don't you know a dead man when you see one?"

Undaunted, Kong sat on him.

"Here, boy." Vanessa walked to the door and opened it. Delighted to have his needs understood, Kong bounded outside into the pattering rain. When she looked back, Brady was sitting up, the sleeping bag pooled around his waist. Bleary-eyed, he scowled at her.

"How come you look so damn good?"

The same could be said about him, she thought. As he'd claimed, he'd filled out a bit. His naked chest looked rock-firm, his shoulders leanly muscled. Because her nerves were beginning to jump, she concentrated on his face.

Why was it he looked all the more attractive with a night's stubble and a surly set to his mouth?

"I used your shower. I hope you don't mind." When he just grunted, she worked up a smile. If she felt this awkward now, she wondered, how would she have felt if he'd joined her in the bed? "I appreciate the night's sanctuary, Brady. Really. Why don't I pay you back by making some coffee?"

"How fast can you make it?"

"Faster than room service." She slipped past him to the adjoining kitchen. "I learned to keep a travel pot with me in hotels." She found a glass pot and a plastic cone filter. "But I think this is a little out of my league."

"Put some water in the kettle. I'll walk you through it."

Grateful for the occupation, she turned on the tap. "I'm sorry about all this," she said. "I know I dumped on you last night, and you were very…" She turned, and her words trailed off. He was standing now, tugging jeans over his hips. Her mouth went bone-dry.

"Stupid," he finished for her. Metal rasped on metal as he pulled up the zipper. "Insane."

"Understanding," she managed. He started toward her. Her feet knocked up against the unfinished counter as she took a hasty step in retreat.

"Don't mention it," he said. "And I do mean don't mention it. I've had an entire sleepless night to regret it."

She lifted a hand to his cheek, then hastily dropped it when she saw his eyes darken. "You should have told me to go home. It was childish of me not to. I'm sure my mother was worried."

"I called her after you went up."

She looked down at the floor. "You're much kinder than I am."

He didn't want her gratitude, he thought. Or her embarrassment. Annoyed, he passed her a paper filter. "You put this in the cone and put the cone on the glass pot. Six scoops of coffee in the filter, then pour the hot water through. Got it?"

"Yes." There was no need for him to be so snotty when she was trying to thank him.

"Terrific. I'll be back in a minute."

She set her hands on her hips as he padded upstairs. An exasperating man, she thought. Sweet and compassionate one minute, surly and rude the next. With a half laugh, she turned back to scowl at the teakettle. And wasn't that just the combination that had always fascinated her? At least she was no longer a naive girl certain he would turn into a prince.

Determined to finish what she had started, she measured out the coffee. She loved the rich morning aroma of it, and wished she hadn't had to stop drinking it. Caffeine, she thought with a wistful sigh. It no longer seemed to agree with her.

She was pouring the boiling water over the coffee when Brady came back. His hair was damp, she noted. And there was the lingering scent of soap around him. Because her mind was set to be friendly, she smiled at him.

"That had to be the quickest shower on record."

"I learned to be quick when I was an intern." He took a long, deep sniff of the coffee. It was his bad luck that he could also smell his shampoo on her hair. "I'm going to feed Kong," he said abruptly, and left her alone again.

When he returned, she was smiling at the coffee, which had nearly dripped through. "I remember one of these in your kitchen on Main Street."

"My mother always made drip coffee. The best."

"Brady, I haven't told you how sorry I am. I know how close you were."

"She never gave up on me. Probably should have more than once, but she never did." His eyes met Vanessa's. "I guess mothers don't."

Uncomfortable, Vanessa turned away. "I think it's ready." When he reached for two mugs, she shook her head. "No, I don't want any, thanks. I've given it up."

"As a doctor, I can tell you that's commendable." He poured a full mug. "As a human being, I have to ask how you function."

She smiled. "You just start a little slower, that's all. I have to go."

He simply put a hand on the counter and blocked her way. There was rain on his hair now, and his eyes were very clear. "You didn't sleep well."

"I'd say that makes two of us."

He took a casual sip of his coffee as he completed a thorough study of her face. The fatigue he saw was due to more than one restless night. "I want you to do something for me."

"If I can."

"Go home, pull the covers over your head, and tune out until noon."

Her lips curved. "I might just do that."

"If those shadows under your eyes aren't gone in forty-eight hours, I'm going to sic my father on you."

"Big talk."

"Yeah." He set the mug aside and then, leaning his other hand on the counter, effectively caged her. "I seem to remember a comment last night about no action."

Since she couldn't back up, she held her ground. "I was trying to make you mad."

"You did." He leaned closer until their thighs met.

"Brady, I don't have the time or patience for this. I have to go."

"Okay. Kiss me goodbye."

Her chin tilted. "I don't want to."

"Sure you do." His mouth whispered over hers before she could jerk her head back. "You're just afraid to."

"I've never been afraid of you."

"No." He smiled an infuriating smile. "But you've learned to be afraid of yourself."

"That's ridiculous."

"Prove it."

Seething, she leaned forward, intent on giving him a brief, soulless kiss. But her heart was in her throat almost instantly. He used no pressure, only soft, soft persuasion. His lips were warm and mobile against hers, his tongue cleverly tracing the shape of her mouth before dipping inside to tease and tempt.

On a breathless murmur, she took her hands up and over his naked chest to his shoulders. His skin was damp and cool.

He nipped gently at her lips, drowning in the taste of her. Using all his control, he kept his tensed hands on the counter. He knew that if he touched her now, even once, he wouldn't stop.

She would come to him. He had promised himself that as he'd sweated through the night. She would come to him, and not because of a memory, not because of grief. Because of need.

Slowly, while he still had some control, he lifted his head and backed away. "I want to see you tonight, Van."

"I don't know." She put a hand to her spinning head.

"Then you think about it." He picked up his mug again, surprised the handle didn't shatter in his grip. "You can call me when you make up your mind."

Her confusion died away, to be replaced by anger. "I'm not playing games."

"Then what the hell are you doing?"

"I'm just trying to survive." She snatched up her purse and ran out into the rain.

Chapter 5

Bed sounded like a wonderful idea, Vanessa decided as she pulled up in front of the house. Maybe if she drew down the shades, put the music on low and willed herself to relax, she would find the sleep she had lost the night before. When she felt more rested, she might have a clearer idea of what to say to her mother.

She wondered if a few hours' sleep would help her resolve her feelings about Brady.

It was worth a shot.

She stepped out of the car and rounded the hood to the sidewalk. When she heard her name called, she turned. Mrs. Driscoll was lumbering toward her, clutching her purse and a stack of mail. A huge, wood-handled black umbrella was tight in her fist. Vanessa's smile came naturally as she moved forward to greet her.

"Mrs. Driscoll. It's good to see you again."

Only a little winded, Mrs. Driscoll peered out of sharp little eyes. "Heard you were back. Too skinny."

With a laugh, Vanessa bent to kiss her leathery cheek. As always, her former teacher smelled of lavender sachet. "You look wonderful."

"Take care of yourself." She sniffed. "That snippy Brady tells me I need a cane. He thinks he's a doctor. Hold on to this." Bossy by nature, she shoved the umbrella into Vanessa's hand. She opened her purse to stuff her mail inside, stubbornly keeping her balance. The rain made her bones ache all the more, but she had always loved to walk in it. "It's about time you came home. You staying?"

"Well, I haven't—"

"About time you gave your mother some attention," she interrupted, leaving Vanessa with nothing to say. "I heard you playing when I walked to the bank yesterday, but I couldn't stop."

Vanessa struggled with the heavy umbrella, and with her manners. "Would you like to come in, have some tea?"

"Too much to do. You still play real nice, Vanessa."

"Thank you."

When Mrs. Driscoll took the umbrella back, Vanessa thought the little visit was over. She should have known better. "I've got a grandniece. She's been taking piano lessons in Hagerstown. Puts a strain on her ma, having to haul her all that way. Figured now that you're back, you could take over."

"Oh, but I—"

"She's been taking them nigh on a year, an hour once a week. She played 'Jingle Bells' real well at Christmas. Did a fair turn on 'Go Tell Aunt Rhody,' too."

"That's very nice," Vanessa managed, beginning to feel desperate, as well as wet. "But since she's already got a teacher, I wouldn't want to interfere."

"Lives right across from Lester's. Could walk to your place. Give her ma a breather. Lucy—that's my niece, my younger brother's second girl—she's expecting another next month. Hoping for a boy this time, since they've got the two girls. Girls just seem to run in the family."

"Ah…"

"It's hard on her driving clear up to Hagerstown."

"I'm sure it is, but—"

"You have a free hour once a week, don't you?"

Exasperated, Vanessa dragged a hand through her rapidly dampening hair. "I suppose I do, but—"

Violet Driscoll knew when to spring. "How about today? The school bus drops her off just after three-thirty. She can be here at four."

She had to be firm, Vanessa told herself. "Mrs. Driscoll, I'd love to help you out, but I've never given instruction."

Mrs. Driscoll merely blinked her little black eyes. "You know how to play the thing, don't you?"

"Well, yes, but—"

"Then you ought to be able to show somebody else how. Unless they're like Dory—that's my oldest girl. Never could teach her how to crochet. Clumsy hands. Annie's got good hands. That's my grandniece. Smart, too. You won't have any trouble with her."

"I'm sure I won't—I mean, I'm sure she is. It's just that—"

"Give you ten dollars a lesson." A smug smile creased Mrs. Driscoll's face as Vanessa rattled her brain for excuses. "You were always quick in school, Vanessa. Quick and well behaved. Never gave me any grief like Brady. That boy was trouble from the get-go. Couldn't help but like him for it. I'll see that Annie's here at four."

She trundled off, sheltered under the enormous umbrella, leaving Vanessa with the sensation of having been flattened by an antique but very sturdy steamroller.

Piano lessons, she thought on a little groan. How had it happened? She watched the umbrella disappear around the corner. It had happened the same way she had "volunteered" to clean the blackboard after school.

Dragging a hand through her hair, she walked to the house. It was empty and quiet, but she'd already given up on the idea of going back to bed. If she was going to be stuck running scales with a fledgling virtuoso, then she'd better prepare for it. At least it would keep her mind occupied.

In the music room, she went to the gracefully curved new cabinet. She could only hope that her mother had saved some of her old lesson books. The first drawer contained sheet music she considered too advanced for a first-year student. But her own fingers itched to play as she skimmed the sheets.

She found what she was looking for in the bottom drawer. There they were, a bit dog-eared, but neatly stacked. All of her lesson books, from primer to level six. Struck by nostalgia, she sat cross-legged on the floor and began to pore through them.

How well she remembered those first heady days of lessons. Finger exercises, scales, drills, those first simple melodies. She felt an echo of that rush of emotion that had come when she had learned that she had the power to turn those printed notes into music.

More than twenty years had passed since that first day, that first lesson. Her father had been her teacher then, and though he had been a hard taskmaster, she had been a willing student. How proud she had been the first time he had told her she'd done well. Those small and rare words of praise had driven her to work all the harder.

With a sigh, she dipped into the drawer for more books. If young Annie had been taking lessons for a year, she should have advanced beyond the primary level. It was then that she found the thick scrapbook, the one she knew her mother had started years before. With a smile, she opened the first page.

There were pictures of her at the piano. It made her laugh to see herself in pigtails and neat white ankle socks. Sentimentally she paged through photos of her first recital, her early certificates of accomplishment. And here were the awards that had once hung on her walls, the newspaper clippings from when she had won her first regional competition, her first national.

How terrified she'd been. Sweaty hands, buzzing ears, curdling stomach. She'd begged her father to let her withdraw. He'd refused to listen to her fears. And she'd won, Vanessa mused.

It surprised her that the clippings continued. Here was an article from the London *Times,* written a full year after she had left Hyattown. And here a picture of her in Fort Worth after she'd won the Van Cliburn.

There were dozens—no, hundreds—Vanessa realized. Hundreds of pictures, snippets of news, pieces of gossip, magazine articles—many she had never seen herself. It seemed that everything that had ever been printed about her was here, carefully preserved. Everything, Vanessa thought, down to the last interview she had granted before her concerts in D.C.

First the letters, she thought, the book weighing heavily on her thighs, and now this. What was she supposed to think? What was she supposed to feel? The mother she had believed had forgotten her had written her religiously, even when there had been no answer. Had followed every step of her career, though she'd been allowed no part in it.

And, Vanessa added with a sigh, had opened the door to her daughter again without question.

But it didn't explain why Loretta had let her go without a murmur. It didn't explain the years away.

I had no choice.

She remembered her mother's words. But what had she meant? An affair would have destroyed her marriage. There was no doubt of that. Vanessa's father would never have forgiven her. But why had it severed her relationship with her daughter?

She had to know. She would know. Vanessa rose and left the books scattered on the rug. She would know today.

The rain had stopped, and the watery sunlight was already struggling through the clouds. Birdsong competed with the sound of a children's television show that chirped through the window of the house next door. Though it was only a few blocks away, she drove to the antique shop. Under other circumstances she would have enjoyed the walk, but she wanted no interruptions from old friends and acquaintances. The old two-story house was just on the edge of town. The sign that read Loretta's Attic was a graceful arch over the front door.

There was an old-fashioned sleigh in the yard, its metal fittings polished to a gleam. A scarred whiskey barrel was filled to overflowing with petunias, their purple-and-white petals drenched with rain. On either side of the entrance, well-groomed beds spilled over with spring color. A beribboned grapevine wreath hung on the door. When she pushed it open, bells jingled.

"It's circa 1860," she heard her mother say. "One of my finest sets. I had it refinished locally by a man who does a great deal of work for me. You can see what a wonderful job he does. The finish is like glass."

Vanessa half listened to the exchange coming from the next room. Though she was frustrated to find her mother with a customer, the shop itself was a revelation.

No dusty, cramped antique shop this. Exquisite glass-fronted cabinets displayed china, statuettes, ornate perfume bottles and slender goblets. Wood gleamed on each individual piece. Brass shone. Crystal sparkled. Though every inch of space was utilized, it was more like a cozy family home than a place of business. The scent of rose-and-spice potpourri wafted from a simmer pot.

"You're going to be very happy with that set," Loretta was saying as she walked back into the main room. "If you find it doesn't suit after you get it home, I'll be more than willing to buy it back from you. Oh, Vanessa." After fumbling a moment, she turned to the young executive type beside her. "This is my daughter. Vanessa, this is Mr. Peterson. He's from Montgomery County."

"Damascus," he explained. He looked like a cat who'd been given a whole pitcher of cream. "My wife and I just bought an old farmhouse. We saw that dining room set here a few weeks ago. My wife hasn't been able to talk about anything else. Thought I'd surprise her."

"I'm sure she'll be thrilled."

Vanessa watched as her mother accepted his credit card and went briskly about completing the transaction.

"You've got a terrific place here, Mrs. Sexton," he went on. "If you came over the county line, you'd have to beat off customers."

"I like it here." She handed him his receipt. "I've lived here all my life."

"Cute town." He pocketed the receipt. "After our first dinner party, I can guarantee you some new customers."

"And I can guarantee I won't beat them off." She smiled at him. "Will you need some help Saturday when you pick it up?"

"No, I'll drag a few friends with me." He shook her hand. "Thanks, Mrs. Sexton."

"Just enjoy it."

"We will." He turned to smile at Vanessa. "Nice meeting you. You've got a terrific mother."

"Thank you."

"Well, I'll be on my way." He stopped halfway to the door. "Vanessa Sexton." He turned back. "The pianist. I'll be damned. I just saw your concert in D.C. last week. You were great."

"I'm glad you enjoyed it."

"I didn't expect to," he admitted. "My wife's the classical nut. I figured I'd catch a nap, but, man, you just blew me away."

She had to laugh. "I'll take that as a compliment."

"No, really. I don't know Mozart from Muzak, but I was—well, I guess enthralled's a good word. My wife'll just about die when I tell her I met you." He pulled out a leather-bound appointment book. "Would you sign this for her? Her name's Melissa."

"I'd be glad to."

"Who'd have expected to find someone like you in a little place like this?" He shook his head as she handed the book back to him.

"I grew up here."

"I can guarantee my wife'll be back." He winked at Loretta. "Thanks again, Mrs. Sexton."

"You're welcome. Drive carefully." She laughed a little after the bells had jingled at his exit. "It's an amazing thing, watching your own child sign an autograph."

"It's the first one I've signed in my hometown." She took a deep breath. "This is a beautiful place. You must work very hard."

"I enjoy it. I'm sorry I wasn't there this morning. I had an early delivery coming."

"It's all right."

Loretta picked up a soft rag, then set it down again. "Would you like to see the rest of the shop?"

"Yes. Yes, I would."

Loretta led the way into the adjoining room. "This is the set your admirer just bought." She ran a fingertip over the top of a gleaming mahogany table. "It has three leaves and will sit twelve comfortably when extended. There's some beautiful carving on the chairs. The buffet and server go with it."

"They're beautiful."

"I bought them at an estate sale a few months ago. They'd been in the same family for over a hundred years. It's sad." She touched one of the glass knobs on the server. "That's why I'm so happy when I can sell something like this to people who will care for it."

She moved to a curved glass china cabinet and opened the door. "I found this cobalt glass at a flea market, buried in a box. Now, the cranberry I got at auction, and paid too much. I couldn't resist it. These saltcellars are French, and I'll have to wait for a collector to take them off my hands."

"How do you know about all of this?" Vanessa asked.

"I learned a lot by working here before I bought it. From reading, from haunting other shops and auctions." She laughed a little as she closed the cabinet door. "And through trial and error. I've made some costly mistakes, but I've also wangled some real bargains."

"You have so many beautiful things. Oh, look at this." Almost reverently, she picked up a Limoges ring box. It was perhaps six inches high and fashioned in the shape of a young girl in a blue bonnet and blue checkered dress. There was a look of smug pleasure on her glossy face. "This is charming."

"I always try to keep in a few Limoges pieces. Whether they're antique or new."

"I have a small collection myself. It's difficult to travel with fragile things, but they always make hotel suites more like home."

"I'd like you to have it."

"I couldn't."

"Please," Loretta said before Vanessa could set it down again. "I've missed a number of birthdays. It would give me a great deal of pleasure if you'd accept it."

Vanessa looked up. They had to turn at least the first corner, she told herself. "Thank you. I'll treasure it."

"I'll get a box for it. Oh, there's the door. I get a lot of browsers on weekday mornings. You can take a look upstairs if you like."

Vanessa kept the little box cupped in her hands. "No, I'll wait for you." Loretta gave her a pleased look before she walked away to greet her customer. When she heard Dr. Tucker's voice join her mother's, Vanessa hesitated, then went in to meet him.

"Well, Van, getting a look at your mother at work?"

"Yes."

He had his arm around her mother's shoulders. Loretta's color had risen. He's just kissed her, Vanessa realized, trying to analyze her feelings. "It's a wonderful place."

"Keeps her off the streets. Of course, I'm going to be doing that myself from now on."

"Ham!"

"Don't tell me you haven't told the child yet." He gave her a quick, impatient squeeze. "Good grief, Loretta, you've had all morning."

"Tell me what?"

With these two, Ham thought, a man had to take the bull by

the horns. "It's taken me two years to wear her down, but she finally gave me a yes."

"A yes?" Vanessa repeated.

"Don't tell me you're as thickheaded as your mother?" He kissed the top of Loretta's head and grinned like a boy. "We're getting married."

"Oh." Vanessa stared blankly. "Oh."

"Is that the best you can do?" he demanded. "Why don't you say congratulations and give me a kiss?"

"Congratulations," she said mechanically, and walked over to peck his cheek.

"I said a kiss." He swung his free arm around her and squeezed. Vanessa found herself hugging him back.

"I hope you'll be happy," she managed, and discovered she meant it.

"Of course I will. I'm getting two beauties for the price of one."

"Quite a bargain," Vanessa said with a smile. "When's the big day?"

"As soon as I can pin her down." It hadn't escaped him that Vanessa and Loretta hadn't exchanged a word or an embrace. "Joanie's fixing dinner for all of us tonight," he decided on the spot. "To celebrate."

"I'll be there."

When she stepped back, he grinned wickedly. "After the piano lesson."

Vanessa rolled her eyes. "News travels fast."

"Piano lesson?" Loretta repeated.

"Annie Crampton, Violet Driscoll's grandniece." He gave a hearty laugh as Vanessa wrinkled her nose. "Violet snagged Vanessa this morning."

Loretta smiled. "What time's the lesson?"

"Four. She made me feel like I was the second-grade milk monitor again."

"I can speak to Annie's mother if you'd like," Loretta said.

"No, it's all right. It's only an hour a week while I'm here. But I'd better get back." This was not the time for questions and demands. "I have to put some kind of program together. Thank you again for the box."

"But I haven't wrapped it."

"It's all right. I'll see you at Joanie's, Dr. Tucker."

"Maybe you could call me Ham now. We're family."

"Yes. Yes, I guess we are." It was less effort than she had expected to kiss her mother's cheek. "You're a very lucky woman."

"I know." Loretta's fingers dug into Ham's.

When the bells jingled behind Vanessa, Ham took out a handkerchief.

"I'm sorry," Loretta said as she sniffled into it.

"You're entitled to shed a few. I told you she'd come around."

"She has every reason to hate me."

"You're too hard on yourself, Loretta, and I won't have it."

She merely shook her head as she balled the handkerchief in her hand. "Oh, the choices we make in this life, Ham. And the mistakes. I'd give anything in the world to have another chance with her."

"Time's all you need to give." He tilted her chin up and kissed her. "Just give her time."

Vanessa listened to the monotonous plunk of the keys as Annie ground out "Twinkle, Twinkle, Little Star." She might have good hands, but so far Vanessa hadn't seen her put them to good use.

She was a skinny girl with pale flyaway hair, a sulky disposition and knobby knees. But her twelve-year old hands were wide-palmed. Her fingers weren't elegant, but they were as sturdy as little trees.

Potential, Vanessa thought as she tried to smile her encouragement. Surely there was some potential buried there somewhere.

"How many hours a week do you practice, Annie?" Vanessa asked when the child had mercifully finished.

"I don't know."

"Do you do your finger exercises every day?"

"I don't know."

Vanessa gritted her teeth. She had already learned this was Annie's standard answer for all questions. "You've been taking lessons regularly for nearly a year."

"I don't—"

Vanessa put up a hand. "Why don't we make this easy? What do you know?"

Annie just shrugged and swung her feet.

Giving up, Vanessa sat beside her on the stool. "Annie—and give me a real answer—do you want to take piano lessons?"

Annie knocked the heels of her orange sneakers together. "I guess."

"Is it because your mother wants you to?"

"I asked if I could." She stared sulkily down at the keys. "I thought I would like it."

"But you don't."

"I kinda do. Sometimes. But I just get to play baby songs."

"Mmm." Sympathetic, Vanessa stroked her hair. "And what do you want to play?"

"Stuff like Madonna sings. You know, good stuff. Stuff like you hear on the radio." She slanted Vanessa a look. "My other teacher said that's not real music."

"All music is real music. We could make a deal."

Suspicion lighted in Annie's pale eyes. "What kind of deal?"

"You practice an hour every day on your finger exercises and the lesson I give you." She ignored Annie's moan. "And I'll buy some sheet music. One of Madonna's songs. I'll teach you to play it."

Annie's sulky mouth fell open. "For real?"

"For real. But only if you practice every day, so that when you come next week I see an improvement."

"All right!" For the first time in nearly an hour, she grinned, nearly blinding Vanessa with her braces. "Wait till I tell Mary Ellen. She's my best friend."

"You've got another fifteen minutes before you can tell her." Vanessa rose, inordinately pleased with herself. "Now, why don't you try that number again?"

Her face screwed up with concentration, Annie began to play. A little incentive, Vanessa thought with a lifted brow, went a long way.

An hour later, she was still congratulating herself. Tutoring the girl might be fun, after all. And she could indulge her own affection for popular music.

Later in her room, Vanessa ran a finger down the Limoges box her mother had given her. Things were changing for her, faster than she had expected. Her mother wasn't the woman she had thought she would find. She was much more human. Her home was still her home. Her friends still her friends.

And Brady was still Brady.

She wanted to be with him, to have her name linked with his as it once had been. At sixteen she had been so sure. Now, as a woman she was afraid, afraid of making a mistake, of being hurt, of losing.

People couldn't just pick up where they had left off. And she could hardly start a new beginning when she had yet to resolve the past.

She took her time dressing for the family dinner. It was to be a festive occasion, and she was determined to be a part of it. Her deep blue dress was cut slimly, with a splash of multicolored beadwork along one shoulder. She left her hair loose, and added braided earrings studded with sapphires.

Before she closed her jewelry box, she took out a ring with a tiny emerald. Unable to resist, she slipped it on. It still fit, she thought, and smiled at the way it looked on her finger. With a shake of her head, she pulled it off again. That was just the sort of sentiment she had to learn to avoid. Particularly if she was going to get through an evening in Brady's company.

They were going to be friends, she reminded herself. Just friends. It had been a long time since she had been able to indulge in the luxury of a friendship. And if she was still attracted to him—well, that would just add a touch of spice, a little excitement. She wouldn't risk her heart, or his, on anything more.

She pressed a hand to her stomach, swearing at the discomfort. Out of her drawer she took an extra roll of antacids. Festive the evening might be, she thought as she took a pill. But it would still be stressful.

It was time she learned to deal with stress better, she told herself as she stared at her reflection. It was time she refused to allow her body to revolt every time she had to deal with something uncomfortable or unpleasant. She was a grown woman, after all, and a disciplined one. If she could learn to tolerate emotional distress, she could certainly overcome the physical.

After checking her watch, she started downstairs. Vanessa Sexton was never late for a performance.

"Well, well." Brady was lounging at the base of the steps. "You're still Sexy Sexton."

Just what she needed, she thought, her stomach muscles knotting. Did he have to look so gorgeous? She glanced at the front door that he'd left open behind him, then back at him.

"You're wearing a suit."

He glanced down at the gray tweed. "Looks like."

"I've never seen you in a suit," she said foolishly. She stopped a step above him. Eye-to-eye. "Why aren't you at Joanie's?"

"Because I'm taking you to Joanie's."

"That's silly. I have my own—"

"Shut up." Taking her shoulders, he hauled her against him for a kiss. "Every time I do that, you taste better."

She had to wait for her heart to flutter back into place. "Look, Brady, we're going to have to set up some ground rules."

"I hate rules." He kissed her again, lingering over it this time. "I'm going to get a real kick out of being related to you." He drew back, grinning. "Sis."

"You're not acting very brotherly," she murmured.

"I'll boss you around later. How do you feel about it?"

"I've always loved your father."

"And?"

"And I hope I'm not hard-hearted enough to begrudge my mother any happiness she might have with him."

"That'll do for now." He narrowed his eyes as she rubbed her temple. "Headache?"

She dropped her hand quickly. "Just a little one."

"Take anything?"

"No, it'll pass. Shouldn't we go?"

"All right." He took her hand to lead her out. "I was thinking... why don't we drop by Molly's Hole on the way home?"

She couldn't help but laugh. "You still have a one-track mind."

He opened the car door for her. "Is that a yes?"

She tilted her head, slanted him a look. "That's an I'll-think-about-it."

"Brat," he muttered as he closed the door.

Ten minutes later, Joanie was bursting through her front door to greet them. "Isn't it great? I can hardly stand it!" She grabbed Vanessa to swing her around. "We're really going to be sisters now. I'm so happy for them, for us!" She gave Vanessa another crushing hug.

"Hey, how about me?" Brady demanded. "Don't I even get a hello?"

"Oh, hi, Brady." At his disgusted look, she laughed and launched herself at him. "Wow! You wore a suit and everything!"

"So I'm told. Dad said we had to dress up."

"And did you ever." She pulled back. "Both of you. Lord, Van, where did you get that dress? Fabulous," she said, before Vanessa could answer. "I'd kill to be able to squeeze my hips into that.

Well, don't just stand out here, come on in. We've got a ton of food, champagne, the works."

"Hell of a hostess, isn't she?" Brady commented as Joanie rushed inside, shouting for her husband.

Joanie hadn't exaggerated about the food. There was a huge glazed ham, with a mountain of whipped potatoes, an array of vegetables, fluffy homemade biscuits. The scent of cooling apple pies wafted in from the kitchen. The home's festive air was accented by candles and the glint of crystal wineglasses.

The conversation was loud and disjointed, punctuated by Lara's cheerful banging of her spoon against the tray of her high chair.

Vanessa heard her mother laughing, more freely, more openly, than she could ever remember. And she looked lovely, Vanessa thought, smiling at Ham, leaning over to stroke Lara. It was happiness, she realized. True happiness. In all her memories, she could pull out no picture of her mother's face when it had been truly happy.

As the meal wore on, she nibbled lightly, certain that no one would notice her lack of appetite in the confusion. But when she saw Brady watching her, she forced herself to take another bite, to sip at the iced champagne, to laugh at one of Jack's jokes.

"I think this occasion calls for a toast." Brady rose. He shot Lara a look as she squealed. "You have to wait your turn," he told her, hefting his glass. "To my father, who turned out to be smarter than I always figured. And to his beautiful bride-to-be, who used to look the other way when I'd sneak into the backyard to neck with her daughter." Over the ensuing laughter, glasses were clinked.

Vanessa drank the bubbly wine and hoped she wouldn't pay for it later.

"Anyone for dessert?" Joanie's question was answered by communal moans. "Okay, we'll hold off on that. Jack, you help me clear the table. Absolutely not," she said when Loretta stood to stack plates. "The guest of honor does not do dishes."

"Don't be silly—"

"I mean it."

"All right, then I'll just clean Lara up."

"Fine, then you and Dad can spoil her until we're done here. Not you, either," she added when Vanessa began to clear the table. "You're not doing dishes on your first dinner in my home."

"She's always been bossy," Brady commented when his sister disappeared into the kitchen. "Would you like to go into the living room? We can put on some music."

"No, actually, I'd like some air."

"Good. There's nothing I like better than walking in the twilight with a beautiful woman." He gave her a cocky grin and held out a hand.

Chapter 6

The evening was soft and smelled of rain. There were lilacs blooming, their scent an elegant whisper on the air. She remembered they had been Joanie's favorite. To the west, the sun was sinking below the mountains in a blaze of red. Cows stood slack-hipped in the fading light. They walked around the side of the house toward a field thick with hay.

"I hear you've taken on a student."

"Mrs. Driscoll gets around."

"Actually, I heard it from John Cory while I was giving him a tetanus shot. He heard it from Bill Crampton—that's Annie's father's brother. He runs a repair shop out of his garage. All the men hang around over there to tell lies and complain about their wives."

Despite her dragging discomfort, Vanessa had to laugh. "At least it's reassuring to know the grapevine still works."

"So how'd the lesson go?"

"She has...possibilities."

"How does it feel to be on the other end?"

"Odd. I promised I'd teach her how to play rock."

"You?"

Vanessa bristled. "Music," she said primly, "is music."

"Right." He put a fingertip behind her earlobe so that he could watch the jewels she wore there catch the last light of the setting sun. And so that he could touch her. "I can see it now, Vanessa Sexton on keyboards with a heavy metal band." He considered a minute. "Do you think you could wear one of those metal corsets, or whatever they're called?"

"No, I couldn't, no matter what they're called. And if you're only along to make fun of me, I can walk by myself."

"Touchy." He draped an arm around her shoulders. He was glad the scent of his shampoo was still in her hair. He wondered if any of the men he'd seen her linked with in magazines and newspapers had felt the same way.

"I like Jack," she said.

"So do I." They walked along a fence thick with honeysuckle.

"Joanie seems so happy here, on the farm, with her family. I often wondered about her."

"Did you ever think about me? After you'd left, after you'd hit it so big, did you ever think about me?"

She looked out over the fields. "I suppose I did."

"I kept thinking you would write."

Too much, she thought. Too often. "Time passed, Brady. And at first I was too angry and hurt. At you and at my mother." Because she wanted to lighten the mood, she smiled. "It took me years to forgive you for dumping me the night of the prom."

"I didn't." He swore and stuck his hands in his pockets. "Look, it's a stupid thing and long over, but I'm tired of taking the rap."

"What are you talking about?"

"I didn't dump you, damn it. I'd rented my first tux, bought my first corsage. Pink and yellow roses." Now that he had brought it up, he felt like a total fool. "I guess I was probably as excited about that night as you were."

"Then why did I sit in my room wearing my new dress for two and a half hours?"

He blew out a long breath. "I got arrested that night."

"What?"

"It was a mistake," he said carefully. "But by the time it was straightened out, it was too late to explain. The charges were pretty thin, to say the least, but I hadn't exactly been a Boy Scout up until then."

"But what were you arrested for?"

"Statutory rape." At her astonished look, he shrugged. "I was over eighteen. You weren't."

It took almost a full minute before it could sink in, before she could find her voice. "But that's ridiculous. We never..."

"Yeah." To his undying regret. "We never."

She pulled both hands through her hair as she tried to reason it out. "Brady, it's almost too ludicrous to believe. Even if we had been intimate, it wouldn't have had anything to do with rape. You were only two years older than I was, and we loved each other."

"That was the problem."

She put a hand on her stomach, kneading a deep ache. "I'm sorry, so sorry. How miserable you must have been. And your parents. Oh, God. What a horrible thing for anyone to go through. But who in the world would have had you arrested? Who would have—" She saw his face, and her answer. "Oh, no!" she moaned, turning away. "Oh, God!"

"He was dead sure I'd taken advantage of you. And he was dead sure I would ruin your life." And maybe, Brady thought as he stared out over the fields, he wouldn't have been far off. "The way he put it, he was going to see I paid for the first, and he was going to do what needed to be done to prevent the second."

"He could have asked me," she whispered. "For once in my life, he could have asked me." She shivered against a quick chill. "It's my fault."

"That's a stupid response."

"No," she said quietly. "It's my fault, because I could never make him understand how I felt. Not about you, not about anything." She took a long breath before she looked at Brady again. "There's nothing I can say that can make up for what he did."

"There's nothing you have to say." He put his hands on her shoulders, and would have drawn her back against him if she hadn't held herself so stiff. Instead, he massaged her knotted muscles, patiently, with his competent physician's hands. "You were as innocent as I was, Van. We never straightened it out, because for the first few days I was too mad to try and you were too mad to ask. Then you were gone."

Her vision blurred before she blinked back the tears. She could picture him all too easily—young, rebellious, angry. Afraid. "I don't know what to say. You must have been terrified."

"Some," he admitted. "I was never formally charged, just held for questioning. You remember old Sheriff Grody—he was a hard-edged, potbellied bully. And he didn't like me one little bit. Later I realized he was just taking the opportunity to make me sweat. Someone else might have handled it differently."

There was no use bringing up the way he'd sat in the cell, bone-scared, helplessly angry, waiting to be allowed his phone call, while the sheriff and Sexton consulted in the next room.

"There was something else that happened that night. Maybe it balanced the scales some. My father stood up for me. I'd never known he would stand up for me that way, no questions, no doubts, just total support. I guess it changed my life."

"My father," Vanessa said. "He knew how much that night meant to me. How much you meant to me. All my life I did what he wanted—except for you. He made sure he had his way even there."

"It's a long way behind us, Van."

"I don't think I can—" She broke off on a muffled gasp of pain. He turned her quickly. "Vanessa?"

"It's nothing. I just—" But the second wave came too sharp, too fast, doubling her over. Moving fast, he scooped her up and headed back for the house. "No, don't. I'm all right. It was just a twinge."

"Breathe slow."

"Damn it, I said it's nothing." Her head fell back as the burning increased. "You're not going to cause a scene," she said between shallow breaths.

"If you've got what I think you've got, you're going to see one hell of a scene."

The kitchen was empty as he came in, so he took the back stairs. At least she'd stopped arguing, Brady thought as he laid her on Joanie's bed. When he switched on the lamp, he could see that her skin was white and clammy.

"I want you to try to relax, Van."

"I'm fine." But the burning hadn't stopped. "It's just stress, maybe a little indigestion."

"That's what we're going to find out." He eased down beside her. "I want you to tell me when I hurt you." Very gently, he pressed on her lower abdomen. "Have you ever had your appendix out?"

"No."

"Any abdominal surgery?"

"No, nothing."

He kept his eyes on her face as he continued the examination. When he pressed just under her breastbone, he saw the flare of pain in her eyes before she cried out. Though his face was grim, he took her hand soothingly.

"Van, how long have you been having pain?"

She was ashamed to have cried out. "Everyone has pain."

"Answer the question."

"I don't know."

He struggled for patience. "How does it feel now?"

"It's fine. I just want—"

"Don't lie to me." He wanted to curse her as pungently as he was cursing himself. He'd known she wasn't well, almost from the moment he'd seen her again. "Is there a burning sensation?"

Because she saw no choice, she relented. "Some."

It had been just about an hour since they'd eaten, he thought. The timing was right. "Have you had this happen before, after you've had alcohol?"

"I don't really drink anymore."

"Because you get this reaction?"

She closed her eyes. Why didn't he just go and leave her alone? "I suppose."

"Do you get gnawing aches, here, under the breastbone?"

"Sometimes."

"And in your stomach?"

"It's more of a grinding, I guess."

"Like acute hunger pangs."

"Yes." The accuracy of his description made her frown. "It passes."

"What are you taking for it?"

"Just over-the-counter stuff." And enough was enough. "Brady, becoming a doctor's obviously gone to your head. You're making a case out of nothing. I'll take a couple of antacids and be fine."

"You don't treat an ulcer with antacids."

"I don't have an ulcer. That's ridiculous. I'm never sick."

"You listen to me." He propped a hand on either side of her head. "You're going into the hospital for tests—X-rays, an upper G.I. And you're going to do what I tell you."

"I'm not going to the hospital." The very idea of it made her remember the horror of her father's last days. "You're not my doctor."

He swore at her richly.

"Nice bedside manner. Now get out of my way."

"You stay right here. And I mean right here."

She obeyed, only because she didn't know if she could manage to stand. Why now? she wondered as she fought against the pain. Why here? She'd had nasty attacks like this before, but she'd always been alone, and she'd always been able to weather them.

And she would weather it this time. Just as she was struggling to sit up, Brady came back with his father.

"Now, what's all this?" Ham said.

"Brady overreacting." She managed to smile, and would have swung her legs off the bed if Brady hadn't stopped her.

"She doubled up with pain when we were outside. There's burning in the abdomen, acute tenderness under the breastbone."

Ham sat on the bed and began his own gentle probing. His questions ran along the same lines as Brady's, and his face became more and more sober at her answers. At last he sat back.

"Now what's a young girl like you doing with an ulcer?"

"I don't have an ulcer."

"You've got two doctors telling you different. I assume that's your diagnosis, Brady."

"It is."

"Well, you're both wrong." Vanessa struggled to push herself up. Ham merely shifted the pillows behind her and eased her back. With a nod, he looked back at his son.

"Of course, we'll confirm it with X-rays and tests."

"I'm not going in the hospital." She was desperately hanging on to one small bit of control. "Ulcers are for Wall Street brokers and CEOs. I'm a musician, for God's sake. I'm not a compulsive worrier, or someone who lets tension rule my life."

"I'll tell you what you are," Brady said, anger shimmering in his voice. "You're a woman who hasn't bothered to take care of herself, who's too damn stubborn to sit back and admit when she's taken on too much. And you're going to the hospital if I have to hog-tie you."

"Easy there, Dr. Tucker," Ham said mildly. "Van, have you had any vomiting, any traces of blood?"

"No, of course not. It's just a little stress, maybe a little overwork—"

"A little ulcer," he told her firmly. "But I think we can treat it with medication if you're going to hang tough about the hospital."

"I am. And I don't see that I need medication, or two doctors hovering over me."

"Testy," Ham commented. "You'll have medication or the hospital, young lady. Remember, I'm the one who treated you for damn near everything, starting with diaper rash. I think a cimetidine might clear this up," he said to Brady. "As long as she stays away from spicy food and alcohol for the length of the treatment."

"I'd like it better if she had the tests."

"So would I," he agreed. "But short of dosing her with morphine and dragging her in, I think this is the cleanest way to treat it."

"Let me think about the morphine," Brady grumbled, and made his father chuckle.

"I'm going to write you a prescription," he told Vanessa. "You get it filled tonight. You have twenty minutes before the pharmacy in Boonsboro closes."

"I'm not sick," she said, pouting.

"Just humor your soon-to-be-stepfather. I've got my bag downstairs. Brady, why don't you come along with me?"

Outside the door, Ham took his son's arm and pulled him to the head of the stairs. "If the medication doesn't clear it up within three or four days, we'll put some pressure on her to have the tests. Meanwhile, I think the less stress the better."

"I want to know what caused it." Fury vibrated through his voice as he stared at the closed bedroom door.

"So do I. She'll talk to you," Ham said quietly. "Just give her some room. I'm going to tell Loretta. Vanessa won't like that, but I'm going to do it. See that she gets the first dose in her tonight."

"I will. Dad, I'm going to take care of her."

"You always meant to." Ham put a hand on Brady's shoulder. "Just don't push too hard too fast. She's like her mother in that way, tends to pull back when you get close." He hesitated, and though he reminded himself that his son was a grown man, he could only think that the grown man was his son. "Are you still in love with her?"

"I don't know. But this time I'm not going to let her get away until I do."

"Just remember, when a man holds on to something too tight, it slips right through his fingers." He gave Brady's shoulder a final squeeze. "I'll go write that prescription."

When Brady walked back into the bedroom, Vanessa was sitting on the edge of the bed, embarrassed, humiliated, furious.

"Come on." His voice was brisk and unsympathetic. "We can just get to the pharmacy before it closes."

"I don't want your damn pills."

Because he was tempted to throttle her, he dipped his hands into his pockets. "Do you want me to carry you out of here, or do you want to walk?"

She wanted to cry. Instead, she rose stiffly. "I'll walk, thank you."

"Fine. We'll take the back stairs."

She didn't want to be grateful that he was sparing her the explanations and sympathy. She walked with her chin up and her shoulders squared. He didn't speak until he slammed the car door.

"Somebody ought to give you a swift right hook." His engine roared into life. Gravel spit from under the tires.

"I wish you'd just leave me alone."

"So do I," he said fervently. He turned off the lane onto asphalt. By the time he'd hit fifth gear, he was calmer. "Are you still having pain?"

"No."

"Don't lie to me, Van. If you can't think of me as a friend, think of me as a doctor."

She turned to stare out the darkened window. "I've never seen your degree."

He wanted to gather her close then, rest her head on his shoulder. "I'll show it to you tomorrow." He slowed as they came to the next town. He said nothing until they pulled up at the pharmacy. "You can wait in the car. It won't take long."

She sat, watching him stride under the lights through the big glass windows of the pharmacy. They were having a special on a popular brand of soft drink. There was a tower of two-liter bottles near the window. There were a few stragglers left inside, most of whom obviously knew Brady, as they stopped to chat while he stood by the drug counter. She hated the feeling of being trapped inside the car with the pain gnawing inside her.

An ulcer, she thought. It wasn't possible. She wasn't a workaholic, a worrier, a power-mad executive. And yet, even as she denied it, the grinding ache dragged through her, mocking her.

She just wanted to go home to lie down, to will the pain away into sleep. Oblivion. It would all be gone tomorrow. Hadn't she been telling herself that for months and months?

When he came back, he set the small white bag in her lap before he started the car. He said nothing as she sat back in the seat with her eyes closed. It gave him time to think.

It didn't do any good to snap at her. It did even less good to be angry with her for being sick. But it hurt and infuriated him that she hadn't trusted him enough to tell him she was in trouble. That she hadn't trusted herself enough to admit it and get help.

He was going to see that she got that help now, whether she wanted it or not. As a doctor, he would do the same for a stranger. How much more would he do for the only woman he had ever loved?

Had loved, he reminded himself. In this case, the past tense was vital. And because he had once loved her with all the passion and purity of youth, he wouldn't see her go through this alone.

At the curb in the front of her house, he parked, then walked around the car to open her door. Vanessa climbed out and began the speech she'd carefully planned on the drive.

"I'm sorry if I acted childishly before. And ungrateful. I know you and your father only want to help. I'll take the medication."

"Damn right you will." He took her arm.

"You don't have to come in."

"I'm coming in," he said as he pulled her up the walk. "I'm watching you take the first dose, and then I'm putting you to bed."

"Brady, I'm not an invalid."

"That's right, and if I have anything to say about it, you won't become one."

He pushed open the door—it was never locked—and hauled her directly upstairs. He filled a glass in the bathroom, handed it to her, then opened the bottle of medication and shook out a pill himself.

"Swallow."

She took a moment to scowl at him before she obeyed. "Are you going to charge me for a house call?"

"The first one's for old times' sake." Gripping her arm again, he pulled her into the bedroom. "Now take off your clothes."

Pain or no pain, she tossed back her head. "Aren't you supposed to be wearing a lab coat and a stethoscope when you say that?"

He didn't even bother to swear. Turning, he yanked open a drawer and searched until he found a nightshirt. She would wear silk to bed, he thought, clenching his teeth. Of course she would. After tossing it on the bed, he pushed her around and dragged down her zipper.

"When I undress you for personal reasons, you'll know it."

"Cut it out." Shocked, she caught the dress as it pooled at her waist. He merely tugged the nightshirt over her head.

"I can control my animal lust by thinking of your stomach lining."

"That's disgusting."

"Exactly." He tugged the dress over her hips. The nightshirt drifted down to replace it. "Stockings?"

Unsure if she should be mortified or infuriated, she unrolled them down the length of her legs. Brady gritted his teeth again. No amount of hours in anatomy class could have prepared him for the sight of Vanessa slowly removing sheer stockings in lamplight.

He was a doctor, he reminded himself, and tried to recite the first line of the Hippocratic oath.

"Now get in bed." He pulled down the quilt, then carefully tucked it up to her chin after she climbed in. Suddenly she looked sixteen again. He clung to his professionalism, setting the bottle of pills on her nightstand. "I want you to follow the directions."

"I can read."

"No drinking." A doctor, he repeated to himself. He was a doctor, and she was a patient. A beautiful patient with sinfully soft skin and big green eyes. "We don't use bland diets so much anymore, just common sense. Stay away from spicy foods. You're going to get some relief fairly quickly. In all probability you won't even remember you had an ulcer in a few days."

"I don't have one now."

"Vanessa." With a sigh, he brushed back her hair. "Do you want anything?"

"No." Her hand groped for his before he could rise. "Can you—? Do you have to go?"

He kissed her fingers. "Not for a while."

Satisfied, she settled back. "I was never supposed to let you come up here when we were teenagers."

"Nope. Remember the night I climbed in the window?"

"And we sat on the floor and talked until four in the morning. If my father had known, he would have—" She broke off, remembering.

"Now isn't the time to worry about all that."

"It isn't a matter of worry, really, but of wondering. I loved you, Brady. It was innocent, and it was sweet. Why did he have to spoil that?"

"You were meant for big things, Van. He knew it. I was in the way."

"Would you have asked me to stay?" She hadn't thought she would ask, but she had always wanted to know. "If you had known about his plans to take me to Europe, would you have asked me to stay?"

"Yes. I was eighteen and selfish. And if you had stayed, you wouldn't be what you are. And I wouldn't be what I am."

"You haven't asked me if I would have stayed."

"I know you would have."

She sighed. "I guess you only love that intensely once. Maybe it's best to have it over and done with while you're young."

"Maybe."

She closed her eyes, drifting. "I used to dream that you would come and take me away. Especially before a performance, when I stood in the wings, hating it."

His brows drew together. "Hating what?"

"The lights, the people, the stage. I would wish so hard that you would come and we would go away together. Then I knew you wouldn't. And I stopped wishing. I'm so tired."

He kissed her fingers again. "Go to sleep."

"I'm tired of being alone," she murmured before she drifted off.

He sat, watching her, trying to separate his feelings for what had been from what was. And that was the problem, he realized. The longer he was with her, the more the edges between the past and present blurred.

There was one and only one thing that was clear. He had never stopped loving her.

After touching his lips to hers, he turned off the bedside light and left her to sleep.

Chapter 7

Bundled in her ratty blue terry-cloth robe, her hair tousled and her disposition grim, Vanessa trudged downstairs. Because she'd been hounded, she'd been taking the medication Ham Tucker had prescribed for two days. She felt better. It annoyed her to have to admit it, but she was a long way from ready to concede that she'd needed it.

More, she was embarrassed that it was Brady who had supervised her first dose and tucked her into bed. It hadn't been so bad when they'd been sniping at each other, but when she'd weakened and asked him to stay with her, he'd been kind. Doctor to patient, she reminded herself. But she had never been able to resist Brady when he was kind.

The morning suited her mood. Thick gray clouds, thick gray rain. It was, she thought, a perfect day to sit alone in the house and brood. In fact, it was something to look forward to. Rain, depression, and a private pity party. At least solitary sulking would be a change. She'd had little time to be alone since the night of Joanie's dinner party.

Her mother tended to hover, finding excuses to come home two or three times each workday. Dr. Tucker checked in on her twice a day, no matter how much Vanessa protested. Even Joanie had come by, to cluck and fuss, bringing armfuls of lilacs and bowls of chicken soup. Neighbors peeped in from time to time to measure her progress. There were no secrets in Hyattown. Vanessa was certain she'd had good wishes and advice from all two hundred and thirty-three residents of the town.

Except one.

Not that she cared that Brady hadn't found time to come by. She scowled and tugged at the belt of her robe. In fact, she told herself as her fingers trailed over the newel post, she was glad he had been conspicuously absent. The last thing she wanted was Brady Tucker—Hyattown's own Dr. Kildare—looming over her, poking at her and shaking his head in his best I-told-you-so manner. She didn't want to see him. And she certainly didn't need to.

She hated making a fool of herself, she thought as she scuffed barefoot down the hallway to the kitchen. And what other term was there for all but keeling over in Joanie's backyard? Then being carried to bed and having Brady treat her like some whining patient.

An ulcer. That was ridiculous, of course. She was strong, competent and self-sufficient—hardly ulcer material. But she unconsciously pressed a hand to her stomach.

The gnawing ache she'd lived with longer than she could remember was all but gone. Her nights hadn't been disturbed by the slow, insidious burning that had so often kept her awake and miserable. In fact, she'd slept like a baby for two nights running.

A coincidence, Vanessa assured herself. All she'd needed was rest. Rest and a little solitude. The grueling schedule she'd maintained the past few years was bound to wear even the strongest person down a bit.

So she'd give herself another month—maybe two—of Hyattown's version of peace, quiet and restoration before making any firm career decisions.

At the kitchen doorway, she came to an abrupt halt. She hadn't expected to find Loretta there. In fact, she had purposely waited to come down until after she'd heard the front door open and close.

"Good morning." Loretta, dressed in one of her tidy suits, hair and pearls in place, beamed a smile.

"I thought you'd gone."

"No, I ran up to Lester's for a paper." She gestured toward the newspaper folded neatly beside the single place setting. "I thought you might want to see what's happening in the world."

"Thank you." Exasperated, Vanessa stood where she was. She hated the fact that she still fumbled whenever Loretta made a gentle maternal gesture. She was grateful for the consideration, but she realized it was the gratitude of a guest for a hostess's generosity. And so it left her feeling guilty and disheartened. "You didn't have to bother."

"No bother. Why don't you sit down, dear? I'll fix you some tea. Mrs. Hawbaker sent some of her own chamomile over from her herb garden."

"Really, you don't have to—" Vanessa broke off at the sound of a knock on the back door. "I'll get it."

She opened the door, telling herself she didn't want it to be Brady. She didn't care if it was Brady. Then she told herself she wasn't the least bit disappointed when the visitor turned out to be female.

"Vanessa." A brunette who huddled under a dripping umbrella was smiling at her. "You probably don't remember me. I'm Nancy Snooks—used to be Nancy McKenna, Josh McKenna's sister."

"Well, I—"

"Nancy, come in." Loretta hurried to the door. "Lord, it's really coming down, isn't it?"

"Doesn't look like we'll have to worry about a drought this year. I can't stay." She remained on the stoop, shifting from foot to foot.

"It's just that I heard Vanessa was back and giving piano lessons. My boy Scott's eight now."

Vanessa saw the blow coming and braced herself. "Oh, well, I'm not really—"

"Annie Crampton's just crazy about you," Nancy said quickly. "Her mama's my second cousin, you know. And when I was talking it over with Bill—Bill's my husband—we agreed that piano lessons would be real good for Scott. Mondays right after school would work out best for us—if you don't have another student then."

"No, I don't, because—"

"Great. Aunt Violet said ten dollars is what you're charging for Annie. Right?"

"Yes, but—"

"We can swing that. I'm working part-time over to the feed and grain. Scott'll be here sharp at four. Sure is nice to have you back, Vanessa. I gotta go. I'll be late for work."

"You be careful driving in this rain," Loretta put in.

"I will. Oh, and congratulations, Mrs. Sexton. Doc Tucker's the best."

"Yes, he is." Loretta managed to smile without laughing out loud as she shut the door on a whoosh of rain. "Nice girl," she commented. "Takes after her aunt Violet."

"Apparently."

"I should warn you." Loretta walked over to set a cup of tea on the table. "Scott Snooks is a terror."

"It figures." It was too early in the morning to think, Vanessa decided. She sat, dropped her heavy head in her hands. "She wouldn't have trapped me if I'd been awake."

"Of course not. How about some nice French toast?"

"You don't have to fix me breakfast." Vanessa's voice was muffled by her hands.

"No trouble at all." Loretta was humming as she poured milk into a bowl. She'd been cheated out of being a mother for twelve years. There was nothing she'd rather do than pamper her daughter with a hot breakfast.

Vanessa scowled down at her tea. "I don't want to keep you. Don't you have to open the shop?"

Still humming, Loretta broke an egg into the bowl. "The beauty of having your own place is calling your own hours." She added touches of cinnamon, sugar and vanilla. "And you need a good breakfast. Ham says you're on the mend, but he wants you to put on ten pounds."

"Ten?" Vanessa nearly choked on her tea. "I don't need—" She bit off an oath as another knock sounded.

"I'll get it this time," Loretta announced. "If it's another hopeful parent, I'll shoo them away."

But it was Brady who stood dripping on the back stoop this time. Without the shelter of an umbrella, he grinned at Vanessa while rain streamed from his dark hair. Instant pleasure turned to instant annoyance the moment he opened his mouth.

"Morning, Loretta." He winked at Vanessa. "Hi, gorgeous."

With something close to a snarl, Vanessa huddled over her steaming tea.

"Brady, what a nice surprise." After accepting his kiss on the cheek, Loretta closed the door on the rain. "Have you had breakfast?" she asked as she went back to the stove to soak the bread.

"No, ma'am." He took an appreciative sniff and hoped he was about to. "Is that French toast?"

"It will be in just a minute. You sit down and I'll fix you a plate."

He didn't have to be asked twice. After dragging his hands through his dripping hair and scattering rain all over creation, he joined Vanessa at the table. He flashed her a smile, a cheerful, friendly look that neatly disguised the fact that he was studying her color. The lack of shadows under her eyes gratified him as much as the mutinous expression in them.

"Beautiful day," he said.

Vanessa lifted her gaze to the rain-lashed windows. "Right."

Undaunted by her grudging response, he shifted in his chair to chat with Loretta as she flipped the browning bread in the skillet.

Not a peep from him in two days, Vanessa thought, and now he pops up on the doorstep, big as life and twice as irritating. He hadn't even asked her how she was feeling—not that she wanted to be fussed over, she reminded herself. But he was a doctor—and he was the one who'd come up with that ridiculous diagnosis.

"Ah, Loretta." Brady all but drooled when she set a heaping plate of fragrant bread in front of him. "My father's a lucky man."

"I suppose cooking's the first priority when a Tucker goes looking for a wife," Vanessa said, feeling nasty.

Brady only smiled as he glopped on maple syrup. "It couldn't hurt."

Vanessa felt her temper rise. Not because she couldn't cook. Certainly not. It was the narrow-minded, sexist idea that infuriated her. Before she could think of a suitably withering reply, Loretta set a plate in front of her.

"I can't eat all of this."

"I can," Brady said as he started on his own meal. "I'll finish up what you don't."

"If you two are set, I'd best go open the shop. Van, there's plenty of that chicken soup left that Joanie brought over yesterday. It'll heat up fine in the microwave for lunch. If this rain keeps up, I'll probably be home early. Good luck with Scott."

"Thanks."

"Scott?" Brady asked, as Loretta went out.

Vanessa merely propped her elbows on the table. "Don't ask."

Brady waited until Loretta had left them alone before rising to help himself to coffee. "I wanted to talk to you about the wedding."

"The wedding?" She looked over. "Oh, the wedding. Yes, what about it?"

"Dad's been applying a little Tucker pressure. He thinks he's got Loretta convinced to take the plunge over the Memorial Day weekend."

"Memorial Day? But that's next week."

"Why wait?" Brady said after a sip, echoing his father's sentiments. "That way they can use the annual picnic as a kind of town wedding reception."

"I see." But it was so soon, Vanessa thought frantically. She hadn't even adjusted to being with her mother again, to living in the same house with her, and now… But it wasn't her decision, she reminded herself. "I suppose they'll move into your father's house."

"I think that's the plan." He sat again. "They've been kicking around the idea of renting this one eventually. Does that bother you?"

She concentrated on cutting a neat slice of the bread. How could she know? She hadn't had time to find out if it was home or not. "No, I suppose not. They can hardly live in two houses at once."

Brady thought he understood. "I can't see Loretta selling this place. It's been in your family for years."

"I often wondered why she kept it."

"She grew up here, just as you did." He picked up his coffee again. "Why don't you ask her what she plans to do about it?"

"I might." She moved her shoulders restlessly. "There's no hurry."

Because he knew her, he let it go at that. "What I really wanted to talk to you about was a wedding present. Obviously they won't need a toaster or a set of china."

"No." Vanessa frowned down at her plate. "I suppose not."

"I was thinking—I ran it by Joanie and she likes the idea. Why don't we pool our resources and give them a honeymoon? A couple weeks in Cancún. You know, a suite overlooking the Caribbean, tropical nights, the works. Neither one of them has ever been to Mexico. I think they'd get a charge out of it."

Vanessa looked up at him again. It was a lovely idea, she decided. And it was typical of him to have thought of it. "As a surprise?"

"I think we can pull it off. Dad's been trying to juggle his schedule to get a week free. I can sabotage that so he'll think he can only manage a couple of days. Getting the tickets, making some reservations, that's the easy part. Then we have to pack their bags without getting caught."

Warming to the idea, she smiled. "If your father has the same stars in his eyes my mother does, I think we can manage that. We could give them the tickets at the picnic, then bundle them into a limo. Is there a limo service around here?"

"There's one in Frederick. I hadn't thought of that." He pulled out a pad to make a note.

"Get them the bridal suite," Vanessa said. When he looked up and grinned, she shrugged. "If we're going to do it, let's do it right."

"I like it. One limo, one bridal suite, two first-class tickets. Anything else?"

"Champagne. A bottle in the limo, and another in the room when they arrive. And flowers. Mom likes gardenias." She stopped abruptly as Brady continued to write. She'd called Loretta "Mom." It had come out naturally. It sounded natural. "She—she used to like gardenias."

"Terrific." He slipped the pad back in his jacket pocket. "You didn't leave me any."

Baffled, she followed his gaze to her own empty plate. "I... I guess I was hungrier than I thought."

"That's a good sign. Any burning?"

"No." Off balance, she rose to take her plate to the sink.

"Any pain?"

"No. I told you before, you're not my doctor."

"Um-hmm." He was standing behind her when she turned. "We'll just figure I'm taking Doc Tucker's appointments today. Let's have a little vertical examination." Before she could move aside, he pressed gentle fingers to her abdomen. "Hurt?"

"No, I told you I—"

He pressed firmly under her breastbone. She winced. "Still tender?"

"A little."

He nodded. When he'd touched that spot two days before, she'd nearly gone through the roof. "You're coming along nicely. Another few days and you can even indulge in a burrito."

"Why is it that everyone who comes in here is obsessed with what I eat?"

"Because you haven't been eating enough. Understandable, with an ulcer."

"I don't have an ulcer." But she was aching from his touch—for an entirely different reason. "And would you move?"

"Right after you pay your bill." Before she could object or respond, he pressed his lips to hers, firmly, possessively. Murmuring her name, he took her deeper, until she was clinging to him for balance. The floor seemed to drop away from her feet so that he, and only he, was touching her. His thighs against hers, his fingers knotted in her hair, his mouth, hungry and impatient, roaming her face.

She smelled of the morning, of the rain. He wondered what it would be like to love her in the gloomy light, her sigh whispering against his cheek. And he wondered how much longer he would have to wait.

He lifted his head, keeping his hands in her hair so that her face was tilted toward his. In the misty green of her eyes, he saw himself. Lost in her. Gently now, and with an infinite care that stilled her wildly beating heart, he touched his lips to hers again.

Her arms tightened around him, strengthening, even as every bone in her body seemed to melt. She tilted her head so that their lips met in perfect alignment, with equal demand.

"Vanessa—"

"Don't say anything, not yet." She pressed her mouth to his throat and just held on. She knew she would have to think, but for now, for just a moment, she wanted only to feel.

His pulse throbbed, strong and fast, against her lips. His body was firm and solid. Gradually his hands relaxed their desperate grip and stroked through her hair. She became aware of the hiss and patter of rain, of the cool tiles under her bare feet, of the morning scents of coffee and cinnamon.

But the driving need would not abate, nor would the confusion and fear that blossomed inside her.

"I don't know what to do," she said at length. "I haven't been able to think straight since I saw you again."

Her murmured statement set off dozens of new fires. His hands moved up to her shoulders and gripped harder than he had meant them to. "I want you, Van. You want me. We're not teenagers anymore."

She stepped back as far as his hands would allow. "It's not easy for me."

"No." He studied her as he struggled to examine his own emotions. "I'm not sure I'd want it to be. If you want promises—"

"No," she said quickly. "I don't want anything I can't give back."

He'd been about to make them, hundreds of them. With an effort, he swallowed them all, reminding himself that he'd always moved too fast when it involved Vanessa. "What can you give back?"

"I don't know." She lifted her hands to his and squeezed before she stepped away. "God, Brady, I feel as though I'm slipping in and out of the looking glass."

"This isn't an illusion, Van." It was a struggle to keep from reaching for her again. But he knew that what his father had told him was true. When you held too tight, what you wanted most slipped through your fingers. "This is just you and me."

She studied him, the eyes so blue against the dark lashes, the damp, untidy hair, the stubborn set of his jaw, the impossibly romantic shape of his mouth. It was so easy to remember why she had loved him. And so easy to be afraid she still did.

"I won't pretend I don't want to be with you. At the same time, I want to run the other way, as fast as I can." Her sigh was long and shaky. "And hope like hell you catch up with me. I realize my behavior's been erratic since I've come home, and a big part of that is because I never expected to find you here, or to have all these old feelings revived. And that's part of the problem. I don't know how much of what I feel for you is just an echo and how much is real."

He found himself in the frustrating position of competing with himself. "We're different people now, Van."

"Yes." She looked at him, her eyes level and almost calm. "When I was sixteen, I would have gone anywhere with you, Brady. I imagined us together forever, a house, a family."

"And now?" he said carefully.

"Now we both know things aren't that simple, or that easy. We're different people, Brady, with different lives, different dreams. I had problems before—we both did. I still have them." She lifted her hands, let them fall. "I'm not sure it's wise to begin a relationship with you, a physical relationship, until I resolve them."

"It's more than physical, Vanessa. It's always been more."

She nodded, taking a moment to calm a fresh flood of emotion. "All the more reason to take it slowly. I don't know what I'm going to do with my life, with my music. Having an affair will only make it that much more difficult for both of us when I leave."

Panic. He tasted it. When she left again, it would break his heart. He wasn't sure that particular organ would survive a second time. "If you're asking me to turn off my feelings and walk away, I won't." In one swift movement, he pulled her against him again. The hell with what was right. "And neither will you."

She felt the thrill race up her spine, those twin sprinters—excitement and alarm. The ghost of the boy she had known and loved was in his eyes, reckless, relentless. She'd never been able to resist him.

"I'm asking you to let me sort this through." If he wanted to use anger, then she would match him blow for blow. "The decision's mine, Brady," she said, jerking away. "I won't be pressured or threatened or seduced. Believe me, it's all been tried before."

It was the wrong switch to pull. His eyes, already hot, turned to blue fire. "I'm not one of your smooth, well-mannered lovers, Van. I won't pressure or threaten or seduce. When the time comes, I'll just take."

Challenged, she tossed her head back. "You won't take anything I don't give. No man does. Oh, I'd like to toss those smooth, well-mannered lovers in your face." She gave him a shove as she walked past him to the stove. "Just to see you squirm. But I'll do better than that." She whirled back, hair flying. "I'll tell you the truth. There haven't been any lovers. Because I haven't wanted there to be." Insolent and mocking, she leaned against the stove. "And if I decide I don't want you, you'll just have to join the ranks of the disappointed."

No one. There had been no one. Almost before he could absorb it, she was hurling her final insult. He bristled, took a step toward her, then managed to stop himself. If he touched her now, one of them would crawl. He didn't want it to be him. He stalked to the back door, and had wrenched it open before he got his temper under control enough to realize that his retreat was exactly what she'd wanted.

So he'd throw her a curve.

"How about going to the movies tonight?"

If he'd suggested a quick trip to the moon, she would have been no less surprised. "What?"

"The movies. Do you want to go to the movies?"

"Why?"

"Because I have a craving for popcorn," he snapped. "Do you want to go or not?"

"I... Yes," she heard herself say.

"Fine." He slammed the door behind him.

Life was a puzzle, Vanessa decided. And she was having a hard time fitting the pieces together. For a week she'd been whirled into wedding and picnic plans. Coleslaw and potato salad, long-stemmed roses and photographers. She was dead sure it was a mistake to try to coordinate a town picnic with an intimate family wedding. It was like trying to juggle bowling balls and feathers.

As the final week passed, she was too busy and too confused to notice that she felt better than she had in years. There was the secret honeymoon, and Joanie's enthusiastic bubbling over every aspect of the upcoming nuptials. There were flowers to be ordered and arranged—and a hundred hamburger patties to make.

She went out with Brady almost every night. To the movies, to dinner. To a concert. He was such an easy and amusing companion that she began to wonder if she had dreamed the passion and anger in the gloomy kitchen.

But each night when he walked her to the door, each night when he kissed her breathless, she realized he was indeed giving her time to think things through. Just as he was making certain she had plenty to think about.

The night before the wedding, she stayed at home. But she thought of him, even as she and Loretta and Joanie bustled around the kitchen putting last-minute touches on a mountain of food.

"I still think the guys should be here helping," Joanie muttered as she slapped a hamburger patty between her hands.

"They'd just be in the way." Loretta molded another hunk of meat into shape. "Besides, I'm too nervous to deal with Ham tonight."

Joanie laughed. "You're doing fine. Dad's a basket case. When he came by the farm today, he asked me three times for a cup of coffee. He had one in his hand the whole time."

Pleased, Loretta chuckled. "It's nice to know he's suffering, too." She looked at the kitchen clock for the fifth time in five minutes. Eight o'clock, she thought. In fourteen hours she would be married. "I hope it doesn't rain."

Vanessa, who'd been deemed an amateur, looked up from her task of arranging the patties in layers between waxed paper. "The forecast is sunny and high seventies."

"Oh, yes." Loretta managed a smile. "You told me that before, didn't you?"

"Only fifty or sixty times."

Her brows knitted, Loretta looked out the window. "Of course, if it did rain, we could move the wedding indoors. It would be a shame to have the picnic spoiled, though. Ham enjoys it so."

"It wouldn't dare rain," Joanie stated, taking the forgotten patty from the bride-to-be's hands. Unable to resist, she tucked her tongue in her cheek. "It's too bad you had to postpone your honeymoon."

"Oh, well." With a shrug, Loretta went back to work. She didn't want to show her disappointment. "Ham just couldn't manage to clear his schedule. I'll have to get used to that sort of thing, if I'm going to be a doctor's wife." She pressed a hand to her nervous stomach. "Is that rain? Did I hear rain?"

"No," Vanessa and Joanie said in unison.

With a weak laugh, Loretta washed her hands. "I must be hearing things. I've been so addled this past week. Just this morning I couldn't find my blue silk blouse—and I've misplaced the linen slacks I got on sale just last month. My new sandals, too, and my good black cocktail dress. I can't think where I might have put them."

Vanessa shot Joanie a warning look before her friend could chuckle. "They'll turn up."

"What? Oh, yes...yes, of course they will. Are you sure that's not rain?"

Exasperated, Vanessa put a hand on her hip. "Mom, for heaven's sake, it's not rain. There isn't going to be any rain. Go take a hot bath." When Loretta's eyes filled, Vanessa rolled her eyes. "I'm sorry. I didn't mean to snap at you."

"You called me 'Mom,'" Loretta said, her breath hitching. "I never thought you would again." As tears overflowed, she rushed from the room.

"Damn it." Vanessa leaned her hands on the counter. "I've been working overtime to keep the peace all week, and I blow it the night before the wedding."

"You didn't blow anything." Joanie put a hand on her shoulder and rubbed. "I'm not going to say it's none of my business, because we're friends, and tomorrow we'll be family. I've watched you and Loretta walk around each other ever since you got back. And I've seen the way she looks at you when your back is turned, or when you leave a room."

"I don't know if I can give her what she wants."

"You're wrong," Joanie said quietly. "You can. In a lot of ways you already have. Why don't you go upstairs, make sure she's all right? I'll give Brady a call and have him help me load most of this food up and take it down to Dad's."

"All right."

Vanessa went upstairs quietly, slowly, trying to work out the right things to say. But when she saw Loretta sitting on the bed, nothing seemed right.

"I'm sorry." Loretta dabbed at her eyes with a tissue. "I guess I'm overly emotional tonight."

"You're entitled." Vanessa hesitated in the doorway. "Would you like to be alone?"

"No." Loretta held out a hand. "Would you sit awhile?"

Unable to refuse, Vanessa crossed the room to sit beside her mother.

"For some reason," Loretta began, "I've been thinking about what you were like as a baby. You were so pretty. I know all mothers say that, but you were. So bright and alert, and all that hair." She reached out to touch the tips of Vanessa's hair. "Sometimes I would just sit and watch you as you slept. I couldn't believe you were mine. As long as I can remember, I wanted to have a home and children. Oh, I wanted to fill a house with children. It was my only ambition." She looked down at the tissue she had shredded. "When I had you, it was the happiest day of my life. You'll understand that better when you have a baby of your own."

"I know you loved me." Vanessa chose her words carefully. "That's why the rest was so difficult. But I don't think this is the time for us to talk about it."

"Maybe not." Loretta wasn't sure it would ever be the time for a full explanation. One that might turn her daughter away again, just when she was beginning to open her heart. "I just want you to know that I understand you're trying to forgive, and to forgive without explanations. That means a great deal to me." She took a chance and gripped her daughter's hand. "I love you now even more than I did that first moment, when they put you into my arms. No matter where you go or what you do, I always will."

"I love you, too." Vanessa brought their joined hands to her cheek for a moment. "I always have." And that was what hurt the most. She rose and managed to smile. "I think you should get some sleep. You want to look your best tomorrow."

"Yes. Good night, Van."

"Good night." She closed the door quietly behind her.

Chapter 8

Vanessa heard the hiss at her window and blinked groggily awake. Rain? she thought, trying to remember why it was so important there be no rain that day.

The wedding, she thought with a start, and sat straight up. The sun was up, she realized as she shook herself. It was streaming through her half-opened window like pale gold fingers. But the hiss came again—and a rattle.

Not rain, she decided as she sprang out of bed. Pebbles. Rushing to the window, she threw it all the way up.

And there he was, standing in her backyard, dressed in ripped sweats and battered sneakers, his legs spread and planted, his head back and a fistful of pebbles in his hand.

"It's about time," Brady whispered up at her. "I've been throwing rocks at your window for ten minutes."

Vanessa leaned an elbow on the sill and rested her chin in her palm. "Why?"

"To wake you up."

"Ever hear of a telephone?"

"I didn't want to wake your mother."

She yawned. "What time is it?"

"It's after six." He glanced over to see Kong digging at the marigolds and whistled the dog to him. Now they both stood, looking up at her. "Well, are you coming down?"

She grinned. "I like the view from here."

"You've got ten minutes before I find out if I can still shimmy up a drainpipe."

"Tough choice." With a laugh, she shut the window. In less than ten minutes, she was creeping out the back door in her oldest jeans and baggiest sweater. Thoughts of a romantic assignation were dispelled when she saw Joanie, Jack and Lara.

"What's going on?" she demanded.

"We're decorating." Brady hefted a cardboard box and shoved it at her. "Crepe paper, balloons, wedding bells. The works. We thought we'd shoot for discreet and elegant here for the ceremony, then go all out down at Dad's for the picnic."

"More surprises." The box weighed a ton, and she shifted it. "Where do we start?"

They worked in whispers and muffled laughter, arguing about the proper way to drape crepe paper on a maple tree. Brady's idea of discreet was to hang half a dozen paper wedding bells from the branches and top it off with balloons. But it wasn't until they had carted everything down the block to the Tuckers that he really cut loose.

"It's a reception, not a circus," Vanessa reminded him. He had climbed into the old sycamore and was gleefully shooting out strips of crepe paper.

"It's a celebration," he replied. "It reminds me of when we'd roll old Mr. Taggert's willow every Halloween. Hand me some more pink."

Despite her better judgment, Vanessa obeyed. "It looks like a five-year-old did it."

"Artistic expression."

With a muttered comment, Vanessa turned. She saw that Jack had climbed on the roof and was busily anchoring a line of balloons along the gutter. While Lara sat on a blanket with a pile of plastic blocks and Kong for company, Joanie tied the last of the wedding bells to the grape arbor. The result of their combined efforts wasn't elegant, and it certainly wasn't artistic. But it was terrific.

"You're all crazy," Vanessa decided when Brady jumped from the tree to land softly beside her. He smelled lightly of soap and sweat. "What's next? A calliope and a snake charmer?"

He reached into a box and drew out another roll of white and a roll of pink. "The mall was out of calliopes, but we've still got some of this left."

Vanessa thought a moment, then grinned. "Give me the tape." With it in her hand, she raced to the house. "Come on," she said, gesturing to Brady. "Give me a boost."

"A what?"

"I need to get up on your shoulders." She got behind him and leaped up nimbly to hook her legs around his waist. "Try to stand still," she muttered as she inched her way upward. He tried not to notice that her thighs were slender and only a thin layer of denim away. "Now I need both rolls."

They juggled the paper and tape between them.

"I like your knees," Brady commented, turning his head to nip at one.

"Just consider yourself a stepladder." She secured the tips of the streamers to the eaves of the house. "Move back, but slowly. I'll twist as you go."

"Go where?"

"To the back of the yard—to that monstrosity that used to be a sycamore tree."

Balancing her and craning his neck behind him to be sure he didn't step on an unwary dog—or his niece—or in a gopher hole, he walked backward. "What are you doing?"

"I'm decorating." She twisted the strips of pink and white together, letting the streamer droop a few inches above Brady's head. "Don't run into the tree." When they reached it, she hooked her feet around Brady's chest and leaned forward. "I just have to reach this branch. Got it."

"Now what?"

"Now we do another from the tree to the other side of the house. Balance," she said, leaning forward to look at him. "That's artistic."

When the deed was done, and the last scrap of colored paper used, she put her hands on her hips and studied the results. "Nice," she decided. "Very nice—except for the mess you made of the sycamore."

"The sycamore is a work of art," he told her. "It's riddled with symbolism."

"It looks like Mr. Taggert's willow on Halloween," Joanie chimed in as she plucked up Lara and settled her on her hip. "One look at that and he's going to know who rolled it in toilet paper every year." She grinned up at Vanessa, who was still perched on Brady's shoulders. "We'd better run. Only two hours until countdown." She poked a finger in Brady's chest. "You're in charge of Dad until we get back."

"He's not going anywhere."

"I'm not worried about that. He's so nervous he might tie his shoelaces together."

"Or forget to wear shoes at all," Jack put in, taking Joanie's arm to lead her away. "Or he could wear his shoes and forget his pants, all because you were standing here worrying about it so you didn't get home and change and get back in time to nag him."

"I don't nag," she said with a chuckle as he pulled her along. "And, Brady, don't forget to check with Mrs. Leary about the cake. Oh, and—" The rest was muffled when Jack clamped a hand over her mouth.

"And I used to put my hands over my ears," Brady murmured. He twisted his head to look up at Vanessa. "Want a ride home?"

"Sure."

He trooped off, still carrying her, through the neighboring yards. "Putting on weight?" He'd noticed she was filling out her jeans very nicely.

"Doctor's orders." She gave his hair an ungentle tug. "So watch your step."

"Purely a professional question. How about I give you an exam?" He turned his head to leer at her.

"Look out for the—" She ducked down so that the clotheslines skimmed over her head. "You might have walked around it."

"Yeah, but now I can smell your hair." He kissed her before she could straighten up again. "Are you going to make me some breakfast?"

"No."

"Coffee?"

She chuckled as she started to squirm down his back. "No."

"Instant?"

"No." She was laughing when her feet hit the ground. "I'm going to take a long, hot shower, then spend an hour primping and admiring myself in the mirror."

He gathered her close, though the dog was trying to wiggle between them. "You look pretty good right now."

"I can look better."

"I'll let you know." He tipped her face up to his. "After the picnic, you want to come by, help me look at paint chips?"

She gave him a quick, impulsive kiss. "I'll let you know," she said before she dashed inside.

Loretta's nerves seemed to have transferred to her daughter. While the bride calmly dressed for her wedding day, Vanessa fussed with the flower arrangements, checked and rechecked the bottle of champagne that had been set aside for the first family toast, and paced from window to window looking for the photographer.

"He should have been here ten minutes ago," she said when she heard Loretta start downstairs. "I knew it was a mistake to hire Mrs. Driscoll's grandson's brother-in-law. I don't understand why—" She turned, breaking off when she saw her mother.

"Oh. You look beautiful."

Loretta had chosen a pale, pale green silk with only a touch of ecru lace along the tea-length hem. It was simple—simply cut, simply beautiful. On an impulse, she'd bought a matching picture hat, and she'd fluffed her hair under the brim.

"You don't think it's too much?" She reached up, her fingers skimming the hat. "It is just a small, informal wedding."

"It's perfect. Really perfect. I've never seen you look better."

"I feel perfect." She smiled. As a bride should, she was glowing. "I don't know what was wrong with me last night. Today I feel perfect. I'm so happy." She shook her head quickly. "I don't want to cry. I spent forever on my face."

"You're not going to cry," Vanessa said firmly. "The photographer— Oh, thank God, he's just pulling up outside. I'll— Oh, wait. Do you have everything?"

"Everything?"

"You know, something old, something new?"

"I forgot." Struck by bridal superstition, Loretta started a frantic mental search. "The dress is new. And these…" She touched a finger to her pearls. "These were my mother's—and her mother's, so they're old."

"Good start. Blue?"

Color rose in Loretta's cheeks. "Yes, actually, under the dress. I have, ah… My camisole has little blue ribbons down the front. I suppose you think I'm foolish buying fancy lingerie."

"No, I don't." Vanessa touched her mother's arm, and was surprised by the quick impulse she had to hug her. Instead, she stepped back. "That leaves borrowed."

"Well, I—"

"Here." Vanessa unclasped the thin gold braided bracelet she wore. "Take this, and you'll be all set." She peeked out the window again. "Oh, here comes Doc Tucker and the rest of them." With a laugh, she waved. "They look like a parade. Go into the music room until I can hustle them outside."

"Van." Loretta was still standing, holding the bracelet in her hand. "Thank you."

Vanessa waited until her mother was out of sight before opening the door. Mass confusion entered. Joanie was arguing with Brady about the proper way to pin a boutonniere. Jack claimed his wife had tied his tie so tight that he couldn't breathe, much less talk. Ham paced the length of the house and back again before Vanessa could nudge him outside.

"You brought the dog," Vanessa said, staring at Kong, who had a red carnation pinned jauntily to his collar.

"He's family," Brady claimed. "I couldn't hurt his feelings."

"Maybe a leash?" she suggested.

"Don't be insulting."

"He's sniffing at Reverend Taylor's shoes."

"With any luck, that's all he'll do to Reverend Taylor's shoes." He turned back to her as she stifled a giggle. "You were right."

"About what?"

"You can look better."

She was wearing a thin, summery dress with yards of skirt in a bold floral print. Its snug contrasting bodice was a rich teal blue, with a bandeau collar that left the curve of her shoulders bare. The gold rope around her neck, and her braided earrings, matched the bracelet she had given Loretta.

"So can you." In a natural movement, she reached up to

straighten the knot in the dark blue tie he was wearing with an oyster-colored suit. "I guess we're all set."

"We're still missing something."

She looked around quickly. The baskets of flowers were in place. Joanie was brushing imaginary dust off her father's sleeve while Reverend Taylor cooed over Lara and tried to avoid Kong. The wedding bells were twirling slowly in the light breeze.

"What?"

"The bride."

"Oh, Lord. I forgot. I'll go get her." Turning, Vanessa raced into the house. She found Loretta in the music room, sitting on the piano stool taking long, deep breaths. "Are you ready?"

She took one more. "Yes." Rising, she walked through the house. But at the back door she paused and groped for Vanessa's hand. Together they crossed the lawn. With each step, Ham's smile grew wider, her mother's hand steadier. They stopped in front of the minister. Vanessa released her mother's hand, stepped back and took Brady's.

"Dearly beloved..." the minister began.

She watched her mother marry under the shade of the maple with paper wedding bells swaying.

"You may kiss the bride," the minister intoned. A cheer went up from neighboring yards where people had gathered. The camera clicked as Ham brought Loretta close for a long, full-bodied kiss that brought on more whistles and shouts.

"Nice job," Brady said as he embraced his father.

Vanessa put her confused emotions on hold and turned to hug her mother. "Best wishes, Mrs. Tucker."

"Oh, Van."

"No crying yet. We've still got lots of pictures to take."

With a squeal, Joanie launched herself at them both. "Oh, I'm so happy." She plucked Lara from Jack's arms. "Give your grandma a kiss."

"Grandma," Loretta whispered, and with a watery laugh she swung Lara into her arms. "Grandma."

Brady laid an arm over Vanessa's shoulders. "How do you feel, Aunt Van?"

"Amazed." She laughed up at him as Mrs. Driscoll's grandson's brother-in-law scurried around snapping pictures. "Let's go pour the champagne."

Two hours later, she was in the Tucker backyard, hauling a tray of hamburger patties to the grill.

"I thought your father always did the honors," she said to Brady.

"He passed his spatula down to me." He had his suit coat off now, his sleeves rolled up and his tie off. Smoke billowed up from the grill as meat sizzled. He flipped a patty expertly.

"You do that very well."

"You should see me with a scalpel."

"I'll pass, thanks." She shifted to avoid being mowed down by two running boys. "The picnic's just like I remember. Crowded, noisy and chaotic."

People milled around in the yard, in the house, even spilled out along the sidewalks. Some sat at the long picnic tables or on the grass. Babies were passed from hand to hand. The old sat in the shade waving at flies as they gossiped and reminisced. The young ran in the sunshine.

Someone had brought a huge portable stereo. Music poured from the rear corner of the yard, where a group of teenagers had gathered to flirt.

"We'd have been there just a few years back," Brady commented.

"You mean you're too old to hang around a boom box now?"

"No. But they think I am. Now I'm Dr. Tucker—as opposed to my father, who's Doc Tucker—and that automatically labels me an adult." He skewered a hot dog. "It's hell growing up."

"Being dignified," she added as he popped it into a bun and slathered on mustard.

"Setting an example for the younger generation. Say 'ah,'" he told her, then shoved the hot dog in her mouth.

She chewed and swallowed in self-defense. "Maintaining a certain decorum."

"Yeah. You've got mustard on your mouth. Here." He grabbed her hand before she could wipe it off. "I'll take care of it." He leaned down and slid the tip of his tongue over the corner of her mouth. "Very tasty," he decided, then nipped lightly at her bottom lip.

"You're going to burn your burgers," she murmured.

"Quiet. I'm setting an example for the younger generation."

Even as she chuckled, he covered her mouth fully with his, lengthening the kiss, deepening it, drawing it out, until she forgot she was surrounded by people. And so did he.

When he released her, she lifted a hand to her spinning head and tried to find her voice.

"Just like old times," someone shouted.

"Better," Brady said quietly, and would have pulled her close again, but for a tap on his shoulder.

"Let that girl go and behave yourself, Brady Tucker." Violet Driscoll shook her head at the pair of them. "You've got hungry people here. If you want to smooch with your girl, you just wait till later."

"Yes, ma'am."

"Never had a lick of sense." She winked at Vanessa as she started back to the shade. "But he's a handsome so-and-so."

"She's right." Vanessa tossed back her hair.

"I'm a handsome so-and-so?"

"No, you've never had a lick of sense."

"Hey!" he called after her. "Where are you going?"

Vanessa shot him a long, teasing look over her shoulder and kept walking.

It was like old times, Vanessa thought as she stopped to talk to high school friends and watched children race and shout and gobble down food. Faces had aged, babies had been born, but the mood was the same. There was the smell of good food, the sounds of laughter and of a cranky baby being lulled to sleep. She heard arguments over the Orioles' chances for a pennant this year, talk about summer plans and gardening tips.

She could smell the early roses blooming and see the tangle of morning glories on the trellis next door.

When Brady found her again, she was sitting on the grass with Lara.

"What're you doing?"

"Playing with my niece." They both lifted their heads to smile at him.

Something shifted inside him. Something fast and unexpected. And something inevitable, he realized. Seeing her smiling up at him, a child's head on her shoulder, sunlight pouring over her skin. How could he have known he'd been waiting, almost his entire life, for a moment like this? But the child should be his, he thought. Vanessa and the child should be his.

"Is something wrong?" she asked.

"No." He brought himself back with a long, steadying breath. "Why?"

"The way you were staring at me."

He sat beside her, touched a hand to her hair. "I'm still in love with you, Vanessa. And I don't know what the hell to do about it."

She stared. Even if she could have latched on to the dozens of emotions swirling through her, she couldn't have put any into words. It wasn't a boy she was looking at now. He was a man, and what he had spoken had been said deliberately. Now he was waiting for her to move, toward him or away. But she couldn't move at all.

Lara bounced in her lap and squealed, shattering the silence. "Brady, I—"

"There you are." Joanie dropped down beside them. "Whoops,"

she said as the tension got through to her. "I'm sorry. I guess it's bad timing."

"Go away, Joanie," Brady told her. "Far away."

"I'd already be gone, since you've asked so nicely, but the limo's here. People are already heading around front to stare at it. I think it's time to see the newlyweds off."

"You're right." Almost using Lara as a shield, Vanessa scrambled to her feet. "We don't want them to miss their plane." She braced herself and looked at Brady again. "You've got the tickets?"

"Yeah, I got them." Before she could skirt around him, he cupped her chin in his hand. "We've still got unfinished business, Van."

"I know." She was grateful her voice could sound so calm when her insides were knotted. "Like Joanie said, it's bad timing." With Lara on her hip, she hurried off to find her mother.

"What's all this about a limo?" Ham demanded as Joanie began unrolling his pushed-up sleeves. "Did somebody die?"

"Nope." Joanie fastened the button on his cuff. "You and your new wife are going on a little trip."

"A trip?" Loretta repeated, as Vanessa handed her her purse.

"When newlyweds take a trip," Brady explained, "it's called a honeymoon."

"But I've got patients all next week."

"No, you don't." With Brady and Jack on either side of Ham, and Vanessa and Joanie flanking Loretta, they led the baffled bride and groom to the front of the house.

"Oh, my" was all Loretta could say as she spotted the gleaming white stretch limo.

"Your plane leaves at six." Brady took an envelope out of his pocket and handed it to his father. "*Vaya con Dios.*"

"What is all this?" Ham demanded. Vanessa noted with a chuckle that old shoes and cans were already being tied to the bumper. "My schedule—"

"Is cleared." Brady gave Ham a slap on the back. "See you in a couple weeks."

"A couple weeks?" His eyebrows shot up. "Where the hell are we going?"

"South of the border," Joanie chimed in, and gave her father a hard, smacking kiss. "Don't drink the water."

"Mexico?" Loretta's eyes widened. "Are we going to Mexico? But how can we— The shop. We haven't any luggage."

"The shop's closed," Vanessa told her. "And your luggage is in the trunk." She kissed Loretta on each cheek. "Have a good time."

"In the trunk?" Her baffled smile widened. "My blue silk blouse?"

"Among other things."

"You all did this." Despite the persistent photographer, Loretta began to cry. "All of you."

"Guilty." Brady gave her a huge hug. "Bye, Mom."

"You're a sneaky bunch." Ham had to take out his handkerchief. "Well, Loretta, I guess we've got ourselves a honeymoon."

"Not if you miss your plane." Joanie, always ready to worry, began to push them toward the limo. "Don't sit in the sun too long. It's much more intense down there. Oh, and whatever you buy, make sure you shop around and bargain first. You can change your money at the hotel—there's a phrase book in the carry-on. And if you need—"

"Say goodbye, Joanie," Jack told her.

"Oh, shoot." She rubbed her knuckles under her damp eyes. "Bye. Wave bye-bye, Lara."

"Oh, Ham. Gardenias." Loretta began to weep again.

With shouts and waves from the entire town, the limo began to cruise sedately down Main Street, followed by the clang and thump of cans and shoes, and an escort of running children.

"There they go," Joanie managed, burying her face in Jack's shoulder. He patted her hair.

"It's okay, honey. Kids have to leave home sometime. Come on, I'll get you some potato salad." He grinned at Brady as he led her away.

Vanessa cleared the lump in her throat. "That was quite a send-off."

"I want to talk to you. We can go to your house or mine."

"I think we should wait until—"

"We've already waited too long."

Panicked, she looked around. How was it that they were alone again so quickly? "The party— You have guests."

"Nobody'll miss us." With a hand on her arm, he turned toward his car.

"Dr. Tucker, Dr. Tucker!" Annie Crampton was racing around the corner of the house. "Come quick! Something's wrong with my grandpa!"

He moved quickly. By the time Vanessa reached the backyard, he was already kneeling beside the old man, loosening his collar.

"Pain," the old man said. "In my chest...can't breathe."

"I got Dad's bag," Joanie said as she passed it to Brady. "Ambulance is coming."

Brady just nodded. "Take it easy, Mr. Benson." He took a small bottle and a syringe out of the bag. "I want you to stay calm." He continued to talk as he worked, calming and soothing with his voice. "Joanie, get his file," he murmured.

Feeling helpless, Vanessa put an arm around Annie's shoulders and drew her back. "Come on, Annie."

"Is Grandpa going to die?"

"Dr. Tucker's taking care of him. He's a very good doctor."

"He takes care of my mom." She sniffled and wiped at her eyes. "He's going to deliver the baby and all, but Grandpa, he's real old. He fell down. He just got all funny-looking and fell down."

"Dr. Tucker was right here." She stroked Annie's flyaway hair. "If he was going to get sick, it was the best place for it. When he's better, you can play your new song for him."

"The Madonna song?"

"That's right." She heard the wail of an ambulance. "They're coming to take him to the hospital."

"Will Dr. Tucker go with him?"

"I'm sure he will." She watched as the attendants hurried out with a stretcher. Brady spoke to them briskly, giving instructions. She saw him put his hands on Annie's mother's shoulders, speaking slowly, calmly, while she looked up at him with trust and tears in her eyes. When Brady started after the stretcher, Vanessa gave Annie a last squeeze.

"Why don't you go sit with your mother for a minute? She'll be scared." How well she knew, Vanessa thought. She remembered the fear and despair she had felt when they had taken her own father. Turning, she rushed after Brady.

"Brady." She knew she couldn't waste his time. When he turned, she saw the concern, the concentration and the impatience in his eyes. "Please let me know how—what happens."

He nodded, then climbed in the rear of the ambulance with his patient.

It was nearly midnight when Brady pulled up in front of his house. There was a sliver of a moon, bone-white against a black sky studded with stars as clear as ice. He sat where he was for a moment, letting his muscles relax one by one. With his windows down he could hear the wind sighing through the trees.

The fatigue of an eighteen-hour-day had finally caught up with him on the drive home. He was grateful Jack had brought his car to the hospital. Without it, he would have been tempted to stretch out in the lounge. Now all he wanted was to ease his tired body into a hot tub, turn on the jets and drink a cold beer.

The lights were on downstairs. He was glad he'd forgotten to turn them off. It was less depressing to come home to an empty house if the lights were on. He'd detoured into town on the way home and driven by Vanessa's. But her lights had been out.

Probably for the best, he thought now. He was tired and edgy. Hardly the mood for patient, sensible talk. Maybe there was an advantage to letting her stew over the fact that he was in love with her.

And maybe there wasn't. He hesitated, his hand on the door. What the hell was wrong with him, he wondered. He'd always been a decisive man. When he'd decided to become a doctor, he'd gone after his degree with a vengeance. When he'd decided to leave his hospital position in New York and come home to practice general medicine, he'd done so without a backward glance or a whisper of regret.

Life-altering decisions, certainly. So why the hell couldn't he decide what to do about Vanessa?

He was going back to town. If she didn't answer her door, he would climb up the damn rainspout and crawl in her bedroom window. One way or the other, they were going to straighten this mess out tonight.

He'd already turned away and started back to his car when the door to the house opened.

"Brady?" Vanessa stood in the doorway, the light at her back. "Aren't you coming in?"

He stopped dead and stared at her. In a gesture of pure frustration, he dragged a hand through his hair. Was it any wonder he couldn't decide what to do about her? She'd never been predictable. Kong raced out of the house, barking, and jumped on him.

"Jack and Joanie dropped us off." Vanessa stood, twisting the doorknob back and forth. "I hope you don't mind."

"No." With the dog racing in circles around him, he started back to the house. Vanessa stepped back, out of reach.

"I brought some leftovers from the picnic. I didn't know if you'd have a chance to get any dinner."

"No, I didn't."

"Mr. Benson?"

"Stabilized. It was shaky for a while, but he's tough."

"I'm glad. I'm so glad. Annie was frightened." She rubbed her hands on her thighs, linked her fingers together, pulled them apart, then stuck them in the pockets of her skirt. "You must be exhausted—and hungry. There's plenty of food in the fridge. The, ah, kitchen looks wonderful." She gestured vaguely. "The new cabinets, the counters, everything."

"It's coming along." But he made no move toward it. "How long have you been here?"

"Oh, just a couple of hours." Five, to be exact. "You had some books, so I've been reading."

"Why?"

"Well, to pass the time."

"Why are you here, Van?"

She bent to stroke the dog. "That unfinished business you mentioned. It's been a long day, and I've had plenty of time to think."

"And?"

Why didn't he just sweep her away, carry her upstairs? And shut her up. "And I... About what you said this afternoon."

"That I'm in love with you."

She cleared her throat as she straightened. "Yes, that. I'm not sure what I feel—how I feel. I'm not sure how you feel, either."

"I told you how I feel."

"Yes, but it's very possible that you think you feel that way because you used to—and because falling back into the same routine, the same relationship—with me—is familiar, and comfortable."

"The hell it is. I haven't had a comfortable moment since I saw you sitting at the piano."

"Familiar, then." She began to twist the necklace at her throat. "But I've changed, Brady. I'm not the same person I was when I left here. We'll never be able to pretend those years away. So, no matter how attracted we are to each other, it could be a mistake to take it any further."

He crossed to her, slowly, until they were eye to eye. He was ready to make a mistake. More than ready. "Is that what you were waiting here to tell me?"

She moistened his lips. "Partly."

"Then I'll have my say."

"I'd like to finish first." She kept her eyes level. "I came here tonight because I've never been able to get you completely out of my mind. Or my..." Heart. She wanted to say it, but couldn't. "My system," she finished. "I've never stopped caring about you, or wondering. Because of something we had no control over, we were cheated out of growing up enough to make the decision to move apart or to become lovers." She paused, but only for a moment. "I came here tonight because I realized I want what was taken away from us. I want you." She stepped closer and put her arms around him. "Is that clear enough?"

"Yeah." He kissed her gently. "That's clear enough."

She smiled at him. "Make love with me, Brady. I've always wanted you to."

With their hands joined, they walked upstairs together.

Chapter 9

She had already been upstairs while she had waited for him to come home—smoothing and straightening the covers on the bed, fluffing the pillows, standing and looking at the room and wondering what it would be like to walk into it with him.

He turned on the lamp beside the bed. It was a beautiful old rose-tinted globe that sat on a packing crate. The floors were unfinished, the walls spackled with drywall mud. The bed was only a mattress on the floor beneath the windows. It was the most beautiful room she'd ever seen.

He wished he could have given her candles and roses, a huge four-poster with satin sheets. All he could give her was himself.

And suddenly he was as nervous as a boy on his first date.

"The atmosphere's a little thin in here."

"It's perfect," she told him.

He took her hands and raised them to his lips. "I won't hurt you, Van."

"I know." She kissed his hands in turn. "This is going to sound stupid, but I don't know what to do."

He lowered his mouth to hers, testing, tempting. "You'll catch on."

Her lips curved as her hands slid up his back. "I think you're right." With an instinct that was every bit as potent as experience, she let her head fall back, let her hands glide and press and wander.

Her lips parted for his, and she tasted his little groan of pleasure. Then she shivered with pleasure of her own as his strong, clever hands skimmed down her body, his thumb brushing down the side of her breast, his fingers kneading at her waist, his palm cupping her hip, sliding down her thigh, before its upward journey.

She pressed against him, delighting in the shower of sensations. When his teeth scraped lightly down her throat, over her bare shoulder, she murmured his name. Like the wind through the trees, she sighed for him, and swayed. Pliant and willing, she waited to be molded.

Her absolute trust left him shaken. No matter how hot her passion, she was innocent. Her body might be that of a woman, but she was still as untouched as the girl he had once loved and lost. He wouldn't forget it. As the need flamed inside him, he banked it. This time it would be for her. All for her.

Compassion and tenderness were as much a part of his nature as his recklessness. He showed her only the gentle side now, as he eased the snug top down to her hips. He kissed her, soothing her with murmurs even as his hands set off millions of tiny explosions as they tugged her dress to the floor.

She wore a swatch of white lace that seemed to froth over the swell of her breasts before skimming down to nip at her waist. For his own pleasure, he held her at arm's length and just looked.

"You stop my heart," he told her.

With unsteady hands, she reached out to unbutton his shirt. Though her breath was already ragged, she kept her eyes on his as she slid the shirt from his shoulders and let it fall to join her dress on the floor. With her heart pounding wildly in her ears, she linked her arms around his neck.

"Touch me." She tilted her head back, offered her mouth. "Show me."

Though the kiss was hard, demanding, ruthless, he forced his hands to be gentle. Her own were racing over him, bringing a desperate edge to an already driving need. When he lowered her onto the bed, he watched her eyes close on a sigh, then open again, clouded with desire.

He dipped his head to absorb her taste on his tongue as it skimmed along the verge of lace, as it slid beneath to tease her taut nipples. Her hips ached and her fingers dug into his back as the pleasure rocketed through her.

With a flick of the wrist, he unsnapped her garters, then sent her churning as he slowly peeled down her stockings, blazing the newly bared flesh with his lips. It seemed he found every inch of her, every curve, fascinating. His gentle fingers played over her, everywhere, until the music roared in her head.

As patient as he was ruthless, he drove her closer and closer to the edge she'd never seen. Her body was like a furnace, pumping out heat, pulsing with needs as sharp as his. He drove himself mad watching her, seeing the way everything she felt, each new sensation he brought to her, raced over her face, into her eyes.

Desire. Passion. Pleasure. Excitement. They flowed from him to her, then back again. Familiar. Oh, yes. They recognized each other. That brought comfort. Yet it was new, unique, gloriously fresh. That was the adventure.

He reveled in the way her skin flowed through his hands, the way her body tensed and arched at his touch. The way the lamplight slanted over her, over his hands as he peeled the last barrier of lace away.

Naked, she reached for him, tugging frantically at his slacks. Because he knew his own needs were tearing his control to shreds, he cupped her in his hand and sent her flying over the last line.

She cried out, stunned, helpless, her eyes glazing over, as her hand slipped limply from his shoulder. Even as she shuddered, he eased into her, slowly, gently, murmuring her name again and again as the blood roared in his ears and pushed him to take his pleasure quickly. Love demanded gentleness.

She lost her innocence sweetly, painlessly, and with simple joy.

She lay in Brady's bed, tangled in Brady's sheets. A sparrow heralded the dawn. During the night, the dog had crept in to take his rightful place at the foot of the bed. Lazily Vanessa opened her eyes.

Brady's face was barely an inch from hers, and she had to ease back and blink to focus on him. He was deep in sleep, his arm heavy around her waist, his breathing slow and even. Now, completely relaxed and vulnerable, he looked more like the boy she remembered than the man she was beginning to know.

She loved. There was no doubt in her mind that she loved. Her heart nearly burst with it. But did she love the boy or the man?

Very gently, she brushed at the hair on his forehead. All she was really sure of was that she was happy. And, for now, it was enough.

More than enough, she thought as she slowly stretched. During the night he had shown her how beautiful making love could be when two people cared about each other. And how exciting it could be when needs were met and desires reached. Whatever happened tomorrow, or a year from tomorrow, she would never forget what they had shared.

Lightly, not wanting to wake him, she touched her lips to his. Even that quiet contact stirred her. Hesitant, curious, she trailed her fingertips over his shoulders, down the length of his back. The need grew and spread inside her.

As dreams went, Brady thought, this was one of the best. He was under a warm quilt in the first light of day. Vanessa was in bed beside him. Her body was pressed against his, shifting gently, arousing quickly. Those beautiful, talented fingers were stroking along his skin. That soft, sulky mouth was toying with his. When he reached for her, she sighed, arching under his hand.

Everywhere he touched she was warm and smooth. Her arms were around him, strong silken ropes that trapped him gloriously against her. When she said his name, once, then twice, the words slipped under the gauzy curtain of his fantasy. He opened his eyes and saw her.

This was no dream. She was smiling at him. Those misty green eyes were heavy with sleep and passion. Her body was slim and soft and curved against his.

"Good morning," she murmured. "I wasn't sure if you—"

He closed his mouth over hers. Dream and reality melded seductively as he slipped inside her.

The sunlight was stronger when she lay over him, her head on his heart, her body still pulsing.

"You were saying?"

"Hmm." The effort to open her eyes seemed wasted, so she kept them closed. "Was I?"

"You weren't sure if I what?"

She sifted through her thoughts. "Oh. I wasn't sure if you had any morning appointments."

He continued to comb his fingers through her hair. "It's Sunday," he reminded her. "Office is closed. But I have to run into the hospital and check on Mr. Benson and a couple of other patients. How about you?"

"Nothing much. Some lesson plans, now that I have ten students."

"Ten?" There was more snicker than surprise in his voice.

She shifted then, folding her arms over his chest and resting her chin on them. "I was ambushed at the picnic yesterday."

"Ten students." He grinned at her. "That's quite a commitment. Does that mean you're planning to settle in town again?"

"At least for the summer. I haven't decided whether I'll agree to a fall tour."

So he had the summer to convince her, he thought. "How about dinner?"

She narrowed her eyes. "We haven't even had breakfast yet."

"I mean tonight. We could have our own picnic with the leftovers. Just you and me."

Just you and me. "I'd like that."

"Good. Now why don't we start the day off right?"

After a chuckle, she pressed her lips to his chest. "I thought we already had."

"I meant you could wash my back." Grinning, he sat up and dragged her out of bed.

Vanessa discovered she didn't mind being alone in the house. After Brady dropped her off, she changed into jeans and a short-sleeved sweatshirt. She wanted to spend the day at the piano, planning the lessons, practicing and, if her current mood held, composing.

There had never been enough time for composing on tour, she thought as she tied her hair back. But now she had the summer. Even if ten hours a week would be taken up by lessons, and nearly that many again by planning them, she had plenty of time to indulge in her first love.

Her first love, she repeated with a smile. No, that wasn't composing. That was Brady. He had been her first love. Her first lover. And it was more than probable he would be her last.

He loved her. Or believed he did. He would never have used the words unless he believed it. Nor could she, Vanessa reflected. She had to be sure of what was best for herself, for him, for everyone, before she risked her heart with those three words.

Once she said them, he wouldn't let go again. However much he had mellowed over the years, however responsible he had become, there was still enough of that wild and willful boy in him to have him tossing her over his shoulder and carrying her off. While that fantasy might have its appeal, a daydream appeal, she was too sensible a woman to tolerate it in reality.

The past was done, she thought. Mistakes had been made. She wouldn't risk the future.

She didn't want to think about tomorrow. Not yet. She wanted only to think of, and enjoy, today.

As she started toward the music room, the phone rang. She debated just letting it ring—a habit she'd developed in hotel rooms when she hadn't wanted to be disturbed. On the fifth ring, she gave in and answered.

"Hello."

"Vanessa? Is that you?"

"Yes. Frank?" She recognized the voice of her father's nervous and devoted assistant.

"Yes. It's me—I," he corrected.

Vanessa could all but see him running a soothing hand over the wide bald spot on top of his head. "How are you, Frank?"

"Fine. Fine. Oh—how are you?"

"I'm fine, too." She had to smile. Though she knew her father had tolerated Frank Margoni only because the man would work an eighty-hour week without complaint, Vanessa was fond of him. "How's the new protégé?"

"Protégé—? Oh, you mean Francesco. He's brilliant, really brilliant. Temperamental, of course. Throws things. But then, he's an artist. He's going to be playing at the benefit in Cordina."

"Princess Gabriella's benefit? The Aid to Handicapped Children?"

"Yes."

"I'm sure he'll be wonderful."

"Oh, of course. No doubt. Certainly. But, you see, the princess... she's terribly disappointed that you won't perform. She asked me—" there was an audible gulp "—personally, if I would persuade you to reconsider."

"Frank—"

"You'd stay at the palace, of course. Incredible place."

"Yes, I know. Frank, I haven't decided if I'm going to perform again."

"You know you don't mean that, Vanessa. With your gift—"

"Yes, *my* gift," she said impatiently. "Isn't it about time I realized it is mine?"

He was silent a moment. "I know your father was often insensitive to your personal needs, but that was only because he was so aware of the depth of your talent."

"You don't have to explain him to me, Frank."

"No…no, of course I don't."

She let out a long sigh. It wasn't fair to take out her frustrations on the hapless Frank Margoni, as her father always had. "I understand the position you're in, Frank, but I've already sent my regrets, and a donation, to Princess Gabriella."

"I know. That's why she contacted me. She couldn't get ahold of you. Of course, I'm not officially your manager, but the princess knew our connection, so…"

"If I decide to tour again, Frank, I'll depend on you to manage me."

"I appreciate that, Vanessa." His glum voice brightened perceptibly. "And I realize that you've needed some time for yourself. The last few years—grueling, I know. But this benefit is important." He cleared his throat with three distinct clicks. "And the princess is very stubborn."

Reluctantly Vanessa smiled. "Yes, I know."

"It's only one performance," he continued, sensing a weak spot. "Not even a full concert. You'll have carte blanche on the material. They'd like you to play two pieces, but even one would make such a tremendous difference. Your name on the program would add so much." He paused only long enough to suck in a breath. "It's a very worthy cause."

"When is the benefit?"

"Next month."

She cast her eyes to the ceiling. "Next month. It's practically next month already, Frank."

"The third Saturday in June."

"Three weeks." She let out a long breath. "All right, I'll do it. For you, and for Princess Gabriella."

"Vanessa, I can't tell you how much I—"

"Please don't." She softened the order with a laugh. "It's only one night."

"You can stay in Cordina as long as you like."

"One night," she repeated. "Send me the particulars here. And give my best to Her Highness."

"I will, of course. She'll be thrilled. Everyone will be thrilled. Thank you, Vanessa."

"It's all right, Frank. I'll see you in a few weeks."

She hung up and stood silent and still. Odd, but she didn't feel tensed and keyed up at the thought of a performance. And a huge one, she considered. The theater complex in Cordina was exquisite and enormous.

What would happen if she clutched in the wings this time? She would get through it somehow. She always had. Perhaps it was fate that she had been called now, when she was teetering on some invisible line. To go forward, or backward, or to stay.

She would have to make a decision soon, she thought as she walked to the piano. She prayed it would be the right one.

She was playing when Brady returned. He could hear the music, romantic and unfamiliar, flowing through the open windows. There was the hum of bees in the flowers, the purr of a lawn mower, and the music. The magic of it. He saw a woman and a young child standing on the sidewalk, listening.

She had left the door open for him. He had only to push the screen to be inside. He moved quietly. It seemed he was stepping through the liquid notes.

She didn't see him. Her eyes were half-closed. There was a smile on her face, a secret smile. As if whatever images she held in her mind were pouring out through her fingers and onto the keys.

The music was slow, dreamy, enriched by an underlying passion. He felt his throat tighten.

When she finished, she opened her eyes and looked at him. Somehow she had known he would be there when the last note died away.

"Hello."

He wasn't sure he could speak. He crossed to her and lifted her hands. "There's magic here. It astonishes me."

"Musician's hands," she said. "Yours are magic. They heal."

"There was a woman standing on the sidewalk with her little boy. I saw them when I drove up. She was listening to you play, and there were tears on her cheeks."

"There's no higher compliment. Did you like it?"

"Very much. What was it called?"

"I don't know. It's something I've been working on for a while. It never seemed right until today."

"You wrote it?" He looked at the music on the piano and saw the neatly written notes on the staff paper. "I didn't know you composed."

"I'm hoping to do more of it." She drew him down to sit beside her. "Aren't you going to kiss me hello?"

"At least." His lips were warm and firm on hers. "How long have you been writing?"

"For several years—when I've managed to sneak the time. Between traveling, rehearsals, practice and performances, it hasn't been much."

"But you've never recorded anything of your own."

"None of it's really finished. I—" She stopped, tilted her head. "How do you know?"

"I have everything you've ever recorded." At her smug smile, he continued. "Not that I actually play any of them." He gave an exaggerated yelp when her elbow connected with his ribs. "I suppose that's the sign of a temperamental artist."

"That's *artiste* to you, philistine."

"Why don't you tell this philistine about your composing?"

"What's to tell?"

"Do you like it?"

"I love it. It's what I like best."

He was playing with her fingers. "Then why haven't you finished anything?" He felt the tension the moment it entered her.

"I told you. There hasn't been time. Touring isn't all champagne and caviar, you know."

"Come on." Keeping her hands in his, he pulled her to her feet.

"Where are we going?"

"In here, where there's a comfortable couch. Sit." He eased her down, then put his hands on her shoulders. His eyes were dark and searching on her face. "Talk to me."

"About what?"

"I wanted to wait until you were recovered." He felt her stiffen, and shook his head. "Don't do that. As your friend, as a doctor, and as the man who loves you, I want to know what made you ill. I want to make sure it never happens again."

"You've already said I've recovered."

"Ulcers can reoccur."

"I didn't have an ulcer."

"Can it. You can deny it all you want—it won't change the facts. I want you to tell me what's been going on the last few years."

"I've been touring. Performing." Flustered, she shook her head. "How did we move from composing to all this?"

"Because one leads to the other, Van. Ulcers are often caused by emotion. By frustrations, angers, resentments that are bottled up to fester instead of being aired out."

"I'm not frustrated." She set her chin. "And you, of all people, should know I don't bottle things up. Ask around, Brady. My temper is renowned on three continents."

He nodded, slowly. "I don't doubt it. But I never once remember you arguing with your father."

She fell silent at that. It was nothing more than the truth.

"Did you want to compose, or did you want to perform?"

"It's possible to do both. It's simply a matter of discipline and priorities."

"And what was your priority?"

Uncomfortable, she shifted. "I think it's obvious it was performing."

"You said something to me before. You said you hated it."

"Hated what?"

"You tell me."

She pulled away to rise and pace the room. It hardly mattered now, she told herself. But he was sitting here, watching her, waiting. Past experience told her he would dig and dig until he uncovered whatever feelings she wanted to hide.

"All right. I was never happy performing."

"You didn't want to play?"

"No," she corrected. "I didn't want to perform. I have to play, just as I have to breathe, but..." She let her words trail off, feeling like an imbecile. "It's stage fright," she snapped. "It's stupid, it's childish, but I've never been able to overcome it."

"It's not stupid or childish." He rose, and would have gone to her, but she was already backing away. "If you hated performing, why did you keep going on? Of course," he said, before she could answer.

"It was important to him." She sat on the arm of a chair, then stood again, unable to settle. "He didn't understand. He'd put his whole life into my career. The idea that I couldn't perform, that it frightened me—"

"That it made you ill."

"I was never ill. I never missed one performance because of health."

"No, you performed despite your health. Damn it, Van, he had no right."

"He was my father. I know he was a difficult man, but I owed him something."

He was a selfish son of a bitch, Brady thought. But he kept his silence. "Did you ever consider therapy?"

Vanessa lifted her hands. "He opposed it. He was very intolerant of weakness. I suppose that was his weakness." She closed her eyes a moment. "You have to understand him, Brady. He was the kind of man who would refuse to believe what was inconvenient for him. And, as far as he was concerned, it just ceased to exist." Like my mother, she thought with a weary sigh. "I could never find the way to make him accept or even understand the degree of the phobia."

"I'd like to understand."

She cupped her hands over her mouth a moment, then let them fall. "Every time I would go to the theater, I would tell myself that this time, this time, it wouldn't happen. This time I wouldn't be afraid. Then I would stand in the wings, shaking and sick and miserable. My skin would be clammy, and the nausea would make me dizzy. Once I started playing, it would ease off. By the end I'd be fine, so I would tell myself that the next time..." She shrugged.

He understood, too well. And he hated the idea of her, of anyone, suffering time after time, year after year. "Did you ever stop to think that he was living his life through you?"

"Yes." Her voice was dull. "He was all I had left. And, right or wrong, I was all he had. The last year, he was so ill, but he never let me stop, never let me care for him. In the end, because he had refused to listen, refused the treatments, he was in monstrous pain. You're a doctor—you know how horrible terminal cancer is. Those last weeks in the hospital were the worst. There was nothing they could do for him that time. So he died a little every day. I went on performing, because he insisted, then flying back to the hospital in Geneva every chance I had. I wasn't there when he died. I was in Madrid. I got a standing ovation."

"Can you blame yourself for that?"

"No. But I can regret." Her eyes were awash with it.

"What do you intend to do now?"

She looked down at her hands, spread her fingers, curled them into her palms. "When I came back here, I was tired. Just worn out, Brady. I needed time—I still do—to understand what I feel, what I want, where I'm going." She stepped toward him and lifted her hands to his face. "I didn't want to become involved with you, because I knew you'd be one more huge complication." Her lip curved a little. "And I was right. But when I woke up this morning in your bed, I was happy. I don't want to lose that."

He took her wrists. "I love you, Vanessa."

"Then let me work through this." She went easily into his arms. "And just be with me."

He pressed a kiss to her hair. "I'm not going anywhere."

Chapter 10

"That was the last patient, Dr. Tucker."

Distracted, Brady looked up from the file on his desk and focused on his nurse. "What?"

"That was the last patient." She was already swinging her purse over her shoulder and thinking about putting her feet up. "Do you want me to lock up?"

"Yeah. Thanks. See you tomorrow." He listened with half an ear to the clink of locks and the rattle of file drawers. The twelve-hour day was almost at an end. The fourth twelve-hour day of the week. Hyattown was a long way from New York, but as far as time served was concerned, Brady had found practicing general medicine in a small town as demanding as being chief resident in a major hospital. Along with the usual stream of patients, hospital rounds and paperwork, an outbreak of chicken pox and strep throat had kept him tied to his stethoscope for over a week.

Half the town was either scratching or croaking, he thought as he settled down to his paperwork. The waiting room had been packed since the end of the holiday weekend. As the only doctor in residence, he'd been taking office appointments, making house calls, doing rounds. And missing meals, he thought ruefully, wishing they still stocked lollipops, rather than balloons and plastic cars, for their younger patients.

He could get by with frozen microwave meals and coffee for a few days. He could even get by with only patches of sleep. But he couldn't get by without Vanessa. He'd barely seen her since the weekend of the wedding—since the weekend they had spent almost exclusively in bed. He'd been forced to cancel three dates. For some women, he thought, that alone would have been enough to have them stepping nimbly out of a relationship.

Better that she knew up front how bad it could get. Being married to a doctor was being married to inconvenience. Canceled dinners, postponed vacations, interrupted sleep.

Closing the file, he rubbed his tired eyes. She was going to marry him, he determined. He was going to see to that. If he ever wangled an hour free to set the stage and ask her.

He picked up the postcard on the corner of his desk. It had a brilliant view of the sun setting on the water, palm trees and sand—and a quickly scrawled note from his father on the back.

"You'd better be having a good time, Dad," Brady mused as he studied it. "Because when you get back, you're going to pay up."

He wondered if Vanessa would enjoy a tropical honeymoon. Mexico, the Bahamas, Hawaii. Hot, lazy days. Hot, passionate nights. Moving too fast, he reminded himself. You couldn't have a honeymoon until you had a wedding. And you couldn't have a wedding until you'd convinced your woman she couldn't live without you.

He'd promised himself he would take it slowly with Vanessa. Give her all the romance they'd missed the first time around. Long walks in the moonlight. Champagne dinners. Evening drives and quiet talks. But the old impatience pulled at him. If they were married now, he could drag his weary bones home. She'd be there.

Perhaps playing the piano. Or curled up in bed with a book. In the next room, there might be a child sleeping. Or two.

Much too fast, Brady warned himself. But he hadn't known, until he'd seen her again, how much he'd wanted that basic and traditional home. The woman he loved, and the children they made between them. Christmas mornings and Sunday afternoons.

Leaning back, he let his eyes close. He could picture it perfectly. Too perfectly, he admitted. He knew his vision left questions unanswered and problems unresolved. They were no longer children who could live on dreams. But he was too tired to be logical. Too needy to be sensible.

Vanessa stood in the doorway and watched him with a mixture of surprise and awe. This was Brady, she reminded herself. Her Brady. But he looked so different here, so professional, in his white lab coat with the framed diplomas and certificates surrounding him. There were files neatly stacked on his desk, and there was an ophthalmoscope in his pocket.

This wasn't the wild youth hell-bent on giving the world a left jab. This was a settled, responsible man who had hundreds of people depending on him. He had already made his niche.

And where was hers? she wondered. He had made his choices and found his place. She was still floundering. Yet, however much she flailed or stumbled, she was always drawn to him. Always back to him.

With a faint smile on her face, she stepped into the office. "You've got another appointment, Dr. Tucker."

"What?" His eyes snapped open. He stared at her as dream and reality merged. She was standing on the other side of his desk, her hair pulled back, in a breezy cotton blouse and slacks.

"I was going to say code blue, or red alert, one of those things you hear on TV, but I didn't know which would fit." She put the basket she carried on the desk.

"I'd settle for 'Hi.'"

"Hi." With a quick laugh, she looked around the office. "I almost didn't come in," she told him. "When I came to the door, you looked so...intimidating."

"Intimidating?"

"Like a doctor. A real doctor," she said on another laugh. "The kind who uses needles and makes terrifying noncommittal noises and scribbles things on charts."

"Hmm," Brady said. "Ah."

"Exactly."

"I can take off the lab coat."

"No, actually, I think I like it. As long as you promise not to whip out a tongue depressor. I saw your nurse as she was leaving. She said you were through for the day."

"Just." The rest of the paperwork would have to wait. "What's in the basket?"

"Dinner—of sorts. Since you wouldn't make a house call, I decided to see if you could fit me into your office schedule."

"It's an amazing coincidence, but I've just had a cancellation." The fatigue simply drained away as he looked at her. Her mouth was naked, and there was a dusting of freckles across the bridge of her nose. "Why don't you sit down and tell me what the problem is?"

"Well." Vanessa sat in the chair in front of the desk. "You see, doctor, I've been feeling kind of light-headed. And absentminded. I forget what I'm doing in the middle of doing it and catch myself staring off into space."

"Hmmm."

"Then there have been these aches. Here," she said, and put a hand on her heart.

"Ah."

"Like palpitations. And at night..." She caught her lower lip between her teeth. "I've had these dreams."

"Really?" He came around to sit on the corner of the desk. There was her scent, whispery light, to flirt with him. "What kind of dreams?"

"They're personal," she said primly.

"I'm a doctor."

"So you say." She grinned at him. "You haven't even asked me to take off my clothes."

"Good point." Rising, he took her hand. "Come with me."

"Where?"

"Your case warrants a full examination."

"Brady—"

"That's Dr. Brady to you." He hit the lights in examining room 1. "Now about that ache."

She gave him a slow, measured look. "Obviously you've been dipping into the rubbing alcohol."

He merely took her by the hips and boosted her onto the examining table. "Relax, sweetie. They don't call me Dr. Feelgood for nothing." He took out his ophthalmoscope and directed the light into her eyes. "Yes, they're definitely green."

"Well, that's a relief."

"You're telling me." He set the instrument aside. "Okay, lose the blouse and I'll test your reflexes."

"Well..." She ran her tongue over her teeth. "As long as I'm here." She let her fingers wander down the buttons, unfastening slowly. Under it she wore sheer blue silk. "I'm not going to have to wear one of those paper things, am I?"

He had to catch his breath as she peeled off the blouse. "I think we can dispense with that. You look to be in excellent health. In fact, I can say without reservation that you look absolutely perfect."

"But I have this ache." She took his hand and pressed it to her breast. "Right now my heart's racing. Feel it?"

"Yeah." Gently he absorbed the feeling of silk and flesh. Her flesh. "I think it's catching."

"My skin's hot," she murmured. "And my legs are weak."

"Definitely catching." With a fingertip he slid a thin silk strap from her shoulder. "You may just have to be quarantined."

"With you, I hope."

He unhooked her slacks. "That's the idea."

When she toed off her sandals, the other strap slithered down her shoulders. Her voice was husky now, and growing breathless. "Do you have a diagnosis?"

He eased the slacks down her hips. "Sounds like the rocking pneumonia and the boogie-woogie flu."

She'd arched up to help him remove her slacks, and now she just stared. "What?"

"Too much Mozart."

"Oh." She twined her arms around his shoulders. It seemed like years since she'd been able to hold him against her. When his lips found the little hollow near her collarbone, she smiled. "Can you help me, Doctor?"

"I'm about to do my damnedest."

His mouth slid over hers. It was like coming home. Her little sigh merged with his as she leaned into him. Dreamily she changed the angle of the kiss and let his taste pour into her. Whatever illness she had, he was exactly the right medicine.

"I feel better already." She nibbled on his lip. "More."

"Van?"

Her heavy eyes opened. While her fingers combed through his hair, she smiled. The light glowed in her eyes. Again he could see himself there, trapped in the misty green. Not lost this time. Found.

Everything he'd ever wanted, ever needed, ever dreamed of, was right here. He felt the teasing pleasure turn to grinding ache in the flash of an instant. With an oath, he dragged her mouth back to his and feasted.

No patience this time. Though the change surprised her, it didn't frighten her. He was her friend, her lover. Her only. There was a desperation and a fervency that thrilled, that demanded, that possessed. As the twin of his emotions rose in her, she pulled him closer.

More, she thought again, but frantically now. She could never get enough of being wanted this wildly. She dragged at his lab coat, even as her teeth scraped over his lip. Desire pumped through her like a drug and had her yanking at his T-shirt before the coat hit the floor. She wanted the feel of his flesh, the heat of it, under her hands. She wanted the taste of that flesh, the succulence of it, under her lips.

The loving he had shown her until now had been calm and sweet and lovely. This time she craved the fire, the dark, the madness.

Control broken, he pushed her back on the narrow padded table, tearing at the wisp of silk. He could tolerate nothing between them now—only flesh against flesh and heart against heart. She was a wonder of slender limbs and subtle curves, of pale skin and delicate bones. He wanted to taste, to touch, to savor every inch.

But her demands were as great as his. She pulled him to her, sliding agilely over him so that her lips could race from his to his throat, his chest, beyond. Rough and greedy, his hands streaked over her, exploiting everywhere, as her questing mouth drove him mad.

His taste. Hot and dark and male, it made her giddy. His form. Firm and hard and muscled, it made her weak. Already damp, his skin slid under her seeking fingers. And she played him deftly, as she would her most passionate concerto.

She feared her heart would burst from its pounding rhythm. Her head spun with it. Her body trembled. Yet there was a power here. Even through the dizziness she felt it swelling in her. How could she have known she could give so much—and take so much?

His pulse thundered under her fingertips. Between his frenzied murmurs, his breath was ragged. She saw the echo of her own passion in his eyes, tasted it when she crushed her mouth to his. For her, she thought as she let herself drown in the kiss. Only for her.

He grasped her hips, fingers digging in. With each breath he took, her scent slammed into his system, potent as any narcotic. Her hair curtained his face, blocking the light and letting him see only her. The faint smile of knowledge was in her eyes. With her every movement, she enticed.

"For God's sake, Van." Her name was part oath, part prayer. If he didn't have her now, he knew he would die from the need.

She shifted, arching back, as she took him into her. For an instant, time stopped, and with it his breath, his thoughts, his life. He saw only her, her hair streaming back like a wild red river, her body pale and gleaming in the harsh light, her face glowing with the power she had only just discovered.

Then it was all speed and sound as she drove them both.

This was glory. She gave herself to it, her arms reaching up before she lost her hands in her own hair. This was wonder. And delight. No symphony had ever been so rousing. No prelude so passionate. Even as sensation shuddered through her, she begged for more.

There was freedom in the greed. Ecstasy in the knowledge that she could take as much as she wanted. Excitement in understanding that she could give just as generously.

Her heart was roaring in her ears. When she groped for his hands, his fingers clamped on to hers. They held tight as they burst over the peak together.

She slid down to him, boneless, her head spinning and her heart racing still. His skin was damp, as hers was, his body as limp. When she pressed her lips to his throat, she could feel the frantic beating of his pulse.

She had done that, Vanessa realized, still dazed. She had taken control and given them both pleasure and passion. She hadn't even had to think, only to act, only to feel. Sailing on this new self-awareness, she propped herself up on an elbow and smiled down at him.

His eyes were closed, his face so completely relaxed that she knew he was next to sleep. His heartbeat, was settling down to a purr, as was hers. Through the contentment, she felt need bloom anew.

"Doctor," she murmured, nibbling at his ear.

"Hmm."

"I feel a lot better."

"Good." He drew in a deep breath, let it out. He figured that was the most exercise he would be able to handle for days. "Remember, your health is my business."

"I'm glad to hear that." She ran a fingertip down his chest experimentally. And felt muscles jump. "Because I think I'm going to need more treatments." She trailed the tip of her tongue down his throat. "I still have this ache."

"Take two aspirin and call me in an hour."

She laughed, a low, husky sound that had his blood humming again. "I thought you were dedicated." Slowly, seductively, she roamed his face with kisses. "God, you taste good." She lowered her mouth to his and sunk in.

"Vanessa." He could easily have floated off to sleep with her gentle stroking. But when her hand slid downward, contentment turned into something more demanding. He opened his eyes and saw that she was smiling at him. She was amused, he noted. And—pun intended—completely on top of things. "You're asking for trouble," he told her.

"Yeah." She lowered her head again to nip at his lip. "But am I going to get it?"

He answered the question to their mutual satisfaction.

"Good God," he said when he could breathe again. "I'm going to have this table bronzed."

"I think I'm cured." She pushed the hair from her face as she slid to the floor. "For now."

Groaning a little, he swung his legs off the table. "Wait till you get my bill."

"I'm looking forward to it." She handed him his pants, then

slithered into her teddy. She didn't know about him, but she'd never think the same way about examining room 1 again. "And to think I came by to offer you some ham sandwiches."

"Ham?" His fingers paused on the snap of his jeans. "As in food? Like meat and bread?"

"And potato chips."

His mouth was already watering. "Consider yourself paid in full."

She shook back her hair, certain that if she felt any better she'd be breaking the law. "I take it to mean you're hungry."

"I haven't eaten since breakfast. Chicken pox," he explained as she pulled on her blouse. "If someone was to offer me a ham sandwich, I'd kiss her feet."

She wiggled her toes. "I like the sound of that. I'll go get the basket."

"Hold it." He took her arm. "If we stay in this room, my nurse is going to get a shock when she opens up tomorrow."

"Okay." She picked up his T-shirt. "Why don't we take it back to my house?" She rubbed the soft cotton against her cheek before handing it to him. "And eat in bed."

"Good thinking."

An hour later, they were sprawled across Vanessa's bed as Brady poured the last drop from a bottle of chardonnay. Vanessa had scoured the house for candles. Now they were set throughout the room, flickering while Chopin played quietly on the bedside radio.

"That was the best picnic I've had since I was thirteen and raided the Girl Scout overnight jamboree."

She scrounged for the last potato chip, then broke it judiciously in half. "I heard about that." There hadn't been time for Girl Scouts with her training. "You were always rotten."

"Hey, I got to see Betty Jean Baumgartner naked. Well, almost naked," he corrected. "She had on a training bra and panties, but at thirteen that's pretty erotic stuff."

"A rotten creep."

"It was hormones." He sipped his wine. "Lucky for you, I've still got plenty." With a satisfied sigh, he leaned back against the pillow. "Even if they're aging."

Feeling foolish and romantic, she bent over to kiss his knee. "I've missed you, Brady."

He opened his eyes again. "I've missed you, too. I'm sorry this week's been so messed up."

"I understand."

He reached out to twine a lock of her hair around his finger. "I hope you do. Office hours alone doubled this week."

"I know. Chicken pox. Two of my students are down with it. And I heard you delivered a baby—boy, seven pounds six ounces—took out a pair of tonsils… Is it pair or set?" she wondered. "Sewed up a gash in Jack's arm, and splinted a broken finger. All that being above and beyond the day-to-day sniffles, sneezes, aches and exams."

"How do you know?"

"I have my sources." She touched his cheek. "You must be tired."

"I was before I saw you. Anyway, it'll ease off when Dad gets back. Did you get a postcard?"

"Yes, just today." She settled back with her wine. "Palm trees and sand, mariachi players and sunsets. It sounds like they're having a wonderful time."

"I hope so, because I intend to switch places with them when they get back."

"Switch places?"

"I want to go away with you somewhere, Van." He took her hand, kissed it. "Anywhere you want."

"Away?" Her nerves began to jump. "Why?"

"Because I want to be alone with you, completely alone, as we've never had the chance to be."

She had to swallow. "We're alone now."

He set his wine aside, then hers. "Van, I want you to marry me."

She couldn't claim surprise. She had known, once he had used the word *love*, that marriage would follow. Neither did she feel fear, as she'd been certain she would. But she did feel confusion.

They had talked of marriage before, when they'd been so young and marriage had seemed like such a beautiful dream. She knew better now. She knew marriage was work and commitment and a shared vision.

"Brady, I—"

"This isn't the way I planned it," he interrupted. "I'd wanted it to be very traditional—to have the ring and a nicely poetic speech. I don't have a ring, and all I can tell you is that I love you. I always have, I always will."

"Brady." She pressed his hand to her cheek. Nothing he could have said would have been more poetic. "I want to be able to say yes. I didn't realize until just this moment how much I want that."

"Then say it."

Her eyes were wide and wet when they lifted to his. "I can't. It's too soon. No," she said, before he could explode. "I know what you're going to say. We've known each other almost our whole lives. It's true. But in some ways it's just as true that we only met a few weeks ago."

"There was never anyone but you," he said slowly. "Every other woman I got close to was only a substitute. You were a ghost who haunted me everywhere I went, who faded away every time I tried to reach out and touch."

Nothing could have moved her or unnerved her more. "My life's turned upside down since I came back here. I never thought I would see you again—and I thought that if I did it wouldn't matter, that I wouldn't feel. But it does matter, and I do feel, and that only makes it more difficult."

She was saying almost what he wanted to hear. Almost. "Shouldn't that make it easier?"

"No. I wish it did. I can't marry you, Brady, until I look into the mirror and recognize myself."

"I don't know what the hell you're talking about."

"No, you can't." She dragged her hands through her hair. "I barely do myself. All I know is that I can't give you what you want. I may never be able to."

"We're good together, Van." He had to fight to keep from holding too tight. "Damn it, you know that."

"Yes." She was hurting him. She could hardly bear it. "Brady, there are too many things I don't understand about myself. Too many questions I don't have the answers to. Please, I can't talk about marriage, about lifetimes, until I do."

"My feelings aren't going to change."

"I hope not."

He reeled himself back, slowly. "You're not going to get away from me this time, Van. If you cut and run, I'll come after you. If you try to sneak off, I'll be right there."

Pride rose instantly to wage war with regret. "You make that sound like a threat."

"It is."

"I don't like threats, Brady." She tossed her hair back in a gesture as much challenge as annoyance. "You should remember I don't tolerate them."

"And you should remember I make good on them." Very deliberately, he took her by the shoulders and pulled her against him. "You belong to me, Vanessa. Sooner or later you're going to get that through your head."

The thrill raced up her spine, as it always did when she saw that dangerous light in his eyes. But her chin came up. "I belong to myself first, Brady. Or I intend to. You'll have to get that through your head. Then, maybe, we'll have something."

"We have something now." When his mouth came to hers, she tasted the anger, the frustration, and the need. "You can't deny it."

"Then let it be enough." Her eyes were as dark and intent as his. "I'm here, with you. While I am, there's nothing and no one else." Her arms went around him, enfolding. "Let it be enough."

But it wasn't enough. Even as he rolled onto her, as his mouth fastened hungrily on hers, as his blood fired, he knew it wasn't enough.

In the morning, when she woke—alone, with his scent on sheets that were already growing cold—she was afraid it would never be.

Chapter 11

Nice, very nice, Vanessa thought as Annie worked her way through one of her beloved Madonna's compositions. She had to admit it was a catchy tune, bold and sly by turns. She'd had to simplify it a bit for Annie's inexperienced fingers, but the heart was still there. And that was what counted.

Perhaps the improvement in Annie's technique wasn't radical, but there was improvement. And, as far as enthusiasm went, Annie Crampton was her prize student.

Her own attitude had changed, as well Vanessa admitted. She hadn't known she would enjoy quite so much influencing young hearts and minds with music. She was making a difference here—perhaps only a small one so far, but a difference.

Then there was the added benefit of the lessons helping her keep her mind off Brady. At least for an hour or two every day.

"Well done, Annie."

"I played it all the way through." The wonder on Annie's face was worth the few sour notes she had hit. "I can do it again."

"Next week." Vanessa picked up Annie's book just as she heard the front screen slam. "I want you to work on this next lesson. Hi, Joanie."

"I heard the music." She shifted Lara to her other hip. "Annie Crampton, was that you playing?"

Braces flashed. "I played it all the way through. Miss Sexton said I did a good job."

"And you did. I'm impressed—especially because she could never teach me anything beyond 'Heart and Soul.'"

Vanessa placed a hand on Annie's head. "Mrs. Knight didn't practice."

"I do. And my mom says I've learned more in three weeks than I did in three months up at the music store." She flashed a final grin as she gathered up her books. "And it's more fun, too. See you next week, Miss Sexton."

"I really was impressed," Joanie said as Annie slammed out the front door.

"She has good hands." She held out her own for the baby. "Hello, Lara."

"Maybe you could give her lessons one day."

"Maybe." She cuddled the baby.

"So, other than Annie, how are the lessons going? You're up to, what—?"

"Twelve students. And that's my absolute limit." She pressed her nose against Lara's and had the baby giggling. "Absolutely. But, all in all, they're going fairly well. I've learned to check students' hands before they sit at the piano. I never did figure out what Scott Snooks smeared on the keys."

"What did it look like?"

"Green." She laughed and bounced Lara. "Now we have an inspection before each lesson."

"If you can teach Scott Snooks anything other than murder and mayhem, you're a miracle worker."

"That's the challenge." And she was beginning to enjoy it. "If you've got time, I can defrost a can of lemonade."

"Miss Domesticity." Joanie grinned. "No, really, I only have a couple of minutes. Don't you have another student coming?"

"Saved by the chicken pox." With Lara in tow, Vanessa moved to the living room. "What's your hurry?"

"I just stopped by to see if you needed anything in town. Dad and Loretta will be back in a few hours, and I want to see them. Meanwhile, I've got three dozen errands to run. Hardware store, grocery store, the lumber place. I still can't believe Jack sweet-talked me into that one." She plopped into a chair. "I've spent most of the morning picking up behind Lara the Wrecking Crew as she single-handedly totaled the house. And to think I was thrilled when she took her first step."

"I could use some sheet music." Vanessa gently removed Lara's grasping fingers from her necklace. "I tell you what, I'll write down the titles for you, and in exchange I'll babysit."

Joanie shook her head and rubbed a hand over her ear. "Excuse me, did you say babysit?"

"Yes. As in you-can-leave-Lara-with-me-for-a-couple-of-hours."

"A couple of hours," she repeated slowly. "Do you mean I can go to the mall, alone, by myself?"

"Well, if you'd rather not—"

Joanie let out a whoop as she jumped up to kiss Vanessa and Lara in turn. "Lara, baby, I love you. Goodbye."

"Joanie, wait." Laughing, Vanessa sprang up to grab her arm. "I haven't written down the titles for the sheet music."

"Oh, yeah. Right. I guess I got a little too excited." She blew her hair out of her eyes. "I haven't been shopping by myself in... I forget." Her smile faded to a look of dismay. "I'm a terrible mother. I was happy about leaving her behind. No, not happy. Thrilled. Ecstatic. Delirious. I'm a terrible mother."

"No, you're a crazy person, but you're a wonderful mother."

Joanie steadied herself. "You're right, it was just the thrill of going to the hardware store without a stroller and a diaper bag that went to my head. Are you sure you can handle it?"

"We'll have a great time."

"Of course you will." Keen-eyed, she surveyed the living room. "Maybe you should move anything important up a couple of feet. And nail it down."

"We'll be fine." She set Lara on the floor and handed her a fashion magazine to peruse—and tear up. "See?"

"Okay... I nursed her before I left home, and there's an emergency bottle of apple juice in her diaper bag. Can you change a diaper?"

"I've seen it done before. How hard can it be?"

"Well, if you're sure you don't have anything you have to do."

"My evening is free. When the newlyweds get home, I only have to walk a half a block to see them."

"I guess Brady will be coming by."

"I don't know."

Joanie kept her eye on Lara as the baby pushed herself up and toddled to the coffee table. "Then it hasn't been my imagination."

"What?"

"That there's been a lot of tension between you two the last week or so."

"You're stalling, Joanie."

"Maybe—but I am interested. The couple of times I've seen Brady recently, he's been either snarling or distracted. I don't want you to tell me it was wishful thinking when I hoped you two would get back together."

"He asked me to marry him."

"He— Wow! Oh, that's wonderful! That's terrific!" As Joanie launched herself into Vanessa's arms, Lara began to bang on the table and squeal. "See, even Lara's excited."

"I said no."

"What?" Slowly, Joanie stepped back. "You said no?"

She turned away from the stunned disappointment in Joanie's face. "It's too soon for all of this, Joanie. I've only been back a few weeks, and so much has happened. My mother, your father..." She walked over to move a vase out of Lara's reach. "When I got here, I wasn't even sure how long I would stay, a couple of weeks, maybe a month. I've been considering a tour next spring."

"But that doesn't mean you can't have a personal life. If you want one."

"I don't know what I want." Feeling helpless, she looked back at Joanie. "Marriage is... I don't even know what it means, so how can I consider marrying Brady?"

"But you love him."

"Yes, I think I do." She lifted her hands, fingers spread. "I don't want to make the same mistake my parents did. I need to be sure we both want the same things."

"What do you want?"

"I'm still figuring it out."

"You'd better figure fast. If I know my brother, he won't give you a lot of time."

"I'll take what I need this time." Before Joanie could argue, she shook her head. "You'd better go if you want to get back before my mother and Ham come home."

"Oh, you're right. I'll go get the diaper bag." She paused at the door. "I know we're already stepsisters, but I'm still holding out for sisters-in-law."

Brady knew he was asking for more grief when he started up the walk to Vanessa's house. During the past week, he had tried to keep his distance. When the woman you loved refused to marry you, it didn't do much for your ego.

He wanted to believe she was just being stubborn, and that backing off and playing it light would bring her around. But he was afraid it went much deeper than that. She'd taken a stand. He could walk away, or he could pound down her door. It wouldn't make any difference.

Either way, he needed to see her.

He knocked on the wooden frame of the screen but got no answer. Hardly surprising, he thought, as the banging and crashing from inside would have drowned out any other sound. Maybe she was in a temper, he thought hopefully. Enraged with herself for turning her back on her chance at happiness.

The image appealed to him. He was almost whistling when he opened the screen and walked down the hall.

Whatever he'd been expecting, it hadn't been his niece gleefully banging pots and pans together on the floor while Vanessa, dusted with flour, stood at the counter. Spotting him, Lara hoisted a stainless steel lid and brought it down with a satisfied bang.

"Hi."

With a hand full of celery, Vanessa turned. She expected her heart to do a quick flip-flop when she saw him. It always did. But she didn't smile. Neither did he.

"Oh. I didn't hear you come in."

"I'm not surprised." He reached down to pick up Lara and give her a quick swing. "What are you doing?"

"Babysitting." She rubbed more flour on her nose. "Joanie had to go into town, so I volunteered to watch Lara for a couple of hours."

"She's a handful, isn't she?"

Vanessa blew out a weary breath. She couldn't bear to think about the mess they had left in the living room. "She likes it in here."

He set the baby down, gave her padded bottom a light pat and sent her off to play with a small tower of canned goods. "Wait until she figures out how to rip the labels off. Got anything to drink?"

"Lara's got a bottle of apple juice."

"I wouldn't want to deprive her."

"There's a can of lemonade in the freezer." She went back to chopping celery. "If you want it, you'll have to make it yourself. My hands are full."

"So I see." He opened the freezer. "What are you making?"

"A mess." She brought the knife down with a thunk. "I thought since my mother and Ham were due back soon it would be nice to have a casserole or something. Joanie's already done so much, I wanted to try to—" She set the knife down in disgust. "I'm no good at this. I'm just no good at it. I've never cooked a meal in my life." She whirled as Brady came to the sink to run cold water into a pitcher. "I'm a grown woman, and if it wasn't for room service and prepackaged meals I'd starve to death."

"You make a great ham sandwich."

"I'm not joking, Brady."

With a wooden spoon, he began to stir the lemonade. "Maybe you should be."

"I came in here thinking I'd try to put myself into this little fantasy. What if I were a doctor's wife?"

He stopped stirring to look at her. "What if you were?"

"What if he were coming home after taking appointments and doing hospital rounds all day? Wouldn't I want to fix him a meal, something we could sit down to together, something we could talk over? Isn't that something he would want? Expect?"

"Why don't you ask him?"

"Damn it, Brady, don't you see? I couldn't make it work."

"All I see is that you're having trouble putting—" He leaned forward to look at the disarray on the counter. "What is this?"

Her mouth moved into a pout. "It's supposed to be a tuna casserole."

"You're having trouble putting a tuna casserole together. And, personally, I hope you never learn how to do it."

"That's not the point."

Struck by tenderness, he brushed at a streak of flour on her cheek. "What is the point?"

"It's a little thing, maybe even a stupid thing. But if I can't even do this—" she shoved and sent an onion scampering down the counter "—how can I work out the bigger ones?"

"Do you think I want to marry you so that I can have a hot meal every night?"

"No. Do you think I want to marry you and feel inept and useless?"

Truly exasperated, he gestured toward the counter. "Because you don't know what to do with a can of tuna?"

"Because I don't know how to be a wife." When her voice rose, she struggled to calm it. Perhaps Lara was too young, and too interested in her pans and cans, to detect an argument, but Vanessa had lived through too many of her own. "And, as much as I care for you, I don't know if I want to be. There's one thing I do well, Brady, and that's my music."

"No one's asking you to give that up, Van."

"And when I go on tour? When I'm gone weeks at a time, when I have to devote endless hours to rehearsals and practicing? What kind of marriage would we have, Brady, in between performances?"

"I don't know." He looked down at his niece, who was contentedly placing cans inside of pots. "I didn't know you were seriously considering going on tour again."

"I have to consider it. It's been a part of my life for too long not to." Calmer now, she went back to dicing vegetables. "I'm a musician, Brady, the same way you're a doctor. What I do doesn't save lives, but it does enrich them."

He pushed an impatient hand through his dark hair. He was in the business of soothing doubts and fears, as much as he was in the business of healing bodies. Why couldn't he soothe Vanessa's?

"I know what you do is important, Van. I admire it. I admire you. What I don't see is why your talent would have to be an obstacle to our being together."

"It's just one of them," she murmured.

He took her arm, slowly turning her to face him. "I want to marry you. I want to have children with you and make a home for them. We can do that here, where we both belong, if you just trust me."

"I need to trust myself first." She took a bracing breath. "I leave for Cordina next week."

His hand slid away from her arm. "Cordina?"

"Princess Gabriella's annual benefit."

"I've heard of it."

"I've agreed to give a performance."

"I see." Because he needed to do something, he opened a cupboard and took out a glass. "And when did you agree?"

"I signed almost two weeks ago."

His fingers tensed on the glass. "And didn't mention it."

"No, I didn't mention it." She wiped her hands on her thighs. "With everything that was happening between us, I wasn't sure how you would react."

"Were you going to wait until you were leaving for the airport, or were you just going to send me a postcard when you got there? Damn it, Van." He barely controlled the urge to smash the glass against the wall. "What the hell kind of games have you been playing with me? Was all this just killing time, lighting up an old flame?"

She went pale, but her voice was strong. "You know better."

"All I know is that you're leaving."

"It's only a single performance, a few days."

"And then?"

She turned to look out the window. "I don't know. Frank, my manager, is anxious to put a tour together. That's in addition to some special performances I've been asked to do."

"In addition," he repeated. "You came here with an ulcer because you could barely make yourself go out onstage, because you pushed yourself too far too often. And you're already talking about going back and doing it again."

"It's something I have to work out for myself."

"Your father—"

"Is dead," she cut in. "He can't influence me to perform. I hope you won't try to influence me not to." She took a calming breath, but it didn't help. "I don't believe I pushed myself too far. I did what I needed to do. All I want is the chance to decide what that is."

As the war inside him continued, Brady wondered if there could be a victor. Or if there would only be victims. "You've been thinking about going back, starting with Cordina, but you never talked to me about it."

"No. However selfish it sounds, Brady, this is something I needed to decide for myself. I realize it's unfair for me to ask you to wait. So I won't." She closed her eyes tight, then opened them again. "Whatever happens, I want you to know that the last few weeks, with you, have meant everything to me."

"The hell with that." It was too much like a goodbye. He yanked her against him. "You can go to Cordina, you can go anywhere, but you won't forget me. You won't forget this."

There was fury in the kiss. And desperation. She fought neither. How could she when their mirror images raged within her? She thought that if her life was to end that instant, she would have known nothing but this wild wanting.

"Brady." She brought her hands to his face. When her brow rested against his, she drew a deep breath. "There has to be more than this. For both of us."

"There is more." With his thumbs under her jaw, he tilted her head back. "You know there is."

"I made a promise to myself today. That I would take the time to think over my life, every year of it, every moment that I remembered that seemed important. And when I had done that, I would make the right decision. No more hesitations or excuses or doubts. But for now you have to let me go."

"I let you go once before." Before she could shake her head, he tightened his grip. "You listen to me. If you leave, like this, I won't spend the rest of my life wishing for you. I'll be damned if you'll break my heart a second time."

As they stood close, their eyes locked on each other's, Joanie strolled into the room.

"Well, some babysitters." With a laugh, she plucked Lara up and hugged her. "I can't believe I actually missed this monster. Sorry it took so long." She smiled at Lara and kept babbling as she fought her way through the layers of tension. "There was a line a mile long at the grocery." She glanced down at the scattered pots and canned goods. "It looks like she kept you busy."

"She was fine," Vanessa managed. "She ate about half a box of crackers."

"I thought she'd gained a couple pounds. Hi, Brady. Good timing." His one-word comment had her rolling her eyes. "I meant I'm glad you're here. Look who I ran into outside." She turned just as Ham and Loretta walked in, arm in arm. "Don't they look great?" Joanie wanted to know. "So tanned. I know tans aren't supposed to be healthy, but they look so good."

"Welcome back." Vanessa smiled, but stayed where she was. "Did you have a good time?"

"It was wonderful." Loretta set a huge straw bag down on the table. There was warm color on her cheeks, on her bare arms. And, Vanessa noted, that same quiet happiness in her eyes. "It has to be the most beautiful place on earth, all that white sand and clear water. We even went snorkeling."

"Never seen so many fish," Ham said as he dropped yet another straw bag on the table.

"Ha!" Loretta gave him a telling look. "He was looking at all those pretty legs under water. Some of those women down there wear next to nothing." Then she grinned. "The men, too. I stopped looking the other way after the first day or two."

"Hour or two," Ham corrected.

She only laughed and dug into her bag. "Look here, Lara. We brought you a puppet." She dangled the colorful dancer from its strings.

"Among a few dozen other things," Ham put in. "Wait until you see the pictures. I even rented one of those underwater cameras and got shots of the, ah, fish."

"It's going to take us weeks to unpack it all. I can't even think about it." With a sigh, Loretta sat down at the table. "Oh, and the silver jewelry. I suppose I went a little wild with it."

"Very wild," Ham added with a wink.

"I want you both to pick out the pieces you like best," she said to Vanessa and Joanie. "Once we find them. Brady, is that lemonade?"

"Right the first time." He poured her a glass. "Welcome home."

"Wait until you see your sombrero."

"My sombrero?"

"It's red and silver—about ten feet across." She grinned over at Ham. "I couldn't talk him out of it. Oh, it's good to be home." She glanced at the counter. "What's all this?"

"I was..." Vanessa sent a helpless look at the mess she'd made. "I was going to try to fix some dinner. I... I thought you might not want to fuss with cooking your first night back."

"Good old American food." Ham took the puppet to dangle it for the giggling Lara. "Nothing would hit the spot better right now."

"I haven't exactly—"

Catching her drift, Joanie moved over to the counter. "Looks like you were just getting started. Why don't I give you a hand?"

Vanessa stepped back, bumped into Brady, then moved away again. "I'll be back in a minute."

She hurried out and took the stairs at a dash. In her room, she sat on the bed and wondered if she was losing her mind. Surely it was a close thing when a tuna casserole nearly brought her to tears.

"Van." Loretta stood with her hand on the knob. "May I come in a minute?"

"I was coming back down. I just—" She started to rise, then sat again. "I'm sorry. I don't want to spoil your homecoming."

"You haven't. You couldn't." After a moment, she took a chance. Closing the door, she walked over to sit on the bed beside her daughter. "I could tell you were upset when we came in. I thought it was just because...well, because of me."

"No. No, not entirely."

"Would you like to talk about it?"

She hesitated so long that Loretta was afraid she wouldn't speak at all.

"It's Brady. No, it's me," Vanessa corrected, impatient with herself. "He wants me to marry him, and I can't. There are so many reasons, and he can't understand. *Won't* understand. I can't cook a meal or do laundry or any of the things that Joanie just breezes right through."

"Joanie's a wonderful woman," Loretta said carefully. "But she's different from you."

"I'm the one who's different, from Joanie, from you, from everyone."

Lightly, afraid to go too far, Loretta touched her hair. "It's not a crime or an abnormality not to know how to cook."

"I know." But that only made her feel more foolish. "It's simply that I wanted to feel self-sufficient and ended up feeling inadequate."

"I never taught you how to cook, or how to run a household. Part of that was because you were so involved with your music, and there wasn't really time. But another reason, maybe the true one, is that I didn't want to. I wanted to have that all to myself. The house, the running of it, was all I really had to fulfill me." She gave a little sigh as she touched Vanessa's rigid arm. "But we're not really talking about casseroles and laundry, are we?"

"No. I feel pressured, by what Brady wants. Maybe by who he wants. Marriage, it sounds so lovely. But—"

"But you grew up in a household where it wasn't." With a nod, Loretta took Vanessa's hand. "It's funny how blind we can be. All the time you were growing up, I never thought what was going on between your father and me affected you. And of course it did."

"It was your life."

"It was our lives," Loretta told her. "Van, while we were away, Ham and I talked about all of this. He wanted me to explain everything to you. I didn't agree with him until right now."

"Everyone's downstairs."

"There have been enough excuses." She couldn't sit, so she walked over to the window. The marigolds were blooming, a brilliant orange and yellow against the smug-faced pansies.

"I was very young when I married your father. Eighteen." She gave a little shake of her head. "Lord, it seems like a lifetime ago. And certainly like I was another person. How he swept me off my feet! He was almost thirty then, and had just come back after being in Paris, London, New York, all those exciting places."

"His career had floundered," Vanessa said quietly. "He'd never talk about it, but I've read—and, of course, there were others who loved to talk about his failures."

"He was a brilliant musician. No one could take that away from him." Loretta turned. There was a sadness in her eyes now, lingering. "But he took it away from himself. When his career didn't reach the potential he expected, he turned his back on it. When he came back home, he was troubled, moody, impatient."

She took a moment to gather her courage, hoping she was doing the right thing. "I was a very simple girl, Van. I had led a very simple life. Perhaps that was what appealed to him at first. His sophistication—his, well, worldliness—appealed to me. Dazzled me. We made a mistake—as much mine as his. I was overwhelmed by him, flattered, infatuated. And I got pregnant."

Shock robbed Vanessa of speech as she stared at her mother. With an effort, she rose. "Me? You married because of me?"

"We married because we looked at each other and saw only what we wanted to see. You were the result of that. I want you to know that when you were conceived, you were conceived in what we both desperately believed was love. Maybe, because we did believe it, it was love. It was certainly affection and caring and need."

"You were pregnant," Vanessa said quietly. "You didn't have a choice."

"There is always a choice." Loretta stepped forward, drawing Vanessa's gaze to hers. "You were not a mistake or an inconvenience or an excuse. You were the best parts of us, and we both knew it. There were no scenes or recriminations. I was thrilled to be carrying his child, and he was just as happy. The first year we were married, it was good. In many ways, it was even beautiful."

"I don't know what to say. I don't know what to feel."

"You were the best thing that ever happened to me, or to your father. The tragedy was that we were the worst thing that ever happened to each other. You weren't responsible for that. We were. Whatever happened afterward, having you made all the difference."

"What did happen?"

"My parents died, and we moved into this house. The house I had grown up in, the house that belonged to me. I didn't understand then how bitterly he resented that. I'm not sure he did, either. You were three then. Your father was restless. He resented being here, and couldn't bring himself to face the possibility of failure if he tried to pick up his career again. He began to teach you, and almost overnight it seemed that all of the passion, all of the energy he had had, went into making you into the musician, the performer, the star he felt he would never be again."

Blindly she turned to the window again. "I never stopped him. I never tried. You seemed so happy at the piano. The more promise you showed the more bitter he became. Not toward you, never toward you. But toward the situation, and, of course, toward me. And I toward him. You were the one good thing we had ever done together, the one thing we could both love completely. But it wasn't enough to make us love each other. Can you understand that?"

"Why did you stay together?"

"I'm not really sure. Habit. Fear. The small hope that somehow we would find out we really did love each other. There were too many fights. Oh, I know how they used to upset you. When you were older, a teenager, you used to run from the house just to get away from the arguing. We failed you, Van. Both of us. And, though I know he did things that were selfish, even unforgivable, I failed you more, because I closed my eyes to them. Instead of making things right, I looked for an escape. And I found it with another man."

She found the courage to face her daughter again. "There is no excuse. Your father and I were no longer intimate, were barely even civil, but there were other alternatives open to me. I had thought about divorce, but that takes courage, and I was a coward. Suddenly there was someone who was kind to me, someone who found me attractive and desirable. Because it was forbidden, because it was wrong, it was exciting."

Vanessa felt the tears burn the back of her eyes. She had to know, to understand. "You were lonely."

"Oh, God, yes." Loretta's voice was choked. She pressed her lips together. "It's no excuse—"

"I don't want excuses. I want to know how you felt."

"Lost," she whispered. "Empty. I felt as though my life were over. I wanted someone to need me again, to hold me. To say pretty things to me, even if they were lies." She shook her head, and when she spoke again her voice was stronger. "It was wrong, Vanessa, as wrong as it was for your father and I to rush together without looking closely." She came back to the bed, took Vanessa's hand. "I want it to be different for you. It will be different. Holding back from something that's right for you is just as foolish as rushing into something that's wrong."

"And how do I know the difference?"

"You will." She smiled a little. "It's taken me most of my life to understand that. With Ham, I knew."

"It wasn't." She was afraid to ask. "It wasn't Ham that you... He wasn't the one."

"All those years ago? Oh, no. He would never have betrayed

Emily. He loved her. It was someone else. He wasn't in town long, only a few months. I suppose that made it easier for me somehow. He was a stranger, someone who didn't know me, didn't care. When I broke it off, he moved on."

"You broke it off? Why?"

Of all the things that had gone before, Loretta knew this would be the most difficult. "It was the night of your prom. I'd been upstairs with you. Remember, you were so upset?"

"He had Brady arrested."

"I know." She tightened her grip on Vanessa's hand. "I swear to you, I didn't know it then. I finally left you alone because, well, you needed to be alone. I was thinking about how I was going to give Brady Tucker a piece of my mind when I got ahold of him. I was still upset when your father came home. But he was livid, absolutely livid. That's when it all came out. He was furious because the sheriff had let Brady go, because Ham had come in and raised holy hell."

She let Vanessa's hands go to press her fingers to her eyes. "I was appalled. He'd never approved of Brady—I knew that. But he wouldn't have approved of anyone who interfered with his plans for you. Yet this—this was so far beyond anything I could imagine. The Tuckers were our friends, and anyone with eyes could see that you and Brady were in love. I admit I had worried about whether you would make love, but we'd talked about it, and you'd seemed very sensible. In any case, your father was raging, and I was so angry, so incensed by his insensitivity, that I lost control. I told him what I had been trying to hide for several weeks. I was pregnant."

"Pregnant," Vanessa repeated. "You— Oh, God."

Loretta sprang up to pace the room. "I thought he would go wild, but instead he was calm. Deadly calm." There was no use telling her daughter what names he had called her in that soft, controlled voice. "He said that there was no question about our remaining together. He would file for divorce. And would take you. The more I shouted, begged, threatened, the calmer he became. He would take you because he was the one who would give you the proper care. I was—well, it was obvious what I was. He already had tickets for Paris. Two tickets. I hadn't known about it, but he had been planning to take you away in any case. I was to say nothing, do nothing to stop him, or he would drag me through a custody suit that he would win when it came out that I was carrying another man's bastard." She began to weep then, silently. "If I didn't agree, he would wait until the child was born and file charges against me as an unfit mother. He swore he would make it his life's work to take that child, as well. And I would have nothing."

"But you…he couldn't…"

"I had barely been out of this county, much less the state. I didn't know what he could do. All I knew was that I was going to lose one child, and perhaps two. You were going to go to Paris, see all those wonderful things, play on all those fabulous stages. You would be someone, have something." Her cheeks drenched, she turned back. "As God is my witness, Vanessa, I don't know if I agreed because I thought it was what you would want, or because I was afraid to do anything else."

"It doesn't matter." She rose and went to her mother. "It doesn't matter anymore."

"I knew you would hate me—"

"No, I don't." She put her arms around Loretta and brought her close. "I couldn't. The baby," she murmured. "Will you tell me what you did?"

Grief, fresh and vital, swam through her. "I miscarried, just shy of three months. I lost both of you, you see. I never had all those babies I'd once dreamed of."

"Oh, Mom." Vanessa rocked as she let her own tears fall. "I'm sorry. I'm so sorry. It must have been terrible for you. Terribly hard."

With her cheek against Vanessa's, she held tight. "There wasn't a day that went by that I didn't think of you, that I didn't miss you. If I had it to do over—"

But Vanessa shook her head. "No, we can't take the past back. We'll start right now."

Chapter 12

She sat in her dressing room, surrounded by flowers, the scent and the color of them. She barely noticed them. She'd hoped, perhaps foolishly, that one of the luscious bouquets, one of the elegant arrangements, had been sent by Brady.

But she had known better.

He had not come to see her off at the airport. He had not called to wish her luck, or to tell her he would miss her while she was gone. Not his style, Vanessa thought as she studied her reflection in the mirror. It never had been. When Brady Tucker was angry, he was angry. He made no polite, civilized overtures. He just stayed mad.

He had the right, she admitted. The perfect right.

She had left him, after all. She had gone to him, given herself to him, made love to him with all the passion and promise a woman could bring to a man. But she had held back the words. And, by doing so, she had held back herself.

Because she was afraid, she thought now. Of making that dreadful, life-consuming mistake. He would never understand that her caution was as much for him as it was for herself.

She understood now, after listening to her mother. Mistakes could be made for the best of reasons, or the worst of them. It was too late to ask her father, to try to understand his feelings, his reasons.

She only hoped it wasn't too late for herself.

Where were they now, those children who had loved so fiercely and so unwisely? Brady had his life, his skill, and his answers. His family, his friends, his home. From the rash, angry boy he had been had grown a man of integrity and purpose.

And she? Vanessa stared down at her hands, the long, gifted fingers spread. She had her music. It was all she had ever really had that belonged only to her.

Yes, she understood now, perhaps more than she wanted to, her mother's failings, her father's mistakes. They had, in their separate ways, loved her. But that love hadn't made them a family. Nor had it made any of the three of them happy.

So while Brady was setting down his roots in the fertile soil of the town where they had both been young, she was alone in a dressing room filled with flowers, waiting to step onto another stage.

At the knock on her door, she watched the reflection in the dressing room mirror smile. The show started long before the key light clicked on.

"*Entrez.*"

"Vanessa." The Princess Gabriella, stunning in blue silk, swept inside.

"Your Highness." Before she could rise and make her curtsy, Gabriella was waving her to her seat in a gesture that was somehow imperious and friendly all at once.

"Please, don't get up. I hope I'm not disturbing you."

"Of course not. May I get you some wine?"

"If you're having some." Though her feet ached after a backbreaking day on her feet, she only sighed a little as she took a chair. She had been born royal, and royalty was taught not to complain. "It's been so hectic today, I haven't had a chance to see you, make certain you've been comfortable."

"No one could be uncomfortable in the palace, Your Highness."

"Gabriella, please." She accepted the glass of wine. "We're alone." She gave brief consideration to slipping out of her shoes, but thought better of it. "I wanted to thank you again for agreeing to play tonight. It's so important."

"It's always a pleasure to play in Cordina." The lights around the mirror sent the dozens of bugle beads on Vanessa's white dress dancing. "I'm honored that you wanted to include me."

Gabriella gave a quick laugh before she sipped. "You're annoyed that I bothered you while you were on vacation." She tossed back her fall of red-gold hair. "And I don't blame you. But for this, I've learned to be rude—and ruthless."

Vanessa had to smile. Royalty or not, the Princess Gabriella was easy to be with. "Honored and annoyed, then. I hope tonight's benefit is a tremendous success."

"It will be." She refused to accept less. "Eve— You know my sister-in-law?"

"Yes, I've met Her Highness several times."

"She's American—and therefore pushy. She's been a tremendous help to me."

"Your husband, he is also American?"

Gabriella's topaz eyes lit. "Yes. Reeve is also pushy. This year we involved our children quite a bit, so it's been even more of a circus than usual. My brother, Alexander, was away for a few weeks, but he returned in time to be put to use."

"You are ruthless with your family, Gabriella."

"It's best to be ruthless with those you love." She saw something, some cloud, come and go in Vanessa's eyes. She would get to that. "Hannah apologizes for not coming backstage before your performance. Bennett is fussing over her."

"Your younger brother is entitled to fuss when his wife is on the verge of delivering their child."

"Hannah was interested in you, Vanessa." Gabriella couldn't resist a smile. "As your name was linked with Bennett's before his marriage."

Along with half the female population of the free world, Vanessa thought, but she kept her smile bland. "His Highness was the most charming of escorts."

"He was a scoundrel."

"Tamed by the lovely Lady Hannah."

"Not tamed, but perhaps restrained." The princess set her glass aside. "I was sorry when your manager informed us that you wouldn't spend more than another day in Cordina. It's been so long since you visited us."

"There is no place I've felt more welcome." She toyed with the petals of a pure white rose. "I remember the last time I was here, the lovely day I spent at your farm, with your family."

"We would love to have you to ourselves again, whenever your schedule permits." Compassionate by nature, she reached out a hand. "You are well?"

"Yes, thank you. I'm quite well."

"You look lovely, Vanessa, perhaps more so because there's such sadness in your eyes. I understand the look. It faced me in the mirror once, not so many years ago. Men put it there. It's one of their finest skills." Her fingers linked with Vanessa's. "Can I help you?"

"I don't know." She looked down at their joined hands, then up into Gabriella's soft, patient eyes. "Gabriella, may I ask you, what's the most important thing in your life?"

"My family."

"Yes." She smiled. "You had such a romantic story. How you met and fell in love with your husband."

"It becomes more romantic as time passes, and less traumatic."

"He's an American, a former policeman?"

"Of sorts."

"If you had had to give up your position, your, well, birthright, to have married him, would you have done so?"

"Yes. But with great pain. Does this man ask you to give up something that's so much a part of you?"

"No, he doesn't ask me to give up anything. And yet he asks for everything."

Gabriella smiled again. "It is another skill they have."

"I've learned things about myself, about my background, my family, that are very difficult to accept. I'm not sure if I give this man what he wants, for now, that I won't be cheating him and myself in the bargain."

Gabriella was silent a moment. "You know my story, it has been well documented. After I had been kidnapped, and my memory was gone, I looked into my father's face and didn't know him. Into my brothers' eyes and saw the eyes of strangers. However much this hurt me, it hurt them only more. But I had to find myself, discover myself in the most basic of ways. It's very frightening, very frustrating. I'm not a patient or a temperate person."

Vanessa managed another smile. "I've heard rumors."

With a laugh, Gabriella picked up her wine and sipped again. "At last I recognized myself. At last I looked at my family and knew them. But differently," she said, gesturing. "It's not easy to explain. But when I knew them again, when I loved them again, it was with a different heart. Whatever flaws they had, whatever mistakes they had made, however they had wounded me in the past, or I them, didn't matter any longer."

"You're saying you forgot the past."

She gave a quick shake of her head, and her diamonds sizzled. "The past wasn't forgotten. It can't be. But I could see it through different eyes. Falling in love was not so difficult after being reborn."

"Your husband is a fortunate man."

"Yes. I remind him often." She rose. "I'd better leave you to prepare."

"Thank you."

Gabriella paused at the door. "Perhaps on my next trip to America you will invite me to spend a day in your home."

"With the greatest pleasure."

"And I'll meet this man."

"Yes." Vanessa's laugh was quick and easy. "I think you will."

When the door closed, she sat again. Very slowly she turned her head, until she faced herself in the mirror, ringed by bright lights. She saw dark green eyes, a mouth that had been carefully painted a deep rose. A mane of chestnut hair. Pale skin over delicate features. She saw a musician. And a woman.

"Vanessa Sexton," she murmured, and smiled a little.

Suddenly she knew why she was there, why she would walk out onstage. And why, when she was done, she would go home.

Home.

It was too damn hot for a thirty-year-old fool to be out in the afternoon sun playing basketball. That was what Brady told himself as he jumped up and jammed another basket.

Even though the kids were out of school for the summer, he had the court, and the park, to himself. Apparently children had more sense than a lovesick doctor.

The temperature might have taken an unseasonable hike into the nineties, and the humidity might have decided to join it degree for degree, but Brady figured sweating on the court was a hell of a lot better than brooding alone at home.

Why the hell had he taken the day off?

He needed his work. He needed his hours filled.

He needed Vanessa.

That was something he was going to have to get over. He dribbled into a fast layup. The ball rolled around the rim, then dropped through.

He'd seen the pictures of Vanessa. They'd been all over the

damn television, all over the newspaper. People in town hadn't been able to shut up about it—about her—for two days.

He wished he'd never seen her in that glittery white dress, her hair flaming down her back, those gorgeous hands racing over the keys, caressing them, drawing impossible music from them. Her music, he thought now. The same composition she'd been playing that day he'd walked into her house to find her waiting for him.

Her composition. She'd finished it.

Just as she'd finished with him.

He scraped his surgeon's fingers on the hoop.

How could he expect her to come back to a one-horse town, her high school sweetheart? She had royalty cheering her. She could move from palace to palace for the price of a song. All he had to offer her was a house in the woods, an ill-mannered dog and the occasional baked good in lieu of fee.

That was bull, he thought viciously as the ball rammed onto the backboard and careened off. No one would ever love her the way he did, the way he had all of his damn life. And if he ever got his hands on her again, she'd hear about it. She'd need an otolaryngologist by the time her ears stopped ringing.

"Stuff it," he snapped at Kong as the dog began to bark in short, happy yips. He was out of breath, Brady thought as he puffed toward the foul line. Out of shape. And—as the ball nipped the rim and bounced off—out of luck.

He pivoted, grabbed the rebound, and stopped dead in his tracks.

There she was, wearing those damn skimpy shorts, an excuse for a blouse that skimmed just under her breasts, carrying a bottle of grape soda and sporting a bratty smile on her face.

He wiped the sweat out of his eyes. The heat, his mood—and the fact that he hadn't slept in two days—might be enough to bring on a hallucination. But he didn't like it. Not a bit.

"Hi, Brady." Though her heart was jolting against her ribs, she schooled her voice. She wanted it cool and low and just a little snotty. "You look awful hot." With her eyes on his, Vanessa took a long sip from the bottle, ran her tongue over her upper lip and sauntered the rest of the way to him. "Want a sip?"

He had to be going crazy. He wasn't eighteen anymore. But he could smell her. That floaty, flirty scent. He could feel the hard rubber of the ball in his bare hands, and the sweat dripping down his bare chest and back. As he watched, she leaned over to pet the dog. Still bent, she tossed her hair over her shoulder and sent him one of those taunting sidelong smiles.

"Nice dog."

"What the hell are you doing?"

"I was taking a walk." She straightened, then tipped the bottle to her lips again, draining it before she tossed the empty container into the nearby trash bin. "Your hook shot needs work." Her mouth moved into a pout. "Aren't you going to grab me?"

"No." If he did, he wasn't sure if he would kiss her or strangle her.

"Oh." She felt the confidence that had built up all during the flight, all during the interminable drive home, dry up. "Does that mean you don't want me?"

"Damn you, Vanessa."

Battling tears, she turned away. This wasn't the time for tears. Or for pride. Her little ploy to appeal to his sentiment had been an obvious mistake. "You have every right to be angry."

"Angry?" He heaved the ball away. Delighted, the dog raced after it. "That doesn't begin to describe what I'm feeling. What kind of game are you playing?"

"It's not a game." Eyes brilliant, she turned back to him. "It's never been a game. I love you, Brady."

He didn't know if her words slashed his heart or healed it. "You took your damn time telling me."

"I took what I had to take. I'm sorry I hurt you." Any moment now, her breath would begin to hitch, mortifying her. "If you decide you want to talk to me, I'll be at home."

He grabbed her arm. "Don't you walk away from me. Don't you walk away from me ever again."

"I don't want to fight with you."

"Tough. You come back here, stir me up. You expect me to let things go on as they have been. To put aside what I want, what I need. To watch you leave time and time again, with never a promise, never a future. I won't do it. It's all or nothing, Van, starting now."

"You listen to me."

"The hell with you." He grabbed her then, but there was no fumbling in this kiss. It was hot and hungry. There was as much pain as pleasure here. Just as he wanted there to be.

She struggled, outraged that he would use force. But his muscles were like iron, sleeked with the sweat that heat and exercise had brought to his skin. The violence that flamed inside him was more potent than any she had known before, the need that vibrated from him more furious.

She was breathless when she finally tore away. And would have struck him if she hadn't seen the dark misery in his eyes.

"Go away, Van," he said tightly. "Leave me alone."

"Brady."

"Go away." He rounded on her again, the violence still darkening his eyes. "I haven't changed that much."

"And neither have I." She planted her feet. "If you've finished playing the macho idiot, I want you to listen to me."

"Fine. I'm going to move to the shade." He turned away from her, snatching up a towel from the court and rubbing it over his head as he walked onto the grass.

She stormed off after him. "You're just as impossible as you ever were."

After a quick, insolent look, he dropped down under the shade of an oak. To distract the dog, he picked up a handy stick and heaved it. "So?"

"So I wonder how the hell I ever fell in love with you. Twice."

She took a deep, cleansing breath. This was not going as she had hoped. So she would try again. "I'm sorry I wasn't able to explain myself adequately before I left."

"You explained well enough. You don't want to be a wife."

She gritted her teeth. "I believe I said I didn't know how to be one—and that I didn't know if I wanted to be one. My closest example of one was my mother, and she was miserably unhappy as a wife. And I felt inadequate and insecure."

"Because of the tuna casserole."

"No, damn it, not because of the tuna casserole, because I didn't know if I could handle being a wife and a woman, a mother and a musician. I hadn't worked out my own definition of any of those terms." She frowned down at him. "I hadn't really had the chance to be any of them."

"You were a woman and a musician."

"I was my father's daughter. Before I came back here, I'd never been anything else." Impassioned, she dropped down beside him. "I performed on demand, Brady. I played the music he chose, went where he directed. And I felt what he wanted me to feel."

She let out a long breath and looked away, to those distant Blue Mountains. "I can't blame him for that. I certainly don't want to—not now. You were right when you said I'd never argued with him. That was my fault. If I had, things might have changed. I'll never know."

"Van—"

"No, let me finish. Please. I've spent so much time working all this out." She could still feel his anger, but she took heart from the fact that he didn't pull his hand away when she touched it. "My coming back here was the first thing I'd done completely on my own in twelve years. And even that wasn't really a choice. I had to come back. Unfinished business." She looked back at him then, and smiled. "You weren't supposed to be a part of that. And when you were, I was even more confused."

She paused to pluck at the grass, to feel its softness between her fingers. "Oh, I wanted you. Even when I was angry, even when I still hurt, I wanted you. Maybe that was part of the problem. I couldn't think clearly around you. I guess I never have been able to. Things got out of control so quickly. I realized, when you talked about marriage, that it wasn't enough just to want. Just to take."

"You weren't just taking."

"I hope not. I didn't want to hurt you. I never did. Maybe, in some ways, I tried too hard not to. I knew you would be upset that I was going to Cordina to perform."

He was calm again. After the roller-coaster ride she'd taken his emotions on, his anger had burned itself out. "I wouldn't ask you to give up your music, Van. Or your career."

"No, you wouldn't." She rose to walk out of the shade into the sun and he followed her. "But I was afraid I would give up everything, anything, to please you. And if I did, I wouldn't be. I wouldn't be, Brady."

"I love what you are, Van." His hands closed lightly over her shoulders. "The rest is just details."

"No." She turned back. Her eyes were passionate, and her grip was tight. "It wasn't until I was away again that I began to see what I was pulling away from, what I was moving toward. All my life I did what I was told. Decisions were made for me. The choice was always out of my hands. This time *I* decided. I chose to go to Cordina. I chose to perform. And when I stood in the wings, I waited for the fear to come. I waited for my stomach to clutch and the sweat to break out, and the dizziness. But it didn't come." There were tears in her eyes again, glinting in the sunlight. "It felt wonderful. I felt wonderful. I wanted to step out on the stage, into those lights. I wanted to play and have thousands of people listen. *I* wanted. And it changed everything."

"I'm glad for you." He ran his hands up and down her arms before he stepped back. "I am. I was worried."

"It was glorious." Hugging her arms, she spun away. "And in my heart I know I never played better. There was such…freedom. I know I could go back to all the stages, all the halls, and play like that again." She turned back, magnificent in the streaming sunlight. "I know it."

"I am glad for you," he repeated. "I hated thinking about you performing under stress. I'd never be able to allow you to make yourself ill again, Van, but I meant it when I said I wouldn't ask you to give up your career."

"That's good to hear."

"Damn it, Van, I want to know you'll be coming back to me. I know a house in the woods doesn't compare with Paris or London, but I want you to tell me you'll come back at the end of your tours. That when you're here we'll have a life together, and a family. I want you to ask me to go with you whenever I can."

"I would," she said. "I would promise that, but—"

Rage flickered again. "No buts this time."

"But," she repeated, eyes challenging, "I'm not going to tour again."

"You just said—"

"I said I could perform, and I will. Now and then, if a particular engagement appeals, and if I can fit it comfortably into the rest of my life." With a laugh, she grabbed his hands. "Knowing I can perform, when I want, when I choose. That's important to me. Oh, it's not just important, Brady. It's like suddenly realizing I'm a real person. The person I haven't had a chance to be since I was sixteen. Before I went onstage this last time, I looked in the mirror. I knew who I was, I liked who I was. So instead of there being fear when I stepped into the light, there was only joy."

He could see it in her eyes. And more. "But you came back."

"I chose to come back." She squeezed his fingers. "I needed to come back. There may be other concerts, Brady, but I want to compose, to record. And as much as it continues to amaze me, I want to teach. I can do all of those things here. Especially if someone was willing to add a recording studio onto the house he's building."

Closing his eyes, he brought her hands to his lips. "I think we can manage that."

"I want to get to know my mother again—and learn how to cook. But not well enough so you'd depend on it." She waited until he looked at her again. "I chose to come back here, to come back to you. About the only thing I didn't choose to do was love you." Smiling, she framed his face in her hands. "That just happened, but I think I can live with it. And I do love you, Brady, more than yesterday."

She brought her lips to his. Yes, more than yesterday, she realized. For this was richer, deeper, but with all the energy and hope of youth.

"Ask me again," she whispered. "Please."

He was having trouble letting her go, even far enough that he could look down into her eyes. "Ask you what?"

"Damn you, Brady."

His lips were curved as they brushed through her hair. "A few minutes ago, I was mad at you."

"I know." Her sigh vibrated with satisfaction. "I could always wrap you around my little finger."

"Yeah." He hoped she'd keep doing it for the next fifty or sixty years. "I love you, Van."

"I love you, too. Now ask me."

With his hands on her shoulders, he drew her back. "I want to do it right this time. There's no dim light, no music."

"We'll stand in the shade, and I'll hum."

"Anxious, aren't you?" He laughed and gave her another bruising kiss. "I still don't have a ring."

"Yes, you do." She'd come, armed and ready. Reaching into her pocket, she pulled out a ring with a tiny emerald. She watched Brady's face change when he saw it, recognized it.

"You kept it," he murmured before he lifted his gaze to hers. Every emotion he was feeling had suddenly doubled.

"Always." She set it in the palm of his hand. "It worked before. Why don't you try it again?"

His hand wasn't steady. It hadn't been before. He looked at her. There was a promise in her eyes that spanned more than a decade. And that was absolutely new.

"Will you marry me, Van?"

"Yes." She laughed and blinked away tears. "Oh, yes."

He slipped the ring on her finger. It still fit.

* * * * *

Megan's Mate

For Laura Sparrow—old friends are the best friends.

Chapter 1

She wasn't a risk-taker. She was always absolutely sure a step was completed before she took the next. It was part of her personality—at least it had been for nearly ten years. She'd trained herself to be practical, to be cautious. Megan O'Riley was a woman who double-checked the locks at night.

To prepare for the flight from Oklahoma to Maine, she had meticulously packed carry-on bags for herself and her son, and had arranged for the rest of their belongings to be shipped. It was foolish, she thought, to waste time at baggage claim.

The move east wasn't an impulse. She had told herself that dozens of times during the past six months. It was both a practical and an advantageous step, not only for herself, but for Kevin, too. The adjustment shouldn't be too difficult, she thought as she glanced over to the window seat where her son was dozing. They had family in Bar Harbor, and Kevin had been beside himself with excitement ever since she'd told him she was considering moving near his uncle and his half brother and sister. And cousins, she thought. Four new babies had been born since she and

Kevin had first flown to Maine, to attend her brother's wedding to Amanda Calhoun.

She watched him sleep, her little boy. Not so little anymore, she realized. He was nearly nine. It would be good for him to be a part of a big family. The Calhouns were generous, God knew, with their affection.

She would never forget how Suzanna Calhoun Dumont, now Bradford, had welcomed her the year before. Even knowing that Megan had been Suzanna's husband's lover just prior to Suzanna's marriage, had borne Baxter Dumont a child, Suzanna had been warm and open.

Of course, Megan was a poor example of the classic other woman. She hadn't known Suzanna even existed when she fell for Baxter. She'd been only seventeen, naive, and ready to believe all the promises and the vows of undying love. No, she hadn't known Bax was engaged to Suzanna Calhoun.

When she'd given birth to Baxter's child, he'd been on his honeymoon. He had never seen or acknowledged the son Megan O'Riley had borne him.

Years later, when fate tossed Megan's brother, Sloan, and Suzanna's sister Amanda together, the story had come out.

Now, through the twists and turns of fate, Megan and her son would live in the house where Suzanna and her sisters had grown up. Kevin would have family—a half brother and sister, cousins, and a houseful of aunts and uncles. And what a house.

The Towers, Megan mused. The glorious old stone structure Kevin still called a castle. She wondered what it would be like to live there, to work there. Now that the renovations on The Towers Retreat were completed, a large portion of the house served as a hotel. A St. James hotel, she added thoughtfully, the brainstorm of Trenton St. James III, who had married the youngest Calhoun, Catherine.

St. James hotels were known worldwide for their quality and

class. The offer to join the company as head accountant had, after much weighing and measuring, simply been too good to resist.

And she was dying to see her brother, Sloan, the rest of the family, The Towers itself.

If she was nervous, she told herself it was foolish to be. The move was a very practical, very logical step. Her new title, accounts manager, soothed frustrated ambitions, and though money had never been a problem, her new salary didn't hurt the ego, either.

And most important of all, she would have more time to spend with Kevin.

As the approach for landing was announced, Megan reached over, brushed a hand through Kevin's hair. His eyes, dark and sleepy, blinked open.

"Are we there yet?"

"Just about. Put your seat back up. Look, you can see the bay."

"We're going to go boating, right?" If he'd been fully awake, he might have remembered he was too old to bounce on his seat. But he bounced now, his face pressed to the window in his excitement. "And see whales. We'll go on Alex's new dad's boat."

The idea of boating made her stomach turn, but she smiled gamely. "You bet we will."

"And we're really going to live in that castle?" He turned back to her, her beautiful boy with his golden skin and tousled black hair.

"You'll have Alex's old room."

"And there's ghosts." He grinned, showing gaps where baby teeth had been.

"So they say. Friendly ones."

"Maybe not all of them." At least Kevin hoped not. "Alex says there's lots of them, and sometimes they moan and scream. And last year a man fell right out of the tower window and broke all his bones on the rocks."

She shuddered, knowing that part was sterling truth. The Calhoun emeralds, discovered a year before, had drawn out more than a legend and romance. They'd drawn out a thief and a murderer.

"That's over with now, Kevin. The Towers is safe."

"Yeah." But he was a boy, after all, and hoped for at least a little danger.

There was another boy who was already plotting adventures. It felt as though he'd been waiting forever at the airport gate for his brother to arrive. Alex had one hand in his mother's, the other in Jenny's—because, as his mother had told him, he was the oldest and had to keep his sister close.

His mother was holding the baby, his brand-new brother. Alex could hardly wait to show him off.

"Why aren't they here yet?"

"Because it takes time for people to get off the plane and out the gate."

"How come it's called a gate?" Jenny wanted to know. "It doesn't look like a gate."

"I think they used to have gates, so they still call them that." It was the best Suzanna could come up with after a frazzling half hour at the airport with three children in tow.

Then the baby cooed and made her smile.

"Look, Mom! There they are!"

Before Suzanna could respond, Alex had broken away and made a beeline toward Kevin, Jenny hot on his heels. She winced as they barely missed plowing into other passengers, then raised a resigned hand to wave at Megan.

"Hi!" Alex, having been schooled in airport procedure by his mother, manfully took Kevin's carry-on. "I'm supposed to take this 'cause we're picking you up." It bothered him a little that, even though his mother claimed he was growing like a weed, Kevin was still taller.

"Have you still got the fort?"

"We got the one at the big house," Alex told him. "*And* we got a new one at the cottage. We live at the cottage."

"With our dad," Jenny piped up. "We got new names and everything. He can fix anything, and he built me a new bedroom."

"It has pink curtains," Alex said with a sneer.

Knowing a brawl was dangerously close, Suzanna neatly stepped between her two children. "How was your flight?" She bent down, kissed Kevin, then straightened to kiss Megan.

"It was fine, thanks." Megan still didn't know quite how to respond to Suzanna's easy affection. There were still times she wanted to shout, *I slept with your husband. Don't you understand? Maybe he wasn't your husband yet, and I didn't know he would be, but facts are facts.* "A little delayed," she said instead. "I hope you haven't been waiting long."

"Hours," Alex claimed.

"Thirty minutes," Suzanna corrected with a laugh. "How about the rest of your stuff?"

"I had it shipped. This is it for now." Megan tapped her garment bag. Unable to resist, she peeked down at the bright-eyed baby in Suzanna's arms. He was all pink and smooth, with the dark blue eyes of a newborn and a shock of glossy black hair. She felt the foolish smile that comes over adults around babies spread over her face as he waved an impossibly small fist under her nose.

"Oh, he's beautiful. So tiny."

"He's three weeks old," Alex said importantly. "His name is Christian."

"'Cause that was our great-grandfather's name," Jenny supplied. "We have new cousins, too. Bianca and Cordelia—but we call her Delia—and Ethan."

Alex rolled his eyes. "Everybody had babies."

"He's nice," Kevin decided after a long look. "Is he my brother, too?"

"Absolutely," Suzanna said, before Megan could respond. "I'm afraid you've got an awfully big family now."

Kevin gave her a shy look and touched a testing finger to Christian's waving fist. "I don't mind."

Suzanna smiled over at Megan. "Want to trade?"

Megan hesitated a moment, then gave in. "I'd love to." She cradled the baby while Suzanna took the garment bag. "Oh, Lord." Unable to resist, she nuzzled. "It's easy to forget how tiny they are. How wonderful they smell. And you..." As they walked through the terminal, she took a good look at Suzanna. "How can you look so terrific, when you had a baby only three weeks ago?"

"Oh, bless you. I've been feeling like such a frump. Alex, no running."

"Same goes, Kevin. How's Sloan taking to fatherhood?" Megan wanted to know. "I hated not coming out when Mandy had the baby, but with selling the house and getting things in order to make the move, I just couldn't manage it."

"Everyone understood. And Sloan's a terrific daddy. He'd have Delia strapped on his back twenty-four hours a day if Amanda let him. He designed this incredible nursery for the babies. Window seats, cubbyholes, wonderful built-in cupboards for toys. Delia and Bianca share it, and when C.C. and Trent are in town—which, since The Retreat opened, is more often than not—Ethan's in there, too."

"It's wonderful that they'll all grow up together." She looked at Kevin, Alex and Jenny, thinking as much about them as about the babies.

Suzanna understood perfectly. "Yes, it is. I'm so glad you're here, Megan. It's like getting another sister." She watched Megan's lashes lower. Not quite ready for that, Suzanna surmised, and switched subjects. "And it's going to be a huge relief to hand over the books to you. Not only for The Retreat, but for the boat business, too."

"I'm looking forward to it."

Suzanna stopped by a new minivan, unlocked the doors. "Pile in," she told the kids, then slipped the baby out of Megan's arms. "I hope you say that after you get a look at the ledgers." Competently she strapped the baby into his car seat. "I'm afraid Holt's a pathetic record keeper. And Nathaniel..."

"Oh, that's right. Holt has a partner now. What did Sloan tell me? An old friend?"

"Holt and Nathaniel grew up together on the island. Nathaniel moved back a few months ago. He used to be in the merchant marine. There you go, sweetie." She kissed the baby, then shot an eagle eye over the rest of the children to make sure seat belts were securely buckled. She clicked the sliding door into place, then rounded the hood as Megan took the passenger seat. "He's quite a character," Suzanna said mildly. "You'll get a kick out of him."

The character was just finishing up an enormous lunch of fried chicken, potato salad and lemon meringue pie. With a sigh of satisfaction, he pushed back from the table and eyed his hostess lustfully.

"What do I have to do to get you to marry me, darling?"

She giggled, blushed and waved a hand at him. "You're such a tease, Nate."

"Who's teasing?" He rose, grabbed her fluttering hand and kissed it lavishly. She always smelled like a woman—soft, lush, glorious. He winked and skimmed his lips up to nibble on her wrist. "You know I'm crazy about you, Coco."

Cordelia Calhoun McPike gave another delighted giggle, then patted his cheek. "About my cooking."

"That, too." He grinned when she slipped away to pour him coffee. She was a hell of a woman, he thought. Tall, stately, striking. It amazed him that some smart man hadn't scooped up the widow McPike long ago. "Who do I have to fight off this week?"

"Now that The Retreat's open, I don't have time for romance." She might have sighed over it if she wasn't so pleased with her life. All her darling girls were married and happy, with babies of their own. She had grandnieces and grandnephews to spoil, nephews-in-law to coddle, and, most surprising of all, a full-fledged career as head chef for the St. James Towers Retreat. She offered Nathaniel the coffee and, because she caught him eyeing the pie, cut him another slice.

"You read my mind."

Now she did sigh a little. There was nothing quite so comforting to Coco as watching a man enjoy her food. And he was some man. When Nathaniel Fury rolled back into town, people had noticed. Who could overlook tall, dark and handsome? Certainly not Coco McPike. Particularly not when the combination came with smoky gray eyes, a cleft chin and wonderfully golden skin over sharp cheekbones—not to mention considerable charm.

The black T-shirt and jeans he wore accented an athletic, rangy body—broad shoulders, muscular arms, narrow hips.

Then there was that aura of mystery, a touch of the exotic. It went deeper than his looks, though the dark eyes and the waving mane of deep mahogany hair was exotic enough. It was a matter of presence, she supposed, the culmination of what he'd done and what had touched him in all those years he traveled to foreign ports.

If she'd been twenty years younger... Well, she thought, patting her rich chestnut hair, maybe ten.

But she wasn't, so she had given Nathaniel the place in her heart of the son she'd never had. She was determined to find the right woman for him and see him settled happily. Like her beautiful girls.

Since she felt she had personally arranged the romances and resulting unions of all four of her nieces, she was confident she could do the same for Nathaniel.

"I did your chart last night," she said casually, and checked the fish stew she had simmering for tonight's menu.

"Oh, yeah?" He scooped up more pie. God, the woman could cook.

"You're entering a new phase of your life, Nate."

He'd seen too much of the world to totally dismiss astrology—or anything else. So he smiled at her. "I'd say you're on target there, Coco. Got myself a business, a house on land, retired my seabag."

"No, this phase is more personal." She wiggled her slim brows. "It has to do with Venus."

He grinned at that. "So, are you going to marry me?"

She wagged a finger at him. "You're going to say that to someone, quite seriously, before the summer's over. Actually, I saw you falling in love twice. I'm not quite sure what that means." Her forehead wrinkled as she considered. "It didn't really seem as if you'd have to choose, though there was quite a bit of interference. Perhaps even danger."

"If a guy falls for two women, he's asking for trouble." And Nathaniel was content, at least for the moment, to have no females in his life. Women simply didn't come without expectations, and he planned to fulfill none but his own. "And since my heart already belongs to you..." He got up to go to the stove and kiss her cheek.

The tornado blew in without warning. The kitchen door slammed open, and three shrieking whirlwinds spun through.

"Aunt Coco! They're here!"

"Oh, my." Coco pressed a hand to her speeding heart. "Alex, you took a year off my life." But she smiled, studying the dark-eyed boy beside him. "Can this be Kevin? You've grown a foot! Don't you have a kiss for Aunt Coco?"

"Yes, ma'am." He went forward dutifully, still unsure of his ground. He was enveloped against soft breasts, in soft scents. It eased his somewhat nervous stomach.

"We're so glad you're here." Coco's eyes teared up sentimentally. "Now the whole family's in one place. Kevin, this is Mr. Fury. Nate, my grandnephew."

Nathaniel knew the story, how the scum Baxter Dumont had managed to get some naive kid pregnant shortly before he married Suzanna. The boy was eyeing him now, nervous but contained. Nathaniel realized Kevin knew the story, as well—or part of it.

"Welcome to Bar Harbor." He offered his hand, which Kevin took politely.

"Nate runs the boat shop and stuff with my dad." The novelty of saying "my dad" had yet to wear thin with Alex. "Kevin wants to see whales," he told Nathaniel. "He comes from Oklahoma, and they don't have any. They hardly have any water at all."

"We've got some." Kevin automatically defended his homeland. "And we've got cowboys," he added, one-upping Alex. "You don't have any of those."

"Uh-huh." This from Jenny. "I got a whole cowboy suit."

"Girl," Alex corrected. "It's a cowgirl, 'cause you're a girl."

"It is not."

"Is too."

Her eyes narrowed dangerously. "Is not."

"Well, I see everything's normal in here." Suzanna entered, aiming a warning look at both of her children. "Hello, Nate. I didn't expect to see you here."

"I got lucky." He slipped an arm around Coco's shoulders. "Spent an hour with my woman."

"Flirting with Aunt Coco again?" But Suzanna noted that his gaze had already shifted. She remembered that look from the first time they'd met. The way the gray eyes measured, assessed. Automatically she put a hand on Megan's arm. "Megan O'Riley, Nathaniel Fury, Holt's partner—and Aunt Coco's latest conquest."

"Nice to meet you." She was tired, Megan realized. Had to be, if that clear, steady gaze put her back up. She dismissed him, a little too abruptly for politeness, and smiled at Coco. "You look wonderful."

"Oh, and here I am in my apron. I didn't even freshen up." Coco gave her a hard, welcoming hug. "Let me fix you something. You must be worn-out after the flight."

"Just a little."

"We took the bags up, and I put Christian in the nursery." While

Suzanna herded the children to the table and chatted, Nathaniel took a good long survey of Megan O'Riley.

Cool as an Atlantic breeze, he decided. A little frazzled and unnerved at the moment, he thought, but not willing to show it. The peach-toned skin and long, waving strawberry blond hair made an eye-catching combination.

Nathaniel usually preferred women who were dark and sultry, but there was something to be said for all that rose and gold. She had blue eyes, the color of a calm sea at dawn. Stubborn mouth, he mused, though it softened nicely when she smiled at her son.

A bit on the skinny side, he thought as he finished off his coffee. Needed some of Coco's cooking to help her fill out. Or maybe she just looked skinny—and prim—because she wore such a severely tailored jacket and slacks.

Well aware of his scrutiny, Megan forced herself to keep up her end of the conversation with Coco and the rest. She'd grown used to stares years before, when she was young, unmarried, and pregnant by another woman's husband.

She knew how some men reacted to her status as a single mother, how they assumed she was an easy mark. And she knew how to disabuse them of the notion.

She met Nathaniel's stare levelly, frostily. He didn't look away, as most would, but continued to watch her, unblinkingly, until her teeth clenched.

Good going, he thought. She might be skinny, but she had grit. He grinned, lifted his coffee mug in a silent toast, then turned to Coco. "I've got to go, got a tour to do. Thanks for lunch, Coco."

"Don't forget dinner. The whole family will be here. Eight o'clock."

He glanced back at Megan. "Wouldn't miss it."

"See that you don't." Coco looked at her watch, closed her eyes. "Where is that man? He's late again."

"The Dutchman?"

"Who else? I sent him to the butcher's two hours ago."

Nathaniel shrugged. His former shipmate, and The Towers' new assistant chef, ran on his own timetable. "If I see him down at the docks, I'll send him along."

"Kiss me goodbye," Jenny demanded, delighted when Nathaniel hauled her up.

"You're the prettiest cowboy on the island," he whispered in her ear. Jenny shot a smug look at her brother when her feet touched the floor again. "You let me know when you're ready for a sail," he said to Kevin. "Nice meeting you, Ms. O'Riley."

"Nate's a sailor," Jenny said importantly when Nathaniel strolled out. "He's been everywhere and done everything."

Megan didn't doubt it for a minute.

So much had changed at The Towers, though the family rooms on the first two floors and the east wing were much the same. Trent St. James, with Megan's brother, Sloan, as architect, had concentrated most of the time and effort on the ten suites in the west wing, the new guest dining area and the west tower. All of that area comprised the hotel.

From the quick tour Megan was given, she could see that none of the time and effort that had gone into the construction and renovations had been wasted.

Sloan had designed with an appreciation for the original fortresslike structure, retaining the high-ceilinged rooms and circular stairs, ensuring that the many fireplaces were working, preserving the mullioned windows and French doors that led out onto terraces, balconies, parapets.

The lobby was sumptuous, filled with antiques and designed with a multitude of cozy corners that invited guests to lounge on a rainy or wintry day. The spectacular views of bay or cliffs or sea or Suzanna's fabulous gardens were there to be enjoyed, or tempted guests to stroll out onto terraces and balconies.

When Amanda, as hotel manager, took over the tour, Megan was told that each suite was unique. The storage rooms of The Towers had been full of old furniture, mementos and art. What hadn't been sold prior to Trent's having invested the St. James money in the transformation now graced the guest rooms.

Some suites were two levels, with an art deco staircase connecting the rooms, some had wainscoting or silk wallpaper. There was an Aubusson rug here, an old tapestry there. And all the rooms were infused with the legend of the Calhoun emeralds and the woman who had owned them.

The emeralds themselves, discovered after a difficult and dangerous search—some said with the help of the spirits of Bianca Calhoun and Christian Bradford, the artist who had loved her—resided now in a glass case in the lobby. Above the case was a portrait of Bianca, painted by Christian more than eighty years before.

"They're gorgeous," Megan whispered. "Stunning." The tiers of grass green emeralds and white diamonds almost pulsed with life.

"Sometimes I'll just stop and look at them," Amanda admitted, "and remember all we went through to find them. How Bianca tried to use them to escape with her children to Christian. It should make me sad, I suppose, but having them here, under her portrait, seems right."

"Yes, it does." Megan could feel the pull of them, even through the glass. "But isn't it risky, having them out here this way?"

"Holt arranged for security. Having an ex-cop in the family means nothing's left to chance. The glass is bulletproof." Amanda tapped her finger against it. "And wired to some high-tech sensor." Amanda checked her watch and judged that she had fifteen minutes before she had to resume her managerial duties. "I hope your rooms are all right. We've barely scratched the surface on the family renovations."

"They're fine." And the truth was, it relaxed Megan a bit to see cracked plaster and gnawed woodwork. It made it all less intimidating. "Kevin's in paradise. He's outside with Alex and Jenny, playing with the new puppy."

"Our Fred and Holt's Sadie are quite the proud parents." With a laugh, Amanda tossed back her swing of sable hair. "Eight pups."

"As Alex said, everyone's having babies. And your Delia is beautiful."

"She is, isn't she?" Maternal pride glowed in Amanda's eyes. "I can't believe how much she's grown already. You should have been around here six months ago. All four of us out to here." She laughed again as she held out her arms. "Waddling everywhere. The men strutting. Do you know they took bets to see if Lilah or I would deliver first? She beat me by two days." And since she'd bet twenty on herself, it still irritated her a little. "It's the first time I've known her to be in a hurry about anything."

"Her Bianca's beautiful, too. She was awake and howling for attention when I was in the nursery. Your nanny has her hands full."

"Mrs. Billows can handle anything."

"Actually, I wasn't thinking about the babies. It was Max." She grinned remembering how Bianca's daddy had come running in, abandoning his new novel on the typewriter to scoop his daughter out of her crib.

"He's such a softie."

"Who's a softie?" Sloan strode into the room to swing his sister off her feet.

"Not you, O'Riley," Amanda murmured, watching the way his face softened like butter as he pressed his cheek to Megan's.

"You're here." He twirled her again. "I'm so glad you're here, Meg."

"Me too." She felt her eyes tear and squeezed him tight. "Daddy."

With a laugh, he set her down, slipped his free arm around his wife. "Did you see her yet?"

Megan feigned ignorance. "Who?"

"My girl. My Delia."

"Oh, her." Megan shrugged, chuckled, then kissed Sloan on his sulking mouth. "Not only did I see her, I held her, I sniffed her, and have already decided to spoil her at every opportunity. She's gorgeous, Sloan. She looks just like Amanda."

"Yeah, she does." He kissed his wife. "Except she's got my chin."

"That's a Calhoun chin," Amanda claimed.

"Nope, it's O'Riley all the way. And speaking of O'Rileys," he continued, before Amanda could argue, "where's Kevin?"

"Outside. I should probably go get him. We haven't even unpacked yet."

"We'll go with you," Sloan said.

"You go. I'm covering." Even as Amanda spoke, the phone on the mahogany front desk rang. "Break's over. See you at dinner, Megan." She leaned up to kiss Sloan again. "See you sooner, O'Riley."

"Mmm..." Sloan gave a satisfied sigh as he watched his wife stride off. "I do love the way that woman eats up the floor."

"You look at her just the way you did a year ago, at your wedding." Megan tucked her hand in his as they walked out of the lobby and onto the stone terrace steps. "It's nice."

"She's..." He searched for a word, then settled on the simplest truth. "Everything. I'd like you to be as happy as I am, Megan."

"I am happy." A breeze flitted through her hair. On it carried the sound of children's laughter. "Hearing that makes me happy. So does being here." They descended another level and turned west. "I have to admit I'm a little nervous. It's such a big step." She saw her son scramble to the top of the fort in the yard below, arms raised high in victory. "This is good for him."

"And you?"

"And me." She leaned against her brother. "I'll miss Mom and Dad, but they've already said that with both of us out here, it gives them twice as much reason to visit twice as often." She pushed the blowing hair from her face while Kevin played sniper, fighting off Alex and Jenny's assault on the fort. "He needs to know the rest of his family. And I...needed a change. And as to that—"

she looked back at Sloan "—I tried to get Amanda to show me the setup."

"And she told you that you couldn't sharpen your pencils for a week."

"Something like that."

"We decided at the last family meeting that you'd have a week to settle in before you started hammering the adding machine."

"I don't need a week. I only need—"

"I know, I know. You'd give Amanda a run for the efficiency crown. But orders are you take a week off."

She arched a brow. "And just who gives the orders around here?"

"Everybody." Sloan grinned. "That's what makes it interesting."

Thoughtful, she looked out to sea. The sky was as clear as blown glass, and the breeze warm with early summer. From her perch at the wall, she could see the small clumps of islands far out in the diamond-bright water.

A different world, she thought, from the plains and prairies of home. A different life, perhaps, for her and her son.

A week. To relax, to explore, to take excursions with Kevin. Tempting, yes. But far from responsible. "I want to pull my weight."

"You will, believe me." He glanced out at the clear sound of a boat horn. "That's one of Holt and Nate's," Sloan told her, pointing to the long terraced boat that was gliding across the water. "The *Mariner*. Takes tourists out for whale-watching."

The kids were all atop the fort now, shouting and waving at the boat. When the horn blasted again, they cheered.

"You'll meet Nate at dinner," Sloan began.

"I met him already."

"Flirting a meal out of Coco?"

"It appeared that way."

Sloan shook his head. "That man can eat, let me tell you. What did you think?"

"Not much," she muttered. "He seemed a little rough-edged to me."

"You get used to him. He's one of the family now."

Megan made a noncommittal sound. Maybe he was, but that didn't mean he was part of hers.

Chapter 2

As far as Coco was concerned, Niels Van Horne was a thoroughly unpleasant man. He did not take constructive criticism, or the subtlest of suggestions for improvement, well at all. She tried to be courteous, God knew, as he was a member of the staff of The Towers and an old, dear friend of Nathaniel's.

But the man was a thorn in her side, an abrasive grain of sand in the cozy slipper of her contentment.

In the first place, he was simply too big. The hotel kitchen was gloriously streamlined and organized. She and Sloan had worked in tandem on the design, so that the finished product would suit her specifications and needs. She adored her huge stove, her convection and conventional ovens, the glint of polished stainless steel and glossy white counters, and her whisper-silent dishwasher. She loved the smells of cooking, the hum of her exhaust fans, the sparkling cleanliness of her tile floor.

And there was Van Horne—or Dutch, as he was called—a bull in her china shop, with his redwood-size shoulders and cinder-block arms rippling with tattoos. He refused to wear the neat white bib aprons she'd ordered, with their elegant blue lettering, preferring his rolled-up shirts and tatty jeans held up by a hank of rope.

His salt-and-pepper hair was tied back in a stubby ponytail, and his face, usually scowling, was as big as the rest of him, scored with lines around his light green eyes. His nose, broken several times in the brawls he seemed so proud of, was mashed and crooked. His skin was brown, and leathery as an old saddle.

And his language... Well, Coco didn't consider herself a prude, but she was, after all, a lady.

But the man could cook. It was his only redeeming quality.

As Dutch worked at the stove, she supervised the two line chefs. The specials tonight were her New England fish stew and stuffed trout à la française. Everything appeared to be in order.

"Mr. Van Horne," she began, in a tone that never failed to put his back up. "You will be in charge while I'm downstairs. I don't foresee any problems, but should any arise, I'll be in the family dining room."

He cast one of his sneering looks over his shoulder. Woman was all slicked up tonight, like she was going to some opera or something, he thought. All red silk and pearls. He wanted to snort, but knew her damned perfume would interfere with the pleasure he gained from the smell of his curried rice.

"I cooked for three hundred men," he said in his raspy, sandpaper-edged voice. "I can deal with a couple dozen pasty-faced tourists."

"Our guests," she said between her teeth, "may be slightly more discriminating than sailors trapped on some rusty boat."

One of the busboys swung through, carrying plates. Dutch's eyes zeroed in on one that still held half an entrée. On *his* ship, men had cleaned their plates. "Not too damn hungry, were they?"

"Mr. Van Horne." Coco drew air through her nose. "You will remain in the kitchen at all times. I will not have you going out into the dining room again and berating our guests over their eating habits. A bit more garnish on that salad, please," she said to one of the line chefs, and glided out the door.

"Can't stand fancy-faced broads," Dutch muttered. And if it wasn't for Nate, he thought sourly, Dutch Van Horne wouldn't be taking orders from a dame.

Nathaniel didn't share his former shipmate's disdain of women. He loved them, one and all. He enjoyed their looks, their smells, their voices, and was more than satisfied to settle in the family parlor with six of the best-looking women it had been his pleasure to meet.

The Calhoun women were a constant delight to him. Suzanna, with her soft eyes, Lilah's lazy sexuality, Amanda's brisk practicality, C.C.'s cocky grin, not to mention Coco's feminine elegance.

They made The Towers Nathaniel's little slice of heaven.

And the sixth woman... He sipped his whiskey and water as he watched Megan O'Riley. Now there was a package he thought might be full of surprises. In the looks department, she didn't take second place to the fabulous Calhouns. And her voice, with its slow Oklahoma drawl, added its own appeal. What she lacked, he mused, was the easy warmth that flowed from the other women.

He hadn't decided as yet whether it was the result of a cold nature or simple shyness. Whatever it was, it ran deep. It was hard to be cold or shy in a room filled with laughing people, cooing babies and wrestling children.

He was holding one of his favorite females at the moment. Jenny was bouncing on his lap and barraging him with questions.

"Are you going to marry Aunt Coco?"

"She won't have me."

"I will." Jenny beamed up at him, an apprentice heartbreaker with a missing front tooth. "We can get married in the garden, like Mom and Daddy did. Then you can come live with us."

"Now that's the best offer I've had in a long time." He stroked a callused finger down her cheek.

"But you have to wait until I get big."

"It's always wise to make a man wait." This from Lilah, who slouched on a sofa, her head in the crook of her husband's arm, a baby in her own. "Don't let him rush you into anything, Jenny. Slow is always best."

"She'd know," Amanda commented. "Lilah's spent her life studying slow."

"I'm not ready to give up my girl." Holt scooped Jenny up. "Especially to a broken-down sailor."

"I can outpilot you blindfolded, Bradford."

"Nuh-uh." Alex popped up to defend the family honor. "Daddy sails the best. He can sail better than anybody. Even if bad guys were shooting at him." Territorial, Alex wrapped an arm around Holt's leg. "He even got shot. He's got a bullet hole in him."

Holt grinned at his friend. "Get your own cheering gallery, Nate."

"Did you ever get shot?" Alex wanted to know.

"Can't say that I have." Nathaniel swirled his whiskey. "But there was this Greek in Corfu that wanted to slit my throat."

Alex's eyes widened until they were like saucers. From his spot on the rug, Kevin inched closer. "Really?" Alex looked for signs of knife wounds. He knew Nathaniel had a tattoo of a fire-breathing dragon on his shoulder, but this was even better. "Did you stab him back and kill him dead?"

"Nope." Nathaniel caught the look of doubt and disapproval in Megan's eyes. "He missed and caught me in the shoulder, and the Dutchman knocked him cold with a bottle of ouzo."

Desperately impressed, Kevin slid closer. "Have you got a scar?"

"Sure do."

Amanda slapped Nathaniel's hand before he could tug up his shirt. "Cut it out, or every man in the room will be stripping to show off war wounds. Sloan's really proud of the one he got from barbed wire."

"It's a beaut," Sloan agreed. "But Meg's is even better."

"Shut up, Sloan."

"Hey, a man's gotta brag on his only sister." Enjoying himself, Sloan draped an arm around her shoulders. "She was twelve—hardheaded little brat. We had a mustang stallion nearly as bad-tempered as she was. She snuck him out one day, determined that she could break him. Well, she got about a half a mile before he shook her off."

"He did not shake me off," Megan said primly. "The bridle snapped."

"That's her story." Sloan gave her a quick squeeze. "Fact is, that horse tossed her right into a barbed-wire fence. She landed on her rump. I don't believe you sat down for six weeks."

"It was two," she said, but her lips twitched.

"Got herself a hell of a scar." Sloan gave her butt a brotherly pat.

"Wouldn't mind taking a look at it," Nathaniel said under his breath, and earned an arched-eyebrow look from Suzanna.

"I think I'll put Christian down before dinner."

"Good idea." C.C. took Ethan from Trent just as the baby began to fuss. "Somebody's hungry."

"I know I am." Lilah rose.

Megan watched mothers and babies head upstairs to nurse, and was surprised by a quick tug of envy. Funny, she mused, she hadn't even thought of having more babies until she came here and found herself surrounded by them.

"So sorry I'm late." Coco glided into the room, patting her hair. "We had a few problems in the kitchen."

Nathaniel recognized the look of frustration on her face and fought back a grin. "Dutch giving you trouble, darling?"

"Well…" She didn't like to complain. "We simply have different views on how things should be done. Oh, bless you, Trent," she said when he offered her a glass. "Oh, dear, where is my head? I forgot the canapés."

"I'll get them." Max unfolded himself from the sofa and headed toward the family kitchen.

"Thank you, dear. Now..." She took Megan's hand, squeezed. "We've hardly had a moment to talk. What do you think of The Retreat?"

"It's wonderful, everything Sloan said it would be. Amanda tells me all ten suites are booked."

"It's been a wonderful first season." She beamed at Trent. "Hardly more than a year ago, I was in despair, so afraid my girls would lose their home. Though the cards told me differently. Did I ever tell you that I foresaw Trent in the tarot? I really must do a spread for you, dear, and see what your future holds."

"Well..."

"Perhaps I can just look at your palm."

Megan let go with a sigh of relief when Max came back with a tray and distracted Coco.

"Not interested in the future?" Nathaniel murmured.

Megan glanced over, surprised that he had moved beside her without her being aware of it. "I'm more interested in the present, one step at a time."

"A cynic." He took her hand and, though it went rigid in his, turned it palm up. "I met an old woman on the west coast of Ireland. Molly Duggin was her name. She said I had the sight." His smoky eyes stayed level with hers for a long moment before they shifted to her open palm. Megan felt something skitter down her spine. "A stubborn hand. Self-sufficient, for all its elegance."

He traced a finger over it. Now there was more than a skitter. There was a jolt.

"I don't believe in palmistry."

"You don't have to. Shy," he said quietly. "I wondered about that. The passions are there, but repressed." His thumb glided gently over her palm's mound of Venus. "Or channeled. You'd prefer to say channeled. Goal-oriented, practical. You'd rather make decisions with your head, no matter what your heart tells you." His eyes lifted to hers again. "How close am I?"

Much too close, she thought, but drew her hand coolly from his. "An interesting parlor game, Mr. Fury."

His eyes laughed at her as he tucked his thumbs in his pockets. "Isn't it?"

By noon the next day, Megan had run out of busywork. She hadn't the heart to refuse Kevin's plea to be allowed to spend the day with the Bradfords, though his departure had left her very much to her own devices.

She simply wasn't used to free time.

One trip to the hotel lobby had aborted her idea of convincing Amanda to let her study the books and files. Amanda, she was told by a cheerful desk clerk, was in the west tower, handling a small problem.

Coco wasn't an option, either. Megan had halted just outside the door of the kitchen when she heard the crash of pots and raised voices inside.

Since Lilah had gone back to work as a naturalist in the park, and C.C. was at her automotive shop in town, Megan was left on her own.

In a house as enormous as The Towers, she felt like the last living soul on the island.

She could read, she mused, or sit in the sun on one of the terraces and contemplate the view. She could wander down to the first floor of the family area and check out the progress of the renovations. And harass Sloan and Trent, she thought with a sigh, as they tried to get some work done.

She didn't consider disturbing Max in his studio, knowing he was working on his book. As she'd already spent an hour in the nursery playing with the babies, she felt another visit was out.

She wandered her room, smoothed down the already smooth coverlet on the marvelous four-poster. The rest of her things had arrived that morning, and in her perhaps too-efficient way, she'd already unpacked. Her clothes were neatly hung in the rosewood armoire or folded in the Chippendale bureau. Framed photos of her family smiled from the gateleg table under the window.

Her shoes were aligned, her jewelry was tucked away and her books were stored on the shelf.

And if she didn't find something to do, she would go mad.

With this in mind, she picked up her briefcase, checked the contents one last time and headed outside, to the car Sloan had left at her disposal.

The sedan ran like a top, courtesy of C.C.'s mechanical skills. Megan drove down the winding road toward the village.

She enjoyed the bright blue water of the bay, and the colorful throngs of tourists strolling up and down the sloped streets. But the glistening wares in the shop windows didn't tempt her to stop and do any strolling of her own.

Shopping was something she did out of necessity, not for pleasure.

Once, long ago, she'd loved the idle pleasure of window-shopping, the careless satisfaction of buying for fun. She'd enjoyed empty, endless summer days once, with nothing more to do than watch clouds or listen to the wind.

But that was before innocence had been lost, and responsibilities found.

She saw the sign for Shipshape Tours by the docks. There were a couple of small boats in drydock, but the *Mariner* and its sister ship, the *Island Queen*, were nowhere to be seen.

Her brows knit in annoyance. She'd hoped to catch Holt before he took one of the tours out. Still, there was no reason she couldn't poke inside the little tin-roofed building that housed the offices. After all, Shipshape was now one of her clients.

Megan pulled the sedan behind a long, long T-Bird convertible. She had to admire the lines of the car, and the glossy black paint job that highlighted the white interior.

She paused a moment, shielding her eyes as she watched a two-masted schooner glide over the water, its rust-colored sails full, its decks dotted with people.

There was no denying the beauty of the spot, though the smell and look of the water was so foreign, compared to what she'd known most of her life. The midday breeze was fresh and carried the scent of the sea and the aromas of lunch from the restaurants nearby.

She could be happy here, she told herself. No, she *would* be happy here. Resolutely she turned toward the building and rapped on the door.

"Yeah. It's open."

There was Nathaniel, his feet propped on a messy and ancient metal desk, a phone at his ear. His jeans were torn at the knee and smeared with something like motor oil. His mane of dark mahogany hair was tousled by the wind, or his hands. He crooked his finger in a come-ahead gesture, his eyes measuring her as he spoke on the phone.

"Teak's your best bet. I've got enough in stock, and can have the deck finished in two days. No, the engine just needed an overhaul. It's got a lot of life left in it. No problem." He picked up a smoldering cigar. "I'll give you a call when we're finished."

He hung up the phone, clamped the cigar between his teeth. Funny, he thought, Megan O'Riley had floated into his brain that morning, looking very much as she did at this moment. All spit and polish, that pretty rose-gold hair all tucked up, her face calm and cool.

"Just in the neighborhood?" he asked.

"I was looking for Holt."

"He's out with the *Queen*." Idly Nathaniel checked the diver's watch on his wrist. "Won't be back for about an hour and a half." His cocky mouth quirked up. "Looks like you're stuck with me."

She fought back the urge to shift her briefcase from hand to hand, to back away. "I'd like to see the books."

Nathaniel took a lazy puff on his cigar. "Thought you were on vacation."

She fell back on her best defense. Disdain. "Is there a problem with the books?" she said frostily.

"Couldn't prove it by me." In a fluid move, he reached down and opened a drawer in the desk. He took out a black-bound ledger. "You're the expert." He held it out to her. "Pull up a chair, Meg."

"Thank you." She took a folding chair on the other side of the desk, then slipped dark-framed reading glasses from her briefcase. Once they were on, she opened the ledger. Her accountant's heart contracted in horror at the mess of figures, cramped margin notes and scribbled-on Post-its. "These are your books?"

"Yeah." She looked prim and efficient in her practical glasses and scooped-up hair. She made his mouth water. "Holt and I sort of take turns with them—that's since Suzanna tossed up her hands and called us idiots." He smiled charmingly. "We figured, you know, with her being pregnant at the time, she didn't need any more stress."

"Hmmm…" Megan was already turning pages. For her, the state of the bookkeeping didn't bring on anxiety so much as a sense of challenge. "Your files?"

"We got 'em." Nathaniel jerked a thumb at the dented metal cabinet shoved in the corner. There was a small, greasy boat motor on top of it.

"Is there anything in them?" she said pleasantly.

"Last I looked there was." He couldn't help it. The more prim and efficient her voice, the more he wanted to razz her.

"Invoices?"

"Sure."

"Expense receipts?"

"Absolutely." He reached in another drawer and took out a large cigar box. "We got plenty of receipts."

She took the box, opened the lid and sighed. "This is how you run your business?"

"No. We run the business by taking people out to sea, or repairing their boats. Even building them." He leaned forward on the desk, mostly so he could catch a better whiff of that soft, elusive scent that clung to her skin. "Me, I've never been much on paperwork, and Holt had his fill of it when he was on the force." His smile spread. He didn't figure she wore prim glasses, pulled-back hair and buttoned-up blouses so that a man would yearn to toss aside, muss up and unbutton. But the result was the same. "Maybe that's why the accountant we hired to do the taxes this year developed this little tic." He tapped a finger beside his left eye. "I heard he moved to Jamaica to sell straw baskets."

She had to laugh. "I'm made of sterner stuff, I promise you."

"Never doubted it." He leaned back again, his swivel chair squeaking. "You've got a nice smile, Megan. When you use it."

She knew that tone, lightly flirtatious, unmistakably male. Her defenses locked down like a vault. "You're not paying me for my smile."

"I'd rather it came free, anyhow. How'd you come to be an accountant?"

"I'm good with numbers." She spread the ledger on the desk before opening her briefcase and taking out a calculator.

"So's a bookie. I mean, why'd you pick it?"

"Because it's a solid, dependable career." She began to run numbers, hoping to ignore him.

"And because numbers only add up one way?"

She couldn't ignore that—the faint hint of amusement in his voice. She slanted him a look, adjusted her glasses. "Accounting may be logical, Mr. Fury, but logic doesn't eliminate surprises."

"If you say so. Listen, we may have both come through the side door into the Calhouns' extended family, but we're there. Don't you feel stupid calling me Mr. Fury?"

Her smile had all the warmth of an Atlantic gale. "No, I don't."

"Is it me, or all men, you're determined to beat off with icicles?"

Patience, which she'd convinced herself she held in great store, was rapidly being depleted. "I'm here to do the books. That's all I'm here for."

"Never had a client for a friend?" He took a last puff on the cigar and stubbed it out. "You know, there's a funny thing about me."

"I'm sure you're about to tell me what it is."

"Right. I can have a pleasant conversation with a woman without being tempted to toss her on the floor and tear her clothes off. Now, you're a real treat to look at, Meg, but I can control my more primitive urges—especially when all the signals say stop."

Now she felt ridiculous. She'd been rude, or nearly so, since the moment she'd met him. Because, she admitted to herself, her reaction to him made her uncomfortable. But, damn it, he was the one who kept looking at her as though he'd like to nibble away.

"I'm sorry." The apology was sincere, if a trifle stiff. "I'm making a lot of adjustments right now, so I haven't felt very congenial. And the way you look at me puts me on edge."

"Fair enough. But I have to tell you I figure it's a man's right to look. Anything more takes an invitation—of one kind or the other."

"Then we can clear the air and start over, since I can tell you I won't be putting out the welcome mat. Now, Nathaniel—" it was a concession she made with a smile "—do you suppose you could dig up your tax returns?"

"I can probably put my hands on them." He scooted back his chair. The squeak of the wheels ended on a high-pitched yelp that had Megan jolting and scattering papers. "Damn it—forgot you were back there." He picked up a wriggling, whimpering black puppy. "He sleeps a lot, so I end up stepping on him or running the damn chair over his tail," he said to Megan as the pup licked frantically at his face. "Whenever I try to leave him home, he cries until I give in and bring him with me."

"He's darling." Her fingers were already itching to stroke. "He looks a lot like the one Coco has."

"Same litter." Because he could read the sentiment in Megan's eyes perfectly, Nathaniel handed the pup across the desk.

"Oh, aren't you sweet? Aren't you pretty?"

When she cooed to the dog, all defenses dropped, Nathaniel noted. She forgot to be businesslike and cool, and instead was all feminine warmth—those pretty hands stroking the pup's fur, her smile soft, her eyes alight with pleasure.

He had to remind himself the invitation was for a dog, not for him.

"What's his name?"

"Dog."

She looked up from the puppy's adoring eyes. "Dog? That's it?"

"He likes it. Hey, Dog." At the sound of his master's voice, Dog immediately cocked his head at Nathaniel and barked. "See?"

"Yes." She laughed and nuzzled. "It seems a bit unimaginative."

"On the contrary. How many dogs do you know named Dog?"

"I stand corrected. Down you go, and don't get any ideas about these receipts."

Nathaniel tossed a ball, and Dog gave joyful chase. "That'll keep him busy," he said as he came around the desk to help her gather up the scattered papers.

"You don't seem the puppy type to me."

"Always wanted one." He crouched down beside her and began to toss papers back into the cigar box. "Fact is, I used to play around with one of Dog's ancestors over at the Bradfords', when I was a kid. But it's hard to keep a dog aboard a ship. Got a bird, though."

"A bird?"

"A parrot I picked up in the Caribbean about five years ago. That's another reason I bring Dog along with me. Bird might eat him."

"Bird?" She glanced up, but the laugh froze in her throat. Why was he always closer than she anticipated? And why did those long, searching looks of his slide along her nerve ends like stroking fingers?

His gaze dropped to her mouth. The hesitant smile was still there, he noted. There was something very appealing about that touch of shyness, all wrapped up in stiff-necked confidence. Her eyes weren't cool now, but wary. Not an invitation, he reminded himself, but close. And damn tempting.

Testing his ground, he reached out to tuck a stray curl behind her ear. She was on her feet like a woman shot out of a cannon.

"You sure spook easily, Megan." After closing the lid on the cigar box, he rose. "But I can't say it isn't rewarding to know I make you nervous."

"You don't." But she didn't look at him as she said it. She'd never been a good liar. "I'm going to take all this back with me, if you don't mind. Once I have things organized, I'll be in touch with you, or Holt."

"Fine." The phone rang. He ignored it. "You know where to find us."

"Once I have the books in order, we'll need to set up a proper filing system."

Grinning, he eased a hip onto the corner of the desk. Lord, she was something. "You're the boss, sugar."

She snapped her briefcase closed. "No, you're the boss. And don't call me 'sugar.'" She marched outside, slipped into her car and eased away from the building and back into traffic. Competently she drove through the village, toward The Towers. Once she'd reached the bottom of the long, curving road that led home, she pulled the car over and stopped.

She needed a moment, she thought, before she faced anyone. With her eyes closed, she rested her head against the back of the seat. Her insides were still jittering, dancing with butterflies that willpower alone couldn't seem to swat away.

The weakness infuriated her. Nathaniel Fury infuriated her. After all this time, she mused, all this effort, it had taken no more than a few measuring looks to remind her, all too strongly, that she was still a woman.

Worse, much worse, she was sure he knew exactly what he was doing and how it affected her.

She'd been susceptible to a handsome face and smooth words before. Unlike those who loved her, she refused to blame her youth and inexperience for her reckless actions. Once upon a time, she'd listened to her heart, had believed absolutely in happy-ever-after. But no longer. Now she knew there were no princes, no pumpkins, no castles in the air. There was only reality, one a woman had to make for herself—and sometimes had to make for her child, as well.

She didn't want her pulse to race or her muscles to tense. She didn't want to feel that hot little curl in her stomach that was a yearning hunger crying to be filled. Not now. Not ever again.

All she wanted was to be a good mother to Kevin, to provide him with a happy, loving home. To earn her own way through her own skills. She wanted so badly to be strong and smart and self-sufficient.

Letting out a long sigh, she smiled to herself. And invulnerable.

Well, she might not quite achieve that, but she would be sensible. Never again would she permit a man the power to alter her life—and certainly not because he'd made her glands stand at attention.

Calmer, more confident, she started the car. She had work to do.

Chapter 3

"Have a heart, Mandy." Megan had sought her sister-in-law out the moment she returned to The Towers. "I just want to get a feel for my office and the routine."

Cocking her head, Amanda leaned back from her own pile of paperwork. "Horrible when everyone's busy and you're not, isn't it?"

Megan let out a heartfelt sigh. A kindred spirit. "Awful."

"Sloan wants you to relax," Amanda began, then laughed when Megan rolled her eyes. "But what does he know? Come on." Ready to oblige, she pushed back from the desk, skirted it. "You're practically next door." She led the way down the corridor to another thick, ornately carved door. "I think you've got just about everything you'll need. But if we've missed something, let me know."

Some women felt that frisson of excitement and anticipation on entering a department store. For some, that sensory click might occur at the smell of fresh paint, or the glint of candlelight, or the fizz of champagne just opened.

For Megan, it was the sight of a well-ordered office that caused that quick shiver of pleasure.

And here was everything she could have wanted.

The desk was glorious, gleaming Queen Anne, with a spotless rose-toned blotter and ebony desk set already in place. A multi-lined phone and a streamlined computer sat waiting.

She nearly purred.

There were wooden filing cabinets still smelling of lemon oil, their brass handles shining in the sunlight that poured through the many-paned windows. The Oriental rug picked up the hues of rose and slate blue in the upholstered chairs and love seat. There were shelves for her accounting books and ledgers, and a hunt table that held a coffeemaker, fax and personal copier.

Old-world charm and modern technology blended into tasteful efficiency.

"Mandy, it's perfect."

"I'd hoped you'd like it." Fussing, Amanda straightened the blotter, shifted the stapler. "I can't say I'm sorry to be handing over the books. It's more than a full-time job. I've filed everything, invoices, expenses, credit-card receipts, accounts payable, et cetera, by department." She opened a file drawer to demonstrate.

Megan's organized heart swelled at the sight of neatly color-coded file folders. Alphabetized, categorized, cross-referenced.

Glorious.

"Wonderful. Not a cigar box in sight."

Amanda hesitated, and then threw back her head and laughed. "You've seen Holt and Nate's accounting system, I take it."

Amused, and comfortable with Amanda, Megan patted her briefcase. "I *have* their accounting system." Unable to resist, she sat in the high-backed swivel chair. "Now this is more like it." She took up a sharpened pencil, set it down again. "I don't know how to thank you for letting me join the team."

"Don't be silly. You're family. Besides, you may not be so grateful after a couple of weeks in chaos. I can't tell you how many interruptions—" Amanda broke off when she heard her name bellowed. Her brow lifted. "See what I mean?" She swung to the door to answer her husband's shout. "In here, O'Riley." She shook her head as Sloan and Trent trooped up to the door. Both of them were covered with dust. "I thought you were breaking down a wall or something."

"We were. Had some more old furniture to haul out of the way. And look what we found."

She examined what he held in his hands. "A moldy old book. That's wonderful, honey. Now why don't you and Trent go play construction?"

"Not just a book," Trent announced. "Fergus's account book. For the year of 1913."

"Oh." Amanda's heart gave one hard thud as she grabbed for the book.

Curiosity piqued, Megan rose to join them in the doorway. "Is it important?"

"It's the year Bianca died." Sloan laid a comforting hand on Amanda's shoulder. "You know the story, Meg. How Bianca was trapped in a loveless, abusive marriage. She met Christian Bradford, fell in love. She decided to take the children and leave Fergus, but he found out. They argued up in the tower. She fell through the window."

"And he destroyed everything that belonged to her." Amanda's voice tightened, shook. "Everything—her clothes, her small treasures, her pictures. Everything but the emeralds. Because she'd hidden those. Now we have them, and the portrait Christian had painted. That's all we have of her." She let out a long breath. "I suppose it's fitting that we should have this of his. A ledger of profit and loss."

"Looks like he wrote in the margins here and there." Trent reached over to flip a page open. "Sort of an abbreviated journal."

Amanda frowned and read a portion of the cramped handwriting aloud.

"Too much waste in kitchen. Fired cook. B. too soft on staff. Purchased new cuff links. Diamond. Good choice for opera tonight. Showier than J. P. Getty's."

She let out a huff of breath. "It shows just what kind of man he was, doesn't it?"

"Darling, I wouldn't have brought it out if I'd known it would bother you."

Amanda shook her head. "No, the family will want it." But she set it down, because her fingers felt coated with more than dust and mold. "I was just showing Megan her new domain."

"So I see." Sloan's eyes narrowed. "What happened to relaxing?"

"This is how I relax," Megan responded. "Now why don't you go away and let me enjoy myself?"

"An excellent idea." Amanda gave her husband a kiss and a shove. "Scram." Even as she was hurrying the men along, Amanda's phone rang. "Give me a call if you need anything," she told Megan, and rushed to answer.

Feeling smug, Megan shut the door of her office. She was rubbing her hands together in anticipation as she crossed to her briefcase. She'd show Nathaniel Fury the true meaning of the word *shipshape*.

Three hours later, she was interrupted by the thunder of little feet. Obviously, she thought even before her door crashed open, someone had given Kevin the directions to her office.

"Hi, Mom!" He rushed into her arms for a kiss, and all thoughts of balancing accounts vanished from her mind. "We had the best time. We played with Sadie and Fred and had a war in the new fort. We got to go to Suzanna's flower place and water millions of plants."

Megan glanced down at Kevin's soggy sneakers. "And yourselves, I see."

He grinned. "We had a water battle, and I won."

"My hero."

"We had pizza for lunch, and Carolanne—she works for Suzanna—said I was a bottomless pit. And tomorrow Suzanna has to landscape, so we can't go with her, but we can go out on the whale boat if you want. You want to, don't you? I told Alex and Jenny you would."

She looked down at his dark, excited eyes. He was as happy as she'd ever seen him. At that moment, if he'd asked if she wanted to take a quick trip to Nairobi and hunt lions, she'd have been tempted to agree.

"You bet I do." She laughed when his arms flew around her and squeezed. "What time do we sail?"

At ten o'clock sharp the next morning, Megan had her three charges on the docks. Though the day was warm and balmy for June, she'd taken Suzanna's advice and brought along warm jackets and caps for the trip out into the Atlantic. She had binoculars, a camera, extra film.

Though she'd already downed a dose of motion-sickness pills, her landlubber's stomach tilted queasily as she studied the boat.

It looked sturdy. She could comfort herself with that. The white paint gleamed in the sun, the rails shone. When they stepped on board, she saw that there was a large interior cabin ringed with windows on the first deck. For the less hearty, she assumed. It boasted a concession stand, soft-drink machines and plenty of chairs and benches.

She gave it a last longing look as the children pulled her along. They wouldn't settle for a nice cozy cabin.

"We get to go to the bridge." Alex strutted along importantly, waving to one of the mates. "We own the *Mariner*. Us and Nate."

"Daddy says the bank owns it." Jenny scrambled up the iron steps, a red ribbon trailing from her hair. "But that's a joke. Dutch says it's a crying shame for a real sailor to haul around weak-bellied tourists. But Nate just laughs at him."

Megan merely lifted a brow. She had yet to meet the infamous Dutchman, but Jenny, clever as any parrot, would often quote him word for word. And all too often, those words were vividly blue.

"We're here." Alex burst onto the bridge, breathless with excitement. "Kevin, too."

"Welcome aboard." Nathaniel glanced up from the chart he was studying. His eyes fastened unerringly on Megan's.

"I was expecting Holt."

"He's helming the *Queen*." He picked up his cigar, clamped it between his teeth, grinned. "Don't worry, Meg, I won't run you aground."

She wasn't concerned about that. Exactly. In his black sweater and jeans, a black Greek fisherman's cap on his head and that gleam in his eye, he looked supremely competent. As a pirate might, she mused, upon boarding a merchant ship. "I started on your books." There, she thought, the ground was steady under her feet.

"I figured you would."

"They're a disorganized mess."

"Yeah. Kevin, come on over and take a look. I'll show you where we're heading."

Kevin hesitated, clinging to his mother's hand another moment. But the lure of those colorful charts was too much for him. He dashed over, dozens of questions tripping off his tongue.

"How many whales will we see? What happens if they bump the boat? Will they shoot water up from that hole on their back? Do you steer the boat from way up here?"

Megan started to interrupt and gently tell her son not to badger Mr. Fury, but Nathaniel was already answering questions, hauling Jenny up on one hip and taking Alex's finger to slide over the lines of the chart.

Pirate or not, she thought with a frown, he had a way with children.

"Ready to cast off, Captain."

Nathaniel nodded to the mate. "Quarter speed astern." Still holding Jenny, he walked to the wheel. "Pilot us out of here, sailor," he said to her, and guided her eager hands.

Curiosity got the better of Megan. She inched closer to study the instruments. Depth sounders, sonar, ship-to-shore radio. Those, and all the other equipment, were as foreign to her as the cockpit of a spaceship. She was a woman of the plains.

As the boat chugged gently away from the docks, her stomach lurched, reminding her why.

She clamped down on the nausea, annoyed with herself. It was in her mind, she insisted. A silly, imaginary weakness that could be overcome through willpower.

Besides, she'd taken seasickness pills, so, logically, she couldn't be seasick.

The children cheered as the boat made its long, slow turn in the bay. Megan's stomach turned with it.

Alex was generous enough to allow Kevin to blow the horn. Megan stared straight out the bridge window, her eyes focused above the calm blue water of Frenchman Bay.

It was beautiful, wasn't it? she told herself. And it was hardly tilting at all.

"You'll see The Towers on the starboard side," Nathaniel was saying.

"That's the right," Jenny announced. "Starboard's right and port's left."

"Stern's the back and the bow's in front," said Alex, not to be outdone. "We know all about boats."

Megan shifted her eyes to the cliffs, struggling to ignore another twist in her stomach. "There it is, Kevin." She gripped the brass rail beneath the starboard window for balance. "It looks like it's growing right out of the rock."

And it did look like a castle, she mused as she watched it with her son beside her. The turrets spearing up into the blue summer sky, the somber gray rock glistening with tiny flecks of mica.

Even the scaffolding and the antlike figures of men working didn't detract from the fairy-tale aura. A fairy tale, she thought, with a dark side.

And that, she realized, was what made it all the more alluring. It was hardly any wonder that Sloan, with his love of buildings, adored it.

"Like something you'd expect to see on some lonely Irish coast." Nathaniel spoke from behind her. "Or on some foggy Scottish cliff."

"Yes. It's even more impressive from the sea." Her eyes drifted up, to Bianca's tower. She shivered.

"You may want to put your jacket on," Nathaniel told her. "It's going to get chillier when we get out to sea."

"No, I'm not cold. I was just thinking. When you've heard all the stories about Bianca, it's hard not to imagine what it was like."

"She'd sit up there and watch the cliffs for him. For Christian. And she'd dream—guiltily, I imagine, being a proper lady. But propriety doesn't have a snowball's chance in hell against love."

She shivered again. The statement hit much too close to home. She'd been in love once, and had tossed propriety aside, along with her innocence.

"She paid for it," Megan said flatly, and turned away. To distract herself, she wandered over to the charts. Not that she could make head or tail of them.

"We're heading north by northeast." As he had with Alex, Nathaniel took Megan's hand and guided it along the chart. "We've got a clear day, good visibility, but there's a strong wind. It'll be a little choppy."

Terrific, she thought, and swallowed hard. "If you don't come up with whales, you're going to have some very disappointed kids."

"Oh, I think I can provide a few." She bumped against him as bay gave way to sea. His hands came up to steady her shoulders, and remained. The boat might have swayed, but he stood solid as a rock. "You want to brace your feet apart. Distribute the weight. You'll get your sea legs, Meg."

She didn't think so. Already she could feel the light coating of chilly sweat springing to her skin. Nausea rolled in an answering wave in her stomach. She would not, she promised herself, spoil Kevin's day, or humiliate herself, by being sick.

"It takes about an hour to get out, doesn't it?" Her voice wasn't as strong, or as steady, as she'd hoped.

"That's right."

She started to move away, but ended by leaning dizzily against him.

"Come about," he murmured, and turned her to face him. One look at her face had his brows drawing together. She was pale as a sheet, with an interesting tinge of green just under the surface. Dead sick, he thought with a shake of his head. And they were barely under way.

"Did you take anything?"

There was no use pretending. And she didn't have the strength to be brave. "Yes, but I don't think it did any good. I get sick in a canoe."

"So you came on a three-hour trek into the Atlantic."

"Kevin had his heart set—" She broke off when Nathaniel put a steadying arm around her waist and led her to a bench.

"Sit," he ordered.

Megan obeyed and, when she saw that the children were occupied staring out the windows, gave in and dropped her head between her legs.

Three hours, she thought. They'd have to pour her into a body bag in three hours. Maybe bury her at sea. God, what had made her think a couple of pills would steady her? She felt a tug on her hand.

"What? Is the ambulance here already?"

"Steady as she goes, sugar." Crouched in front of her, Nathaniel slipped narrow terry-cloth bands over her wrists.

"What's this?"

"Acupressure." He twisted the bands until small metal studs pressed lightly on a point on her wrist.

She would have laughed if she hadn't been moaning. "Great. I need a stretcher and you offer voodoo."

"A perfectly valid science. And I wouldn't knock voodoo, either. I've seen some pretty impressive results. Now breathe slow and easy. Just sit here." He slid open a window behind her and let in a blast of air. "I've got to get back to the helm."

She leaned back against the wall and let the fresh air slap her cheeks. On the other side of the bridge, the children huddled, hoping that Moby Dick lurked under each snowy whitecap. She watched the cliffs, but as they swayed to and fro, she closed her eyes in self-defense.

She sighed once, then began to formulate a complicated trigonometry problem in her mind. Oddly enough, by the time she'd worked it through to the solution, her stomach felt steady.

Probably because I've got my eyes closed, she thought. But she could hardly keep them closed for three hours, not when she was in charge of a trio of active children.

Experimentally, she opened one. The boat continued to rock, but her system remained steady. She opened the other. There was a moment of panic when the children weren't at the window. She jolted upright, illness forgotten, then saw them circled around Nathaniel at the helm.

A fine job she was doing, she thought in disgust, sitting there in a dizzy heap while Nathaniel piloted the ship and entertained three kids. She braced herself for the next slap of nausea as she took a step.

It didn't come.

Frowning, she took another step, and another. She felt a little weak, true, but no longer limp and clammy. Daring the ultimate test, she looked out the window at the rolling sea.

There was a tug, but a mild one. In fact, she realized, it was almost a pleasant sensation, like riding on a smooth-gaited horse. In amazement, she studied the terry-cloth bands on her wrists.

Nathaniel glanced over his shoulder. Her color was back, he noted. That pale peach was much more flattering than green. "Better?"

"Yes." She smiled, trying to dispel the embarrassment as easily as his magic bands had the seasickness. "Thank you."

He waited while she bundled the children, then herself, into jackets. On the Atlantic, summer vanished. "First time I shipped out, we hit a little squall. I spent the worst two hours of my life hanging over the rail. Come on. Take the wheel."

"The wheel? I couldn't."

"Sure you could."

"Do it, Mom. It's fun. It's really fun."

Propelled forward by three children, Megan found herself at the helm, her back pressed lightly into Nathaniel's chest, her hands covered by his.

Every nerve in her body began to throb. Nathaniel's body was hard as iron, and his hands were sure and firm. She could smell the sea, through the open windows and on him. No matter how much she tried to concentrate on the water flowing endlessly around them, he was there, just there. His chin brushing the top of her head, his heartbeat throbbing light and steady against her back.

"Nothing like being in control to settle the system," he commented, and she made some sound of agreement.

But this was nothing like being in control.

She began to imagine what it might be like to have those hard, clever hands somewhere other than on the backs of hers. If she turned so that they were face-to-face, and she tilted her head up at just the right angle...

Baffled by the way her mind was working, she set it to calculating algebra.

"Quarter speed," Nathaniel ordered, steering a few degrees to port.

The change of rhythm had Megan off balance. She was trying to regain it when Nathaniel turned her around. And now she was facing him, her head tilted up. The easy grin on his face made her wonder if he knew just where her mind had wandered.

"See the blips on the screen there, Kevin?" But he was watching her, all but hypnotizing her with those unblinking slate-colored eyes. Sorcerer's eyes, she thought dimly. "Do you know what they mean?" And his lips curved—closer to hers than they should be. "There be whales there."

"Where? Where are they, Nate?" Kevin rushed to the window, goggle-eyed.

"Keep watching. We'll stop. Look off the port bow," he told Megan. "I think you'll get your money's worth."

Still dazed, she staggered away. The boat rocked more enthusiastically when stopped—or was it her system that was so thoroughly rocked? As Nathaniel spoke into the P.A. system, taking over the mate's lecture on whales, she slipped the camera and binoculars out of her shoulder bag.

"Look!" Kevin squealed, jumping like a spring as he pointed. "Mom, look!"

Everything cleared from her mind but wonder. She saw the massive body emerge from the choppy water. Rising, up and up, sleek and grand and otherworldly. She could hear the shouts and cheers from the people on the deck below, and her own strangled gasp.

It was surely some sort of magic, she thought, that something so huge, so magnificent, could lurk under the whitecapped sea. Her fingers rose to her lips, pressed there in awe as the sound of the whale displacing water crashed like thunder.

Water flew, sparkling like drops of diamond. Her camera stayed lowered, useless. She could only stare, an ache in her throat, tears in her eyes.

"His mate's coming up."

Nathaniel's voice broke through her frozen wonder. Hurriedly she lifted the camera, snapping quickly as sea parted for whale.

They geysered from their spouts, causing the children to applaud madly. Megan was laughing as she hauled Jenny up for a better view and the three of them took impatient turns with the binoculars.

She pressed herself to the window as eagerly as the children while the boat cruised, following the glossy humps as they speared through the sea. Then the whales sounded, diving deep with a flap of their enormous tails. Below, people laughed and shouted as they were drenched with water.

Twice more the *Mariner* sought out and found pods, giving her passengers the show of a lifetime. Long after they turned and headed for home, Megan stayed at the window, hoping for one more glimpse.

"Beautiful, aren't they?"

She looked back at Nathaniel, eyes glowing. "Incredible. I had no idea. Photographs and movies don't quite do it."

"Nothing quite like seeing and doing for yourself." He cocked a brow. "Still steady?"

With a laugh, she glanced down at her wrists. "Another minor miracle. I would never have put stock in anything like this."

"'There are more things in heaven and earth, Horatio.'"

A black-suited pirate quoting Hamlet. "So it seems," she murmured. "There's The Towers." She smiled. "Off the port side."

"You're learning, sugar." He gave orders briskly and eased the *Mariner* into the calm waters of the bay.

"How long have you been sailing?"

"All my life. But I ran off and joined the merchant marine when I was eighteen."

"Ran off?" She smiled again. "Looking for adventure."

"For freedom." He turned away then, to ease the boat into its slip as smoothly as a foot slides into an old, comfortable shoe.

She wondered why a boy of eighteen would have to search for

freedom. And she thought of herself at that age, a child with a child. She'd cast her freedom away. Now, more than nine years later, she could hardly regret it. Not when the price of her freedom had been a son.

"Can we go down and get a drink?" Kevin tugged on his mother's hand. "We're all thirsty."

"Sure. I'll take you."

"We can go by ourselves," Alex said earnestly. He knew they were much too big to need an overseer. "I got money and everything. We just want to sit downstairs and watch everybody get off."

"All right, then, but stay inside." She watched them rush off. "They start spreading their wings so soon."

"Your boy's going to be flying back to you for a long time yet."

"I hope so." She cut herself off before she voiced the rest: *He's all I have.* "This has been a terrific day for him. For me, too. Thanks."

"My pleasure." They were alone on the bridge now, the lines secured, the plank down and the passengers disembarking. "You'll come again."

"I don't think I could keep Kevin away. I'd better go down with them."

"They're fine." He stepped closer, before she could evade. "You know, Meg, you forget to be nervous when the kids are around."

"I'm not nervous."

"Jumpy as a fish on a line. It was a pure pleasure watching your face when we sighted whale. It's a pure pleasure anytime, but when you're laughing and the wind's in your hair, it could stop a man's heart."

He took another step and backed her up against the wheel. Maybe it wasn't fair, but he'd think about that later. It was going to take him a good long time to forget the way she'd felt, her back pressed against him, her hands soft and hesitant under his.

"Of course, there's something to be said about the way you're looking right now. All eyes. You've got the prettiest blue eyes I've ever seen. Then there's all that peaches-and-cream." He lifted a finger to her cheek, skimmed it down. She felt as though she'd stepped on a live wire. "Makes a man crave a nice long taste."

"I'm not susceptible to flattery." She'd wanted to sound firm and dismissive, not breathless.

"Just stating a fact." He leaned down until his mouth was a whisper from hers. "If you don't want me to kiss you, you'd better tell me not to."

She would have. Absolutely. If she'd been able to speak. But then his mouth was on hers, warm and firm and every bit as clever as his hands. She would tell herself later that her lips had parted with shock, to protest. But it was a lie.

They opened greedily, with a surge of hunger that went deep, that echoed on a groan that a woman might make who had her first sampling of rich cream after years of thin water.

Her body refused to go rigid in denial, instead humming like a harp string freshly plucked. Her hands dived into his hair and urged him to take the kiss deeper.

He'd expected a cool response, or at least a hesitant one. Perhaps he'd seen a flash of passion in her eyes, deep down, like the heat and rumble in the core of a volcano that seems dormant from the surface.

But nothing had prepared him for this blast of fire.

His mind went blank, then filled with woman. The scent and feel and taste of her, the sound of the moan that caught in her throat when he nipped on her full lower lip. He dragged her closer, craving more, and had the dizzying delight of feeling every slim curve and line of Megan pressed against his body.

The scent of the ocean through the window had him imagining taking her on some deserted beach, while the surf pounded and the gulls screamed.

She felt herself sinking, and gripped him for balance. There was too much, much too much, rioting through her system. It would take a great deal more than the little bands around her wrist to level her now.

It would take control, willpower, and, most of all…remembering.

She drew back, would have stumbled if his arms hadn't stayed clamped around her. "No."

He couldn't get his breath. He told himself he would analyze later why one kiss had knocked him flat, like a two-fisted punch. "You'll have to be more specific. No to what?"

"To this. To any of this." Panic kicked in and had her struggling away. "I wasn't thinking."

"Me, neither. It's a good sign you're doing it right, if you stop thinking when you're kissing."

"I don't want you to kiss me."

He slipped his hands into his pockets. Safer there, he decided, since the lady was thinking again. "Sugar, you were doing more than your share."

There was little use in hotly denying the obvious truth. She fell back on cool logic. "You're an attractive man, and I responded in a natural manner."

He had to grin. "Darling, if kissing like that's in your nature, I'm going to die happy."

"I don't intend for it to happen again."

"You know what they say about the road to hell and intentions, don't you?" She was tensed up again. He could see it in the set of her shoulders. He imagined her experience with Dumont had left plenty of scars. "Relax, Meg," he said, more kindly. "I'm not going to jump you. You want to take it slow, we'll take it slow."

The fact that his tone was so reasonable raised her hackles. "We're not going to take it any way at all."

Better, he decided. He didn't mind riling her. In fact, he was looking forward to doing it. Often.

"I'm going to have to say you're wrong. A man and woman set off a fire like that, they're going to keep coming back to the heat."

She was very much afraid he was right. Even now, part of her yearned to fan that blaze again. "I'm not interested in fires or in heat. I'm certainly not interested in an affair with a man I barely know."

"So, we'll get to know each other better before we have one," Nate responded, in an irritatingly reasonable tone.

Megan clamped her teeth together. "I'm not interested in an affair, period. I know that must be a blow to your ego, but you'll just have to deal with it. Now, if you'll excuse me, I'm going to get the children."

He stepped politely out of her way, waited until she'd reached the glass door leading onto the upper deck. "Meg?" It was only partly ego that pushed him to speak. The rest was pure determination. "The first time I make love with you, you won't think about him. You won't even remember his name."

Her eyes sliced at him, twin ice-edged swords. She abandoned dignity and slammed the door.

Chapter 4

"The woman'll be the death of me." Dutch took a bottle of Jamaican rum from his hidey-hole in the back of the pantry. "Mark my words, boy."

Nathaniel kicked back in the kitchen chair, sated and relaxed after the meal he'd enjoyed in the Calhoun dining room. The hotel kitchen was spotless, now that the dinner rush was over. And Coco, Nathaniel knew, was occupied with family. Otherwise, Dutch wouldn't have risked the rum.

"You're not thinking of jumping ship, are you, mate?"

Dutch snorted at the idea. As if he had to take French leave because he couldn't handle a fussy, snooty-nosed female. "I'm sticking." After one wary glance toward the door, he poured them both a healthy portion of rum. "But I'm warning you, boy, sooner or later that woman's going to get her comeuppance. And she's going to get it from yours truly." He stabbed a thick thumb at his wide chest.

Nathaniel downed a swig of rum, hissing through his teeth as it hit. Smooth as silk it wasn't. "Where's that bottle of Cruzan I got you?"

"Used it in a cake. This is plenty good enough for drinking."

"If you don't want a stomach lining," Nathaniel said under his breath. "So, what's the problem with Coco now?"

"Well, if it's not one thing, it's two." Dutch scowled at the kitchen phone when it rang. Room service, he thought with a sneer. Never had any damn room service aboard one of his ships. "Yeah, what?"

Nathaniel grinned into his rum. Tact and diplomacy weren't Dutch's strong points. He imagined that if Coco heard the man growl at guests that way, she'd faint. Or pop Dutch over the head with a skillet.

"I guess you think we've got nothing better to do down here?" he snarled into the phone. "You'll get it when it's ready." He hung up and snagged a plate. "Ordering champagne and fancy cake this time of night. Newlyweds. Ha! Haven't seen hide nor hair of the two in number three all week."

"Where's your romance, Dutch?"

"I leave that to you, lover boy." His ham-size fists delicately cut into the chocolate *gâteau*. "Seen the way you was eyeing that redhead."

"Strawberry blonde," Nathaniel corrected. "More gold than red." Bravely he took another sip of rum. "She's a looker, isn't she?"

"Never seen you go for one that wasn't." With an artist's flair, Dutch ladled vanilla sauce on the side of the twin slices of cake and garnished them with raspberries. "Got a kid, doesn't she?"

"Yeah." Nathaniel studied the cake and decided he could probably force down a small piece. "Kevin. Dark hair, tall for his age." A smile curved his lips. Damned if the boy hadn't gotten to him. "Big, curious eyes."

"Seen him." Dutch had a weakness for kids that he tried to hide. "Okay-looking boy. Comes around with those other two noisy brats, looking for handouts."

Which, Nathaniel knew, Dutch dispensed with great pleasure behind the mask of a scowl.

"Got herself in trouble pretty young."

Nathaniel frowned at that. It was a phrase, too often used to his way of thinking, that indicated the woman was solely responsible for the pregnancy. "It takes two, Dutch. And the bastard was stringing her along."

"I know. I know. I heard about it. Not much gets past me." It wasn't hard to finesse information out of Coco—if he pushed the right buttons. Though he'd never admit it, that was something he looked forward to doing daily. He buzzed for a waiter, taking delight in holding his thumb down until the kitchen door swung open. "Make up a tray for number three," Dutch ordered. "Two gato's, bottle of house champagne, two flutes, and don't forget the damn napkins."

That done, he tossed back his own rum. "Guess you'll be wanting a piece of this now."

"Wouldn't turn it down."

"Never known you to turn down food—or a female." Dutch cut a slice—a great deal larger than those he'd cut for the newlyweds—and shoved the plate in front of Nathaniel.

"I don't get any raspberries?"

"Eat what's in front of you. How come you ain't out there flirting with that skinny girl?"

"I'm working on it," Nathaniel said with a mouthful of cake. "They're in the dining room, all of them. Family meeting." He rose, poured himself coffee, dumped the rest of his rum in it. "They found some old book. And she's not skinny." He had firsthand knowledge, now that he'd had Megan in his arms. "She's delicate."

"Yeah, right." He thought of Coco, those long, sturdy lines as fine as any well-crafted sloops. And snorted again. "All females are delicate—until they get a ring through your nose."

* * *

No one would have called the women in the dining room delicate—not with a typical Calhoun argument in full swing.

"I say we burn it." C.C. folded her arms across her chest and glared. "After everything we learned about Fergus from Bianca's journal, I don't know why we'd consider keeping his lousy account book around."

"We can't burn it," Amanda fired back. "It's part of our history."

"Bad vibes." Lilah narrowed her eyes at the book, now sitting in the center of the table. "Really bad vibes."

"That may be." Max shook his head. "But I can't go along with burning a book. Any kind of book."

"It's not exactly literature," C.C. mumbled.

Trent patted his wife's stiff shoulder. "We can always put it back where it came from—or give Sloan's suggestion some consideration."

"I think a room designed for artifacts, mementos—" Sloan glanced at Amanda "—the pieces of history that go with The Towers, would add something. Not only to the hotel, but for the family."

"I don't know." Suzanna pressed her lips together and tried to be objective. "I feel odd about displaying Fergus's things with Bianca's, or Aunt Colleen's, Uncle Sean's and Ethan's."

"He might have been a creep, but he's still a piece of the whole." Holt toyed with the last of his coffee. "I'm going with Sloan on this one."

That, of course, enticed a small riot of agreements, disagreements, alternate suggestions. Megan could only sit back and watch in amazement.

She hadn't wanted to be there at all. Not at a family meeting. But she'd been summarily outvoted. The Calhouns could unite when they chose.

As the argument swirled around her, she glanced at the object in question. When Amanda left it in her office, she'd eventually given in to temptation. After cleaning off the leather, she'd flipped through pages, idly totaling up columns, clucking her tongue at the occasional mistake in arithmetic. Of course, she'd scanned a few of the marginal notations, as well, and had found Fergus Calhoun a cold, ambitious and self-absorbed man.

But then, a simple account ledger hardly seemed worth this much trouble. Particularly when the last few pages of the books were merely numbers without any rhyme or reason.

She was reminding herself it wasn't her place to comment when she was put directly on the spot.

"What do you think, Megan, dear?" Coco's unexpected question had Megan blinking.

"Excuse me?"

"What do you think? You haven't told us. And you'd be the most qualified, after all."

"Qualified?"

"It's an account book," Coco pointed out. "You're an accountant."

Somehow, the logic in that defeated Megan. "It's really none of my business," she began, and was drowned out by a chorus of reasons why it certainly was. "Well, I..." She looked around the table, where all eyes were focused on her. "I imagine it would be an interesting memento—and it's kind of fascinating to review bookkeeping from so long ago. You know, expenses, and wages for the staff. It might be interesting to see how it adds up, what the income and outgo was for your family in 1913."

"Of course!" Coco clapped her hands. "Why, of course it would. I was thinking about you last night, Meg, while I was casting my runes. It kept coming back to me that you were to take on a project—one with numbers."

"Aunt Coco," C.C. said patiently, "Megan is our accountant."

"Well, I know that, darling." With a bright smile, Coco patted her hair. "So at first I didn't think much of it. But then I kept having this feeling that it was more than that. And I'm sure, somehow, that the project is going to lead to something wonderful."

Something that will make all of us very happy. I'm so pleased you're going to do it."

"Do it?" Megan looked helplessly at her brother. She got a flash of a grin in return.

"Study Fergus's book. You could even put it all on computer, couldn't you? Sloan's told us how clever you are."

"I could, of course, but—"

She was interrupted by the cry of a baby through the monitor on the sideboard.

"Bianca?" Max said.

"Ethan," C.C. and Lilah said in unison.

And the meeting was adjourned.

What exactly, Megan wondered later, had she agreed to do? Somehow, though she'd barely said a word, she'd been placed in charge of Fergus's book. Surely that was a family matter.

She sighed as she pushed open the doors to her terrace and stepped outside. If she stated that obvious fact, in the most practical, logical of terms, she would be patted on the head, pinched on the cheek and told that she was family and that was all there was to it.

How could she argue?

She took a deep breath of the scented night air, and all but tasted Suzanna's freesias and roses. She could hear the sea in the distance, and the air she moved through was moist and lightly salty from it. Stars wheeled overhead, highlighted by a three-quarter moon, bright as a beacon.

Her son was dreaming in his bed, content and safe and surrounded by people who loved him.

Dissecting Fergus's book was a small favor that couldn't begin to repay what she'd been given.

Peace of mind. Yes, she thought, the Calhouns had opened the gates to that particular garden.

Too charmed by the night to close it out and sleep, she wandered down the curving stone steps to drift through the moon-kissed roses and star-sprinkled peonies, under an arbor where wisteria twisted triumphantly, raining tiny petals onto the path.

"'She was a phantom of delight when first she gleamed upon my sight.'"

Megan jolted, pressing a hand on her heart when a shadow separated itself from the other shadows.

"Did I startle you?" Nathaniel stepped closer, the red tip of his cigar glowing. "Wordsworth usually has a different effect."

"I didn't know you were there." And wouldn't have come out had she known. "I thought you'd gone home."

"I was passing a little time with Dutch and a bottle of rum." He stepped fully into the moonlight. "He likes to complain about Coco, and prefers an audience." He drew slowly on his cigar. For a moment, his face was misted by smoke, making it mysterious and beautiful. An angel cast from grace. "Nice night."

"Yes, it is. Well…"

"No need to run off. You wanted to walk in the garden." He smiled, reaching down to snap a pale pink peony from its bush. "Since it's nearly midnight, there's no better time for it."

She accepted the blossom, told herself she wouldn't be charmed. "I was admiring the flowers. I've never had much luck growing them."

"You have to put your heart in it—along with the water and fertilizer."

Her hair was down, waving softly over her shoulders. She still wore the neatly tailored blue jacket and slacks she'd had on at dinner. A pity, he thought. It would have suited the night, and his mood, if she'd drifted outside in a flowing robe. But then, Megan O'Riley wasn't the type of woman to wander midnight gardens in swirling silks.

Wouldn't let herself be.

The only way to combat those intrusive gray eyes, other than to run like a fool, was conversation. "So, do you garden, as well as sail and quote the classics?" she asked him.

"I've an affection for flowers, among other things." Nathaniel put a hand over the peony she held, and lifted it toward him so that he could enjoy its fragrance, and hers. He smiled at her over the feathered petals.

She found herself caught, as if in some slow-motion dream, between the man and the moonlight. The perfume of the garden seemed to rise up and swirl like the breeze, gently invading her senses. Shadows shifted over his face, highlighting all those fascinating clefts and ridges, luring her gaze to his mouth, curved now and inviting.

They seemed so completely alone, so totally cut off from the reality and responsibilities of day-to-day.

Just a man and a woman among star-dappled flowers and moonlit shadows, and the music of the distant sea.

Deliberately she lowered her lashes, as if to break the spell.

"I'm surprised you'd have time for poetry and flowers, with all the traveling."

"You can always make time for what counts."

The fact that the night held magic hadn't escaped him. But then, he was open to such things. There'd been times he'd seen water rise out of itself like a clenched fist, times he'd heard the siren song of mermaids through shifting fog—he believed in magic. Why else had he waited in the garden, knowing, somehow knowing, she would come?

He released the flower, but took her free hand, linking their fingers before she could think of a reason he shouldn't. "Walk with me, Meg. A night like this shouldn't be wasted."

"I'm going back in." She looked back up just as a breeze stirred in the air. Wisteria petals rained down.

"Soon."

So she was walking with him in the fairy-lit garden, with a flower in her hand and fragrant petals in her hair.

"I...really should check on Kevin."

"The boy have trouble sleeping?"

"No, but—"

"Bad dreams?"

"No."

"Well, then." Taking that as an answer, he continued his stroll down the narrow path. "Does having a man flirt with you always make you turn tail and run?"

"I certainly wasn't running. And I'm not interested in flirtations."

"Funny. When you were standing out on the terrace a bit ago, you looked like a woman ready for a little flirting."

She stopped dead. "You were watching me."

"Mmm." Nathaniel crushed his cigar out into the sand of a nearby urn. "I was thinking it was a shame I didn't have a lute."

Annoyance warred with curiosity. "A lute?"

"A pretty woman standing on a balcony in the moonlight—she should be serenaded."

She had to laugh at that. "I suppose you play the lute."

"Nope. Wished I did, though, when I saw you." He began to walk again. The cliff curved downward, toward the seawall. "I used to sail by here when I was a kid and look up at The Towers. I liked to think there was a dragon guarding it, and that I'd scale the cliffs and slay him."

"Kevin still calls it a castle," she murmured, looking back.

"When I got older and took note of the Calhoun sisters, I figured when I killed the dragon, they'd reward me. In the way a sixteen-year-old walking hormone fantasizes."

She laughed again. "Which one of them?"

"Oh, all of them." Grinning, he sat on the low wall, drew her down beside him. "They've always been...remarkable. Holt had this thing for Suzanna, though he wouldn't admit it. Being as he was my friend, I selflessly crossed her off my list. That left three for me after I conquered that dragon."

"But you never did face the dragon?"

A shadow passed over his face. "I had another to deal with. I guess you could say we left it at a draw, and I went to sea." He shook off the mood, and the uncomfortable past. "But I did have a brief and memorable interlude with the lovely Lilah."

Megan's eyes widened. "You and Lilah?"

"Right before I left the island. She set out to drive me crazy. I think she was practicing." He sighed at the memory. "She was damn good at it."

But they were so easy with each other, Megan thought. So relaxed and friendly.

"You're so easy to read, Meg." He chuckled and slipped his arm around her shoulders. "We weren't exactly Romeo and Juliet. I kissed her a few times, did my damnedest to convince her to do more. She didn't. And she didn't break my heart. Well, dented it a little, maybe," he mused.

"And Max isn't bothered?"

"Why would he be? He's got her. If we'd had a flaming affair—which we didn't—it would be a smoldering matchstick compared to what they've got."

He was right there. Each of the Calhoun women had found her match. "Still, it's interesting," she said quietly. "All these connections within connections."

"Are you thinking of me, or yourself?"

She stiffened, abruptly aware that she was sitting hip-to-hip with him, his arm around her. "That's not something I care to discuss."

"Still raw?" He tightened his arm, comforting. "From what I've heard of Dumont, I wouldn't think he'd be worth it. Settle down," he said when she jerked away. "We'll let it go. Too nice a night to uncover old wounds. Why don't you tell me how they talked you into taking on that old account book?"

"How do you know about that?"

"Holt and Suzanna filled me in." She was still rigid, he noted. But she wasn't running. "I saw them before they left."

She relaxed a little. It was comforting to discuss it with someone else who was just that small step outside the family. "I don't know how they talked me into it. I barely opened my mouth."

"Your first mistake."

She huffed out a breath. "I'd have had to shout to be heard. I don't know why they call it a meeting, when all they do is argue." Her brows knit. "Then they stop arguing and you realize you've been sucked in. If you try to pull yourself out, you find they've united in this solid wall that's impossible to beat."

"I know just what you mean. I still don't know if it was my idea to go into business with Holt. The notion came up, was debated, voted on and approved. The next thing I knew, I was signing papers."

Interesting, she mused, and studied his strong profile. "You don't strike me as someone who could be talked into anything."

"I could say the same."

She considered a moment, then gave up. "You're right. The book's fascinating. I can hardly wait to get at it."

"I hope you're not planning on letting it take up all your free time." He toyed with the ends of her blowing hair. No, not red, he mused. It was gold, enriched by quiet fire. "I want some of it."

Cautiously she inched away. "I explained to you, I'm not interested."

"What you are is worried because you are interested." He cupped a hand under her chin and turned her to face him. "I figure you had a rough time, and maybe it's helped you cope to lump all men in with the bastard who hurt you. That's why I said I'd be patient."

Fury flared in her eyes. "Don't tell me what I am or how I've coped. I'm not asking for your understanding or your patience."

"Okay."

He crushed his mouth to hers, without any patience at all. His lips were demanding, urgent, irresistible, conquering hers before she could draw the breath to deny it.

The embers that had smoldered inside her since the first time he'd kissed her burst into reckless flame. She wanted—craved—this flash point of feeling, this fireball of sensation. Hating herself for the weakness, she let herself burn.

He'd proved his point, Nathaniel thought as he tore his mouth from hers to press it against the thundering pulse in her throat. Proved his point, and wrapped himself up in nasty knots of need.

Needs that would have to wait, because she was far from ready. And because it mattered—she mattered—more than he'd expected.

"Now tell me you're not interested," he muttered against her lips, furious that he was unable to take what was so obviously his. "Tell me you didn't want me to touch you."

"I can't." Her voice broke in despair. She wanted him to touch her, to take her, to throw her on the ground and make wild love to her. And to take the decision, and the responsibility, out of her hands. That made her ashamed. That made her a coward. "But wanting's not enough." Shaken, she pushed away, lurched to her feet. "It's never going to be enough for me. I've wanted before." She stood trembling in the moonlight, her hair blowing free, her eyes fierce and afraid.

Nathaniel cursed himself, then her for good measure. "I'm not Dumont. And you're not a seventeen-year-old girl."

"I know who I am. I don't know who you are."

"You're hedging, Megan. We recognized each other from the first instant."

She stepped back, because she knew he was right. Because it terrified her. "You're talking about chemistry."

"Maybe I'm talking about fate." He said it softly, as he rose. He'd frightened her, and he despised himself for it. Unnerving a woman was one thing, bullying another. "You need time to think about that. So do I. I'll walk you back."

She put out a hand to stop him. "I can find my own way." She whirled and raced up the moonlit path.

Nathaniel swore under his breath. He sat again and took out a fresh cigar, lit it. There wasn't any use heading home yet. He already knew he wouldn't sleep.

Late the following afternoon, Megan roused herself from her ledgers when a knock sounded on her office door.

"Come in."

"Sorry to interrupt." Coco poked her head in the door—a head, Megan noted with surprise, that was now topped with sleek ebony hair—she apparently was a woman who changed her hair color as often as she changed moods. "You didn't break for lunch," Coco said as she stepped through the door with a large and laden silver tray.

"You didn't have to bother." Megan glanced at her watch and was stunned to see it was after three. "You've got enough to do without waiting on me."

"Just part of the service." After setting the tray on a table, Coco began to arrange a place setting. "We can't have you skipping meals." She glanced over at the computer screen, the open ledgers, the calculator and the neatly stacked files. "My goodness, such a lot of numbers. Numbers have always unsettled me. They're so...unyielding."

"You don't have to let them push you around," Megan said with a laugh. "Once you know that one and one always equals two, you can do anything."

Coco studied the screen doubtfully. "If you say so, dear."

"I've just finished up the first quarter on Shipshape. It was...a challenge."

"It's wonderful that you think so." Coco turned her back on the numbers before they could give her a headache. "But none of us wants you overdoing things. Now, here's some iced tea and a nice club sandwich."

It did look tempting, particularly since she'd had no appetite for breakfast. A residual effect, she knew, of her encounter with Nathaniel.

"Thank you, Coco. I'm sorry I took you away from your work."

"Oh." Coco waved a dismissive hand as Megan rose to pick up her plate. "Don't give it a thought. To be frank, dear, I simply had to get out—away from that man."

"The Dutchman?" Megan smiled over her first bite of sandwich. "I met him this morning, when I was coming down. I made a wrong turn and ended up in the hotel wing."

Restless, Coco began to fiddle with the thick gold links around her throat. "I hope he didn't say anything to offend you. He's a bit…rough."

"No." Megan poured two glasses of tea, offered one to Coco. "He sort of glowered and told me I needed some meat on my bones. I thought he was going to start stuffing me with the Greek omelet he was fixing, but one of the busboys dropped a plate. I escaped while he was swearing at the poor kid."

"His language." Coco seated herself, smoothed down her silk trouser leg. "Deplorable. And he's always contradicting me on recipes." She shut her eyes, shuddered. "I've always considered myself a patient woman—and, if I can be immodest for a moment, a clever one. I had to be both to raise four lively girls." Sighing, she tossed up her hands in a gesture of surrender. "But as far as that man's concerned, I'm at my wits' end."

"I suppose you could let him go," Megan said tentatively.

"Impossible. The man's like a father to Nathaniel, and the children, for reasons that escape me, are terribly fond of him." She opened her eyes again and smiled bravely. "I can cope, dear, and I must admit the man has a way with certain rudimentary dishes." She patted her new hairdo. "And I find little ways to distract myself."

But Megan's attention was stuck back at Coco's first statement. "I suppose Mr. Van Horne has known Nathaniel for some time."

"Oh, more than fifteen years, I believe. They served together, sailed together, whatever you call it. I believe Mr. Van Horn took Nate under his wing. Which is something in his favor, I suppose. God knows the boy needed someone, after the miserable childhood he had."

"Oh?" It wasn't in Megan's nature to probe, but Coco needed little prompting.

"His mother died when he was very young, poor boy. And his father." Her lovely mouth went grim. "Well, the man was little more than a beast really. I barely knew John Fury, but there was always talk in the village. And now and then Nathaniel would come along with Holt when Holt brought us fish. I'd see the bruises for myself."

"Bruises," Megan repeated, horrified. "His father beat him?"

Coco's soft heart had tears swimming in her eyes. "I'm very much afraid so."

"But—didn't anyone do anything about it?"

"Whenever there were questions, the man would claim the boy had fallen, or gotten into a fight with another child. Nathaniel never contradicted him. Sad to say, abuse was something people often overlooked back then. Still is, I'm afraid." Tears threatened her mascara. She dabbed at them with Megan's napkin. "Nathaniel ran off to sea the moment he was of age. His father died a few years back. Nate sent money for the funeral, but didn't come. It was hard to blame him."

Coco sighed, shook herself. "I didn't mean to come in with such a sad story. But it has a good ending. Nate turned out to be a fine man." Coco's damp eyes were deceptively guileless. "All he needs is the right woman. He's terribly handsome, don't you think?"

"Yes," Megan said cautiously. She was still trying to equate the abused child with the confident man.

"And dependable. Romantic, too, with all those tales of the sea, and that air of mystery around him. A woman would be very lucky to catch his eye."

Megan blinked her own eyes as the not-so-subtle hint got through. "I couldn't say. I don't know him very well, and I don't really think about men that way."

"Nonsense." Confident in her own matchmaking skills, Coco patted Megan's knee. "You're young, beautiful, intelligent. Having a man in your life doesn't diminish those things, dear—or a woman's independence. The right man enhances them. And I have a feeling that you'll be finding that out, very soon. Now—" she leaned over and kissed Megan's cheek "—I have to get back to the kitchen, before that man does something horrid to my salmon patties."

She started out the door, then paused—timing it, Coco thought, rather beautifully. "Oh, dear, I'm such a scatterbrain. I was supposed to tell you about Kevin."

"Kevin?" Automatically Megan's gaze shifted to the window. "Isn't he outside with Alex and Jenny?"

"Well, yes, but not here." Coco smiled distractedly—it was a pose she'd practiced for years. "It's Nathaniel's day off, and he was by for lunch. Such a wonderful appetite he has, and never seems to gain an ounce. Of course, he does keep active. That's why he has all those marvelous muscles. They are marvelous, aren't they?"

"Coco, where is Kevin?"

"Oh, there I go, running off again. Kevin's with Nate. All of them are. He took the children with him."

Megan was already on her feet. "With him? Where? On a boat?" Visions of squalls and towering waves of water swam through her head, despite the calm, cloudless blue of the sky.

"No, no, to his house. He's building a deck or something, and the children were dying to go along and help. It would be such a favor to me if you could go by and pick them up." And, of course, Coco thought cannily, Megan would then see Nate's lovely little home, and his charming way with children. "Suzanna expects the children to be here, you see, but I didn't have the heart to deny them. She won't be back until five, so there's no hurry."

"But, I—"

"You know where Suzanna and Holt's cottage is, don't you, darling? Nathaniel's is only a half a mile past it. Charming place. You can't miss it."

Before Megan could form another word, the door closed gently in her face.

A job, Coco thought as she strode down the corridor, very well done.

Chapter 5

Kevin didn't know which was the coolest. It was a very close call between the small fire-breathing dragon on the back of Nathaniel's shoulder and the puckered white scar on the front. The scar was the result of the knife wound, which ought to have put it far ahead in the running. But a tattoo, a tattoo of a *dragon*, was pretty hard to beat.

There was another scar, just above Nathaniel's waistline, near the hip. At Alex's eager questioning, Nathaniel had said it was from a moray eel he'd tangled with in the South Pacific.

Kevin could easily imagine Nathaniel, armed with only a knife clenched between his teeth, fighting to the death with a sea creature on the scale of the Loch Ness monster.

And Nathaniel had a parrot, a big, colorful bird who sat right inside the house on a wooden perch and talked. Kevin's current favorite was "Off with her head."

Kevin figured Nathaniel Fury was about the coolest man he'd ever met—a man who had traveled the seven seas like Sinbad, and had the scars and stories to prove it. A man who liked puppies and talking birds.

He didn't seem to mind when Kevin hung back while Alex and Jenny raced around the yard with the puppy and killed each other with imaginary laser pistols. It was more fun to crouch close while Nathaniel hammered nails into boards.

It took Kevin about six boards to start asking questions.

"How come you want a deck out here?"

"So I can sit on it." Nathaniel set another board in place.

"But you've already got one in the back."

"I'll still have it." Three strikes of the hammer and the nail was through board and joist. Nathaniel sat back on his haunches. He wore nothing but a bandanna twisted around his head and a pair of ragged cutoff jeans. His skin was bronzed by the sun and coated lightly with sweat. "See how the frame goes?"

Kevin followed the direction of the deck frame as it skirted around the side of the house. "Uh-huh."

"Well, we'll keep going till we meet the other deck."

Kevin's eyes brightened. "So it'll go all around, like a circle."

"You got it." Nathaniel hammered the next nail, and the next, then shifted positions. "How do you like the island?"

He asked the question in such a natural, adult fashion that Kevin first glanced around to see if Nathaniel was speaking to him. "I like it. I like it a lot. We get to live in the castle, and I can play with Alex and Jenny anytime."

"You had friends back in Oklahoma, too, right?"

"Sure. My best friend is John Curtis Silverhorn. He's part Comanche. My mom said he could come visit anytime, and that we can write letters all we want. I already wrote him about the whale." Kevin smiled shyly. "I liked that the best."

"We'll have to go out again."

"Really? When?"

Nathaniel stopped hammering and looked at the boy. He realized he should have remembered from his exposure to Alex and

Jenny that when children were raised with love and trust, they believed just about everything you told them.

"You can come out with me whenever you want. 'Long as your mother gives the go-ahead."

His reward for the careless offer was a brilliant smile. "Maybe I can steer the boat again?"

"Yeah." Nathaniel grinned and turned Kevin's baseball cap backward. "You could do that. Want to nail some boards?"

Kevin's eyes widened and glowed. "Okay!"

"Here." Nathaniel scooted back so that Kevin could kneel in front of him. "Hold the nail like this." He wrapped his hands over Kevin's, showing him how to hold both the hammer and the nail to guide the stroke.

"Hey!" Alex rose from the dead on Planet Zero and raced over. "Can I do it?"

"Me too." Jenny leaped on Nathaniel's back, knowing she was always welcome.

"I guess I got me a crew." Nathaniel figured that with all the extra help it would only take about twice as long to finish.

An hour later, Megan pulled up beside the long, classic lines of the T-Bird and stared. The house itself surprised her. The charming two-story cottage, with its neatly painted blue shutters and its window boxes bright with pansies, wasn't exactly the image she had of Nathaniel Fury. Nor was the tidy green lawn, the trimmed hedge, the fat barking puppy.

But it was Nathaniel who surprised her most. She was a bit taken aback by all that exposed golden skin, the lithe, muscled body. She was human, after all. But it was what he was doing that really captured her attention.

He was crouched over her son on the partially finished deck, their heads close, his big hand over Kevin's small one. Jenny was sitting adoringly beside him, and Alex was playing highwire on a joist.

"Hi, Megan! Look, I'm the death-defying Alex." In his excitement, Alex nearly lost his balance and almost plunged a harrowing eight inches to the ground. He pinwheeled his arms and avoided disaster.

"Close call," she said, and grinned at him.

"I'm in the center ring, without a net."

"Mom, we're building a deck." Kevin caught his bottom lip between his teeth and pounded a nail. "See?"

"Yes, I do." Briefcase in tow, Megan stopped to pet the eager puppy, who fell over backward in enthusiasm.

"And it's my turn next." Jenny batted her eyes at Nathaniel. "Isn't it?"

"That's right, sugar. Okay, Captain. Let's drive that baby home."

With a grunt of effort, Kevin sent the nail into the board. "I did it. I did the whole board." Proudly Kevin looked back at his mother. "We each get to do a board. This is my third one."

"It looks like you're doing a good job." To give the devil his due, she smiled at Nathaniel. "Not everyone could handle it."

"Just takes a steady eye and a sure hand. Hey, mates, where's my timber?"

"We'll get it." Alex and Kevin scrambled together to heave the next plank.

Standing back, Megan watched the routine they'd worked out. Nathaniel took the board, sighted down it, set it in place. He tapped, shifted, using a small block of wood to measure the distance between the last board and the new one. Once he was satisfied, Jenny wriggled in front of him.

She wrapped both little hands around the hammer, and Nathaniel, a braver soul than Megan had imagined, held the nail.

"Keep your eye on the target," Nathaniel warned, then sat patiently while her little strokes gradually anchored the nail. Then, wrapping his hand over hers, he rammed it home. "Thirsty work," he said casually. "Isn't it, mates?"

"Aye, aye." Alex put his hands to his throat and gagged.

Nathaniel held the next nail. "There's some lemonade in the kitchen. If someone was to go fetch the pitcher and a few glasses…"

Four pairs of eyes turned on her, putting Megan firmly in her place. If she wasn't going to be a carpenter, she'd have to be a gofer.

"All right." She set the briefcase down and crossed the finished portion of the deck to the front door.

Nathaniel said nothing, waited.

Seconds later, a shrill wolf whistle sounded from inside, followed by a muffled scream. He was grinning by the time Bird squawked out his invitation: "Hey, sugar, buy you a drink? Here's looking at you, kid." When Bird began to sing a chorus of "There Is Nothing Like a Dame," the children collapsed into fits of laughter.

A few minutes later, Megan carried out a tray of drinks. Bird's voice followed her. "'Give me a kiss, and to that kiss a score!'"

She arched a brow as she set the tray on the deck. "Bogart, show tunes and poetry. That's quite a bird."

"He has an eye for pretty women." Nathaniel picked up a glass and downed half the contents. He scanned Megan, taking in the tidy French twist, the crisp blouse and slacks. "Can't say I blame him."

"Aunt Coco says Nate needs a woman." Alex smacked his lips over the tart lemonade. "I don't know why."

"To sleep with him," Jenny said, and caused both Nathaniel and Megan to gape. "Grown-ups get lonely at night, and they like to have someone to sleep with. Like Mom and Daddy do. I have my bear," she continued, referring to her favorite stuffed animal. "So I don't get lonely."

"Break time." Nathaniel gamely swallowed his choke of laughter. "Why don't you guys take Dog for a walk down by the water?"

The idea met with unanimous approval. With war whoops and slapping feet, they raced off.

"Kid's got a point." Nathaniel rubbed the cold glass over his sweaty brow. "Nights can get lonely."

"I'm sure Jenny will lend you her bear." Megan stepped away

from him, as if studying the house. "It's a very nice place, Nathaniel." She flicked a finger over the sassy petals of a pansy. "Homey."

"You were expecting a crow's nest, some oilcloth?"

She had to smile. "Something like that. I want to thank you for letting Kevin spend the day."

"I'd say the three of them are working as a team these days."

Her smile softened. She could hear their laughter from behind the house. "Yes, you're right."

"I like having them around. They're good company." He shifted on the deck, folding his legs under him. "The boy's got your eyes."

Her smile faded. "No, Kevin's are brown." Like his father's.

"No, not the color. The look in them. Goes a lot deeper than brown or blue. How much have you told him?"

"I—" She brought herself back, angled her chin. "I didn't come here to discuss my personal life with you."

"What did you come here to discuss?"

"I came to get the children, and to go over your books."

Nathaniel nodded at her briefcase. "Got them in there?"

"Yes." She retrieved it, then, because she saw little choice, sat on the deck facing him. "I've finished the first quarter—that's January, February, March. Your outlay exceeded your income during that period, though you did have some cash flow through boat repairs. There is an outstanding account payable from February." She took out files, flipped through the neat computer-generated sheets. "A Mr. Jacques LaRue, in the amount of twelve hundred and thirty-two dollars and thirty-six cents."

"LaRue's had a tough year." Nathaniel poured more lemonade. "Holt and I agreed to give him some more time."

"That's your business, of course. Traditionally there would be late charges on any outstanding account after thirty days."

"Traditionally, on the island, we're a little friendlier."

"Your choice." She adjusted her glasses. "Now, as you can see, I've arranged the books into logical columns. Expenses—rent, utilities, office supplies, advertising and so forth. Then we have wages and withholding."

"New perfume."

She glanced over. "What?"

"You're wearing a new perfume. There's a hint of jasmine in it."

Distracted, she stared at him. "Coco gave it to me."

"I like it." He leaned closer. "A lot."

"Well." She cleared her throat, flipped a page. "And here we have income. I've added the weekly ticket sales from the tours to give you a month-by-month total, and a year-to-date. I see that you run a package deal with The Retreat, discounting your tour for hotel guests."

"Seemed friendly—and like good business."

"Yes, it's very smart business. On the average, eighty percent of the hotel guests take advantage of the package. I... Do you have to sit so close?"

"Yeah. Have dinner with me tonight, Meg."

"No."

"Afraid to be alone with me?"

"Yes. Now, as you can see, in March your income began an upswing—"

"Bring the boy."

"What?"

"Am I mumbling?" He smiled at her and slipped her glasses off her nose. "I said bring Kevin along. We'll take a drive out to this place I know. Great lobster rolls." He gave the word *lobster* a broad New England twist that made her smile. "I can't claim they're up to Coco's standards, but there's plenty of local color."

"We'll see."

"Uh-uh. Parental cop-out."

She sighed, shrugged. "All right. Kevin would enjoy it."

"Good." He handed her glasses back before he rose to heft another board. "Tonight, then."

"Tonight?"

"Why wait? You can call Suzanna, tell her we'll drop the kids off at her house on the way."

"I suppose I could." Now that his back was to her, she had no choice but to watch the ripple of muscles play as he set the board. She ignored the quick tug at her midsection, and reminded herself that her son would be along as chaperon. "I've never had a lobster roll."

"Then you're in for a treat."

He was absolutely right. The long, winding drive in the spectacular T-Bird was joy enough. The little villages they passed through were as scenic as any postcard. The sun dipped down toward the horizon in the west, and the breeze in the open car smelled of fish, then flowers, then sea.

The restaurant was hardly more than a diner, a square of faded gray wood set on stilts in the water, across a rickety gangplank. The interior decoration ran to torn fishnets and battered lobster buoys.

Scarred tables dotted the equally scarred floor. The booths were designed to rip the hell out of panty hose. A dubious effort at romantic atmosphere was added by the painted tuna can and hurricane globe set in the center of each table. The candles globbed in the base of the cans were unlit. Today's menu was scrawled on a chalkboard hanging beside the open kitchen.

"We got lobster rolls, lobster salad and lobster lobster," a waitress explained to an obviously frazzled family of four. "We got beer, we got milk, iced tea and soft drinks. There's French fries and coleslaw, and no ice cream 'cause the machine's not working. What'll you have?"

When she spotted Nathaniel, she abandoned her customers and gave him a hard punch in the chest. "Where you been, Captain?"

"Oh, out and about, Jule. Got me a taste for lobster roll."

"You came to the right place." The waitress, scarecrow-thin with a puff of steel-gray hair, eyed Megan craftily. "So, who's this?"

"Megan O'Riley, her son Kevin. This is Julie Peterson. The best lobster cook on Mount Desert Island."

"The new accountant from The Towers." Julie gave a brisk nod. "Well, sit down, sit down. I'll fix you up when I get a minute." She swiveled back to her other customers. "You make up your mind yet, or are you just going to sit and take the air?"

"The food's better than the service." Nathaniel winked at Kevin as he led them to a booth. "You've just met one of the monuments of the island, Kevin. Mrs. Peterson's family has been trapping lobster and cooking them up for over a hundred years."

"Wow." He eyed the waitress, who, to almost-nine-year-old eyes, seemed old enough to have been handling that job personally for at least a century.

"I worked here some when I was a kid. Swabbing the decks." And she'd been kind to him, Nathaniel remembered. Giving him ice or salve for his bruises, saying nothing.

"I thought you worked with Holt's family—" Megan began, then cursed herself when he lifted a brow at her. "Coco mentioned it."

"I put in some time with the Bradfords."

"Did you know Holt's grandfather?" Kevin wanted to know. "He's one of the ghosts."

"Sure. He used to sit on the porch of the house where Alex and Jenny live now. Sometimes he'd walk up to the cliffs over by The Towers. Looking for Bianca."

"Lilah says they walk there together now. I haven't seen them." And it was a crushing disappointment. "Have you ever seen a ghost?"

"More than once." Nathaniel ignored the stiff kick Megan gave him under the table. "In Cornwall, where the cliffs are deadly and the fogs roll in like something alive, I saw a woman standing, looking out to sea. She wore a cape with a hood, and there were tears in her eyes."

Kevin was leaning forward now, rapt and eager.

"I started toward her, through the mist, and she turned. She was beautiful, and sad. 'Lost,' was what she said to me. 'He's lost. And so am I.' Then she vanished. Like smoke."

"Honest?" Kevin said in an awed whisper.

Honest wasn't the point, Nathaniel knew. The pull of the story was. "They called her the Captain's Lady, and legend is that her husband and his ship went down in a storm in the Irish Sea. Night after night while she lived, and long after, she walked the cliffs weeping for him."

"Maybe you should be writing books, like Max," Megan murmured, surprised and annoyed at the shiver that raced down her spine.

"Oh, he can spin a tale, Nate can." Julie plopped two beers and a soft drink on the table. "Used to badger me about all the places he was going to see. Well, guess you saw them, didn't you, Captain?"

"Guess I did." Nathaniel lifted the bottle to his lips. "But I never forgot you, darling."

Julie gave another cackling laugh, punched his shoulder. "Sweet-talker," she said, and shuffled off.

Megan studied her beer. "She didn't take our order."

"She won't. She'll bring us what she wants us to have." He took another pull of the beer. "Because she likes me. If you're not up for beer, I can charm her into switching it."

"No, it's fine. I suppose you know a lot of people on the island, since you grew up here."

"A few. I was gone a long time."

"Nate sailed around the whole world. Twice." Kevin slurped soda through his straw. "Through hurricanes and typhoons and everything."

"It must have been exciting."

"It had its moments."

"Do you miss it?"

"I sailed on another man's ship for more than fifteen years. Now I sail my own. Things change." Nathaniel draped his arm over the back of the booth. "Like you coming here."

"We like it." Kevin began to stab his straw in the ice. "Mom's boss in Oklahoma was a skinflint."

"Kevin."

"Granddad said so. And he didn't appreciate you. You were hiding your light under a bushel." Kevin didn't know what that meant, but his grandmother had said so.

"Granddad's biased." She smiled and ruffled her son's hair. "But we do like it here."

"Eat hearty," Julie ordered, and dropped three enormous platters on the table.

The long rolls of crusty bread were filled with chunks of lobster and flanked by a mound of coleslaw and a small mountain of French fries.

"Girl needs weight," Julie proclaimed. "Boy, too. Didn't know you liked 'em skinny, Captain."

"I like them any way I can get them," Nathaniel corrected, which sent Julie off into another gale of laughter.

"We'll never eat all of this." Megan stared, daunted, at her plate.

Nathaniel had already dug in. "Sure we will. So, have you looked over Fergus's book yet?"

"Not really." Megan sampled the first bite. Whatever the atmosphere, the food was four-star. "I want to get the backlog caught up first. Since Shipshape's books were the worst, I dealt with them first. I still have to work on your second quarter, and The Retreat's."

"Your mother's a practical woman, Kev."

"Yeah." Kevin managed to swallow a giant bite of lobster roll. "Granddad says she needs to get out more."

"Kevin."

But the warning came too late. Nathaniel was already grinning. "Does he? What else does Granddad say?"

"She should live a little." Kevin attacked his French fries with the single-minded determination of a child. "'Cause she's too young to hole up like a hermit."

"Your granddad's a smart man."

"Oh, yeah. He knows everything. He's got oil for blood and horses on the brain."

"A quote from my mother," Megan said dryly. "She knows everything, too. But you were asking about Fergus's book."

"Just wondered if it had scratched your curiosity."

"Some. I thought I might take an hour or so at night to work on it."

"I don't think that's what your daddy meant by living a little, Meg."

"Regardless." She turned back to the safer topic of the account book. "Some of the pages are faded badly, but other than a few minor mistakes, the accounts are very accurate. Except for the last couple of pages, where there are just numbers without any logic."

"Really. They don't add up?"

"They don't seem to, but I need to take a closer look."

"Sometimes you miss more by looking too close." Nathaniel winked at Julie as she set another round of drinks on the table. It was coffee for him this time. She knew that when he was driving he kept it to one beer. "I wouldn't mind taking a look at it."

Megan frowned at her. "Why?"

"I like puzzles."

"I don't think it's much of a puzzle, but if it's all right with the family, I don't have any objection." She leaned back, sighed. "Sorry, I just can't eat any more."

"It's okay." Nathaniel switched his empty plate with hers. "I can."

To Megan's amazement, he could. It wasn't much of a surprise that Kevin had managed to clean his plate. The way he was growing he often seemed in danger of eating china and all when he sat down for a meal. But Nathaniel ate his meal, then half of hers, without a blink.

"Have you always eaten like that?" Megan asked when they were driving away from the restaurant.

"Nope. Always wanted to, though. Never could seem to fill up as a kid." Of course, that might have been because there was little to fill up on. "At sea, you learn to eat anything, and plenty of it, while it's there."

"You should weigh three hundred pounds."

"Some people burn it off." He shifted his eyes to hers. "Like you. All that nervous energy you've got just eats up those calories."

"I'm not skinny," she muttered.

"Nope. Thought you were myself, till I got ahold of you. It's more like willowy—and you've got a real soft feel to you when you're pressed up against a man."

She hissed, started to look over her shoulder.

"He conked out the minute I turned on the engine," Nathaniel told her. And, indeed, she could see Kevin stretched out in the back, his head pillowed on his arms, sleeping soundly. "Though I don't see what harm there is for the boy to know a man's interested in his mother."

"He's a child." She turned back, the gentle look in her eyes gone. "I won't have him think that I'm—"

"Human?"

"It's not your affair. He's my son."

"That he is," Nathaniel agreed easily. "And you've done a hell of a job with him."

She slanted him a cautious look. "Thank you."

"No need to. Just a fact. It's tough raising a kid on your own. You found the way to do it right."

It was impossible to stay irritated with him, especially when she remembered what Coco had told her. "You lost your mother when you were young. Ah... Coco mentioned it."

"Coco's been mentioning a lot of things."

"She didn't mean any harm. You know how she is, better than I. She cares so much about people, and wants to see them..."

"Lined up two by two? Yeah, I know her. She picked you out for me."

"She—" Words failed her. "That's ridiculous."

"Not to Coco." He steered easily around a curve. "Of course, she doesn't know that I know she's already got me scheduled to go down on one knee."

"It's fortunate, isn't it, that you're forewarned?"

Her indignant tone had a smile twitching at his lips. "Sure is. She's been singing your praises for months. And you almost live up to the advance publicity."

She hissed like a snake and turned to him. His grin, and the absurdity of the situation, changed indignation to amusement. "Thank you." She stretched out her legs, leaned back and decided to enjoy the ride. "I'd hate to have disappointed you."

"Oh, you didn't, sugar."

"I've been told you're mysterious, romantic and charming."

"And?"

"You almost live up to the advance publicity."

"Sugar—" he took her hand and kissed it lavishly "—I can be a lot better."

"I'm sure you can." She drew her hand away, refusing to acknowledge the rippling thrill up her arm. "If I wasn't so fond of her, I'd be annoyed. But she's so kind."

"She has the truest heart of anyone I've ever met. I used to wish she was my mother."

"I'm sorry." Before she could resist the urge, Megan laid a hand on his. "It must have been so hard, losing your mother when you were only a child."

"It's all right. It was a long time ago." Much too long for him to grieve. "I still remember seeing Coco in the village, or when I'd tag along with Holt to take fish up to The Towers. There she'd be, this gorgeous woman—looked like a queen. Never knew what color her hair would be from one week to the next."

"She's a brunette today," Megan said, and made him laugh.

"First woman I ever fell for. She came to the house a couple times, read my old man the riot act about his drinking. Guess she thought if he was sober he wouldn't knock me around so much."

He took his eyes off the road again, met hers. "I imagine she mentioned that, too?"

"Yes." Uncomfortable, Megan looked away. "I'm sorry, Nathaniel. I hate when people discuss me, no matter how good their intentions. It's so intrusive."

"I'm not that sensitive, Meg. Everybody knew what my old man was like." He could remember, too well, the pitying looks, the glances that slid uneasily away. "It bothered me back then, but not anymore."

She struggled to find the right words. "Did Coco—did it do any good?"

He was silent a moment, staring out at the lowering sun and the bloodred light it poured into the water. "He was afraid of her, so he beat the hell out of me when she left."

"Oh, God."

"I'd just as soon she didn't know that."

"No." Megan had to swallow the hot tears lodged in her throat. "I won't tell her. That's why you ran away to sea, isn't it? To get away from him."

"That's one of the reasons." He reached over, ran a fingertip down her cheek. "You know, if I'd figured out the way to get to you was to tell you I'd taken a strap a few times, I'd have brought it up sooner."

"It's nothing to joke about." Megan's voice was low and furious. "There's no excuse for treating a child that way."

"Hey, I lived through it."

"Did you?" She shifted back to him, eyes steady. "Did you ever stop hating him?"

"No." He said it quietly. "No, I didn't. But I stopped letting it be important, and maybe that's healthier." He stopped the car in front of The Towers, turned to her. "Someone hurts you, in a permanent way, you don't forget it. But the best revenge is seeing that it doesn't matter."

"You're talking about Kevin's father, and it's not at all the same. I wasn't a helpless child."

"Depends on where you draw the line between helpless and innocent." Nathaniel opened the car door. "I'll carry Kevin in for you."

"You don't have to." She hurried out herself, but Nathaniel already had the boy in his arms.

They stood there for a moment, in the last glow of the day, the boy between them, his head resting securely on Nathaniel's shoulder, dark hair to dark hair, honed muscle to young limbs.

Something locked deep inside her swelled, tried to burst free. She sighed it away, stroked a hand over her son's back and felt the steady rhythm of his breathing.

"He's had a long day."

"So have you, Meg. There are shadows under your eyes. Since that means you didn't sleep any better than I did last night, I can't say I mind seeing them there."

It was hard, she thought, so very hard, to keep pulling away from the current that drew her to him. "I'm not ready for this, Nathaniel."

"Sometimes a wind comes up, blows you off course. You're not ready for it, but if you're lucky, you end up in a more interesting place than you'd planned."

"I don't like to depend on luck."

"That's okay. I do." He shifted the boy more comfortably, and carried him to the house.

Chapter 6

"Don't see what all the damn to-do's about," Dutch grumbled as he whipped a delicate egg froth for his angel food cake surprise.

"Trenton St. James II is a member of the family." Running on nerves, Coco checked the temperature on her prime rib. She had a dozen things to deal with since the cucumber facial she'd indulged in had thrown off her timetable. "And the president of the St. James hotels." Satisfied that the beef was coming along nicely, she basted her roast duck. "As this is his first visit to The Retreat, it's important that everything run smoothly."

"Some rich bastard coming around to freeload."

"Mr. Van Horne!" Coco's heart lurched. After six months, she knew she shouldn't be shocked by the man. But, *really.* "I've known Mr. St. James for...well, a great number of years. I can assure you he is a successful businessman, an entrepreneur. *Not* a freeloader."

Dutch sniffed, gave Coco the once-over. She'd done herself up good and proper, he noted. The fancy-shmancy dress glittered and flowed down, stopping plenty short to show off her legs. Her cheeks were all pink, too. And he didn't think it was from kitchen heat. His lips curled back in a sneer.

"So what's he, your boyfriend?"

The pink deepened to rose. "Certainly not. A woman of my... experience doesn't have boyfriends." Surreptitiously she checked her face in the stainless-steel exhaust hood on the stove. "Beaux, perhaps."

Beaux. Ha! "I hear he's been married four times and pays enough alimony to balance the national debt. You looking to be number five?"

Speechless, Coco pressed a hand to her heart. "You are—" She stumbled, stuttered, over the words. "Impossibly rude. Impossibly crude."

"Hey, ain't none of my never-mind if you want to land yourself a rich fish."

She squeaked. Though the rolling temper that caused red dots to swim in front of her eyes appalled her—she was, after all, a civilized woman—she surged forward to ram a coral-tipped nail into his massive chest. "I will not tolerate any more of your insults."

"Yeah?" He poked her right back. "Whatcha gonna do about it?"

She leaned forward until they were nose-to-nose. "I will fire you."

"Now that'll break my heart. Go ahead, fancy face, give me the boot. See how you get by with tonight's dinner rush."

"I assure you, I will 'get by' delightfully." Her heart was beating too fast. Coco wondered it didn't soar right out of her breast.

"Like hell." He hated her perfume. Hated that it made his nostrils twitch and his mouth water. "When I came on board, you were barely treading water."

She couldn't get her breath, simply couldn't. "This kitchen doesn't need you, Mr. Van Horne. And neither do I."

"You need me plenty." How had his hands gotten onto her shoulders? Why were hers pressed to his chest? The hell with how or why, he thought. He'd show her what was what.

Her eyes popped hard when his hard, sneering mouth crushed down on hers in a very thorough kiss. But she didn't see a thing. Her world, so beautifully secure, tilted under her feet. That was why—naturally that was why—she clung to him.

She would slap his face. She certainly would.

In just a few minutes.

Damn women, Dutch thought. Damn them all. Especially tall, curvy, sweet-smelling females with lips like…cooking cherries. He'd always had a weakness for tartness.

He jerked her away, but kept his big hands firm on her shoulders. "Let's get something straight…" he began.

"Now look here…" she said at the same time.

They both leaped apart like guilty children when the kitchen door swung open.

Megan stood frozen in the doorway, her jaw dropping. Surely she hadn't seen what she thought she'd seen. Coco was checking the oven, and Dutch was measuring flour into a bowl. They couldn't have been…embracing. Yet both of them were a rather startling shade of pink.

"Excuse me," she managed. "I'm sorry to, ah…"

"Oh, Megan, dear." Flustered, Coco patted her hair. She was tingling, she realized. From embarrassment—and annoyance, she assured herself. "What can I do for you?"

"I just wanted to check a couple of the kitchen expenses." She was still goggling, her eyes shifting from Coco to Dutch and back. The tension in the room was thicker than Coco's split-pea soup. "But if you're busy, we can do it later."

"Nonsense." Coco wiped her sweaty palms on her apron. "We're just a little frantic preparing for Trenton's arrival."

"Trenton? Oh, I'd forgotten. Trent's father's expected." She was cautiously backing out of the room. "We don't need to do this now."

"No, no." Oh, Lord, Coco thought, don't leave me. "Now's a perfect time. We're under control here. Let's do it in your office, shall we?" She took Megan firmly by the arm. "Mr. Van Horne can handle things for a few minutes." Without waiting for his assent, she hurried from the room. "Details, details," Coco said gaily, and clung to Megan as though she were a life raft in a churning sea. "It seems the more you handle, the more there are."

"Coco, are you all right?"

"Oh, of course." But she pressed a hand to her heart. "Just a little contretemps with Mr. Van Horne. But that's nothing I can't deal with." She hoped. "How are your accounts coming along, dear? I must say I'd hoped you'd find time to glance at Fergus's book."

"Actually, I have—"

"Not that we want you working too hard." With the buzz going on in Coco's head, she didn't hear a word Megan said. "We want you to feel right at home here, to enjoy yourself. To relax. After all the trouble and excitement last year, we all want to relax. I don't think any of us could stand any more crises."

"I do not have, nor do I require, a reservation."

The crackling, irate voice stopped Coco in her tracks. The becoming flush in her cheeks faded to a dead white.

"Dear God, no. It can't be."

"Coco?" Megan took a firmer grip on Coco's arm. She felt the tremor and wondered if she could hold the woman up if she fainted.

"Young man." The voice rose, echoing off the walls. "Do you know who I am?"

"Aunt Colleen," Coco said in a shaky whisper. She let go one last shuddering moan, drew in a bracing breath, then walked bravely into the lobby. "Aunt Colleen," she said in an entirely different tone. "What a lovely surprise."

"Shock, you mean." Colleen accepted her niece's kiss, then rapped her cane on the floor. She was tall, thin as a rail and formidable as iron in a raw-silk suit and pearls as white as her hair. "I see you've filled the place with strangers. Better to have it burned to the ground. Tell this insolent boy to have my bags taken up."

"Of course." Coco gestured for a bellman herself. "In the family wing, second floor, first room on the right," she instructed.

"And don't toss those bags around, boy." Colleen leaned on her gold-tipped cane and studied Megan. "Who's this?"

"You remember Megan, Aunt Colleen. Sloan's sister? You met at Amanda's wedding."

"Yes, yes." Colleen's eyes narrowed, measured. "Got a son, don't you?" Colleen knew all there was to know about Kevin. Had made it her business to know.

"Yes, I do. It's nice to see you again, Miss Calhoun."

"Ha. You'd be the only one of this lot who thinks so." Ignoring them both, she walked to Bianca's portrait, studied it and the emeralds glistening in their case. She sighed, but so quietly no one could hear.

"I want brandy, Cordelia, before I take a look at what you've done to this place."

"Of course. We'll just go into the family wing. Megan, please, join us."

It was impossible to deny the plea in Coco's eyes.

A few moments later, they had settled into the family parlor. Here, the wallpaper was still faded, peeling in spots. There were scars on the floor in front of the fireplace where errant embers had seared and burned.

"Nothing's changed here, I see." Colleen sat like a queen in a wing chair.

"We've concentrated on the hotel wing." Nervous and babbling, Coco poured brandy. "Now that it's done, we're beginning renovations. Two of the bedrooms are finished. And the nursery's lovely."

"Humph." She'd come specifically to see the children—and only secondarily to drive Coco mad. "Where is everyone? I come to see my family and find nothing but strangers."

"They'll be along. We're having a dinner party tonight, Aunt

Colleen." Coco kept the brilliant smile plastered on her face. "Trent's father's joining us for a few days."

"Aging playboy," Colleen mumbled into her brandy. "You." She pointed at Megan. "Accountant, aren't you?"

"Yes, ma'am."

"Megan's a whiz with figures," Coco said desperately. "We're so grateful she's here. And Kevin, too, of course. He's a darling boy."

"I'm talking to the girl, Cordelia. Go fuss in the kitchen."

"But—"

"Go on, go on."

With an apologetic look for Megan, Coco fled.

"The boy'll be nine soon?"

"Yes, in a couple of months." She was prepared, braced, for a scathing comment on his lineage.

Tapping her fingers on the arm of the chair, Colleen nodded. "Get along with Suzanna's brood, does he?"

"Very well. They've rarely been apart since we arrived." Megan did her best not to squirm. "It's been wonderful for him. And for me."

"Dumont bothering you?"

Megan blinked. "I beg your pardon?"

"Don't be a fool, girl, I asked if that excuse for a human being has been bothering you."

Megan's spine straightened like a steel rod. "No. I haven't seen or heard from Baxter since before Kevin was born."

"You will." Colleen scowled and leaned forward. She wanted to get a handle on this Megan O'Riley. "He's been making inquiries."

Megan's fingers clenched on the snifter of brandy. "I don't understand."

"Poking his nose in, asking questions." Colleen gave her cane an imperious thump.

"How do you know?"

"I keep my ear to the ground when it comes to family." Eyes bright, Colleen waited for a reaction, got none. "You moved here, didn't you? Your son's been accepted as Alex and Jenny—and Christian's—brother."

Ice was forming in Megan's stomach, thin, brittle strips of it. "That has nothing to do with him."

"Don't be a fool. A man like Dumont thinks the world revolves around him. His eye's on politics, girl, and the way that particular circus is running, a few well-chosen words from you to the right reporter..." The idea was pleasant enough to make Colleen smile. "Well, his road to Washington would be a steeper climb."

"I've no intention of going to the press, of exposing Kevin to public attention."

"Wise." Colleen sipped again. "A pity, but wise. You tell me if he tries anything. I'd like to tangle with him again."

"I can handle it myself."

Colleen lifted one snowy brow. "Perhaps you can."

"How come I have to wear a dumb tie?" Kevin squirmed while Megan fumbled with the knot. Her fingers had been stiff and cold ever since her talk with Colleen.

"Because it's a special dinner and you need to look your best."

"Ties are stupid. I bet Alex doesn't have to wear a stupid tie."

"I don't know what Alex is wearing," Megan said, with the last of her patience. "But you're doing as you're told."

The sharp tone, rarely heard, had his bottom lip poking out. "I'd rather have pizza."

"Well, you're not having pizza. Damn it, Kevin, hold still!"

"It's choking me."

"*I'm* going to choke you in a minute." She blew her hair out of her eyes and secured the knot. "There. You look very handsome."

"I look like a dork."

"Fine, you look like a dork. Now put your shoes on."

Kevin scowled at the shiny black loafers. "I hate those shoes. I want to wear my sneakers."

Exasperated, she leaned down until their faces were level.

"Young man, you will put your shoes on, and you will watch your tone of voice. Or you'll find yourself in very hot water."

Megan marched out of his room and across the hall to her own. Snatching her brush from the dresser, she began to drag it through her hair. She didn't want to go to the damn dinner party, either. The aspirin she'd downed an hour before hadn't even touched the splitting headache slicing through her skull. But she had to put on her party face and go down, pretend she wasn't terrified and angry and sick with worry over Baxter Dumont.

Colleen might be wrong, she thought. After all, it had been nearly a decade. Why would Baxter bother with her and Kevin now?

Because he wanted to be a United States senator. Megan closed her eyes. She read the paper, didn't she? Baxter had already begun his campaign for the seat. And an illegitimate son, never acknowledged, hardly fit the straight-arrow platform he'd chosen.

"Mom."

She saw Kevin's reflection in the mirror. His shoes were on—and his chin was on his chest. Guilt squeezed its sticky fingers around her heart. "Yes, Kevin."

"How come you're so mad at everything?"

"I'm not." Wearily she sat on the edge of the bed. "I've just got a little headache. I'm sorry I snapped at you." She held out her arms, sighing when he filled them. "You're such a handsome dork, Kev." When he laughed, she kissed the top of his head. "Let's go down. Maybe Alex and Jenny are here."

They were, and Alex was just as disgusted with his tie as Kevin was with his. But there was too much going on for the boys to sulk for long. There were canapés to gobble, babies to play with and adventures to plan.

Everyone, naturally, was talking at once.

The volume in the room cut through Megan's aching head like a rusty saw. She accepted the flute of champagne Trenton II offered her, and did her best to pretend an interest in his flirtation. He was trim and tall and tanned, glossily handsome and charming. And Megan was desperately relieved when he turned his attentions on Coco.

"Make a nice couple, don't they?" Nathaniel murmured in her ear.

"Striking." She took a cube of cheese and forced it down.

"You don't look in the party mood, Meg."

"I'm fine." To distract him, she changed the subject. "You might be interested in what I think I might have walked in on this afternoon."

"Oh?" Taking her arm, he steered her toward the open terrace doors.

"Coco and Dutch."

"Fighting again? Saucepans at twenty paces?"

"Not exactly." She took a deep breath of air, hoping it would clear her head. "They were...at least I think they were..."

Nathaniel's brows shot up. He could fill in the blanks himself. "You're joking."

"No. They were nose-to-nose, with their arms around each other." She managed to smile even as she rubbed at the throbbing in her temple. "At my unexpected and ill-timed entrance, they jumped apart as if they'd been planning murder. And they were blushing. Both of them."

"The Dutchman, blushing?" Nathaniel started to laugh, but it began to sink in. "Good God."

"I think it's sweet."

"Sweet." He looked back inside, where Coco, regally elegant, was laughing over something Trenton had whispered in her ear. "She's out of his league. She'll break his heart."

"What a ridiculous thing to say." Lord, why didn't her head just fall off her shoulders and give her some relief? "Sporting events have leagues, not romances."

"The Dutchman and Coco." It worried him, because they were

two of the very few people in the world he could say he loved. "You're the accountant, sugar, and you're going to tell me that adds up?"

"I'm not telling you anything," she shot back. "Except I think they're attracted to each other. And stop calling me 'sugar.'"

"Okay, simmer down." He looked back down at her, focused on her. "What's the matter?"

Guiltily she dropped her hand. She'd been massaging her temple again. "Nothing."

With an impatient oath, he turned her fully to face him, looked into her eyes. "Headache, huh? Bad one?"

"No, it's— Yes," she admitted. "Vicious."

"You're all tensed up." He began to knead her shoulders. "Tight as a spring."

"Don't."

"This is purely therapeutic." He rubbed his thumbs in gentle circles over her collarbone. "Any pleasure either of us gets out of it is incidental. Have you always been prone to headaches?"

His fingers were strong and male and magical. It was impossible not to stretch under them. "I'm not prone to headaches."

"Too much stress." His hands skimmed lightly up to her temples. She closed her eyes with a sigh. "You bottle too much up, Meg. Your body makes you pay for it. Turn around, let me work on those shoulders."

"It's not—" But the protest died away when his hands began to knead at the knots.

"Relax. Pretty night, isn't it? Moon's full, stars are out. Ever walk up on the cliffs in the moonlight, Megan?"

"No."

"Wildflowers growing right out of the rock, the water thundering. You can imagine those ghosts Kevin's so fond of strolling hand in hand. Some people think it's a lonely place, but it's not."

His voice and his hands were so soothing. She could almost believe there was nothing to worry about. "There's a painting at

Suzanna's of the cliffs in moonlight," Megan offered, trying to focus on the conversation.

"Christian Bradford's work—I've seen it. He had a feel for that spot. But there's nothing like the real thing. You could walk with me there after dinner. I'll show you."

"This isn't the time to fool around with the girl." Colleen's voice cut through the evening air, and she stamped her cane in the doorway.

Though Megan tensed again, Nathaniel kept his hands where they were and grinned. "Seems like a fine time to me, Miss Colleen."

"Ha! Scoundrel." Colleen's lips twitched. Nothing she liked better than a handsome scoundrel. "Always were. I remember you, running wild through the village. Looks like the sea made a man of you, all right. Stop fidgeting, girl. He's not going to let loose of you. If you're lucky."

Nathaniel kissed the top of Megan's head. "She's shy."

"Well, she'll have to get over it, won't she? Cordelia's finally going to feed us. I want you to sit with me, talk about boats."

"It would be a pleasure."

"Well, come on, bring her. Lived on cruise ships half my life or more," Colleen began. "I'll wager I've seen more of the sea than you, boy."

"I wouldn't doubt it, ma'am." Nathaniel kept one hand on Megan and offered Colleen his arm. "With a trail of broken hearts in your wake."

She gave a hoot of laughter. "Damn right."

The dining room was full of the scents of food and flowers and candle wax. The moment everyone was settled, Trenton II rose, glass in hand.

"I'd like to make a toast." His voice was as cultured as his dinner suit. "To Cordelia, a woman of extraordinary talents and beauty."

Glasses were clinked. From his spy hole at the crack in the

doorway, Dutch snorted, scowled, then stomped back to his own kitchen.

"Trent." C.C. leaned toward her husband, her voice low. "You know I love you."

He thought he knew what was coming. "Yes, I do."

"And I adore your father."

"Mmm-hmm…"

"And if he puts the moves on Aunt Coco, I'm going to have to kill him."

"Right." Trent smiled weakly and began on the first course.

At the other end of the table, sublimely ignorant of the threat, Trenton beamed at Colleen. "What do you think of The Retreat, Miss Calhoun?"

"I dislike hotels. Never use them."

"Aunt Colleen." Coco fluttered her hands. "The St. James hotels are world-famous for their luxury and taste."

"Can't stand them," Colleen said complacently as she spooned up soup. "What's this stuff?"

"It's lobster bisque, Aunt Colleen."

"Needs salt," she said, for the devil of it. "You, boy." She jabbed a finger down the table at Kevin. "Don't slouch. You want your bones to grow crooked?"

"No, ma'am."

"Got any ambitions?"

Kevin stared helplessly, and was relieved when his mother's hand closed over his. "I could be a sailor," he blurted out. "I steered the *Mariner*."

"Ha!" Pleased, she picked up her wine. "Good for you. I won't tolerate any idlers in my family. Too thin. Eat your soup, such as it is."

With a quiet moan, Coco rang for the second course.

"She never changes." Lazily content, Lilah rocked while Bianca suckled hungrily at her breast. The nursery was quiet, the lights were low. Megan had headed for it, figuring it would be the perfect escape hatch.

"She's..." Megan searched for a diplomatic phrase. "Quite a lady."

"She's a nosy old nuisance." Lilah laughed lightly. "But we love her."

In the next rocker, Amanda sighed. "As soon as she hears about Fergus's book, she's going to start nagging you."

"And badgering," C.C. put in, cradling Ethan.

"And hounding," Suzanna finished up as she changed Christian's diaper.

"That sounds promising."

"Don't worry." With a laugh, Suzanna slipped Christian into his sleeper. "We're right behind you."

"Notice," Lilah added with a smile, "the direction is *behind*."

"About the book." Megan flicked a finger over a dancing giraffe on a mobile. "I've made copies of several pages I thought you'd be interested in. He made a lot of notations, about business deals, personal business, purchases. At one point he inventories jewelry—Bianca's, I assume—for insurance purposes."

"The emeralds?" Amanda's brow rose at Megan's nod. "And to think of all the hours we spent going through papers, trying to find proof that they existed."

"There's a number of other pieces—hundreds of thousands of dollars' worth in 1913 dollars."

"He sold nearly everything," C.C. murmured. "We found the documents of sale. He got rid of anything that reminded him of Bianca."

"It still hurts," Lilah admitted. "Not the money, though God knows we could have used it. It's the loss of what was hers, what we won't be able to pass on."

"I'm sorry."

"Don't be." Amanda rose to lay a sleeping Delia in her crib. "We're too sentimental. I suppose we all feel such a close connection with Bianca."

"I know what you mean." It felt odd to admit it, but Megan was compelled. "I feel it, too. I suppose from seeing the references to her in the old book, and having her portrait right there in the lobby." A bit embarrassed, she laughed. "Sometimes, when you walk down the halls at night, it's almost as if you could sense her."

"Of course," Lilah said easily. "She's here."

"Excuse me, ladies." Nathaniel stepped inside, obviously comfortable in a nursery inhabited by babies and nursing mothers.

Lilah smiled slowly. "Well, hello, handsome. What brings you to the maternity wing?"

"Just coming to fetch my date."

When he took Megan's arm, she drew back. "We don't have a date."

"A walk, remember?"

"I never said—"

"It's a lovely night for it." Suzanna lifted Christian into her arms, cooed to him.

"I have to put Kevin to bed."

She was digging in her heels, but it didn't seem to be doing any good.

"I've already tucked him in." Nathaniel propelled her toward the doors.

"You put Kevin to bed?"

"Since he'd fallen asleep in my lap, it seemed the thing to do. Oh, Suzanna, Holt said the kids are ready whenever you are."

"I'm on my way." Suzanna waited until Megan and Nate were out of earshot before she turned to her sisters. "What do you think?"

Amanda smiled smugly. "I think it's working perfectly."

"I have to agree." C.C. settled Ethan comfortably in his crib. "I thought Lilah had lost her mind when she came up with the idea of getting those two together."

Lilah yawned, sighed. "I'm never wrong." Then her eyes lit. "I bet we can see them from the window."

"*Spy* on them?" Amanda arched her brows. "Good idea," she said, and darted to the window.

They were outlined in the moonlight that sprinkled the lawn.
"You're complicating things, Nathaniel."
"Simplifying," he corrected. "Nothing simpler than a walk in the moonlight."
"That's not where you expect all this to end."
"Nope. But we're still moving at your pace, Meg." He brought her hand to his lips, kissed it absently, when they began the climb. "I seem to have this need to be around you. It's the damnedest thing. Can't shake it. So I figure, why try? Why not just roll with it?"
"I'm not a simple woman." She wished she could be, just for tonight, just for an hour in the starlight. "I have baggage and resentments and insecurities I didn't even realize were there until I met you. I'm not going to let myself be hurt again."
"No one's going to hurt you." In a subtle gesture of protection, he slipped an arm around her and looked up at the sky. "Look how big the moon is tonight. Just hanging there. You can see Venus, and the little star that dogs her. There's Orion." He lifted her hand, tracing the sky with it as he had once traced his charts. "And the Twins. See?"
"Yes." She watched their joined hands connect stars while the breeze lifted lovingly off the water and stirred the flowers that grew wild in the rock.

Romantic, mysterious, Coco had said. Yes, he was, and Megan realized she was much more susceptible to both than she would have believed.

For she was here, wasn't she, standing on a cliff with a seafaring man whose callused hand held hers, whose voice helped her see the pictures painted by the stars. His body was warm and solid against hers. And her blood was pumping fast and free in her veins.

Alive. The wind and the sea and the man made her feel so alive.

And perhaps there was something more—those ghosts of the Calhouns'. The cliffs seemed to invite spirits to walk, the air filled with contentment. And the glow of love that had outlasted time.

"I shouldn't be here like this." But she didn't move away, not even when his lips brushed over her hair.

"Listen," he murmured. "Close your eyes and listen, and you can hear the stars breathing."

She obeyed, and listened to the whisper and throb of the air. And of her own heart. "Why do you make me feel this way?"

"I don't have an answer. Not everything adds up neat, Meg." Because he had a great need to see her face, he turned her gently. "Not everything has to." And kissed her. His lips skimmed hers, journeyed up to her temple, over her brow and down. "How's the headache?"

"It's gone. Nearly."

"No. Keep your eyes closed." His lips traced over them, soft as air, before trailing slowly over her face. "Kiss me back, will you?"

How could she not, when his mouth was so tempting on hers? With a small sound of surrender, she let her heart lead. Just for tonight, she promised herself. Just for a moment.

That slow, melting change almost undid him. She went pliant in his arms, those hesitant lips heating, parting, offering. It took all his willpower not to drag her against him and plunder.

She wouldn't resist. Perhaps he'd known that there would be enough magic on those cliffs to bewitch them both, to seduce her into surrender—and to remind him to take care.

"I want you, Megan." He took his lips down her throat, up over her jaw. "I want you so much it's got me tied in knots."

"I know. I wish..." She pressed her face to his shoulder. "I'm not playing games, Nathaniel."

"I know." He stroked a hand down her hair. "It would be easier if you were, because I know all the rules." Cupping her face, he lifted it. "And how to break them." He sighed, kissed her again, lightly. "They make it damn hard for me, those eyes of yours." He stepped back. "I'd better take you in."

"Nathaniel." She laid a hand on his chest. "You're the first man who's made me...who I've wanted to be with since Kevin was born."

Something flashed in his eyes, wild, dangerous, before he banked it. "Do you think it makes it easier on me, knowing that?" He would have laughed, if he hadn't felt so much like exploding. "Megan, you're killing me." But he swung an arm around her shoulders and led her down the cliff path.

"I don't know how to handle this," she said under her breath. "I haven't had to handle anything like this before."

"Keep it up," he warned, "and you're over my shoulder, shanghaied straight to bed. Mine."

The image gave her a quick thrill, and a guilty one. "I'm just trying to be honest."

"Try lying," he said with a grimace. "Make it easier on me."

"I'm a lousy liar." She slanted a look at him. Wasn't it interesting, she mused, that for once he was the one at a disadvantage? "It doesn't seem logical that it would bother you to know what I'm feeling."

"I'm having a lot of trouble dealing with what I'm feeling." He took a long, steadying breath. "And I'm not feeling logical." Nor, he thought ruefully, would he sleep tonight. "'Desire hath no rest.'"

"What?"

"Robert Burton. Nothing."

They walked toward the lights of The Towers. The shouting reached them before they crossed the lawn.

"Coco," Megan said.

"Dutch." Taking firm hold of Megan's hand, Nathaniel quickened his pace.

"You're insulting and obnoxious," Coco snapped at Dutch, her chin up, her hands planted on her hips.

His massive arms were folded across his barrel of a chest. "I saw what I saw, said what I said."

"I was not draped all over Trenton like a...a..."

"Barnacle," Dutch said with relish. "Like a barnacle on the hull of a fancy yacht."

"We happen to have been dancing."

"Ha! That's what you call it. We got another name for it. Where I come from, we call it—"

"Dutch!" Nathaniel cut off the undoubtedly crude description.

"There." Mortified, Coco smoothed down her dress. "You've made a scene."

"You were the one making a scene, with that smooth-skinned rich boy. Flaunting yourself."

"F-f-flaunting." Enraged, she drew herself up to her full, and considerable, height. "I have never flaunted in my life. You, sir, are despicable."

"I'll show you despicable, lady."

"Cut it out." Prepared for fists to fly, Nathaniel stepped between them. "Dutch, what the hell's wrong with you? Are you drunk?"

"A nip or two of rum never rattled my brain." He glared over Nathaniel's shoulder at Coco. "It's her that's acting snockered. Out of my way, boy, I've got a thing or two left to say."

"You've finished," Nathaniel corrected.

"Out of his way." All eyes turned to Coco. She was flushed, bright-eyed, and regal as a duchess. "I prefer to handle this matter myself."

Megan tugged gently on her arm. "Coco, don't you think you should go inside?"

"I do not." She caught herself and added a friendly pat. "Now, dear, you and Nate run along. Mr. Van Horne and I prefer to handle this privately."

"But—"

"Nathaniel," Coco said, interrupting her, "take Megan inside now."

"Yes, ma'am."

"Are you sure we should leave them alone?"

Nathaniel continued to steer Megan to the terrace doors. "You want to get in the middle of that?"

Megan glanced back over her shoulder. "No." She chuckled, shook her head. "No, I don't think so."

"Well, Mr. Van Horne," Coco began, when she was certain they were alone again. "Do you have something more to say?"

"I got plenty." Prepared for battle, he stepped forward. "You tell that slick-talking rich boy to keep his hands to himself."

She tossed back her head and enjoyed the mad flutter of her heart when her eyes met his. "And if I don't?"

Dutch growled like a wolf—like a wolf, Coco thought, challenging his mate. "I'll break his puny arms like matchsticks."

Oh, my, she thought. Oh, my goodness. "Will you, really?"

"Just you try me." He gave her a jerk, and she let herself tumble into his arms.

This time she was ready for the kiss, and met it head-on. By the time they broke apart, they were both breathless and stunned.

Sometimes, Coco realized, it was up to the woman. She moistened her lips, swallowed hard.

"My room's on the second floor."

"I know where it is." A ghost of a smile flitted around his mouth. "Mine's closer." He swept her into his arms—very much, Coco thought dreamily, like a pirate taking his hostage.

"You're a fine, sturdy woman, Coco."

She pressed a hand on her thundering heart. "Oh, Niels."

Chapter 7

It wasn't like Megan to daydream. Years of discipline had taught her that dreams were for sleeping, not for rainy mornings when the fog was drifting around the house and the windows ran wet, as if with tears. But her computer hummed, unattended, and her chin was on her fist as her mind wandered back, as it had several times over the past few days, toward moonlight and wildflowers and the distant thunder of surf.

Now and again she caught herself and fell back on logic. It wouldn't pay to forget that the only romance in her life had been an illusion, a lie that betrayed her innocence, her emotions and her future. She'd thought herself immune, been content to be immune. Until Nathaniel.

What should she do, now that her life had taken this fast, unexpected swing? After all, she was no longer a child who believed in or needed promises and coaxing words. Now that her needs had been stirred, could she satisfy them without being hurt?

Oh, how she wished her heart wasn't involved. How she wished she could be smart and savvy and sophisticated and indulge in a purely physical affair, without emotion weighing in so heavily.

Why couldn't attraction, leavened with affection and respect, be enough? It should be such a simple equation. Two consenting adults, plus desire, times understanding and passion, equals mutual pleasure.

She just wished she could be sure there wasn't some hidden fraction that would throw off the simple solution.

"Megan?"

"Hmm?" Dreamily she turned toward the sound of the voice. Her imaginings shattered when she saw Suzanna inside the office, smiling at her. "Oh, I didn't hear you come in."

"You were miles away."

Caught drifting, Megan fought back embarrassment and shuffled papers. "I suppose I was. Something about the rain."

"It's lovely—always sets my mind wandering." Suzanna thought she knew just where Megan's mind had wandered. "Though I doubt the tourists or the children think so."

"Kevin thought the fog was great—until I told him he couldn't climb on the cliffs in it."

"And Alex and Jenny's plans for an assault on Fort O'Riley have been postponed. The kids are in Kevin's room, defending the planet against aliens. It's wonderful watching them together."

"I know. They've blended together so well."

"Like a mud ball," Suzanna said with a laugh, and eased a jean-clad hip on the edge of Megan's desk. "How's the work coming?"

"It's moving along. Amanda kept everything in order, so it's just a matter of shifting it into my own system and computerizing."

"It's a tremendous relief for her, having you take it over. Some days she'd be doing the books with a phone at her ear and Delia at her breast."

The image made Megan grin. "I can see it. She's amazingly organized."

"An expert juggler. Nothing she hates more than to bobble a ball. You'd understand that."

"Yeah, I do." Megan picked up a pencil and ran it between her fingers. "I worried about coming here, Suzanna, bringing Kevin. I was afraid I'd not only bobble a ball, but drop all of them, because I'd be so anxious not to say anything, even think anything, that would make you uncomfortable."

"Aren't we past that, Megan?"

"You were." Sighing, Megan set the pencil down again. "Maybe it's a little harder, being the other woman."

"Were you?" Suzanna said gently. "Or was I?"

Megan could only shake her head. "I can't say I wish I could go back and change things, because if I did I wouldn't have Kevin." She took a long breath, met Suzanna's eyes levelly. "I know you consider Kevin a brother to your children, and that you love him."

"Yes, I do."

"I want you to know that I think of your children as my family and I love them."

Suzanna reached over to lay a hand over Megan's. "I know you do. One of the reasons I dropped in was to ask if you'd mind if Kevin came along with us. I'm going to do some greenhouse work today. Alex and Jenny always enjoy it—especially since it includes pizza for lunch."

"I can't think of anything he'd rather do. And it would make up for having to wear a tie the other night."

Suzanna's eyes lit with humor. "I nearly had to strangle Alex to get him into his. I hope Aunt Coco doesn't plan any more formal dinner parties for some time to come." She tilted her head. "Speaking of Aunt Coco, have you seen her today?"

"Only for a minute, right after breakfast. Why?"

"Was she singing?"

"As a matter of fact, she was." Megan touched her tongue to her top lip. "She's been singing in the morning for several days now."

"She was singing just now, too. And wearing her best perfume."

Uneasy, Suzanna nibbled her lip. "I was wondering if Trent's father... Of course, he's gone back to Boston now, so I thought there was nothing to worry about. He's a lovely man, and we're all very fond of him, but, well, he's been married four times, and he doesn't seem able to keep his eye from roving."

"I noticed." After a quick debate on privacy versus disclosure, Megan cleared her throat. "Actually, I don't think Coco's looking in that direction."

"No?"

"Dutch," Megan said, and watched Suzanna's eyes go blank.

"Excuse me?"

"I think she and Dutch are...infatuated."

"Dutch? Our Dutch? But she's always complaining about him, and he's snarling at her every chance he gets. They're always fighting, and..." She trailed off, pressed her hands to her lips. "Oh..." she said, while her eyes danced over them. "Oh, oh, oh..."

They stared at each other, struggled dutifully for perhaps three seconds before bursting into laughter. Megan fell easily into the sisterly pleasure of discussing a family member. After she told Suzanna about walking in on Coco and Dutch in the kitchen, she followed it up with the scene on the terrace.

"There were sparks flying, Suzanna. At first I thought they were going to come to blows, then I realized it was more of a—well, a mating ritual."

"A mating ritual," Suzanna repeated in a shaky voice. "Do you really think they—?"

"Well." Megan wriggled her eyebrows. "She's been doing a lot of singing lately."

"She certainly has." Suzanna let the idea stew for a moment, found it simmered nicely. "I think I'll drop by the kitchen before I go. Check out the atmosphere."

"I hope I can count on a full report."

"Absolutely." Still chuckling, Suzanna rose to go to the door. "I guess that was some moon the other night."

"It was," Megan murmured. "Some moon."

Suzanna paused with her hand on the knob. "And Nathaniel's some man."

"I thought we were talking about Dutch."

"We were talking about romance," Suzanna corrected. "I'll see you later."

Megan frowned at the closed door. Good Lord, she thought, was she that obvious?

After spending the rest of the morning and the first part of the afternoon on The Retreat's accounts, Megan gave herself the small reward of an hour with Fergus's book. She enjoyed tallying up the costs of stabling horses, maintaining carriages. It was an eye-opener to see how much expense was involved in giving a ball at The Towers in 1913. And, by reading Fergus's margin notes, to come to understand his motives.

> Invitations all accepted. No one dare decline. B. ordered flowers—argued about ostentation. Told her big display equals success and wife must never question husband. She will wear emeralds, not pearl choker as she suggested, show society my taste and means, remind her of her place.

Her place, Megan thought with pity for Bianca, had been with Christian. How sad that it had taken death to unite them.

Wanting to dispel the gloom, she flipped to the back pages. The numbers simply didn't make sense. Not expenses, she mused. Not dates. Account numbers, perhaps. Stock-market prices, lot numbers?

Perhaps it would be worth a trip to the library to see if she could unearth any information from 1913 that correlated. And on the way she could stop by Shipshape to drop off the completed spreadsheet for April and pick up any more receipts.

If she happened to run into Nathaniel, it would be purely coincidental.

* * *

It was a pleasure to drive in the rain. The slow, steady stream of drops had most of the summer people seeking indoor entertainment. A few pedestrians wandered the sidewalks, window-shopping under umbrellas. The water in Frenchman Bay was gray and misted, with the masts and sails of ships spearing through the heavy air.

She could hear the ring of bell buoys, the drone of foghorns. It was as if the entire island were tucked under a blanket, snug and safe and solitary. She was tempted to keep driving, to take the twisting road to Acadia National Park, or the meandering one along the shore.

Maybe she would, she thought. After she completed the day's business, she would take that drive, explore her new home. And maybe she would ask Nathaniel to join her.

But she didn't see his car outside Shipshape. Ridiculous to say it didn't matter whether she saw him or not, she realized. Because it did matter. She wanted to see him, to watch the way his eyes deepened and locked on hers. The way his lips curved.

Maybe he'd parked around the corner, out of sight. Snagging her briefcase, she dashed from her car into the office. It was empty.

The first slap of disappointment was stunning. She hadn't realized just how much she'd counted on him being there until he wasn't. Then she heard, faintly, through the rear wall, the throb of bass from a radio. Someone was in the shop attached to the back of the building, she concluded. Probably working on repairs as the seas were too rough for tours.

She wasn't going to check out who was back there, she told herself firmly. She'd come on legitimate business and she took out the latest spreadsheet and set it on the overburdened desk. But on a purely practical level, she would need to go over, with at least one of them, the second quarter and the projections for the rest of the year. But she supposed it could wait.

A long look around showed her a disorder she couldn't comprehend. How could anyone work, or hope to concentrate, in such a mess?

She was tempted to organize, but turned her back on the chaos and walked to the filing cabinets. She'd take what she needed and leave the rest. Then she would, casually, wander around back, to the shop.

When she heard the door open, she turned, ready with a smile. It faded a little when she saw a stranger in the doorway. "May I help you?"

The man stepped fully inside and shut the door behind him. When he smiled, something jittered inside Megan's brain. "Hello, Megan."

For an instant, time froze, and then it rewound. Slow motion for five years, six, then back a decade, to a time when she'd been young and careless and ready to believe in love at first sight.

"Baxter," she whispered. How odd, she thought dully, that she hadn't recognized him. He'd hardly changed in ten years. He was as handsome, as smooth and polished, as he'd been when she first saw him. A trim, Savile Row–suited Prince Charming with lies on his lips.

Baxter smiled down at Megan. For days he'd been trying to catch her alone. Frustration had pushed him to approach her here and now. Because he was a man concerned with his image, he'd checked the office thoroughly before he stepped through the door. It was easy to see she was alone in the small space. There were things he intended to settle with her once and for all. Calmly, of course, he thought as she stared at him. Reasonably. Privately.

"Pretty as ever, aren't you?" It pleased him to see her eyes go blank with shock. The advantage was with him, as he preferred it. After all, he'd been planning this reunion for several weeks now. "The years have improved your looks, Megan. You've lost that charming baby fat, and you've become almost elegant. My compliments."

When he stepped closer, she didn't move, couldn't make her

legs or her brain respond. Not even when he lifted a finger and trailed it down her cheek, under her chin, to tip it up in an old habit she'd made herself forget.

"You were always a beauty, Megan, with that wide-eyed innocence that makes a man want to corrupt."

She shuddered. He smiled.

"What are you doing here?" *Kevin* was all she could think. Thank God Kevin wasn't with her.

"Funny, I was going to ask you the same. Just what are you doing here, Megan?"

"I live here." She hated hearing the hesitancy in her voice, like the throb of an old scar. "I work here."

"Tired of Oklahoma, were you? Wanted a change of scene?" He leaned closer, until she backed into the filing cabinet. Bribery, he knew, wouldn't work with her. Not with the O'Riley money behind her. Intimidation was the next logical choice. "Don't take me for a fool, Megan. It would be a terrible, costly mistake."

When her back hit the filing cabinet, she realized she was cringing, and her shock melted away, her spine stiffening. She wasn't a child now, she reminded herself, but a woman. Aware, responsible. "It's none of your business why I moved here."

"Oh, but it is." His voice was silky, quiet, reasonable. "I prefer you in Oklahoma, Megan. Working at your nice, steady job, in the midst of your loving family. I really much prefer it."

His eyes were so cold, she thought with dull wonder. Odd, she'd never seen that, didn't remember that. "Your preferences mean nothing to me, Baxter."

"Did you think I wouldn't find out that you'd thrown your lot in with my ex-wife and her family?" he continued, in that same reasonable tone. "That I haven't kept tabs on you over the years?"

With an effort, she steadied her breathing, but when she tried to shift away, he blocked her. She wasn't afraid, yet, but the temper she'd worked so hard to erase from her character was beginning to bubble up toward the surface.

"I never gave a thought to what you'd find out. And no, I wasn't aware you were keeping tabs. Why should you? Neither Kevin nor I ever meant anything to you."

"You've waited a long time to make your move." Baxter paused, struggling to control the fury that had clawed its way into his throat. He'd worked too hard, done too much, to see some old, forgotten mistake rear up and slap him down. "Clever of you, Megan, more clever than I gave you credit for."

"I don't know what you're talking about."

"Do you seriously want me to believe you know nothing about my campaign? I'm not going to tolerate this pathetic stab at revenge."

Her voice was cooler now, despite the fact that she could feel her skin start to tremble with an intense mixture of emotions. "At the risk of repeating myself, I don't know what you're talking about. My life is of no concern to you, Baxter, and yours none of mine. You made that clear a long time ago, when you refused to acknowledge me or Kevin."

"Is that the tack you're going to take?" He'd wanted to be calm, but rage was working through him. Intimidation, he realized, simply wouldn't be enough. "The young, innocent girl, seduced, betrayed, abandoned? Left behind, pregnant and brokenhearted? Please, spare me."

"That's not a tack, it's truth."

"You were young, Megan, but innocent?" His teeth flashed. "Now, that's a different matter. You were willing enough, even eager."

"I believed you!" She shouted it—a mistake, as her own voice tore her composure to pieces. "I believed you loved me, that you wanted to marry me. And you played on that. You never had any intention of making a future with me. You were already engaged. I was just an easy mark."

"You certainly were easy." He pushed her back against the cabinet, kept his hands hard on her shoulders. "And very, very tempting. Sweet, Megan. Very sweet."

"Take your hands off me."

"Not quite yet. You're going to listen to me, carefully. I know why you've come here, linked yourself with the Calhouns. First there'll be whispers, rumors, then a sad story to a sympathetic reporter. The old lady put pressure on me about Suzanna." He thought of Colleen with loathing. "But I've made that work for me. In the interest of the children," he murmured. "Letting Bradford adopt them, selflessly giving up my rights, so the children could be secure in a traditional family."

"You never cared about them, either, did you?" Megan said in a husky voice. "Alex and Jenny never mattered to you, any more than Kevin."

"The point is," he continued, "the old woman has no reason to bother about you. So, Megan, you'd better mind your step and listen to me. Things aren't working out for you here, so you're going to move back to Oklahoma."

"I'm not going anywhere," she began, then gasped when his fingers dug in.

"You're going back to your quiet life, away from here. There will be no rumors, no tearful interviews with reporters. If you try to undermine me, to implicate me in any way, I'll ruin you. When I've finished—and believe me, with the Dumont money I can hire plenty of willing men who'll swear they've enjoyed you—when I've finished," he repeated, "you'll be nothing more than an opportunistic slut with a bastard son."

Her vision hazed. It wasn't the threat that frightened her, or even infuriated her so very much. It was the term *bastard* in connection with her little boy.

Before she fully realized her intent, her hand was swinging up and slapping hard across his face. "Don't you ever speak about my son that way."

When his hand cracked across her cheek, it wasn't pain she felt, or even shock, but rage.

"Don't push me, Megan," he said, breathing hard. "Don't push me, because you'll be the one to take the fall. You, and the boy."

As crazed as any mother protecting her cub, she lunged at him. The power of the attack rammed them both against the wall. She landed two solid blows before he threw her off.

"You still have that passionate nature, I see." He dragged her against him, infuriated, aroused. "I remember how to channel it."

She struck out again, a glancing blow, before he caught her arms and pinned them against her body. So she used her teeth. Even as Baxter cursed in pain, the door burst in.

Nathaniel plucked him off the floor as he might a flea off a dog. Through the haze of her own vision, Megan saw there was murder in his eye. Hot-blooded. Deadly.

"Nathaniel."

But he didn't look at her. Instead, he rapped Baxter hard against the wall. "Dumont, isn't it?" His voice was viciously quiet, terrifyingly pleasant. "I've heard how you like pushing women around."

Baxter struggled for dignity, though his feet were inches off the ground. "Who the hell are you?"

"Well, now, it seems only fair you should know the name of the man who's going to rip out your damn heart with his bare hands." He had the pleasure of seeing Baxter blanch. "It's Fury, Nathaniel Fury. You won't forget it—" he rammed a fist low, into the kidneys "—will you?"

When Baxter could breathe again, his words struggling out weakly, he wheezed, "You'll be in jail before the night's out."

"I don't think so." His head snapped around when Megan started forward. "Stay back," he said between his teeth. The hot leap of fire in his eyes had her coming to a stop.

"Nathaniel." She swallowed hard. "Don't kill him."

"Any particular reason you want him alive?"

She opened her mouth, shut it again. The answer seemed desperately important, so she offered the truth. "No."

Baxter drew in his breath to scream. Nathaniel cut it off neatly with a hand over the windpipe. "You're a lucky man, Dumont. The lady doesn't want me to kill you, and I don't like to disappoint her. We'll leave it to fate." He dragged Baxter outside, hauling him along as if the man were nothing more than a heavily packed seabag.

Megan raced to the door. "Holt." A shiver of relief worked down her spine when she spotted Suzanna's husband near the pier. "Do something."

Holt merely shrugged. "Fury beat me to it. You should go back in, you're getting wet."

"But—he's not really going to kill him, is he?"

Holt considered a moment, narrowing his eyes against the rain as Nathaniel carted Baxter down the pier. "Probably not."

"I hope to God you can't swim," Nathaniel muttered, then threw Baxter off the pier. He turned away and was striding to Megan before the sound of the splash. "Come on."

"But—"

He simply scooped her up in his arms. "I'm knocking off for the day."

"Fine." Holt stood, his thumbs in his pockets, a look of unholy glee in his eyes. "See you tomorrow."

"Nathaniel, you can't—"

"Shut up, Meg." He dumped her in the car. She craned her neck, and wasn't sure whether she was relieved or disappointed to see Baxter heaving himself back onto the pier.

He needed quiet to pull himself back from violence. He detested the temper that lurked inside him, that made him want to raise his fists and pummel. He could rationalize it, under the circumstances, but it always left him sick inside to know what he was capable of if pushed.

There was no doubt in his mind that he would have come very close to murder if Megan hadn't stopped him.

He'd trained himself to use words and wit to resolve a fight. It usually worked. When it didn't, well, it didn't. But he continued, years after the last blow he'd taken from his father, to remember, and regret.

She was shivering by the time he parked the car in his driveway. It didn't occur to him until that moment that he'd forgotten Dog. Holt would see to him, Nathaniel figured, and plucked Megan from her seat.

"I don't—"

"Just be quiet." He carried her in, past the bird, who squawked greetings, and up the stairs. Megan was ready to babble in shock by the time he dumped her in a chair in the bedroom. Without a word, he turned away to rummage through his dresser drawers. "Get out of those wet clothes," he ordered, tossing her a sweatshirt and sweatpants. "I'm going to go down and make you some tea."

"Nathaniel—"

"Just do it!" he shouted, gritting his teeth. "Just do it," he repeated quietly, and shut the door.

He didn't slam it; nor, when he was down in the kitchen, did he put his fist through a wall. He thought about it. But instead, he put on the kettle, got out the brandy. After a moment's consideration, he took a pull of the fiery liquid, straight from the bottle. It didn't calm him very much, but it took the edge off his sense of self-disgust.

When he heard Bird whistle and invite Megan to come to the Casbah, he set her spiked tea on the table.

She was pale, he noted, and her eyes were too big. So were the sweats. He nearly smiled at the picture she made, hesitating in the doorway, with the shirt drooping off her shoulders and the pants bagging at her ankles.

"Sit down and have something to drink. You'll feel better."

"I'm all right, really." But she sat, and lifted the mug in both hands, because they tended to shake. The first sip had her sucking in her breath. "I thought this was tea."

"It is. I just gave it a little help." He sat across from her, waited until she sipped again. "Did he hurt you?"

She stared down at the table. The wood was polished so brightly she could see her own face in it. "Yes."

She said it calmly. She thought she was calm, until Nathaniel put his hand over hers. Her breath hitched once, twice, and then she put her head on the table and wept.

So much washed out with the tears—the hopes she'd once had, the dreams, the betrayal and the disillusionment, the fears and the bitterness. He didn't try to stop her, only waited it out.

"I'm sorry." She let her cheek rest against the table a moment, comforted by the cool, smooth feel of the wood on her skin and Nathaniel's hand on her hair. "It all seemed to happen so fast, and I wasn't prepared." She straightened, started to wipe the tears away, when a new fear glazed her eyes. "Kevin. Oh, God, if Bax—"

"Holt will take care of Kevin. Dumont won't get near him."

"You're right." She gave a shuddering sigh. "Of course, you're right. Holt would see to Suzanna and all the children right away. And all Baxter wanted to do in any case was frighten me."

"Did he?"

Her eyes were still wet, but they were steady. "No. He hurt me, and he infuriated me, and he made me sick that I'd ever let him touch me. But he didn't frighten me. He can't."

"Attagirl."

She sniffled, smiled weakly. "But I frightened him. That's why he came here today, after all this time. Because he's frightened."

"Of what?"

"Of the past, the consequences." She drew another, deeper breath and smelled Nathaniel—tobacco and salt spray. How oddly comforting it was. "He thinks our coming here is some sort of plot against him. He's been keeping track of me all this time. I didn't know."

"He's never contacted you until today?"

"No, never. I suppose he felt safe when I was in Oklahoma and hadn't any connection with Suzanna. Now, not only is there a connection, but I'm living here. And Kevin and Alex and Jenny… Well, he doesn't seem to understand it has nothing to do with him."

She picked up her tea again. Nathaniel hadn't asked anything, he'd simply sat and held her hand. Perhaps that was why she felt compelled to tell him.

"I met him in New York. I was seventeen, and it was my first real trip away from home. It was during the winter break, and several of us went. One of my friends had relatives there. I guess you've been to New York."

"A time or two."

"I'd never experienced anything like it. The people, the buildings. The city was so exciting, and so unlike the West. Everything crowded in and colorful. I loved it—rushing along Fifth Avenue, having coffee in some hole-in-the-wall in Greenwich Village. Gawking. It sounds silly."

"No, it sounds normal."

"I guess it was," she said with a sigh. "Everything was normal, and simple, before… It was at this party, and he looked so handsome and romantic, I suppose. A young girl's dream, with those movie-star looks and that sheen of sophistication. And he was older—just enough older to be fascinating. He'd been to Europe." She stopped herself, squeezed her eyes shut. "Oh, God, how pathetic."

"You know you don't have to do this now, Meg."

"No, I think I do." Steadying herself, she opened her eyes again. "If you can stand listening to it."

"I'm not going anywhere." He gave her hand a comforting squeeze. "Go ahead, then, get rid of it."

"He said all the right things, made all the right moves. He sent a dozen roses the next day, and an invitation to dinner."

She paused to choose her words and pushed absently at a pin that had loosened in her hair. It wasn't so horrible, she realized, to look back. It seemed almost like a play, with her as both actor and audience. Vitally involved and breezily detached.

"So I went. There was candlelight, and we danced. I felt so grown-up. I think you only really feel that way when you're seventeen. We went to museums and window-shopping and to shows. He told me he loved me, and he bought me a ring. It had two little diamond hearts, interconnected. It was very romantic. He slipped it on my finger, and I slipped into his bed."

She stopped, waited for Nathaniel to comment. When he didn't, she worked up the courage to continue.

"He said he would come to Oklahoma, and we'd make our plans for the future. But, of course, he didn't come. At first, when I called, he said he'd been delayed. Then he stopped answering my calls altogether. I found out I was pregnant, and I called, I wrote. Then I heard that he was engaged, that he'd been engaged all along. At first I didn't believe it, then I just went numb. It took me a while before I made myself believe it, made myself understand and deal with it. My family was wonderful. I never would have gotten through it without them. When Kevin was born, I realized I couldn't just feel grown-up. I had to *be* grown-up. Later on, I tried to contact Bax one last time. I thought he should know about Kevin, and that Kevin should have some sort of relationship with his father. But..." She trailed off. "When there was absolutely no interest, only anger and hostility, I began to understand that it was best that that didn't happen. Today, maybe for the first time, I was absolutely sure of it."

"He doesn't deserve either of you."

"No, he doesn't." She managed a small smile. Now that she'd said it all, for the first time in so very long, she felt hollowed out. Not limp, she realized. Just free. "I want to thank you for charging to the rescue."

"My pleasure. He won't touch you again, Meg." He took her hand, brought it to his lips. "You or Kevin. Trust me."

"I do." She turned her hand in his, gripped. "I do trust you." Her pulse was starting to skip, but she kept her eyes on his. "I thought, when you carried me in and upstairs... Well, I didn't think you were going to make me tea."

"Neither did I. But you were trembling, and I knew if I touched you before I cooled off, I'd be rough. That it wouldn't be right, for either of us."

Her heart stuttered, then picked up its pace. "Are you cooled off now?"

His eyes darkened. "Mostly." Slowly, he rose, drew her to her feet. "Is that an invitation, Megan?"

"I—" He was waiting, she realized, for her to agree or refuse. No seduction, no pretty promising words. No illusions. "Yes," she said, and met his lips with hers.

When he swept her up this time, she gave a quick, nervous laugh. It slid back down her throat when she met the look in his eyes.

"You won't think of him," Nathaniel said quietly. "You won't think of anything but us."

Chapter 8

She could hear her own heartbeat pounding, pounding, in counterpoint to the rain that pounded against the windows. She wondered whether Nathaniel could hear it, too, and if he did, whether he knew that she was afraid. His arms were so strong, his mouth was so sure each time it swooped down to claim hers again.

He carried her up the stairs as if she weighed no more than the mist that swirled outside the cottage.

She would make a mistake, she would do something foolish, she wouldn't be what either of them wanted. The doubts pinched at her like fingers as he swept her into his bedroom, where the light was dim and the air was sweet with wisteria.

She saw the spear of purple blooms in an old bottle on a scarred wooden chest, the undraped windows that were opened to welcome the moist breeze. And the bed, with its sturdy iron headboard and taut cotton spread.

He set her down beside it, so that she was all too aware of the weakness in her knees. But she kept her eyes on his and waited, terrified and aching, for him to make the first move.

"You're trembling again." His voice was quiet, the fingers he lifted to stroke her cheek were soothing. Did she think he couldn't see all those fears in her eyes? She couldn't know that they stirred his own.

"I don't know what to do." The moment the words were out, she closed her eyes. She'd done it already, she realized. The first mistake. Determined, she dragged his head down to hers for an aggressive kiss.

A fire kindled in his gut, flames leaping and licking at the ready fuel of his need. Muscles tensed in reaction, he fought back the urge to shove her back on the bed and take, take quickly, fiercely. He kept his hands easy, stroking her face, her shoulders, her back, until she quieted.

"Nathaniel."

"Do you know what I want, Meg?"

"Yes— No." She reached for him again, but he caught her hands, kissed them, fingertip by fingertip.

"I want to watch you relax. I want to watch you enjoy." His eyes on hers, he lowered her hands to her sides. "I want to watch you fill up with me." Slowly he began to take the pins from her hair, setting them on the table beside the bed. "I want to hear you say my name when I'm inside you."

He combed his fingers through her hair, contenting himself with the silky texture. "I want you to let me do all the things I've been dreaming of since I first laid eyes on you. Let me show you."

He kissed her first, his mouth soft, smooth, seductive. Endlessly patient, he parted hers with teasing nips and nibbles, with the persuasive caress of his tongue. Degree by torturous degree, he deepened the kiss, until her hands clutched weakly at his waist and her shudders gave way to pliancy.

The lingering taste of brandy, the faint and very male scrape of a day's beard against her cheek, the patter of rain and the drifting scent of flowers. All this whirled in her head like a drug, both potent and possessing.

His lips left hers to journey over her face, to trace the line of her jaw, to nuzzle at her ear, waiting, patiently waiting, until he felt her slip over to the next stage of surrender.

He stepped back, only an inch, and slipped the shirt up her torso, over her head, let it drop to the floor. His muscles coiled like a snake. She thought she saw the lightning flash of desire that darkened his eyes to soot. But he only skimmed a fingertip down her throat, to the aching tip of her breast.

Her breath caught; her head lolled back.

"You're so beautiful, Meg. So soft." He pressed a kiss to her shoulder while his hands gently molded, caressed, aroused. "So sweet."

He was afraid his hands were too big, too rough. As a result, his touch was stunningly tender, humming over her heating skin. They slicked down her sides, leaving tremors in their wake as he eased the loose pants from her hips.

Then those fingertips moved over her, gliding over curves until her shaking breathing turned to unsteady moans.

He undressed, watching her heavy eyes flutter open, seeing the misty blue focus on him, the pupils dilate.

Now, she thought, and her heart stuttered madly in her throat. He would take her now, and ease this glorious ache he'd stirred to life inside her. Sweet and eager, her mouth lifted to his. He gathered her close, laid her on the bed as gently as he might have laid her in a pool of rose petals. She arched to him, accepting, braced for the torrent. He used only his lips, soft as the rain, savoring her flesh as though it were a banquet of the most delicate flavors. Then his hands, big and hard-palmed, skimmed, lingered, discovered.

Nothing could have prepared her. If she'd had a hundred lovers, none could have given more, or taken more. She was lost in a gently rocking sea of sensation, undone by patience, weakened by tenderness.

Her breathing slowed, deepened, even as her heart rate soared. She felt the brush of his hair on her breast before his mouth claimed it, heard his quiet, satisfied groan of pleasure as he suckled. Heard his sigh as he circled and teased with his tongue.

She sank, fathoms deep, in warm, clear waters.

She didn't know when those waters began to churn. The storm gathered so slowly, so subtly. It seemed one moment she was drifting, and the next floundering. She couldn't get her breath, no matter how deeply she gasped for air. Her mind, suddenly reeling, struggled for the surface, even as her body coiled and tensed.

"Nathaniel." She grabbed at him, her fingers digging into his flesh. "I can't—"

But he covered her mouth with his, swallowing her gasps, savoring her moan, as the first dizzy climax racked her.

She reared against his hand, instinctively urging him on as hot red waves of pleasure swept her up. Her neat, rounded nails scored his shoulders before her hands, her body, even her mind, went limp.

"Megan. God." She was so hot, so wet. He pressed his lips to her throat as he fought to level his own breathing. Pleasuring a woman had always pleasured him. But not like this. Never like this. He felt like a king and a beggar all at once.

Her stunned response aroused him unbearably. All he could do was wallow in her, absorbing her shock waves, and his own, feeling each and every nerve in his body sizzle and spark.

He wanted to give her more. Had to give her more. Strapping down his own grinding needs, he slipped inside her, letting himself rock with the pleasure of her quick shudder, her broken sigh.

She was so small. He had to remind himself again and again that she was small, all delicate bones and fragile skin. That she was innocent, and nearly as untouched as a virgin. So while the blood pounded in his head, his heart, his loins, he took her gently, his hands fisted on the bedspread for fear he would touch her and bruise.

He felt her body contract, explode. And then she said his name.

He pressed his lips to hers again, and followed her over.

* * *

The rain was still drumming. As she slowly swam back to reality, she heard its steady beat on the roof. She lay still, her hand tangled in Nathaniel's hair, her body glowing. She realized she had a smile on her face.

She began to hum.

Nathaniel stirred himself, pushed back lazily to lean on his elbow. "What are you doing?"

"Singing. Sort of."

He grinned, studying her. "I like your looks, sugar."

"I'm getting used to yours." She traced the cleft in his chin with a fingertip. Her lashes lowered. "It was all right, wasn't it?"

"What?" He waited, wisely holding back a chuckle until she looked at him again. "Oh, that. Sure, it was okay for a start."

She opened her mouth, closed it again with a little humming sound that wasn't at all musical. "You could be a little more... flattering."

"You could be a little less stupid." He kissed her frowning mouth. "Making love isn't a quiz, Meg. You don't get graded."

"What I meant was... Never mind."

"What you meant was..." He hauled her over until she was splayed on top of him. "On a scale of one to ten..."

"Cut it out, Nathaniel." She laid her cheek on his chest. "I hate it when you make me feel ridiculous."

"I don't." Possessively he ran a hand down her back. "I love to make you feel ridiculous. I love to make you feel."

He nearly followed that up with a very simple "I love you." But she wouldn't have accepted it. He'd barely done so himself.

"You did." She kept her head over his heart. "You made me feel things I never have before. I was afraid."

Trouble clouded his eyes. "I don't want you to be afraid of me."

"I was afraid of me," she corrected. "Of us. Of letting this happen. I'm glad it did." It was easier than she'd imagined to shift, to smile, to press her mouth to his. For a moment, she thought he tensed, but she dismissed that as foolish and kissed him again.

His system snapped to full alert. How could he want her again, so desperately, so quickly? he wondered. How could he resist those sweet, tantalizing lips?

"Keep that up," he managed, "and it's going to happen again."

The shiver of excitement was glorious. "Okay." She shared her anticipation in the kiss, torturing his mouth, teasing his tongue. Amazed that there could be more, she gave a low sound of delight when he rolled, shoving her beneath him and crushing her mouth.

For a heady moment, he let those violent needs hold sway, trapping her beneath him, devouring her lips, her skin, dragging a hand through her tousled hair until her throat was exposed to his hungry teeth and tongue.

She moaned, writhed under him. Whimpered.

Rolling away, he lay on his back, cursing himself, while his heart pounded the blood through his veins.

Confused, shivering with needs freshly aroused but unmet, Megan laid a tentative hand on his arm. He jerked away.

"Don't." The order came out harsh. "I need a minute."

Her eyes went dead. "I'm sorry. I did something wrong."

"No, you didn't." He scrubbed his hands over his face and sat up. "I'm just not ready. Look, why don't I go down and rustle us up something to eat?"

He was only inches away. It might as well have been miles, and she felt the sharp sting of rejection. "No, that's all right." Her voice was cool and calm again. "I really should get going. I need to pick up Kevin."

"Kevin's fine."

"Regardless." She brushed at her hair, tried to smooth it. She wished desperately for something to wrap around her nakedness.

"Don't pull that door shut on me now." He battled back fury, and a much more dangerous passion.

"I haven't shut any door. I thought—that is, I assumed you wanted me to stay. Since you don't, I'll—"

"Of course I want you to stay. Damn it, Megan." He whirled on her, and wasn't surprised when she jerked back. "I need a bloody minute. I could eat you alive, I want you so much."

In defense, she crossed an arm over her breasts. "I don't understand you."

"Damn right you don't understand me. You'd run like hell if you did." He fought for control, gained a slippery hold. "We'll be fine, Meg, if you wait until I pull myself together."

"What are you talking about?"

Gripped by frustration, he grabbed her hand, pressed it against his, palm to palm. "I've got big hands, Megan. Got them from my father. I know the right way to use them—and the wrong way."

There was a glint in his eyes, like the honed edge of a sword. It should have frightened her, but it only excited. "You're afraid of me," she said quietly. "Afraid you'll hurt me."

"I won't hurt you." He dropped his hand, left it fisted on the bed.

"No, you won't." She lifted a hand to touch his cheek. His jaw was tight, urging her fingers to stroke and soothe. There was a power here, she realized, a power she'd been unaware of possessing. She wondered what they could make between them if she set it free.

"You want me." Feeling reckless, she edged closer, until her mouth slid over his. "You want to touch me." She lifted his fisted hand to her breast, her heart pounding like a drum as his fingers opened, cupped. "And for me to touch you." Her hands stroked down his chest, felt the quiver of his stomach muscles. So much strength, she thought, so ruthlessly chained. What would it be like if those links snapped free?

She wanted to know.

"Make love with me now, Nathaniel." Eyes half-closed, she linked her arms around his neck, pressed her eager body to his. "Show me how much you want me."

He held himself in check, concentrating on the flavor of her mouth. It would be enough, he told himself, to make her float again.

But she had learned quickly. When he sought to soothe, she enticed. Where he tried to gentle, she enraged.

With an oath, he dragged her up until they were kneeling, body-to-body. And his mouth was wild.

She answered avidly each urgent demand, each desperate moan. His hands were everywhere, hard and possessive, taking more only when she cried out for it. There was no calm water to sink in now, but a violent tempest that spun them both over the bed in a tangle of hot flesh and raging needs.

He couldn't stop, no longer gave a damn about control. She was his, and by God, he would have all of her. With something like a snarl, he clamped her hands above her head and ravished her flesh.

She arched like a bow, twisted, and still he plundered, invading that hot, wet core with probing tongue until she was sobbing his name.

And more, still more, wrestling over the bed with her hands as rough and ready as his, her mouth as bold and ravenous.

He drove himself into her, hard and deep, hissing with triumph, eyes glazed and dark. His hands locked on hers as she rose to meet him.

She would remember the speed, and the wild freedom, of their mindless mating. And she would remember the heady flavor of power as they plunged recklessly off the edge together.

She must have slept. When she woke, she was sprawled on her stomach across the bed. The rain had stopped and night had fallen. When her mind cleared, she became aware of dozens of small aches, and a drugged sense of satisfaction.

She thought of rolling over, but it seemed like too much trouble. Instead, she stretched out her arms, searching the tumbled bed, knowing already that she was alone.

She heard the bird squawk slyly. "You know how to whistle, don't you, Steve?"

She was still chuckling when Nathaniel stepped back into the room.

"What do you do, run old movies for him all day?"

"He's a Bogart fan. What can I tell you?" It amazed him that he felt awkward, holding a dinner tray while a naked woman lolled in his bed. "That's a pretty good scar you've got there, sugar."

She was much too content to be embarrassed when she saw where his eyes had focused. "I earned it. That's a pretty good dragon you've got."

"I was eighteen, stupid, and more than a little buzzed on beer. But I guess I earned it, too."

"Suits you. What have you got there?"

"Thought you might be hungry."

"I'm starving." She braced herself on both elbows and smiled at him. "That smells terrific. I didn't know you cooked."

"I don't. Dutch does. I cadge handouts from the kitchen, then nuke them."

"Nuke them?"

"Zap them in the microwave." He set the tray down on the sea chest at the foot of the bed. "We've got some Cajun chicken, some wine."

"Mmm…" She roused herself enough to lean over and peer at it. "Looks wonderful. But I really need to get Kevin."

"I talked to Suzanna." He wondered if he could talk her into eating dinner just as she was, gloriously naked. "Unless she hears from you, Kevin's set to spend the night with them."

"Oh. Well."

"She says he's already knee-deep in video games with Alex and Jenny."

"And if I called, I'd spoil his party."

"Pretty much." He sat on the edge of the bed, ran a fingertip down her spine. "So, how about it? Sleep with me tonight?"

"I don't even have a toothbrush."

"I can dig up an extra." He broke off a piece of chicken, fed it to her.

"Oh." She swallowed, blew out a breath. "Spicy."

"Yeah." He leaned down to sample her lips, then lifted a glass of wine to them. "Better?"

"It's wonderful."

He tipped the glass so that a few drops of wine spilled on her shoulder. "Oops. Better clean that up." He did so with a lingering lick of his tongue. "What do I have to do to convince you to stay?"

She forgot the food and rolled into his arms. "You just did."

In the morning, the mists had cleared. Nathaniel watched Megan pin up her hair in a beam of sunlight. It seemed only right that he move behind her and press his lips to the base of her neck.

He thought it was a sweetly ordinary, sweetly intimate gesture that could become a habit.

"I love the way you polish yourself up, sugar."

"Polish myself up?" Her curious eyes met his in the glass. She had on the same tailored suit she'd worn the day before—now slightly wrinkled. Her makeup was sketchy at best, courtesy of the small emergency cosmetic kit she carried in her purse, and her hair was giving her trouble, as she'd lost half of her pins.

"Like you are now. Like some pretty little cupcake behind the bakery window."

"Cupcake." She nearly choked. "I'm certainly not a cupcake."

"I've got a real sweet tooth." To prove it, he nibbled his way to her ear.

"I've noticed." She turned, but put her hands against his chest to hold him off. "I have to go."

"Yeah, me too. I don't suppose I could talk you into coming with me."

"To sight whales?" She cocked her head. "No more than I could talk you into sitting with me in my office all day, running figures."

He winced. "Guess not. How about tonight?"

She yearned, wished, longed. "I have to think of Kevin. I can't spend my nights here with you while he spends them somewhere else."

"I had that figured. I was thinking if you were to leave your terrace doors open..."

"You could come sneaking in?" she asked archly.

"More or less."

"Good thinking." She laughed and drew away. "Now, are you going to drive me back to my car?"

"Looks that way." He took her hand, holding it as they walked downstairs. "Megan..." He hated to bring it up when the sun was shining and his mood was light. "If you hear from Dumont, if he tries to see you or Kevin, if he calls, sends a damn smoke signal, does anything, I want you to tell me."

She gave his hand a reassuring squeeze. "I doubt I will, after the dunking you gave him. But don't worry, Nathaniel, I can handle Baxter."

"Off with his head," Bird suggested, but Nathaniel didn't smile.

"It's not a matter of what you can handle." He pushed the door open, stepped outside. "Maybe you don't figure that last night gives me the right to look out for you and your boy, but I do. I will. So we'll put it this way." He opened the car door for her. "Either you promise me that you'll tell me, or I go after him now."

She started to protest, but the image, absolutely vivid, of the look on Nathaniel's face when he'd rammed Baxter against the wall stopped her. "You would."

"Bank on it."

She tried to separate annoyance from the simple pleasure of being protected. And couldn't. "I want to say I appreciate the concern, but I'm not sure I do. I've been taking care of myself, and of Kevin, for a long time."

"Things change."

"Yes," she said carefully, wondering what was behind those calm, unblinking gray eyes. "I'm more comfortable when they change slowly."

"I'm doing my best to keep at your pace, Meg." Whatever frustrations he had, he told himself, he could handle. "Just a simple yes or no on this'll do."

It wasn't just herself, Megan thought. There was Kevin. And Nathaniel was offering them both a strong, protecting arm. Pride meant nothing when compared to the welfare of her son.

Not at all sure why she was amused, she turned to him once he'd settled into the driver's seat. "You have an uncanny knack for getting your own way. And when you do, you just accept it as inevitable."

"It usually is." He backed out of the drive and headed for Shipshape.

There was a small greeting party waiting for them. Holt and, to Megan's surprise, her brother, Sloan.

"I dropped the kids off at The Towers," Holt told her, before she could ask. "They've got your dog, Nate."

"Thanks." She'd barely stepped from the car when Sloan grabbed her by the shoulders, stared hard into her eyes.

"Are you all right? Why the hell didn't you call me? Did he put his hands on you?"

"I'm fine. Sloan, I'm fine." Instinctively she cupped his face, kissed him. "I didn't call because I already had two white knights charging into battle. And he may have put his hands on me, but I put my fists on him. I think I split his lip."

Sloan said something particularly foul about Dumont and hugged Megan close. "I should have killed him when you first told me about him."

"Stop it." She pressed her cheek to his. "It's over. I want it put aside. Kevin's not to hear about it. Now come on, I'll drive you back to the house."

"I've got some things to do." He gave Nathaniel a steely stare over Megan's shoulder. "You go on up, Meg. I'll be along later."

"All right, then." She kissed him again. "Holt, thanks again for looking after Kevin."

"No problem." Holt tucked his tongue in his cheek when Nathaniel scooped Megan up for a long, lingering kiss. A glance at Sloan's narrowed eyes had him biting that tongue to keep from grinning.

"See you, sugar."

Megan flushed, cleared her throat. "Yes…well. Bye."

Nathaniel tucked his thumbs in his pockets, waited until she'd driven off before he turned to Sloan. "Guess you want to talk to me."

"Damn right I want to talk to you."

"You'll have to come up to the bridge. We've got a tour going out."

"Want a referee?" Holt offered, and earned two deadly glances. "Too bad. I hate to miss it."

Smoldering, Sloan followed Nathaniel up the gangplank, waited restlessly while he gave orders. Once they were on the bridge, Nathaniel glanced over the charts and dismissed the mate.

"If this is going to take longer than fifteen minutes, you're in for a ride."

"I've got plenty of time." Sloan stepped closer, braced his legs like a gunslinger at high noon. "What the hell were you doing with my sister?"

"I think you have that figured out," Nathaniel said coolly.

Sloan bared his teeth. "If you think I'm going to stand back while you move in on her, you're dead wrong. I wasn't around when she got tangled up with Dumont, but I'm here now."

"I'm not Dumont." Nathaniel's own temper threatened to snap, a dry twig of control. "You want to take out what he did to her on me, that's fine. I've been looking to kick someone's ass ever since

I caught that bastard tossing her around. So you want to take me on?" he said invitingly. "Do it."

Though the invitation tempted some elemental male urge, Sloan pulled back. "What do you mean, he was tossing her around?"

"Just what I said. He had her up against the wall." The rage swept back, almost drowning him. "I thought about killing him, but I didn't think she could handle it."

Sloan breathed deep to steady himself. "So you threw him off the pier."

"Well, I punched him a few times first, then I figured there was a chance he couldn't swim."

Calmer, and grateful, Sloan nodded. "Holt had a few words with him when he dragged his sorry butt out. They've tangled before." He'd missed his chance that time, as well, he thought, thoroughly disgusted. "I don't think Dumont'll come back, chance running into any of us again." Sloan knew he should be glad of it, but he regretted, bitterly, not getting his own licks in.

"I appreciate you looking out for her," he said stiffly. "But that doesn't get us past the rest. She'd have been upset, vulnerable. I don't like a man who takes advantage of that."

"I gave her tea and dry clothes," Nathaniel said between his teeth. "It would have stopped right there, if that was what she wanted. Staying with me was her choice."

"I'm not going to see her hurt again. You might look at her and see an available woman, but she's my sister."

"I'm in love with your sister." Nathaniel snapped his head around when the bridge door opened.

"Ready to cast off, Captain."

"Cast off." He cursed under his breath as he stalked to the wheel.

Sloan stood back while he gave orders and piloted the boat into the bay.

"You want to run that by me again?"

"Have you got a problem with plain English?" Nathaniel tossed back. "I'm in love with her. Damn it."

"Well, now." More than a little taken aback, Sloan sat on the bench closest to the helm.

He wanted to think that one through. After all, Megan had barely met the man. Then again, he remembered, he'd fallen for Amanda in little more time than it took her to snap his head off. If he'd been able to choose a man for his sister, it might have been someone very much like Nathaniel Fury.

"Have you told her that?" Sloan asked, his tone considerably less belligerent.

"Go to hell."

"Haven't," he decided, and braced his booted foot on his knee. "Does she feel the same way about you?"

"She will." Nathaniel set his teeth. "She needs time to work it out, that's all."

"Is that what she said?"

"That's what I say." Nathaniel ran a frustrated hand through his hair. "Look, O'Riley, either mind your own damn business or take a punch at me. I've had enough."

Sloan's smile spread slow and easy. "Crazy about her, aren't you?"

Nathaniel merely grunted and started out to sea.

"What about Kevin?" Sloan studied Nathaniel's profile as he probed. "Some might have a problem taking on another man's son."

"Kevin's Megan's son." His eyes flashed to Sloan's, burned. "He'll be mine."

Sloan waited a moment until he was sure. "So, you're going to take on the whole package."

"That's right." Nathaniel pulled out a cigar, lit it. "You got a problem with that?"

"Can't say as I do." Sloan grinned and accepted the cigar Nathaniel belatedly offered him. "You might, though. My sister's a damn stubborn woman. But seeing as you're almost a member of the family, I'll be glad to offer any help."

A smile finally twitched at Nathaniel's mouth. "Thanks, but I'd like to handle it on my own."

"Suit yourself." Sloan settled back to enjoy the ride.

"Are you sure you're all right?"

Megan had no more than stepped in the door of The Towers when she found herself surrounded by concern.

"I'm fine, really." Her protests hadn't prevented the Calhouns from herding her into the family kitchen and plying her with tea and sympathy. "This has gotten blown out of proportion."

"When somebody messes with one of us," C.C. corrected, "he messes with all of us."

She glanced outside, where the children were playing happily in the yard. "I appreciate it. Really. But I don't think there's anything more to worry about."

"There won't be." Colleen stepped into the room, her gaze scanning each face in turn. "What are you all doing in here, smothering the girl? Get out."

"Aunt Colleen..." Coco began.

"Out, I said, all of you. You, go back to your kitchen and flirt with that big Dutchman you've got sneaking into your room at night."

"Why, I—"

"Go. And you." Now her cane gestured threateningly at Amanda. "You've got a hotel to run, don't you? Go weed some flowers," she ordered Suzanna. "And you go tinker with an engine." She flicked her gaze from C.C. to Lilah.

"Tougher with me, isn't it, Auntie?" Lilah said lazily.

"Take a nap," Colleen snapped.

"Got me," Lilah said with a sigh. "Come on, ladies, we've been dismissed."

Satisfied when the door swung shut behind them, Colleen sat heavily at the table. "Get me some of that tea," she ordered Megan. "See that it's hot."

Though she moved to obey, Megan wasn't cowed. "Do you always find rudeness works to your advantage, Miss Calhoun?"

"That, old age, and a hefty portfolio." She took the tea Megan set in front of her, sipped, nodded grudgingly when she found it hot and strong. "Now then, sit down and listen to what I have to say. And don't prim your mouth at me, young lady."

"I'm very fond of Coco," Megan told her. "You embarrassed her."

"Embarrassed her? Ha! She and that tattooed hulk have been mooning around after each other for days. Gave her a prod is what I did." But she eyed Megan craftily. "Loyal when it's deserved, are you?"

"I am."

"And so am I. I made a few calls this morning, to some friends in Boston. Influential friends. Hush," she ordered when Megan started to speak. "Detest politics myself, but it's often necessary to dance with the devil. Dumont should be being made aware, at this moment, that any contact with you, or your son, will fatally jeopardize his ambitions. He will not trouble you again."

Megan pressed her lips together. She wanted her voice to be steady. No matter what she had said, how she had pretended, there had been an icy fear, like a cold ax balanced over her head, of what Baxter might do. In one stroke, Colleen had removed it.

"Why did you do it?"

"I loathe bullies. I particularly loathe bullies who interfere with the contentment of my family."

"I'm not your family," Megan said softly.

"Ha! Think again. You stuck your toe in Calhoun waters, girl. We're like quicksand. You're a Calhoun now, and you're stuck."

Tears rushed into her eyes, blinding her. "Miss Calhoun—" Megan's words were cut off by the impatient rap of Colleen's cane. After a sniffle, Megan began again. "Aunt Colleen," she corrected, understanding. "I'm very grateful."

"So you should be." Colleen coughed to clear her own husky

voice. Then she raised it to a shout. "Come back in here, the lot of you! Stop listening at the door!"

It swung open, Coco leading the way. She walked to Colleen, bent, kissed the papery cheek.

"Stop all this nonsense." She waved her grandnieces away. "I want the girl to tell me how that strapping young man tossed that bully in the drink."

Megan laughed, wiped her eyes. "He choked him first."

"Ha!" Colleen rapped her cane in appreciation. "Don't spare the details."

Chapter 9

B. behaving oddly. Since return to island for summer she is absentminded, daydreaming. Arrived late for tea, forgot luncheon appointment. Intolerable. Unrest in Mexico annoying. Dismissed valet. Excess starch in shirts.

Unbelievable, Megan thought, staring at the notes Fergus had written in his crabbed hand beside stock quotations. He could speak of his wife, a potential war and his valet in the same faintly irritated tone. What a miserable life Bianca must have had. How terrible to be trapped in a marriage, ruled by a despot and without any power to captain your own destiny.

How much worse, she thought, if Bianca had loved him.

As she often did in the quiet hours before sleep, Megan flipped through the pages to the series of numbers. She had time now to regret that she'd never made it to the library.

Or perhaps Amanda was a better bet. Amanda might know whether Fergus had had foreign bank accounts, safe-deposit boxes.

Peering down, she wondered whether that was the answer. The

man had had homes in Maine and in New York. These could be the numbers of various safe-deposit boxes. Even combinations to safes he'd kept in his homes.

That idea appealed to her, a straightforward answer to a small but nagging puzzle. A man as obsessed with his wealth and the making of money as Fergus Calhoun had been would very likely have kept a few secret stores.

Wouldn't it be fantastic, she thought, if there was some dusty deposit box in an old bank vault? Unopened all these years, she imagined. The key lost or discarded. The contents? Oh…priceless rubies or fat, negotiable bonds. A single faded photograph. A lock of hair wound with a gold ribbon.

She rolled her eyes and laughed at herself. "Imagination's in gear, Megan," she murmured. "Too bad it's so farfetched."

"What is?"

She jumped like a rabbit, her glasses sliding down to her chin. "Damn. Nathaniel."

He was grinning as he closed and locked the terrace doors at his back. "I thought you'd be happy to see me."

"I am. But you didn't have to sneak up on me that way."

"When a man comes through a woman's window at night, he's supposed to sneak."

She shoved her glasses back in place. "They're doors."

"And you're too literal." He leaned over the back of the chair where she sat and kissed her like a starving man. "I'm glad you talk to yourself."

"I do not."

"You were, just now. That's why I decided to stop watching you and come in." He strolled to the hallway door, locked it. "You looked incredibly sexy sitting there at your neat little desk, your hair scooped up, your glasses sliding down your nose. In that cute, no-nonsense robe."

She wished heartily that the practical terry cloth could transform into silk and lace. But she had nothing seductive to adorn herself in, and had settled for the robe and Coco's perfume.

"I didn't think you were coming after all. It's getting late."

"I figured there'd be some hoopla over yesterday, and that you'd need to settle Kevin for the night. He didn't get wind of it, did he?"

"No." It touched her that he would ask, that it would matter to him. "None of the children know. Everyone else has been wonderful. It's like thinking you're alone in a battle and then finding yourself surrounded by a circle of shields." She smiled, tilted her head. "Are you holding something behind your back?"

His brows rose, as if in surprise. "Apparently I am." He drew out a peony, a twin to the one he'd given her before. "'A rose,'" he said, "'without a thorn.'"

He crossed to her as he spoke, and all she could think for one awed moment was that this man, this fascinating man, wanted her. He started to take its faded twin from the bud vase on her desk.

"Don't." She felt foolish, but stayed his hand. "Don't throw it out."

"Sentimental, Meg?" Moved that she had kept his token, he slipped the new bud in with the old. "Did you sit here, working late, looking at the flower and thinking of me?"

"I might have." She couldn't fight the smile in his eyes. "Yes, I thought of you. Not always kindly."

"Thinking's enough." He lifted her hand, kissed her palm. "Nearly." To her surprise, he plucked her from the chair, sat himself down and nestled her in his lap. "But this is a whole lot better."

It seemed foolish to disagree, so she rested her head on his shoulder.

"Everyone's getting prepped for the big Fourth of July celebration," she told him idly. "Coco and Dutch are arguing about recipes for barbecue sauce and the kids are bitterly disappointed we won't let them have small, colorful bombs to set off."

"They'll end up making two kinds of sauce and asking everyone to take sides." It was nice sitting like this, he thought, alone and quiet at the end of the day. "And the kids won't be disappointed after they see the fireworks display Trent organized."

Kevin had talked of nothing else all evening, she remembered. "I've heard it's going to be quite a show."

"Count on it. This bunch won't do anything halfway. Like fireworks, do you, sugar?"

"Almost as much as the kids." She laughed and snuggled against him. "I can't believe it's July already. All I have to do is get about two dozen things out of the way so I can compete in the great barbecue showdown, keep the kids from setting themselves on fire and enjoy the show."

"Business first," he murmured. "Working on Fergus's book?"

"Mmm-hmm... I had no idea how much of a fortune he'd amassed, or how little he considered people. Look here." She tapped her finger to the page. "Whenever he made a note about Bianca, it's as if she were a servant or, worse, a possession. He checked over the household accounts every day, to the penny. There's a notation about how he docked the cook thirty-three cents for a kitchen discrepancy."

"A lot of people think more of money than souls." He flipped idly through the book. "I can be sure you're not sitting on my lap because of my bank balance—since you know it down to the last nickel."

"You're in the black."

"Barely."

"Cash flow is usually thin the first few years in any business—and when you add in the outlay in equipment you've purchased, the down payment for the cottage, insurance premiums and licensing fees—"

"God, I love it when you talk profit and loss." Letting the book close, he nipped playfully at her ear. "Talk to me about checks and balances, or quarterly returns. Quarterly returns make me crazy."

"Then you'll be happy to know you and Holt underestimated your federal payments."

"Mmm…" He stopped, narrowed his eyes. "What do you mean?"

"You owe the government another two hundred and thirty dollars, which can be added to your next quarter due, or, more wisely, I can file an amended return."

He swore halfheartedly. "How come we have to pay them in advance, anyway?"

She gave him a light kiss in sympathy. "Because, Nathaniel, if you don't, the IRS will make your life a living hell. I'm here to save you from them. I'm also, if your system can take the excitement, going to suggest you open a Keogh—a retirement account for the self-employed."

"Retirement? Hell, Meg, I'm thirty-three."

"And not getting a day younger. Do you know what the cost-of-living projections are for your golden years, Mr. Fury?"

"I changed my mind. I don't like it when you talk accountant to me."

"It's also good tax sense," she persisted. "The money you put in won't be taxable until you're of retirement age. When, usually, your bracket is lower. Besides, planning for the future might not be romantic, but it is rewarding."

He slid a hand under the terry cloth. "I'd rather have instant gratification."

Her pulse scrambled. "I have the necessary form."

"Damn right you do."

"For the Keogh. All you need to— Oh." The terry cloth parted like water under his clever hands. She gasped, shuddered, melted. "How did you do that?"

"Come to bed." He lifted her. "I'll show you."

Just past dawn, Nathaniel strolled down the curve of the terrace steps, his hands in his pockets and a whistle on his lips. Dutch, in a similar pose, descended the opposite curve. Both men stopped dead when they met in the center.

They stared, swore.

"What are you doing here at this hour?" Dutch demanded.

"I could ask you the same question."

"I live here, remember?"

Nathaniel inclined his head. "You live down there." He pointed toward the kitchen level.

"I'm taking the air," Dutch said, after a fumble for inspiration.

"Me too."

Dutch flicked a glance toward Megan's terrace. Nathaniel gave Coco's a studying look. Each decided to leave well enough alone.

"Well, then. Suppose you want some breakfast."

Nathaniel ran his tongue around his teeth. "I could do with some."

"Come on, can't dawdle out here all morning."

Relieved with the solution, they walked down together in perfect agreement.

She overslept. It was a breach in character that had her racing out of her room, still buttoning her blouse. She stopped to peek into Kevin's bedroom, spotted the haphazardly made bed and sighed.

Everyone was up and about, it seemed, but her.

She made a dash toward her office, crossing breakfast with her son off her list of small pleasures for the day.

"Oh, dear." Coco fluttered her hands when Megan nearly mowed her down in the lobby. "Is something wrong?"

"No, I'm sorry. I'm just late."

"Did you have an appointment?"

"No." Megan caught her breath. "I meant I was late for work."

"Oh, my, I thought there was a problem. I just this minute left a memo on your desk. Go ahead in, dear, I don't want to hold you up."

"But—" Megan found herself addressing Coco's retreating back, so she turned into her office to read the message.

Coco's idea of an interoffice memo was something less than professional.

> Megan, dear, I hope you slept well. There's fresh coffee in your machine, and I've left you a nice basket of muffins. You really shouldn't skip breakfast. Kevin ate like a young wolf. It's so rewarding to see a boy enjoy his food. He and Nate will be back in a few hours. Don't work too hard.
> Love, Coco
> P.S. The cards say you have two important questions to answer. One with your heart, one with your head. Isn't that interesting?

Megan blew out a breath, and was reading the memo again when Amanda popped in. "Got a minute?"

"Sure." She handed over the paper she held. "Do you think you could interpret this for me?"

"Ah, one of Aunt Coco's convoluted messages." Lips pursed, Amanda studied it. "Well, the coffee and muffins are easy."

"I got that part." In fact, Megan helped herself to both. "Want some?"

"No, thanks, she already delivered mine. Kevin ate a good breakfast. I can vouch for that. When I saw him, he was scarfing down French toast, with Nathaniel battling him for the last piece."

Megan bobbled her coffee. "Nathaniel was here for breakfast?"

"Eating and charming Aunt Coco, while telling Kevin some story about a giant squid. They'll be back in a few hours," she continued, tapping the note, "because Kevin talked Nate into taking him out on the tour again. It didn't take much talking," she added with a smile. "And we didn't think you'd mind."

"No, of course not."

"And the bit about the cards defies interpretation. That's pure Aunt Coco." Amanda set the memo down again. "It's spooky, though, just how often she hits the mark. Been asked any questions lately?"

"No, nothing in particular."

Amanda thought of what Sloan had related to her about Nathaniel's feelings. "Are you sure?"

"Hmmm? Yes. I was thinking about Fergus's book. I suppose it could loosely be considered a question. At least there's one I want to ask you."

Amanda made herself comfortable. "Shoot."

"The numbers in the back. I mentioned them before." She opened a file, handing a copy of the list to Amanda. "I was wondering if they might be passbook numbers, or safe-deposit boxes, safe combinations. Lot numbers, maybe, on some real estate deal?" She moved her shoulders. "I know it's silly to get so hung up on them."

"No." Amanda waved the notion away. "I know just what you mean. I hate it when things don't fit into place. We went through most of the papers from this year when we were looking for clues to find the necklace. I don't recall anything that these figures might connect to, but I can look through the material again."

"Let me do it," Megan said quickly. "I feel like it's my baby."

"Glad to. I've got more than enough on my plate, and with the big holiday tomorrow, barely time to clean up. Everything you'd want is in the storeroom under Bianca's tower room. We've got it all boxed according to year and content, but it's still a nasty, time-consuming job."

"I live for nasty, time-consuming jobs."

"Then you'll be in heaven. Megan, I hate to ask, but it's the nanny's day off, and Sloan's up to his ears in plywood or something. We've been playing pass-the-babies this morning, but I've got an appointment in the village this afternoon. I could reschedule."

"You want me to baby-sit."

"I know you're busy, but—"

"Mandy, I thought you'd never ask me." Megan's eyes lit up. "When can I get my hands on her?"

Kevin figured this was the best summer of his life. He missed his grandparents, and the horses, and his best friend, John Silverhorn, but there was too much to do for him to be really homesick.

He got to play with Alex and Jenny every day, had his own fort, and lived in a castle. There were boats to sail, and rocks to climb—and Coco or Mr. Dutch always had a snack waiting in the kitchen. Max told him really neat stories. Sloan and Trent sometimes let him help with the renovations, and Holt had let him drive the little powerboat.

All his new aunts played games with him, and sometimes, if he was really, really careful, they let him hold one of the babies.

It was, to Kevin's thinking, a really good deal.

Then there was Nathaniel. He snuck a look at the man who sat beside him, driving the big convertible up the winding road to The Towers. Kevin had decided that Nathaniel knew something about everything. He had muscles and a tattoo and most always smelled like the sea.

When he stood at the helm of the big tour boat, his eyes narrowed against the sun and his broad hands on the wheel, he was every little boy's idea of a hero.

"Maybe…" Kevin trailed off until Nathaniel glanced down at him.

"Maybe what, mate?"

"Maybe I could go back out with you sometime," Kevin blurted out. "I won't ask so many questions next time, or get in the way."

Was there ever a man, Nathaniel wondered, who could defend himself against the sweetness of a child? He stopped the car at the family entrance. "I'll pipe you aboard my ship anytime." He flicked a finger down the brim of the captain's hat he'd carelessly dropped on Kevin's head. "And you can ask all the questions you want."

"Really?" Kevin pushed the brim back up, so that he could see.

"Really."

"Thanks!" Kevin threw his arms around Nathaniel in a spontaneous hug that had Nathaniel's heart sliding down the slippery chute toward love. "I gotta tell Mom. Are you going to come in?"

"Yeah." He let his hands linger on the boy a moment before they dropped away.

"Come on." Bursting with tidings, Kevin scrambled out of the car and up the steps. He hit the door running. "Mom! I'm back!"

"What a quiet, dignified child," Megan commented as she stepped into the hallway from the parlor. "It must be my Kevin."

With a giggle, Kevin darted to her, rising on his toes to see which baby she was holding. "Is that Bianca?"

"Delia."

Kevin squinted and studied. "How can you tell them apart? They look the same."

"A mother's eyes," she murmured, and bent to kiss him. "Where've you been, sailor?"

"We went way, way out in the ocean and back, twice. We saw nine whales. One was like a baby. When they're all together, they're called a pod. Like what peas grow in."

"Is that so?"

"And Nate let me steer and blow the horn, and I helped chart the course. And this man on the second deck was sick the whole time, but I wasn't 'cause I've got good sea legs. And Nate says I can go with him again, so can I?"

Nearly nine years as a mother had Megan following the stream of information perfectly. "Well, I imagine you can."

"Did you know whales mate for life, and they're not really fish at all, even though they live in the water? They're mammals, just like us and elephants and dogs, and they've got to breathe. That's how come they come up and blow water out of their spouts."

Nathaniel walked in on the lecture. And stopped, and looked. Megan stood, smiling down at her son, his hand in hers and a baby on her hip.

I want. The desire streamed through Nathaniel like sunlight, warm, bright. The woman—there had never been a question of that. But he wanted, as Sloan had said, the whole package. The woman, the boy, the family.

Megan looked over and smiled at him. His heart all but stopped.

She started to speak, but the look in Nathaniel's eyes had her throat closing. Though she took an unconscious step back, he was already there, his hand on her cheek, his lips on hers with a tenderness that turned her to putty.

The baby laughed in delight and reached for a fistful of Nathaniel's hair.

"Here we go." Nathaniel took Delia, hefted her high so that she could squeal and kick her feet. When he settled her on his hip, both Megan and Kevin were still staring at him. He jiggled the baby and cocked his head at the boy. "Do you have a problem with me kissing your mom?"

Megan made a little strangled sound. Kevin's gaze dropped heavily to the floor. "I don't know," he mumbled.

"She sure is pretty, isn't she?"

Kevin shrugged, flushed. "I guess." He wasn't sure how he was supposed to feel. Lots of men kissed his mother. His granddad and Sloan—and Holt and Trent and Max. But this was different. He knew that. After all, he wasn't a baby. He shot a look up, lowered his eyes again. "Are you going to be her boyfriend now?"

"Ah..." Nathaniel glanced at Megan, was met with a look that clearly stated that he was on his own. "That's close enough. Does that bother you?"

Because his stomach was suddenly jittery, Kevin moved his thin shoulders again. "I don't know."

If the boy wasn't going to look up, Nathaniel figured it was time to move down. He crouched, still holding the baby. "You can take plenty of time to think about it, and let me know. I'm not going anywhere."

"Okay." Kevin's eyes slid up toward his mother's, then back to

Nathaniel's. He sidled closer and leaned toward Nathaniel's ear. "Does she like it?"

Nathaniel clamped down on a chuckle and answered solemnity with solemnity. "Yeah, she does."

After a long breath, Kevin nodded. "Okay, I guess you can kiss her if you want."

"I appreciate it." He offered Kevin a hand, and the man-to-man shake had the boy's chest swelling like a balloon.

"Thanks for taking me today." Kevin took off the captain's hat. "And for letting me wear this."

Nathaniel dropped the hat back on Kevin's head, pushed up the brim. "Keep it."

The boy's eyes went blank with shocked pleasure. "For real?"

"Yeah."

"Wow. Thanks. Thanks a lot. Look, Mom, I can keep it. I'm going to show Aunt Coco."

He raced upstairs with a clatter of sneakers. When Nathaniel straightened again, Megan was eyeing him narrowly.

"What did he ask you?"

"Man talk. Women don't understand these things."

"Oh, really?" Before she could disabuse him of that notion, Nathaniel hooked his fingers in her waistband and jerked her forward.

"I've got permission to do this now." He kissed her thoroughly, while Delia did her best to snuggle between them.

"Permission," Megan said when she could breathe again. "From whom?"

"From your men." He strolled casually into the parlor, laid Delia on her play rug, where she squealed happily at her favorite stuffed bear. "Except your father, but he's not around."

"My men? You mean Kevin and Sloan." Realization dawned, and had her sinking onto the arm of a chair. "You spoke to Sloan about...this?"

"We were going to beat each other up about it, but it didn't come to that." Very much at home, Nathaniel walked to the side table and poured himself a short whiskey from a decanter. "We straightened it out."

"You did. You and my brother. I suppose it didn't occur to either of you that I might have some say in the matter."

"It didn't come up. He was feeling surly about the fact that you'd spent the night with me."

"It's none of his business," Megan said tightly.

"Maybe it is, maybe it isn't. It's water under the bridge now. Nothing to get riled about."

"I'm not riled. I'm irritated that you took it upon yourself to explain our relationship to my family without discussing it with me." And she was unnerved, more than a little, by the worshipful look she'd seen in Kevin's eyes.

Women, Nathaniel thought, and tossed back his whiskey. "I was either going to explain it to Sloan or take a fist in the face."

"That's ridiculous."

"You weren't there, sugar."

"Exactly." She tossed back her head. "I don't like to be discussed. I've had my fill of that over the years."

Very carefully, Nathaniel set his glass down. "Megan, if you're going to circle back around to Dumont, you're just going to get me mad."

"I'm not doing that. I'm simply stating a fact."

"And I stated a fact of my own. I told your brother I was in love with you, and that settled it."

"You should have..." She trailed off, gasped for air that had suddenly gone too thin. "You told Sloan you were in *love* with me?"

"That's right. Now you're going to say I should have told you first."

"I... I don't know what I'm going to say." But she was glad, very glad, that she was already sitting down.

"The preferred response is 'I love you, too.'" He waited, ignored the slow stroke of pain. "Can't get your tongue around that."

"Nathaniel." Be calm, she warned herself. Reasonable. Logical. "This is all moving so fast. A few weeks ago, I didn't even know you. I never expected what's happened between us. And I'm still baffled by it. I have very strong, very real feelings for you, otherwise I couldn't have stayed with you that first night."

She was killing him, bloodlessly. "But?"

"Love isn't something I'll ever be frivolous about again. I don't want to hurt you, or be hurt, or risk a misstep that could hurt Kevin."

"You really think time's the answer, don't you? That no matter what's going on inside you, if you just wait a reasonable period, study all the data, balance all the figures, the right answer comes up."

Her shoulders stiffened. "If you're saying do I need time, then yes, I do."

"Fine, take your time, but add this into your equation." In two strides he was in front of her, dragging her up, crushing her mouth with his. "You feel just what I feel."

She did—she was very much afraid she did. "That's not the answer."

"It's the only answer." His eyes burned into hers. "I wasn't looking for you, either, Megan. My own course was plotted out just fine. You changed everything for me. So you're going to have to adjust your nice neat columns and make room for me. Because I love you, and I'm going to have you. You and Kevin are going to belong to me." He released her. "Think about it," he said, and walked out.

Idiot. Nathaniel continued to curse himself as he spun his wheels pulling up in front of Shipshape. Obviously he'd found a new way to court a woman: Yell and offer ultimatums. Clearly the perfect way to win a heart.

He snatched Dog out of the back seat and received a sympathetic face bath. "Want to get drunk?" he asked the wriggling ball of fur. "Nope, you're right, bad choice." He stepped inside the building, set the dog down and wondered where he might find an alternative.

Work, he decided, was a wiser option than a bottle.

He busied himself with an engine until he heard the familiar blat of a horn. That would be Holt, bringing in the last tour of the day.

His mood still sour, Nathaniel went out and down to the pier to help secure lines.

"The holiday's bringing in a lot of tourists," Holt commented when the lines were secured. "Good runs today."

"Yeah." Nathaniel scowled at the throng of people still lingering on the docks. "I hate crowds."

Holt's brow lifted. "You were the one who came up with the Fourth of July special to lure them in."

"We need the money." Nathaniel stomped back into the shop. "Doesn't mean I have to like it."

"Who's ticked you off?"

"Nobody." Nathaniel took out a cigar, lit it defiantly. "I'm not used to being landlocked, that's all."

Holt very much doubted that was all, but, in the way of men, shrugged his acceptance and picked up a wrench. "This engine's coming along."

"I can pick up and go anytime." Nathaniel clamped the cigar between his teeth. "Nothing holding me. All I got to do is pack a bag, hop a freighter."

Holt sighed, accepted his lot as a sounding board. "Megan, is it?"

"I didn't ask for her to drop in my lap, did I?"

"Well..."

"I was here first." Even when he heard how ridiculous that sounded, Nathaniel couldn't stop. "Woman's got a computer chip in her head. She's not even my type, with those neat little suits and that glossy briefcase. Who ever said I was going to settle down here, lock myself in for life? I've never stayed put anywhere longer than a month since I was eighteen."

Holt pretended to work on the engine. "You started a business, took out a mortgage. And it seems to me you've been here better than six months now."

"Doesn't mean anything."

"Is Megan dropping hints about wedding bells?"

"No." Nathaniel scowled around his cigar and snarled. "I am."

Holt dropped his wrench. "Hold on a minute. Let me get this straight. You're thinking of getting married, and you're kicking around here muttering about hopping a freighter and not being tied down?"

"I didn't ask to be tied down, it just happened." Nathaniel took a deliberate puff, then swore. "Damn it, Holt, I made a fool of myself."

"Funny how we do that around women, isn't it? Did you have a fight with her?"

"I told her I loved her. She started the fight." He paced the shop, nearly gave in to the urge to kick the tool bench. "What happened to the days when women wanted to get married, when that was their Holy Grail, when they set hooks for men to lure them in?"

"What century are we in?"

The fact that Nathaniel could laugh was a hopeful sign. "She thinks I'm moving too fast."

"I'd tell you to slow down, but I've known you too long."

Calmer, he took up a ratchet, considered it, then set it down again. "Suzanna took her lumps from Dumont. How'd you get past it?"

"I yelled at her a lot," Holt said, reminiscing.

"I've tried that."

"Brought her flowers. She's got a real weakness for flowers." Which made him think that perhaps he'd stop on the way home and pick some up.

"I've done that, too."

"Have you tried begging?"

Nathaniel winced. "I'd rather not." His eyes narrowed curiously. "Did you?"

Holt took a sudden, intense interest in the engine. "We're talking about you. Hell, Nate, quote her some of that damn poetry you're so fond of. I don't know. I'm not good at this romance stuff."

"You got Suzanna."

"Yeah." Holt's smile spread. "So get your own woman."

Nathaniel nodded, crushed out his cigar. "I intend to."

Chapter 10

The sun had set by the time Nathaniel returned home. He'd overhauled an engine and repaired a hull, and he still hadn't worked off his foul mood.

He remembered a quote—Horace, he thought—about anger being momentary insanity. If you didn't figure out a way to deal with momentary insanity, you ended up in a padded room. Not a cheerful image.

The only way to deal with it, as far as he could see, was to face it. And Megan. He was going to do both as soon as he'd cleaned up.

"And she'll have to deal with me, won't she?" he said to Dog as the pup scrambled out of the car behind him. "Do yourself a favor, Dog, and stay away from smart women who have more brains than sense."

Dog wagged his tail in agreement or sympathy, then toddled away to water the hedges.

Nathaniel slammed the car door and started across the yard.

"Fury?"

He stopped, squinted into the shadows of dusk, toward the side of the cottage. "Yeah?"

"Nathaniel Fury?"

He watched the man approach, a squat, muscled tank in faded denim. Creased face, strutting walk, a grease-smeared cap pulled low over the brow.

Nathaniel recognized the type. He'd seen the man, and the trouble he carried with him like a badge, in dives and on docks the world over. Instinctively he shifted his weight.

"That's right. Something I can do for you?"

"Nope." The man smiled. "Something *I* can do for *you*."

Even as the first flash of warning lit in Nathaniel's brain, he was grabbed from behind, his arms viciously twisted and pinned. He saw the first blow coming, braced, and took a heavy fist low in the gut. The pain was incredible, making his vision double and waver before the second blow smashed into his jaw.

He grunted, went limp.

"Folded like a girl. Thought he was supposed to be tough." The voice behind him sneered, giving him the height and the distance. In a fast, fluid movement, Nathaniel snapped his head back, rapping his skull hard against the soft tissue of a nose. Using the rear assailant for balance, he kicked up both feet and slammed them into a barrel chest.

The man behind him cursed, loosened his grip enough for Nathaniel to wrest himself away. There were only seconds to judge his opponents and the odds.

He saw that both men were husky, one bleeding profusely now from his broken nose, the other snarling as he wheezed, trying to get back his breath after the double kick to his chest. Nate snapped his elbow back, had the momentary pleasure of hearing the sound of bone against bone.

They came at him like dogs.

He'd been fighting all his life, knew how to mentally go around the pain and plow in. He tasted his own blood, felt the power sing up his arm as his fist connected. His head rang like church bells when he caught a blow to the temple. His breath burned from another in the ribs.

But he kept moving in as they circled him, lashing out, dripping sweat and blood. Avoiding a leap at his throat with a quick pivot, he followed through with a snapping, backhanded blow. The flesh on his knuckles ripped, but the pain was sweet.

He caught the quick move out of the corner of his eye and turned into it. The blow skimmed off his shoulder, and he answered it with two stinging jabs to the throat that had one of the men sinking bonelessly to his knees.

"Just you and me now." Nathaniel wiped the blood from his mouth and measured his foe. "Come on."

The loss of his advantage had his opponent taking a step in retreat. Facing Nathaniel now was like facing a wolf with fangs sharp and exposed. His partner was useless, and the man shifted his eyes for the best route of escape.

Then his eyes lit up.

Lunging, he grabbed one of the boards waiting to be nailed to the deck. He was grinning now, advancing and swinging the board like a bat. Nathaniel felt the wind whistle by his ear as he feinted left, then the wood slapping on his shoulder on the return swing.

He went in low. The rushing power took them both over the deck and smashing through the front door.

"Fire in the hole!" Bird shouted out. "All hands on deck!" His wings flapped frantically as the two men hurtled across the room.

A small table splintered like toothpicks under their combined weight. The wrestling wasn't pretty, nor was there any grace in the short body punches or the gouging fingers. The cottage rang with smashing furniture and harsh breathing.

Something new crept into the jungle scent of sweat and blood. When he recognized fear, Nathaniel's adrenaline pumped faster, and he used the new weapon as ruthlessly as his fists.

He closed his hand around the thick throat, thumb crushing

down on the windpipe. The fight had gone out of his opponent. The man was flailing now, gagging.

"Who sent you?" Nathaniel's teeth were bared in a snarl as he grabbed the man by the hair and rapped his head hard on the floor.

"Nobody."

Breathing through his teeth, Nathaniel hauled him over, twisted his arm and jerked it viciously up his back. "I'll snap it like a twig. Then I'll break the other one, before I start on your legs. Who sent you?"

"Nobody," the man repeated, then screamed thinly when Nathaniel increased the pressure. "I don't know his name. I don't!" He screamed again, almost weeping now. "Some dude outa Boston. Paid us five hundred apiece to teach you a lesson."

Nathaniel kept the arm twisted awkwardly, his knee on the man's spine. "Draw me a picture."

"Tall guy, dark hair, fancy suit." The squat man babbled out curses, unable to move without increasing his own agony. "Name of God, you're breaking my arm."

"Keep talking and it's all I'll break."

"Pretty face—like a movie star. Said we was to come here and look you up. We'd get double if we put you in the hospital."

"Looks like you're not going to collect that bonus." After releasing his arm, Nathaniel dragged the man up by the scruff of his neck. "Here's what you're going to do. You're going to go back to Boston and tell your pretty-faced pal that I know who he is and I know where to find him." For the hell of it, Nathaniel rammed the man against the wall on the way out the door. "Tell him not to bother looking over his shoulder, because if I decide he's worth going after, he won't see me coming. You got that?"

"Yeah, yeah, I got it."

"Now pick up your partner." The other man was struggling onto his hands and knees. "And start running."

They didn't need any more urging. Pressing a hand to his ribs,

Nathaniel watched until they'd completed their limping race out of sight.

He gave in to a groan then, hobbling painfully through the broken door and into the house.

"I have not yet begun to fight," Bird claimed.

"A lot of help you were," Nathaniel muttered. He needed ice, he thought, a bottle of aspirin and a shot of whiskey.

He took another step, stopping, then swearing, when his vision blurred and his legs wobbled like jelly. Dog came out of the corner where he'd huddled, whimpering, and whined at Nate's feet.

"Just need a minute," he said to no one in particular, and then the room tilted nastily on its side. "Oh, hell," he murmured, and passed out cold.

Dog licked at him, tried to nuzzle his nose, then sat, thumped his tail and waited. But the smell of blood made him skittish. After a few moments, he waddled out the door.

Nathaniel was just coming to when he heard the footsteps approaching. He struggled to sit up, wincing at every blow that had gone unfelt during the heat of battle. He knew that if they'd come back for him, they could tap-dance on his face without any resistance from him.

"Man overboard," Bird announced, and earned a hissing snarl from Nathaniel.

Holt stopped in the doorway and swore ripely. "What the hell happened?" Then he was at Nathaniel's side, helping him to stand.

"Couple of guys." Too weak to be ashamed of it, Nathaniel leaned heavily on Holt. It began to occur to him that he might need more than aspirin.

"Did you walk into a robbery?"

"No. They just stopped by to beat me to a pulp."

"Looks like they did a good job of it." Holt waited for Nathaniel to catch his breath and his balance. "Did they mention why?"

"Yeah." He wiggled his aching jaw and saw stars. "They were paid to. Courtesy of Dumont."

Holt swore again. His friend was a mess, bruised, bloodied and torn. And it looked as though he were too late to do anything other than mop up the spills.

"Did you get a good look at them?"

"Yeah, good enough. I kicked their butts back to Boston to deliver a little message to Dumont."

Half carrying Nathaniel to the door, Holt stopped, took another survey. "You look like this, and you won?"

Nathaniel merely grunted.

"Should have known." The news made Holt marginally more cheerful. "Well, we'll get you to the hospital."

"No." Damned if he'd give Dumont the satisfaction. "Son of a bitch told them they'd get a bonus if they put me in the hospital."

"Then that's out," Holt said with perfect understanding. "Just a doctor then."

"It's not that bad. Nothing's broke." He checked his tender ribs. "I don't think. Just need some ice."

"Yeah, right." But, being a man, Holt was in perfect sympathy with the reluctance to be bundled off to a doctor. "Okay, we're going to the next-best place." He eased Nathaniel into the car. "Take it slow, ace."

"I can't take it otherwise."

With a snap of his fingers, Holt ordered Dog into the car. "Hold on a minute while I phone Suzanna, let her know what's going on."

"Feed the bird, will you?"

Nathaniel drifted between pain and numbness until Holt returned.

"How'd you know to come by?"

"Your dog." Holt started the car and eased it as gently as possible out of the drive. "He played Lassie."

"No fooling?" Impressed, Nathaniel made the effort to reach back and pat Dog on the head. "Some dog, huh?"

"It's all in the bloodlines."

Nathaniel roused himself enough to probe his face with cautious fingers. "Where are we going?"

"Where else?" Holt headed for The Towers.

Coco squealed at the sight of him, pressing both hands to her cheeks, as Nathaniel hobbled into the family kitchen with one arm slung over Holt's supporting shoulders.

"Oh, you poor *darling*! What happened? Was there an accident?"

"Ran into something." Nathaniel dropped heavily into a chair. "Coco, I'll trade you everything I own, plus my immortal soul, for a bag of ice."

"Goodness."

Brushing Holt away, she took Nathaniel's battered face in her hands. In addition to bruises and scrapes, there was a jagged cut under one eye. The other was bloodshot and swelling badly. It didn't take her longer than a moment to see that the something he'd run into was fists.

"Don't you worry, sweetheart, we'll take care of you. Holt, run up to my room. There's a bottle of painkillers in the medicine chest, from when I had that nasty root canal."

"Bless you," Nathaniel managed. He closed his eyes, listening to her bustling around the kitchen. Moments later he hissed and jerked when a cool cloth dabbed the cut under his eye.

"There, there, dear," she cooed. "I know it hurts, but we have to get it clean so there's no infection. I'm going to put a little peroxide on it now, so you just be brave."

He smiled, but found that did nothing to help his torn lip. "I love you, Coco."

"I love you, too, sweetie."

"Let's elope. Tonight."

Her answer was to lay her lips gently on his brow. "You shouldn't fight, Nathaniel. It doesn't solve anything."

"I know."

Breathless from the run, Megan burst into the kitchen. "Holt said— Oh, God." She streaked to Nathaniel's side, grabbed his sore hand so tightly he had to bite down to suppress a yelp. There was blood drying on his face, and there were bruises blooming. "How bad are you hurt? You should be in the hospital."

"I've had worse."

"Holt said two men came after you."

"Two?" Coco's hand paused. "*Two* men attacked you?" All the softness fled from her eyes, hardening them to tough blue steel. "Why, that's reprehensible. Someone should teach them how to fight fair."

Despite his lip, Nathaniel grinned. "Thanks, beautiful, but I already did."

"I hope you knocked their heads together." After a huffing breath, Coco went back to work on his face. "Megan, dear, fix Nate an ice bag for his eye. It's going to swell."

Megan obeyed, torn into dozens of pieces, by the damage to his face, by the fact that he hadn't even looked at her.

"Here." She laid the cool bag against his eye while Coco cleaned his torn knuckles.

"I can hold it. Thanks." He took it from her, let the ice numb the pain.

"There's antiseptic in the left-hand cupboard, second shelf," Coco said.

Megan, feeling weepy, turned to get it.

The door opened again, this time letting in a crowd. Nathaniel's initial discomfort with the audience turned to reluctant amusement as the Calhouns fired questions and indignation. Plans for revenge were plotted and discarded while Nathaniel suffered the sting of iodine.

"Give the boy air!" Colleen commanded, parting her angry grandnieces and nephews like a queen moving through her court. She eyed Nathaniel. "Banged you up pretty good, did they?"

"Yes, ma'am."

Her eyes were shrewd. "Dumont," she murmured, so that only he could hear.

Nathaniel winced. "Right the first time."

She glanced at Coco. "You seem to be in able hands, here. I have a call to make." She smiled thinly. It helped to have connections, she thought as she tapped out of the room with her cane. And through them she would see that Baxter Dumont knew he had put a noose around his own neck, and that one false move would mean his career would come to an abrupt and unpleasant stop.

Nobody trifled with Colleen Calhoun's family.

Nathaniel watched Colleen go, then took the pill Coco held out to him and gulped it down. The movement sent fresh pain radiating up his side.

"Let's get that shirt off." Trying to sound cheerful, Coco attacked the torn T-shirt with kitchen shears. The angry mutters died away as Nathaniel's bruised torso was exposed.

"Oh." Tears stung Coco's eyes. "Oh, baby."

"Don't pamper the boy." Dutch came in holding two bottles. Witch hazel and whiskey. One look at Nathaniel had him gritting his teeth together so hard they ached, but he kept his voice careless. "He ain't no baby. Take a shot of this, Captain."

"He's just taken a pill," Coco began.

"Take a shot," Dutch repeated.

Nathaniel winced once as the whiskey stung his lip. But it took the edge off a great many other aches. "Thanks."

"Look at ya." Dutch snorted and dumped the witch hazel onto a cloth. "Let 'em pound all over you, like some city boy with sponges where his fists should be."

"There were two of them," Nathaniel muttered.

"So?" Dutch gently swabbed the bruises. "You getting so outa shape you can't take two?"

"I kicked their butts." Experimentally Nathaniel probed a tooth with his tongue. It hurt, but at least it wasn't loose.

"Better had," Dutch returned, with a flash of pride. "Tried to rob you, did they?"

Nathaniel's gaze flashed to Megan. "No."

"Ribs're bruised." Ignoring Nathaniel's curse, Dutch prodded and poked until he was satisfied. "Not cracked though." He crouched, peered into Nathaniel's eyes. "D'ya pass out?"

"Maybe." It was almost as bad as another thumping to admit it. "For a minute."

"Vision blurred?"

"No, Doc. Not now."

"Don't get smart. How many?" He held up two thick fingers.

"Eighty-seven." Nathaniel would have reached for the whiskey again, but Coco shoved it aside.

"He's not drinking any more on top of the pill I gave him."

"Women think they know every damn thing." But Dutch sent her a look, reassuring her that their charge would be all right. "Bed's what you need now. A hot soak and cool sheets. Want I should carry you?"

"Hell, no." That was one humiliation he could do without. He took Coco's hand, kissed it. "Thanks, darling. I'd do it all again if I knew you'd be my nurse." He looked back at Holt. "I could use a ride home."

"Nonsense." Coco disposed of that idea instantly. "You'll stay here, where we can look after you. You may very well have a concussion, so we'll take shifts waking you up through the night to be sure you don't slip into a coma."

"Wives' tales," Dutch grunted, but nodded at her behind Nathaniel's back.

"I'll turn down the bed in the rose guest room," Amanda stated. "C.C., why don't you run our hero a nice hot bath? Lilah, bring that ice along."

He didn't have the energy to fight the lot of them, so he sat back as Lilah walked over and touched her lips gently to his. "Come on, tough guy."

Sloan moved over to help him to his feet. "Two of them, huh? Puny guys?"

"Bigger than you, pal." He was floating just a little as he hobbled up the stairs between Sloan and Max.

"Let's get those pants off," Lilah said, when they'd eased him down to sit on the side of the bed.

He still had the wit to arch a brow at her. "You never said that when it counted. No offense," he added to Max.

"None taken." With a chuckle, Max bent down to pull off Nathaniel's shoes. He knew what it was to be nursed back to health by the Calhoun women, and he figured that once Nathaniel got past the worst of the pain, he'd realize he'd landed in heaven. "Need some help getting in the tub?"

"I can handle it, thanks."

"Give a call if you run into trouble." Sloan held the door open, waiting until the room cleared. "And, when you're more up to it, I'd like the whole story."

Alone, Nathaniel managed to ease himself into the hot water. The first flash of agony passed, transforming gradually into something closer to comfort. By the time he'd climbed out again, the worst seemed to be over.

Until he looked in the mirror.

There was a bandage under his left eye, another on his temple. His right eye looked like a rotting tomato. That left the bruises, the swollen lip, the nasty scrape on his jaw. All in all, he thought, he looked like hell.

With a towel slung around his waist, he stepped back into the bedroom, just as Megan came in the hallway door.

"I'm sorry." She pressed her lips together to keep herself from saying all manner of foolish things. "Amanda thought you might want another pillow, some more towels."

"Thanks." He made it to the bed and lay back with a sigh of relief.

Grateful for something practical to do, she hurried to the bed, plumped and arranged pillows for him, smoothed the sheets. "Is there anything I can get you? More ice? Some soup?"

"No, this is fine."

"Please, I want to help. I need to help." She couldn't bear it any longer, and she laid a hand to his cheek. "They hurt you. I'm so sorry they hurt you."

"Just bruises."

"Damn it, don't be so stupid—not when I'm looking right at you, not when I can see what they did." She pulled back on the need to rage and looked helplessly into his eyes. "I know you're angry with me, but can't you let me do something?"

"Maybe you'd better sit down." When she did, he took her hand in his. He needed the contact every bit as much as she did. "You've been crying."

"A little." She looked down at his damaged knuckles. "I felt so helpless downstairs, seeing you like this. You let Coco tend you, and you wouldn't even look at me." Drenched with emotion, her eyes came back to his. "I don't want to lose you, Nathaniel. It's only that I've just found you, and I don't want to make another mistake."

"It always comes back to him, doesn't it?"

"No, no. It comes back to me."

"What he did to you," Nathaniel corrected grimly.

"All right, yes." She brought his hand to her cheek. "Please, don't walk away from me. I don't have all the answers yet, but I know when Holt said you'd been hurt—my heart just stopped. I've never been so frightened. You mean so much to me, Nathaniel. Let me just take care of you until you're better."

"Well." He was softening, and he reached out to stroke her hair. "Maybe Dumont did me a favor this time."

"What do you mean?"

He shook his head. Maybe his brain was a little addled by the drug and the pain. He hadn't meant to tell her, at least not yet. But he thought she had the right to know.

"The two guys that jumped me tonight. Dumont hired them."

Every ounce of color faded from her cheeks. "What are you saying? You're saying that Baxter paid them to attack you? To—"

"Rough me up, that's all. I'd say he was sore about me tossing him in the water and was looking for some payback." He shifted, winced. "He'd have been smarter to put his money on a couple of pros. These two were real amateurs."

"*Baxter* did this." Megan's vision hazed. She shut her eyes until she was sure it had cleared again. "My fault."

"Like hell. None of it's been yours, not from the start. He did what he did to you, Suzanna, the kids. Chickenhearted bastard couldn't even fight for himself. Hey." He tugged on her hair. "I won, remember. He didn't get what he'd paid for."

"Do you think that matters?"

"It does to me. If you want to do something for me, Megan, really want to do something for me, you'll push him right out of your head."

"He's Kevin's father," she whispered. "It makes me sick to think it."

"He's nothing. Lie down here with me, will you?"

Because she could see that he was fighting off the drug, she did as he asked. Gently she shifted his head so that it rested on her breast.

"Sleep for a while," she murmured. "We won't think of it now. We won't think of anything."

He sighed, let himself drift. "I love you, Megan."

"I know." She stroked his hair and lay wakeful while he slept.

Neither of them saw the little boy with shattered eyes and pale cheeks in the open doorway.

Nathaniel woke to the rhythm of his own pain. There was a bass drum in his head, pounding low in the skull, with a few more enthusiastic riffs at the left temple. It was more of a snare along his ribs, a solid rat-a-tat that promised to remain steady and persistent. His shoulder sang along in a droning hum.

Experimentally, he sat up. Stiff as a week-old corpse, he thought in disgust. With slow, awkward movements, he eased out of the bed. Except for the pounding in his head, it was clear. Maybe too clear, he thought with a wince as he limped into the shower. His one pleasure was that he knew his two unexpected visitors would be suffering more than he was at the moment.

Even the soft needles of spray brought a bright bloom of pain to the worst of his bruises. Teeth clenched, he waited out the pain until it mellowed to discomfort.

He'd live.

Naked and dripping, he stepped out of the shower, then filled the basin with icy water. Taking one bracing breath, he lowered his face into it until the shocking cold brought on a blessed numbness.

Steadier, he went back into the bedroom, where fresh clothes had been left folded on a chair. With a great deal of swearing, he managed to dress. He was thinking of coffee, aspirin and a full plate when the door creaked open.

"You shouldn't be up." Coco, a tray balanced in both hands, clucked her tongue. "Now get that shirt off and get back into bed."

"Darling, I've been waiting all my life to hear you say that."

"You must be feeling a little better," Coco said, and laughed, then set the tray on the bedside table and fluffed at her hair. It occurred to Nathaniel as he followed the familiar gesture that her hair hadn't changed color in a couple weeks, maybe more. Must be some mood she was in, he decided.

"I'll do."

"Poor dear." She lifted a hand to gently touch the bruises on his face. He looked even worse this morning, but she didn't have the heart to say so. "At least sit down and eat."

"You read my mind." More than willing, he eased himself into a chair. "I appreciate the service."

"It's the least we can do." Coco fit the legs of the bedside table over the chair and unfolded his napkin. Nathaniel thought she would have tucked it into his collar if he hadn't taken it himself. "Megan told me what happened. That Baxter hired those—those thugs. I've a mind to go to Boston myself and deal with that man."

The fierce look in her eyes warmed Nathaniel's heart. She was like some fiery Celtic goddess. "Sugar, he wouldn't have a chance against you." He sampled his eggs, closed his eyes on the simple pleasure of hot, delicious food. "We'll let it go, darling."

"Let it go! You can't. You have to contact the police. Of course, I'd prefer if all you boys got together and took a trip down to blacken that man's eyes..." She pressed a hand to her heart as the image caused it to beat fast. "But," she continued with some regret, "the proper thing to do is contact the authorities and have them handle it."

"No cops." He scooped up delicately fried hash-brown potatoes. "Dumont's going to suffer a lot more, not knowing what I'll do or when I'll do it."

"Well..." Considering that, Coco began to smile. "I suppose he would. Like waiting for the other shoe to drop."

"Yeah. And bringing the police in would make it tough for Megan and the boy."

"You're right, of course." Gently she brushed a hand over his hair. "I'm so glad they have you."

"I wish she felt the same way."

"She does. She's just afraid. Megan's had so much to handle in her life. And you—well, Nathaniel, you're a man who'd leave any woman a bit addled."

"You think so, huh?"

"I know so. Are you having much pain this morning, dear? You can take another pill."

"I'll settle for aspirin."

"I thought you might." Coco took a bottle out of her apron pocket. "Take these with your juice."

"Yes, ma'am." He obeyed, then went back to his eggs. "So, you've seen Megan this morning?"

"It was nearly dawn before I could convince her to leave you and get some sleep."

That information went down even better than the food. "Yeah?"

"And the way she looked at you…" Coco patted his hand. "Well, a woman knows these things. Especially when she's in love herself." A becoming blush bloomed on her cheeks. "I suppose you know that Niels and I—that we're…involved."

He made some sound. He didn't want the image in his brain of them together in the dark. Coco and Dutch were as close to parents as he'd ever had, and no child, even at thirty-three, wanted to think about that side of a parental relationship.

"These past few weeks have been wonderful. I had a lovely marriage, and there are memories I've cherished and will cherish all of my life. And over the years, I've had some nice, compatible relationships. But with Niels…" The dreamy look came into her eyes. "He makes me feel young and vital, and almost delicate. It's not just the sex," she added, and had Nathaniel wincing.

"Aw, jeez, Coco." He took a sip of coffee, as he was rapidly losing his appetite. "I don't want to know about that."

She chuckled, adoring him. "I know how close you are to Niels."

"Well, sure." He was beginning to feel trapped in the chair, barred by the tray. "We sailed together a long time, and he's…"

"Like a father to you," she said gently. "I know. I just wanted you to know I love him, too. We're going to be married."

"What?" His fork clattered against china. "*Married?* You and the Dutchman?"

"Yes." Nervous now, because she couldn't tell whether his expression was horrified or simply shocked, Coco fiddled with the jet beads at her throat. "I hope you don't mind."

"Mind?" His brain had gone blank. Now it began to fill again—the restless movements of her hands, the tone of her voice, the anxious look in her eyes. Nathaniel shifted the table away from his chair and rose. "Imagine a classy woman like you falling for that old tar. Are you sure he hadn't been slipping something into your soup?"

Relieved, she smiled. "If he has, I like it. Do we have your blessing?"

He took her hands, looked down at them. "You know, for nearly as far back as I can remember, I wanted you to be my mother."

"Oh." Her eyes filled, overflowed. "Nathaniel."

"Now I guess you will be." His gaze lifted to hers again before he kissed her, one cheek, the other, then her lips. "He'd better be good to you, or he'll answer to me."

"I'm so happy." Coco sank, weeping, into his arms. "I'm so very happy, Nate. I didn't even see it coming in the cards." Her breath hitched as she pressed her wet face to his throat. "Or the tea leaves, even the crystal. It just happened."

"The best things usually do."

"I want you to be happy." Drawing back, she fumbled in her pocket for one of her lace-trimmed hankies. "I want you to believe in what you have with Megan, and not let it slip away. She needs you, Nate. So does Kevin."

"That's what I told her." He smiled a little as he took the hankie and dried Coco's tears himself. "I don't guess she was ready to hear it."

"You just keep saying it." Her voice became firm. "Keep right on saying it until she is." And if Megan needed an extra push, Coco thought, she'd be happy to supply it herself. "Now, then." She smoothed down her hair, her slacks. "I have a million things to do. I want you to rest, so you'll be up to the picnic and the fireworks."

"I feel okay."

"You feel as if you've been run over by a truck." She marched to the bed, busying herself with smoothing sheets and fluffing pillows. "You can lie down for another hour or two, or you can sit out on the terrace in the sun. It's a lovely day, and we can fix you up a nice chaise. When Megan wakes up, I'll have her come give you a rubdown."

"Now that sounds promising. I'll take the sun." He started toward the terrace doors, but then he heard footsteps hurrying down the hall.

Megan rushed in. "I can't find Kevin," she blurted out. "No one's seen him all morning."

Chapter 11

She was pale as ice, and struggling to be calm. The idea of her little boy running away was so absurd that she continued to tell herself it was a mistake, a prank. Maybe a dream.

"No one's seen him," she repeated, bracing a hand on the doorknob to stay upright. "Some—some of his clothes are gone, and his knapsack."

"Call Suzanna," Nathaniel said quickly. "He's probably with Alex and Jenny."

"No." She shook her head slowly, side to side. Her body felt like glass, as though it would shatter if she moved too quickly. "They're here. They're all here. They haven't seen him. I was sleeping." She said each word deliberately, as if she were having trouble understanding her own voice. "I slept late, then I checked his room, like I always do. He wasn't there, but I thought he'd be downstairs, or outside. But when I went down, Alex was looking for him." The fear began to claw at her, little cat feet up and down her spine. "We hunted around, then I came back up. That's when I saw that some of his things…some of his things…"

"All right, dear, now don't you worry." Coco hurried over to slip a supporting arm around Megan's waist. "I'm sure he's just playing a game. There are so many places to hide in the house, on the grounds."

"He was so excited about today. It's all he could talk about. He's supposed to be playing Revolutionary War with Alex and Jenny. He—he was going to be Daniel Boone."

"We'll find him," Nathaniel told her.

"Of course we will." Gently Coco began to ease Megan along. "We'll organize a search party. Won't he be excited when he finds out?"

An hour later, they were spread throughout the house, searching corners and hidey-holes, retracing and backtracking. Megan kept a steel grip on her composure and covered every inch, starting in the tower and working her way down.

He had to be here, she reassured herself. Of course, she would find him any minute. It didn't make sense otherwise.

Bubbles of hysteria rose in her throat and had to be choked down.

He was just playing a game. He'd gone exploring. He loved the house so much. He'd drawn dozens of pictures of it to send back to Oklahoma so that everyone could see that he lived in a castle.

She would find him behind the next door she opened.

Megan told herself that, repeating it like a litany, as she worked her way from room to room.

She ran into Suzanna in one of the snaking hallways. She felt cold, so cold, though the sun beat hot against the windows. "He doesn't answer me," she said faintly. "I keep calling him, but he doesn't answer."

"It's such a big house." Suzanna took Megan's hands, gripped hard. "Once when we were kids we played hide-and-seek and didn't find Lilah for three hours. She'd crawled into a cabinet on the third floor and had a nap."

"Suzanna." Megan pressed her lips together. She had to face it, and quickly. "His two favorite shirts are missing, and both pairs of his sneakers. His baseball caps. The money he'd been saving in his jar is gone. He's not in the house. He's run away."

"You need to sit down."

"No, I—I need to do something. Call the police. Oh, God—" Breaking, Megan pressed her hands to her face. "Anything could have happened to him. He's just a little boy. I don't even know how long he's been gone. I don't even know." Her eyes, swimming with fear, locked on Suzanna's. "Did you ask Alex, Jenny? Maybe he said something to them. Maybe—"

"Of course I asked them, Megan," Suzanna said gently. "Kevin didn't say anything to them about leaving."

"Where would he go? Why? Back to Oklahoma," she said on a wild, hopeful thought. "Maybe he's trying to get back to Oklahoma. Maybe he's been unhappy, just pretending to like it here."

"He's been happy. But we'll check it out. Come on, let's go down."

"Been over every bit of this section," Dutch told Nathaniel. "The pantries, the storerooms, even the meat locker. Trent and Sloan are going over the renovation areas, and Max and Holt are beating the bushes all over the grounds."

There was worry in his eyes, but he was brewing a pot of fresh coffee with steady hands.

"Seems to me if the kid was just playing and heard all this shouting and calling, he'd come out to see what the excitement was all about."

"We've been over the house twice." Nathaniel stared grimly out the window. "Amanda and Lilah have combed every inch of The Retreat. He's not in here."

"Don't make a lick of sense to me. Kevin's been happy as a clam. He's in here every blessed day, getting under my feet and begging for sea stories."

"Something's got him running." There was a prickle at the back of his neck. Rubbing it absently, Nathaniel looked out toward the cliffs. "Why does a kid run? Because he's scared, or he's hurt, or he's unhappy."

"That boy ain't none of those things," Dutch said staunchly.

"I wouldn't have thought so." Nathaniel had been all three at that age, and he believed he would have recognized the signs. There had been times he ran, too. But he'd had nowhere to go.

The tickle at the back of his neck persisted. Again, he found his gaze wandering toward the cliffs. "I've got a feeling," he said almost to himself.

"What?"

"No, just a feeling." The prickle was in his gut now. "I'm going to check it out."

It was as though he were being pulled to the cliffs. Nathaniel didn't fight it, though the rocky ground jarred the pain back into his bones and the steep climb stole his breath. With one hand pressed to his aching ribs, he continued, his gaze sweeping the rocks and the high wild grass.

It was, he knew, a place that would draw a child. It had drawn him as a boy. And as a man.

The sun was high and white, the sea sapphire blue, then frothy where it lashed and foamed on the rocks. Beautiful and deadly. He thought of a young boy stumbling along the path, missing a step, slipping. The nausea churned so violently he had to stop and choke it back.

Nothing had happened to Kevin, he assured himself. He wouldn't let anything happen to Kevin.

He turned, started to climb higher, calling the boy's name as he searched.

It was the bird that caught his eye. A pure white gull, graceful as a dancer, swooped over the grass and rock, circled back with a musical call that was almost human, eerily feminine. He stood, staring at it. For one sunstruck second, Nathaniel would have sworn the gull's eyes were green, green as emeralds.

It glided down, perched on the ledge below and looked up, as if waiting for him.

Nathaniel found himself clambering down, ignoring the jolts to his abused body. The thunder of the surf seemed to fill his head. He thought he smelled a woman, sweet, soft, soothing, but then it was only the sea.

The bird wheeled away, skyward, joined its mate—another gull, blindingly white. For a moment they circled, calling together in something like joy. Then they winged out to sea.

Wheezing a bit, Nathaniel gained the ledge, and saw the shallow crevice in the rock where the boy was huddled.

His first instinct was to scoop the child up, hold him. But he checked it. He wasn't altogether certain he wasn't the reason Kevin had run.

Instead, he sat down on the ledge and spoke quietly. "Nice view from here."

Kevin kept his face pressed to his knees. "I'm going back to Oklahoma." It was an attempt at defiance that merely sounded weary. "I can take a bus."

"I guess so. You'd see a lot of the country that way. But I thought you liked it here."

His answer was a shrug. "It's okay."

"Somebody give you a hard time, mate?"

"No."

"Did you have a fight with Alex?"

"No, it's nothing like that. I'm just going back to Oklahoma. It was too late to take the bus last night, so I came up here to wait. I guess maybe I fell asleep." He hunched his shoulder, kept his face averted. "You can't make me go back."

"Well, I'm bigger than you, so I could." He said it gently, touched a hand to Kevin's hair. But the boy jerked away. "I'd rather not make you do anything until I understand what's on your mind."

He let some time pass, watching the sea, listening to the wind, until he sensed Kevin relaxing a little beside him.

"Your mother's kind of worried about you. Everybody else is, too. Maybe you ought to go back and tell them goodbye before you leave."

"She won't let me go."

"She loves you a lot."

"She should never have had me." There was bitterness in the words, words that were much too sharp for a little boy.

"That's a stupid thing to say. I figure you've got a right to get mad if you want but there's not much point in just being stupid."

Kevin's head shot up. His face was streaked with tears and dirt, and it sliced through Nathaniel's heart.

"If she hadn't had me, things would be different. She always pretends it doesn't matter. But I know."

"What do you know?"

"I'm not a baby anymore. I know what he did. He made her pregnant, then he went away. He went away, and he never cared. He went away and married Suzanna, and then he left her, too. And Alex and Jenny. That's how come I'm their brother."

Those were stormy seas, Nathaniel thought, that needed to be navigated with care. The boy's eyes, hurt and angry, latched onto his.

"Your mother's the one who has to explain that to you, Kevin."

"She told me that sometimes people can't get married and be together, even when they have kids. But he didn't want me. He never wanted me, and I hate him."

"I'm not going to argue with you about that," Nathaniel said carefully. "But your mother loves you, and that counts for a lot more. If you take off, it's going to hurt her, bad."

Kevin's lips trembled. "She could have you if I was gone. You'd stay with her if it wasn't for me."

"I'm afraid I'm not following you, Kevin."

"He—he had you beaten up." Kevin's voice hitched as he fought to get the words out. "I heard last night. I heard you and Mom, and she said it was her fault, but it's mine. 'Cause he's my father and he did it and now you hate me, too, and you'll go away."

"Little jerk." On a flood of emotion, Nathaniel yanked the boy to his knees and shook him. "You pulled this stunt because I got a few bruises? Do I look like I can't take care of myself? Those other two wimps had to crawl away."

"Really?" Kevin sniffed and rubbed at his eyes. "But still—"

"Still, hell. You didn't have anything to do with it, and I ought to shake you until your teeth fall out for worrying us all this way."

"He's my father," Kevin said, tilting his chin up. "So that means—"

"That means nothing. My father was a drunk who used to kick my butt for the pleasure of it, six days out of seven. Does that make me like him?"

"No." Tears began to roll more freely now. "But I thought you wouldn't like me anymore, and you'd never stay and be my father now, like Holt is with Alex and Jenny."

Nathaniel's hands gentled as he drew the sobbing boy into his arms. "You thought wrong." He rubbed his lips over Kevin's hair, absorbed the jolt of love. "I ought to hang you from the yardarm, sailor."

"What's that?"

"I'll show you later." He tightened his grip. "Did you stop and think that I might be hoping you'd be my son? That I want you and your mom to be mine?"

"Honest?" Kevin's voice was muffled against Nathaniel's chest.

"Do you figure I've been training you to take the helm just to have you walk off?"

"I don't know. I guess not."

"I've been looking for you, Kevin, longer than just today."

With a sigh, Kevin let his head rest in the curve of Nathaniel's shoulder. "I was awful scared. But then the bird came."

"Bird?" Remembering, Nathaniel glanced around. But the rocks were empty.

"Then I wasn't so scared. She stayed all night. She was there whenever I woke up. She flew away with the other one, but then you came. Is Mom mad at me?"

"Probably."

Kevin sighed again—a long-suffering sound that made Nathaniel smile. "I guess I'm in trouble."

"Well, let's get your things and go back and face the music."

Kevin picked up his knapsack and put his hand trustingly in Nathaniel's. "Does it hurt?" he asked, studying Nathaniel's face.

"You bet."

"Later, can I see all your bruises?"

"Sure. I've got some beauts."

Nathaniel felt every one of them as they climbed back up to the cliff path and started down the rocky slope toward home. It was worth it, worth every jar and wince, to see the look on Megan's face.

"Kevin!" She flew across the lawn, hair blowing, cheeks tracked with tears.

"Go on," Nathaniel murmured to the boy. "She'll want to hug you first."

With a nod, Kevin dropped his knapsack and raced into his mother's arms.

"Oh, Kevin..." She couldn't hold him tight enough, even kneeling on the grass, pressing him close, rocking and weeping in terrible relief.

"Where'd you find him?" Trent asked Nathaniel quietly.

"Up on the cliffs, holed up in a crevice in the rocks."

"Good God." C.C. shuddered. "Did he spend the night up there?"

"Looked that way. I had this feeling, I can't explain it. And there he was."

"A feeling?" Trent exchanged a look with his wife. "Remind me to tell you sometime how I found Fred when he was a puppy."

Max gave Nathaniel a pat on the back. "I'll go call the police, let them know we've found him."

"He'll be hungry." Coco swallowed fresh tears and burrowed closer to Dutch. "We'll go fix him something to eat."

"You bring 'em in when she's finished slobbering over him—" Dutch camouflaged the break in his voice with a cough. "Women. Always making a fuss."

"Come on, let's go in." Suzanna tugged on Alex and Jenny's hands.

"But I want to ask if he saw the ghosts," Alex complained.

"Later." Holt solved the problem by hoisting Alex onto his shoulders.

With a shuddering sigh, Megan drew back, ran her hands over Kevin's face. "You're all right? You're not hurt?"

"Nuh-uh." It embarrassed him that he'd cried in front of his brother and sister. After all, he was nearly nine. "I'm okay."

"Don't you *ever* do that again." The swift change from weeping mother to fierce parent had Nathaniel's brows rising. "You had us all worried sick, young man. We've been looking for you for hours, even Aunt Colleen. We've called the police."

"I'm sorry." But the thrill of knowing the police had been alerted overpowered the guilt.

"Sorry isn't enough, Kevin Michael O'Riley."

Kevin's gaze hit the ground. It was big-time trouble when she used all his names. "I won't ever do it again. I promise."

"You had no business doing it this time. I'm supposed to be able to trust you, and now— Oh." On another hitching sob, she pressed his head to her breast. "I was so scared, baby. I love you so much. Where were you going?"

"I don't know. Maybe Grandma's."

"Grandma's." She sat back on her heels and sighed. "Don't you like it here?"

"I like it best of anything."

"Then why did you run away, Kevin? Are you mad at me?"

He shook his head, then dropped his chin on his chest. "I thought you and Nate were mad at me because he got beaten up. But Nate says it's not my fault and you're not mad. He says it doesn't matter about *him*. You're not mad at me, are you?"

Her horrified eyes flew to Nate's, held there as she drew Kevin close again. "Oh, no, baby, I'm not. No one is." She looked at her son again, cupping his face in her hands. "Remember when I told you that sometimes people can't be together? I should explain that sometimes they shouldn't be together. That's the way it was with me and—" She couldn't refer to him as Kevin's father. "With me and Baxter."

"But I was an accident."

"Oh, no." She smiled then, kissed his cheeks. "An accident's something you wish hadn't happened. You were a gift. The best one I ever had in my life. If you ever think I don't want you again, I guess I'll have to stuff you into a box and tie it up with a bow so you'll get the point."

He giggled. "I'm sorry."

"Me too. Now let's go get you cleaned up." She rose, gripped her son's hand in hers and looked at Nathaniel. "Thank you."

In the way of children, Kevin bounced back from his night on the cliffs and threw himself into the holiday. He was, for the moment, a hero, desperately impressing his siblings with his tales of the dark and the sea and a white bird with green eyes.

In keeping with the family gathering, all the dogs attended, so Sadie and Fred raced with their puppies and the children over the rolling lawn. Babies napped in playpens or rocked in swings or charmed their way into willing arms. A few hotel guests wandered over from their own feast provided by The Retreat, drawn by the laughter and raised voices.

Nathaniel passed, reluctantly, on the impromptu softball game, figuring one slide into third would have him down for the count. Instead, he designated himself umpire and had the pleasure of arguing with every batter he called out.

"Are you blind or just stupid?" C.C. tossed down her bat in disgust. "A sock in the eye's no excuse for missing that call. That ball was outside a half a mile."

Nathaniel clamped his cigar in his teeth. "Not from where I'm standing, sugar."

She slapped her hands on her hips. "Then you're standing in the wrong spot." Jenny took the opportunity to attempt a cartwheel over home plate, and earned some applause from the infield.

"C.C., you've got one of the best-looking strike zones I've ever had the pleasure of seeing. And that was strike three. You're out."

"If you weren't already black-and-blue…" She swallowed a laugh, and sneered instead. "You're up, Lilah."

"Already?" In a lazy gesture, Lilah brushed her hair away from her face and stepped into the box.

From her position at short, Megan glanced at her second baseman. "She won't run even if she connects."

Suzanna sighed, shook her head. "She won't have to. Just watch."

Lilah skimmed a hand down her hip, cast a sultry look back at Nathaniel, then faced the pitcher. Sloan went through an elaborate windup that had the children cheering. Lilah took the first strike with the bat still on her shoulder. Yawned.

"We keeping you up?" Nathaniel asked her.

"I like to wait for my pitch."

Apparently the second one wasn't the one she was waiting for. She let it breeze by, and earned catcalls from the opposing team.

She stepped out of the box, stretched, smiled at Sloan. "Okay, big guy," she said as she took her stance again. She cracked the low curveball and sent it soaring for a home run. Amid the cheers, she turned and handed her bat to Nathaniel. "I always recognize the right pitch," she told him, and sauntered around the bases.

When the game broke for the feast, Nathaniel eased down beside Megan. "You've got a pretty good arm there, sugar."

"I coached Kevin's Little League team back in Oklahoma." Her gaze wandered to her son, as it had dozens of times during the afternoon. "He doesn't seem any the worse for wear, does he?"

"Nope. How about you?"

"The bats in my stomach have mellowed out to butterflies." She pressed a hand to them now, lowered her voice. "I never knew he thought about Baxter. About…any of it. I should have."

"A boy's got to have some secrets, even from his mother."

"I suppose." It was too beautiful a day, she decided, too precious a day, to waste on worry. "Whatever you said to him up there, however you said it, was exactly right. It means a lot to me." She looked over at him. "You mean a lot to me."

Nathaniel sipped his beer, studied her. "You're working up to something, Meg. Why don't you just say it?"

"All right. After you left yesterday, I spent a lot of time thinking. About how I'd feel if you didn't come back. I knew there'd be a hole in my life. Maybe I'd be able to fill it again, part of the way, but something would always be missing. When I asked myself what that would be, I kept coming up with the same answer. No matter how many ways I looked at it or juggled it around, the answer never changed."

"So what's the answer, Meg?"

"You, Nathaniel." She leaned over and kissed him. "Just you."

Later, when the sky was dark and the moon floated over the water, she watched the fireworks explode. Color bloomed into color. Waterfalls of glowing sparks rained from sky to water in a celebration of freedom, new beginnings and, Megan thought, hope.

It was a dazzling display that had the children staring upward, wide-eyed and openmouthed. The echoing booms shivered the air until, with a machine-gun crescendo, color and light spewed high in the finale. For a heart-pounding interlude, the sky was bright with golds and reds, blues and blinding whites, circles and spirals, cascades and towers, that shattered into individual stars over the sea.

Long after it was over, the dregs of the party cleared away, the children tucked into bed, she felt the power of the celebration running through her blood. In her own room, she brushed her hair until it flowed over her shoulders. Anticipation vibrating inside her, she belted her borrowed robe loosely at her waist. Quietly she slipped out the terrace doors and walked to Nathaniel's room.

It hadn't taken much pressure to persuade him to stay another night. He'd been tired and aching, and he hadn't relished even the short drive home. But the long soak in the tub hadn't relaxed him, as he hoped. He was still filled with restless urges, and with flashing images of Megan's face, lit with the glow of rockets.

Then he stepped into the bedroom and saw her.

She wore a silky robe of deep blue that flowed down her body and clung to her curves. Her hair glinted, golden fire, and her eyes were as dark and mysterious as sapphires.

"I thought you could use a rubdown." She smiled hesitantly. "I've had a lot of experience loosening stiff muscles. With horses, anyway."

He was almost afraid to breathe. "Where did you get that?"

"Oh." Self-consciously she ran a hand down the robe. "I borrowed it from Lilah. I thought you'd like it better than terry cloth." When he said nothing, her nerve began to slip. "If you'd rather I go, I understand. I don't expect that you'd feel well enough to— We don't have to make love, Nathaniel. I just want to help."

"I don't want you to go."

Her smile bloomed again. "Why don't you lie down, then? I'll start on your back. Really, I'm good at this." She laughed a little. "The horses loved me."

He crossed to the bed, touched her hair, her cheek. "Did you wear silk robes to work the stock?"

"Always." She eased him down. "Roll onto your stomach," she

said briskly. Pleased with the task, she poured liniment into her hands, then rubbed her palms together to warm it. Carefully, so that the movement of the mattress didn't jar him, she knelt over him. "Tell me if I hurt you."

She started on his shoulders, gently over the bruises, more firmly over knotted muscles. He had a warrior's body, she thought, tough and tight, and carrying all the marks of battle.

"You overdid it today."

He only grunted, closing his eyes and letting his body reap the pleasure of her stroking hands. He felt the brush of silk against his skin when she shifted. Drifting through the sharp scent of liniment was her subtle perfume, another balm to the senses.

The aches began to fade, then shifted into a deeper, more primal pain that coursed smoothly through his blood when she lowered her lips to his shoulder.

"Better?" she murmured.

"No. You're killing me. Don't stop."

Her laugh was low and soft as she eased the towel from his hips, and pressed competent fingers low on his spine. "I'm here to make you feel better, Nathaniel. You have to relax for me to do this right."

"You're doing just fine." He moaned as her hands moved lower, circling, kneading. Then her lips, skimming, whisper-soft.

"You have such a beautiful body." Her own breathing grew heavy as she stroked and explored. "I love looking at it, touching it." Slowly she took her lips up his spine, over his shoulder again, to nuzzle at his ear. "Turn over," she whispered. "I'll do the rest."

Her lips were there to meet his when he shifted, to linger, to heat. But when he reached up, groaning, to cup her breasts, she drew back.

"Wait." Though her hands trembled, she freshened the liniment. With her eyes on his, she spread her fingers over his chest. "They put marks on you," she murmured.

"I put more on them."

"Nathaniel the dragon-slayer. Lie still," she whispered, and bent close to kiss the scrapes and bruises on his face. "I'll make it all go away."

His heart was pounding. She could feel it rocket against her palm. In the lamplight, his eyes were dark as smoke. The robe pooled around her knees when she straddled him. She massaged his shoulders, his arms, his hands, kissing the scraped knuckles, laving them with her tongue.

The air was like syrup, thick and sweet. It caught in his lungs with each labored breath. No other woman had ever made him feel helpless, drained and sated, all at once.

"Megan, I need to touch you."

Watching him, she reached for the belt of the robe, loosened it. In one fluid movement, the silk slid from her shoulders. Beneath she wore a short slip of the same color and texture. As he reached up, one thin strap spilled off her shoulder.

She closed her eyes, let her head fall back, as his hands stroked over the silk, then beneath. The colors were back, all those flashing, dazzling lights that had erupted in the sky. Stars wheeled inside her head, beautifully hot. Craving more, she rose over him, took him into her with a delicious slowness that had them both gasping.

She shuddered when he arched up, gripping her hips in his hands. Now the colors seemed to shoot into her blood, white-hot, and her skin grew damp and slick. Suddenly greedy, she swooped down, devouring his lips, fingers clutching the bruised flesh she'd sought to soothe.

"Let me." She moaned and pressed his hands against her breasts. "Let me."

With a wildness that staggered him, she drove him hard, riding him like lightning. He called out her name as his vision dimmed, as the frantic need convulsed like pain inside him. Release was like a whiplash that stung with velvet.

She tightened around him like a fist and shattered him.

Weak as water, she flowed down, rested her head on his chest. "Did I hurt you?"

He couldn't find the strength to wrap his arms around her and let them lie limp on the bed. "I can't feel anything but you."

"Nathaniel." She lifted her head to press a kiss to his thundering heart. "There's something I forgot to tell you yesterday."

"Hmm… What's that?"

"I love you, too." She watched his eyes open, saw the swirl of emotion darken them.

"That's good." His arms, no longer weak, circled her, cradled her.

"I don't know if it's enough, but—"

He turned his lips to hers to quiet her. "Don't mess it up. 'For love's sake only,' Megan. That's enough for tonight." He kissed her again. "Stay with me."

"Yes."

Chapter 12

Fireworks were one thing, but when the Calhouns put their heads together planning Coco's engagement party, there promised to be plenty of skyrockets.

Everything from a masked ball to a moonlight cruise had been considered, with the final vote going to dinner and dancing under the stars. With only a week to complete arrangements, assignments were handed out.

Megan squeezed time out of each day to polish silver, wash crystal and inventory linens.

"All this fuss." Colleen thumped her way to the closet where Megan was counting napkins. "When a woman her age straps herself down to a man, she should have the sense to do it quietly."

Megan lost count and patiently began again. "Don't you like parties, Aunt Colleen?"

"When there's a reason for them. Never considered putting yourself under a man's thumb reason to celebrate."

"Coco's not doing that. Dutch adores her."

"Humph. Time will tell. Once a man's got a ring on your finger, he doesn't have to be so sweet and obliging." Her crafty eyes studied Megan's face. "Isn't that why you're putting off that big-shouldered sailor? Afraid of what happens after the 'I-dos'?"

"Of course not." Megan laid a stack of linens aside before she lost count again. "And we're talking about Coco and Dutch, not me. She deserves to be happy."

"Not everybody gets what they deserve," Colleen shot back. "You'd know that well, wouldn't you?"

Exasperated, Megan whirled around. "I don't know why you're trying to spoil this. Coco's happy, I'm happy. I'm doing my best to make Nathaniel happy."

"I don't see you out buying any orange blossoms for yourself, girl."

"Marriage isn't the answer for everyone. It wasn't for you."

"No, I'm too smart to fall into that trap. Maybe you're like me. Men come and go. Maybe the right one goes with the rest, but we get by, don't we? Because we know what they're like, deep down." Colleen eased closer, her dark eyes fixed on Megan's face. "We've known the worst of them. The selfishness, the cruelty, the lack of honor and ethics. Maybe one steps into our lives for a moment, one who seems different. But we're too wise, too careful, to take that shaky step. If we live our lives alone, at least we know no man will ever have the power to hurt us."

"I'm not alone," Megan said in an unsteady voice.

"No, you have a son. One day he'll be grown, and if you've done a good job, he'll leave your nest and fly off to make his own."

Colleen shook her head, and for one moment she looked so unbearably sad that Megan reached out. But the old woman held herself stiff, her head high.

"You'll have the satisfaction of knowing you escaped the trap of marriage, just as I did. Do you think no one ever asked me? There was one," Colleen went on, before Megan could speak. "One who nearly lulled me in before I remembered, before I turned him away, before I risked the hell my mother had known."

Colleen's mouth thinned at the memory. "He tried to break her in every way, with his rules, his money, his need to own. In the end, he killed her, then he slowly, slowly, went mad. But not with guilt. What ate at him, I think, was the loss of something he'd never been able to fully own. That was why he rid the house of every piece of her, and locked himself in his own private purgatory."

"I'm sorry," Megan murmured. "I'm so sorry."

"For me? I'm old, and long past the time to grieve. I learned from my experience, as you learned from yours. Not to trust, never to risk. Let Coco have her orange blossoms, we have our freedom."

She walked away stiffly, leaving Megan to flounder in a sea of emotion.

Colleen was wrong, she told herself, and began to fuss with napkins again. She wasn't cold and aloof and blocked off from love. Just days ago she'd declared her love. She wasn't letting Baxter's shadow darken what she had with Nathaniel.

Oh, but she was. Wearily she leaned against the doorjamb. She was, and she wasn't sure she could change it. Love and lovemaking didn't equal commitment. No one knew that better than she. She had loved Baxter fully, vitally. And that was the shadow. Even knowing that what she felt for Nathaniel was fuller, richer, and much, much truer, she couldn't dispel that doubt.

She would have to think it through, calmly, as soon as she had time. The answer was always there, she assured herself, if you looked for it long enough, carefully enough. All she had to do was process the data.

She tossed down her neatly counted napkins in disgust. What kind of woman was she? she wondered. She was trying to turn emotions into equations, as if they were some sort of code she had to decipher before she could know her own heart.

That was going to stop. She was going to stop. If she couldn't look into her own heart, it was time to…

Her thoughts trailed off, circled back, swooping down on one errant idea like a hawk on a rabbit.

Oh, God, a code. Leaving the linens in disarray, she flew down the hall to her own bedroom.

Fergus's book was where she'd left it, lying neatly on the corner of her desk. She snatched it up and began flipping frantically through pages.

It didn't have to be stock quotations or account numbers, she realized. It didn't have to be anything as logical as that. The numbers were listed in the back of the book, after dozens of blank sheets—after the final entry Fergus had written. On the day before Bianca died.

Why hadn't she seen it before? There were no journal entries, no careful checks and balances after that date. Only sheet after blank sheet. Then the numbers, formed in a careful hand.

A message, Megan wondered, something he'd been compelled to write down but hadn't wanted prying eyes to read. A confession of guilt, perhaps? Or a plea for understanding?

She sat and took several clearing breaths. They were numbers, after all, she reminded herself. There was nothing she couldn't do with numbers.

An hour passed, then two. As she worked, the desk became littered with discarded slips of paper. Each time she stopped to rest her eyes or her tired brain, she wondered whether she had tumbled into lunacy even thinking she'd found some mysterious code in the back of an old book.

But the idea hooked her, kept her chained to the desk. She heard the blast of a horn as a tour boat passed. The shadows lengthened from afternoon toward evening.

She grew only more determined as each of her efforts failed. She would find the key. However long it took, she would find it.

Something clicked, causing her to stop, sit back and study anew. As if tumblers had fallen into place, she had it. Slowly, painstakingly, she transcribed numbers into letters and let the cryptogram take shape.

The first word to form was *Bianca*.

"Oh, God." Megan pressed her hand to her lips. "It's real."

Step by step she continued, crossing out, changing, advancing letter by letter, word by word. When the excitement began to build in her, she pushed it back. This was an answer she would find only with her mind. Emotions would hurry her, cause mistakes. So she thought of nothing but the logic of the code.

The figures started to blur in front of her eyes. She forced herself to close them, to sit back and relax until her mind was clear again. Then she opened them again, and read.

> Bianca haunts me. I have no peace. All that was hers must be put away, sold, destroyed. Do spirits walk? It is nonsense, a lie. But I see her eyes, staring at me as she fell. Green as her emeralds. I will leave her a token to satisfy her. And that will be the end of it. Tonight I will sleep.

Breathless, Megan read on. The directions were very simple, very precise. For a man going mad with the enormity of his own actions, Fergus Calhoun had retained his conciseness.

Tucking the paper in her pocket, Megan hurried out. She didn't consider alerting the Calhouns. Something was driving her to finish this herself. She found what she needed in the renovation area in the family wing. Hefting a crowbar, a chisel, a tape measure, she climbed the winding iron steps to Bianca's tower.

She had been here before, knew that Bianca had stood by the windows and watched the cliffs for Christian. That she had wept here, dreamed here, died here.

The Calhouns had made it charming again, with plump, colorful pillows on the window seat, delicate tables and china vases. A velvet chaise, a crystal lamp.

Bianca would have been pleased.

Megan closed the heavy door at her back. Using the tape measure, she followed Fergus's directions. Six feet in from the door, eight from the north wall.

Without a thought to the destruction she was about to cause, Megan rolled up the softly faded floral carpet, then shoved the chisel between the slats of wood.

It was hard, backbreaking work. The wood was old, but thick and strong. Someone had polished it to a fine gleam. She pried and pulled, stopping only to flex her straining muscles and, when the light began to fail, to switch on the lamps.

The first board gave with a protesting screech. If she'd been fanciful, she might have thought it sounded like a woman. Sweat dripped down her sides, and she cursed herself for forgetting a flashlight. Refusing to think of spiders, or worse, she thrust her hand into the gap.

She thought she felt the edge of something, but no matter how she stretched and strained, she couldn't get a grip. Grimly resigned, she set to work on the next board.

Swearing at splinters and her own untried muscles, she fought it loose. With a grunt, she tossed the board aside, and panting, stretched out on her stomach to grope into the hole.

Her fingertip rang against metal. She nearly wept. The handle almost slipped out of her sweaty hand, but she pulled the box up and free and set it on her lap.

It was no more than a foot long, a foot wide and a few pounds in weight, and it was grimy from the years it had spent in the darkness. Almost tenderly, she brushed away the worst of the dust. Her fingers hovered at the latch, itching to release it, then dropped away.

It wasn't hers to open.

"I don't know where she could be." Amanda strode back into the parlor, tossing up her hands. "She's not in her office, or her room."

"She was fussing in a closet when I saw her last." Colleen tipped back her glass. "She's a grown woman. Might be taking a walk."

"Yes, but..." Suzanna trailed off with a glance at Kevin. There was no point in worrying the child, she reminded herself. Just because Megan was never late, that was no reason to assume something was wrong. "Maybe she's in the garden." She smiled and handed the baby to Holt. "I can go look."

"I'll do it." Nathaniel stood up. He didn't really believe Megan had forgotten their date for dinner and gone walking in the garden, but looking was better than worrying. "If she comes in while I'm gone—" But then he heard her footsteps and glanced toward the doorway.

Her hair was wild, her eyes were wide. Her face and clothes were smeared with dirt. And she was smiling, brilliantly. "I'm sorry I'm late."

"Megan, what on earth?" Dumbfounded, Sloan stared at her. "You look as if you've been crawling in a ditch."

"Not quite." She laughed and pushed a hand through her disordered hair. "I got a little involved, lost track of the time. Sloan, I borrowed some of your tools. They're in the tower."

"In the—"

But she was crossing the room, her eyes on Colleen. She knelt at the old woman's feet, set the box in her lap. "I found something that belongs to you."

Colleen scowled down at the box, but her heart was thrumming in her ears. "Why would you think it belongs to me?"

Gently Megan took Colleen's hand, laid it on the dusty metal. "He hid it under the floor of the tower, her tower, after she died." Her quiet voice silenced the room like a bomb. "He said she haunted him." Megan pulled the transcribed code out of her pocket, set it on top of the box.

"I can't read it," Colleen said impatiently.

"I'll read it for you." But when Megan took the sheet again, Colleen grabbed her wrist.

"Wait. Have Coco come in. I want her here."

While they waited, Megan got up and went to Nathaniel. "It was a code," she told him, before turning to face the room. "The numbers in the back of the book. I don't know why I didn't see it..." Then she smiled. "I was looking too hard, too closely. And today I knew. I just knew." She stopped, lifted her hands, let them fall. "I'm sorry. I should have told you as soon as I'd solved it. I wasn't thinking."

"You did what you were meant to do," Lilah corrected. "If one of us was supposed to find it, we would have."

"Is it like a treasure hunt?" Kevin wanted to know.

"Yes." Megan drew him close to ruffle his hair.

"I really don't have time right now, dear." Coco was arguing as Amanda dragged her into the room. "It's the middle of the dinner rush."

"Sit and be quiet," Colleen ordered. "The girl has something to read. Get your aunt a drink," she said to C.C. "She may need it. And freshen mine, while you're at it." She lifted her eyes, bird-bright, to Megan's. "Well, go on. Read it."

As she did, Megan slipped her hand into Nathaniel's. She heard Coco's quick gasp and sigh. Her own throat was raw with unshed tears when she lowered the page again.

"So... I went up and I pried up some floorboards. And I found it."

Even the children were silent when Colleen placed her thin hands on the box. They trembled once, then steadied as she worked the latch free, and opened the lid. Now it was her lips that trembled, and her eyes filled. She drew out a small oval frame, tarnished black with age.

"A photograph," she said in a thick voice. "Of my mother with me and Sean and Ethan. It was taken the year before she died. We sat for it in the garden in New York." She stroked it once, then offered it to Coco.

"Oh, Aunt Colleen. It's the only picture we have of all of you."

"She kept it on her dressing table, so that she could look at it every day. A book of poetry." Colleen drew out the slim volume, caressed it. "She loved to read poetry. It's Yeats. She would read it to me sometimes, and tell me it reminded her of Ireland. This brooch." She took out a small, simple enamel pin decorated with violets. "Sean and I gave it to her for Christmas. Nanny helped us buy it, of course. We were too young. She often wore it."

She caressed a marcasite watch, its pin shaped like a bow, and a carved jade dog hardly bigger than her thumb.

There were other small treasures—a smooth white stone, a pair of tin soldiers, the dust of an ancient flower. Then the pearls, an elegant choker of four delicate strands that had slept the decades away in a black velvet pouch.

"My grandparents gave her these as a bridal gift." Colleen ran a fingertip over the smooth orbs. "She told me it would be mine on my wedding day. He didn't like her to wear it. Too plain, he said. Too ordinary. She kept them in the pouch, in her jewel case. She would often take them out and show them to me. She said that pearls given with love were more precious than diamonds given for show. She told me to treasure them as she did, and to wear them often, because—" Her voice broke, and she reached for her glass, sipped to clear her throat. "Because pearls needed warmth."

She closed her eyes and sat back. "I thought he'd sold them, disposed of them with the rest."

"You're tired, Aunt Colleen." Suzanna went quietly to her side. "Why don't I take you upstairs? I can bring you a dinner tray."

"I'm not an invalid." Colleen snapped the words out, but her hand covered Suzanna's and squeezed. "I'm old, but I'm not feeble. I've wit enough to make some bequests. You." She pressed the brooch into Suzanna's hand. "This is yours. I want to see you wear it."

"Aunt Colleen—"

"Put it on now. Put it on." She brushed Suzanna away and picked up the book of poetry. "You spend half your time dreaming," she said to Lilah. "Dream with this."

"Thank you." Lilah bent down, kissed her.

"You'll have the watch," she said to Amanda. "You're the one who's always worrying about what time it is. And you," she continued, looking at C.C. and waving Amanda's thanks away, "take the jade. You like to set things around that gather dust."

Her eyebrow cocked at Jenny.

"Waiting for your turn, are you?"

Jenny smiled guilelessly. "No, ma'am."

"You'll have this." She offered Jenny the stone. "I was younger than you when I gave this to my mother. I thought it was magic. Maybe it is."

"It's pretty." Delighted with her new treasure, Jenny rubbed it against her cheek. "I can put it on my windowsill."

"She'd have been pleased," Colleen said softly. "She kept it on hers." With a harsh cough, she cleared her voice to briskness again. "You boys, take these, and don't lose them. They were my brother's."

"Neat," Alex whispered, reverently holding a perfectly detailed soldier. "Thanks."

"Thanks," Kevin echoed. "It's just like a treasure box," he said, grinning at her. "Aren't you going to give anything to Aunt Coco?"

"She'll have the photograph."

"Aunt Colleen." Overcome, Coco reached for her hankie. "Really, you mustn't."

"You'll take it as a wedding gift, and be grateful."

"I am grateful. I don't know what to say."

"See that you clean that tarnish off the frame." Bracing her weight on the cane, Colleen rose and turned to Megan. "You look pleased with yourself."

Megan's heart was too full for pretense. "I am."

For a moment, Colleen's damp eyes twinkled back. "You should be. You're a bright girl, Megan. And a resourceful one. You remind me of myself, a very long time ago." Gently she picked up the pearls, letting the glowing strands run through her bent fingers.

"Here." Megan stepped toward her. "Let me help you put them on."

Colleen shook her head. "Pearls need youth. They're for you."

Stunned, Megan dropped her hands again. "No, you can't give them away like that. Bianca meant them for you."

"She meant them to be passed on."

"Within the family. They...they should go to Coco, or—"

"They go where I say they go," Colleen said imperiously.

"It isn't right." Megan searched the room for help, but found only satisfied smiles.

"It seems perfectly right to me," Suzanna murmured. "Amanda?"

Amanda touched a hand to the watch she'd pinned to her lapel. "Completely."

"Lovely." Coco wept into her hankie. "Just lovely."

"Fits like a glove," C.C. agreed, and glanced at Lilah.

"Destined." She tilted her face up to Max. "Only a fool fights destiny."

"Then we're agreed?" Suzanna took a quick survey and received nods from the men. "The vote's in."

"Ha!" Though she was enormously proud, Colleen scowled. "As if I needed approval to dispose of what's mine. Take them." She thrust them into Megan's hands. "Go upstairs and clean yourself up. You look like a chimney sweep. I want to see you wearing them when you come down."

"Aunt Colleen..."

"No blubbering. Do as you're told."

"Come on." Suzanna took Megan's arm to lead her from the room. "I'll give you a hand."

Satisfied, Colleen sat again, thumped her cane. "Well, where's my drink?"

Later, when the waning moon had tipped over the edge of the sea, Megan walked with Nathaniel to the cliffs. The breeze whispered secrets in the grass and teased the wildflowers.

She wore blue, a simple summer dress with a full skirt that

swirled in the wind. The pearls, glowing like small, perfect moons, circled her throat.

"You've had quite a day, Megan."

"My head's still spinning. She gave it all away, Nathaniel. I can't understand how she could give away all the things that mattered so much."

"She's a hell of a woman. It takes a special one to recognize magic."

"Magic?"

"My practical, down-to-earth Megan." He tugged on her hand until they sat on a rock together, looking out over the churning water. "Didn't you wonder, even for a moment, why each gift was so perfectly suitable? Why eighty years ago Fergus Calhoun would have been compelled to select just those things to hide away? The flower brooch for Suzanna, the watch for Amanda, Yeats for Lilah and the jade for C.C.? The portrait for Coco?"

"Coincidence," Megan murmured, but there was doubt in her voice.

He only laughed and kissed her. "Fate thrives on coincidence."

"And the pearls?"

"These." He lifted a finger to trace them. "A symbol of family, endurance, innocence. They suit you very well."

"They— I know I should have found a way not to accept them, but when Suzanna put them on me upstairs, they felt as though they were mine."

"They are. Ask yourself why you found them, why, with all the months the Calhouns searched for the emeralds, they never came across a hint of the strongbox. Fergus's book turns up after you move into The Towers. There's a numbered code. Who better to solve it than our logical CPA?"

Megan shook her head and blew out a laughing breath. "I can't explain it."

"Then just accept it."

"A magic rock for Jenny, soldiers for the boys." She rested her head against Nathaniel's shoulder. "I suppose I can't argue with that kind of coincidence. Or fate." Content, she closed her eyes and let the air caress her cheeks. "It's hard to believe that just a few days ago I was frantic with worry. You found him near here, didn't you?"

"Yes." He thought it best for her peace of mind not to mention the dicey climb down to the ledge. "I followed the bird."

"The bird?" Puzzled, she drew back. "That's odd. Kevin told me about a bird. A white one with green eyes that stayed with him that night. He's got a good imagination."

"There was a bird," Nathaniel told her. "A white gull with emerald eyes. Bianca's eyes."

"But—"

"Take magic where you find it." He slipped an arm around her shoulders so that they both could enjoy the sounds of the surf. "I have something for you, Megan."

"Mmm?" She was comfortable, almost sleepy, and she moaned in protest when he shifted away.

Nathaniel reached inside his jacket and drew out a sheaf of papers. "You might have a hard time reading them in this light."

"What's this?" Amused, she took them. "More receipts?"

"Nope. It's a life insurance policy."

"A— For heaven's sake. You shouldn't be carrying this around. You need to put it in a safe-deposit box, or a safe. Fireproof."

"Shut up." His nerves were beginning to stretch, so he stood, then paced to the edge of the cliff and back. "There's a hospitalization policy, too, my mortgage, a couple of bonds. And a damn Keogh."

"A Keogh." Megan held the papers as if they were diamonds. "You filled out the form."

"I can be practical, if that's what it takes. You want security, I'll give you security. There are plenty of figures there for you to tally."

She pressed her lips together. "You did this for me."

"I'd do anything for you. You'd rather I invest in municipal bonds than slay dragons? Fine."

She stared at him as he stood with the sea and sky at his back, his feet braced as if he were riding the deck of a ship, his eyes lit with a power that defeated the dark. And with bruises fading on his face.

"You faced your dragon years ago, Nathaniel." To keep her hands occupied, she smoothed the papers. "I've had trouble facing my own." Rising, she walked to him, slipped the papers back into his pocket. "Aunt Colleen cornered me today. She said a lot of things, how I was too smart to take risks. How I'd never make the mistake of letting a man be too important. That I'd be better off alone than giving someone my trust, my heart. It upset me, and it frightened me. It took me a while to realize that's just what she'd meant to do. She was daring me to face myself."

"Have you?"

"It's not easy for me. I didn't like everything I saw, Nathaniel. All these years I've convinced myself that I was strong and self-reliant. But I'd let someone so unimportant shadow my life, and Kevin's. I thought I was protecting my son, and myself."

"You did a hell of a good job, from where I'm standing."

"Too good, in some ways. I closed myself off because it was safer. Then there was you." She reached up to lay a hand on his cheek. "I've been so afraid of what I feel for you. But that's over. I love you, Nathaniel. It doesn't matter if it was magic or fate, coincidence or sheer luck. I'm just glad I found you."

She lifted her face to his, reveled in the freedom of the kiss, the scent of the sea, the promise of his arms.

"I don't need retirement plans and insurance policies, Nathaniel," she murmured. "Not that you don't. It's very important that you... Stop laughing."

"I'm crazy about you." Still laughing, Nathaniel scooped her off her feet and swung her in dizzying circles.

"Crazy period." She struggled to catch her breath and clung to him. "We're going to fall off the cliff."

"Not tonight we're not. Nothing can happen to us tonight. Can't you feel it? We're the magic now." He set her on her feet again and held her close, so that even the air couldn't come between them. "I love you, Meg, but damned if I'm going to get down on one knee."

She went very still. "Nathaniel, I don't think—"

"Good. Don't think. Just listen. I've sailed around the world more than once, and seen in a decade more than most people see in their lifetimes. But I had to come home to find you. Don't say anything," he murmured. "Sit."

He led her back to the rock and sat with her. "I have something more for you than paperwork. That was just to smooth the path. Take a look at it," he said as he drew a box from his pocket. "Then tell me it wasn't meant."

With trembling fingers, she opened the box. With a sound of wonder, she lifted her eyes to his. "It's a pearl," she whispered.

"I was going to go for the traditional diamond. Seemed like the right thing. But when I saw this, I knew." He took it out of the box. "Coincidence?"

"I don't know. When did you buy this?"

"Last week. I thought about walking here with you, that first time. The moon and the stars." He studied the ring, the single glowing pearl surrounded by small, bright diamonds. "The moon and the stars," he said again, taking her hands. "That's what I want to give you, Megan."

"Nathaniel." She tried to tell herself it was too fast, too foolish, but the thought wouldn't lodge. "It's lovely."

"It's meant." He touched his lips to hers. "Just as we're meant. Marry me, Megan. Start a life with me. Let me be Kevin's father and make more children with you. Let me grow old loving you."

She couldn't find the logic, or think of all the reasons they should wait. So she answered with her heart. "Yes. Yes to everything." Laughing, she threw her arms around him. "Oh, Nathaniel. Yes, yes, yes…"

He squeezed his eyes tight on relief and joy. "You sure you don't want to qualify that?"

"I'm sure. I'm so sure." Drawing back, she held out her left hand. "Please. I want the moon and the stars. I want you."

He slipped the ring on her finger. "You've got me, sugar."

When he drew her close again, he thought he heard the air sigh, like a woman.

Epilogue

"Mom! We're here!"

Megan glanced up from her desk just as Kevin flew in the office door. She lifted her brow at the suit jacket and tie he wore.

"My, my, don't you look handsome!"

"You said I had to dress up 'cause it's Aunt Colleen's birthday dinner. I guess it's okay." He stretched his neck. "Dad showed me how to tie the tie by myself."

"And you did a fine job." She restrained herself from smoothing and straightening the knot. "How was the tour business today?"

"It was great. Calm seas and a freshening breeze. We sighted the first whale off the port bow."

"Oh, I love that nautical talk." She kissed his nose.

"If I didn't have to go to school, I could work with Dad and Holt every day, and not just on Saturday."

"And if you didn't go to school, you'd never know much more than you do today. Saturdays will have to do." She gave his hair a tug. "Mate."

He'd expected as much. And, really, he didn't mind school.

After all, he was a whole year in front of Alex. He grinned at his mother. "Everybody's here. When are the new babies coming?"

"Mmm..." With the Calhoun sisters in varying stages of pregnancy, it was an interesting question. "I'd say on and off starting next month and through the New Year."

He ran a fingertip over the corner of her desk. "Who do you think's going to be first? C.C. or Suzanna?"

"Why?" She glanced up from the ledger, and her eyes narrowed. "Kevin, you are not betting on who has the next baby."

"But, Mom—"

"No betting," she repeated, and smothered a laugh. "Give me just a minute to finish up here, and I'll be along."

"Hurry up." Kevin was bouncing. "The party's already started."

"All right, I'll just—" Just nothing, she thought, and closed the ledger with a snap. "Office hours are over. Let's go party."

"All right!" Grabbing her hand, Kevin hauled her out of the room. "Alex said Dutch made this really big cake and it's going to have about a hundred candles on it."

"Not quite a hundred," Megan said with a laugh. When they neared the family wing, she glanced toward the ceiling. "Honey, I'd better check upstairs first."

"Looking for someone?" Nathaniel came down the steps. There was a twinkle in his eye and a tiny pink bundle in his arms.

"I should have known you'd wake her up."

"She was awake. Weren't you, sugar?" He bent his head to kiss his daughter's cheek. "She was asking for me."

"Really."

"She can't talk yet," Kevin informed his father. "She's only six weeks old."

"She's very advanced for her age. Smart, like her mama."

"Smart enough to know a sucker when she sees one." They made such a picture, she thought, the big man with a boy at his side and a baby in his arms. Her picture, she thought, and smiled. "Come here, Luna."

"She wants to go to the party, too," Kevin declared, reaching up to stroke a finger over his sister's cheek.

"Sure she does. That's what she told me."

"Oh, Dad."

Grinning, Nathaniel ruffled Kevin's hair. "I could eat a pod of whales, mate. How about you?"

"Aye, aye." Kevin made a dash for the parlor. "Come on, come on, everybody's waiting."

"I've got to do this first." Nathaniel leaned over his daughter to kiss Megan.

"Jeez." With a roll of his eyes, Kevin headed for the noise, and the real fun.

"You're looking awfully pleased with yourself," Megan murmured.

"Why shouldn't I? I've got a beautiful wife, a terrific son, an incredible daughter." He ran his knuckles over Megan's pearl choker. "What else could I ask for? How about you?"

Megan lifted her hand to pull his mouth back to hers. "I've got the moon and the stars."

* * * * *